PENGUIN ⊙ CLASSICS

THE BLACK SHEEP

HONORÉ DE BALZAC was born at Tours in 1799, the son of a civil servant. He spent nearly six years as a boarder in a Vendôme school, then went to live in Paris, working as a lawyer's clerk then as a hack writer. Between 1820 and 1824 he wrote a number of novels under various pseudonyms, many of them in collaboration, after which he unsuccessfully tried his luck at publishing, printing and type-founding. At the age of thirty, heavily in debt, he returned to literature with a dedicated fury and wrote the first novel to appear under his own name, *The Chouans*. During the next twenty years he wrote about ninety novels and shorter stories, among them many masterpieces, to which he gave the comprehensive title the *Human Comedy*. He died in 1850, a few months after his marriage to Evelina Hanska, the Polish countess with whom he had maintained amorous relations for eighteen years.

•

DONALD ADAMSON was born in 1939 and educated at Manchester Grammar School, Magdalen College, Oxford and the Sorbonne. He teaches at Goldsmiths' College, London. His first book, *The Genesis of 'Le Cousin Pons'* (1966), was followed by a second Oxford thesis, on Balzac and the visual arts. He is also joint author of a history of the Beauclerk family, *The House of Nell Gwyn*, and has edited the first biographical memoir on T.S. Eliot. He is a Fellow of the Royal Society of Literature. He is currently translating *Germinie Lacerteux*, by the Goncourt brothers, and has also translated *Ursule Mirouët* by Balzac, for the Penguin Classics. He is married, with two sons, and lives in Kent and Cornwall.

Honoré de Balzac

THE BLACK SHEEP

(La Rabouilleuse)

TRANSLATED
WITH AN INTRODUCTION BY
DONALD ADAMSON

PENGUIN BOOKS

PENGUIN BOOKS

Published by the Penguin Group
27 Wrights Lane, London w8 5TZ, England
Viking Penguin Inc., 40 West 23rd Street, New York, New York 10010, USA
Penguin Books Australia Ltd, Ringwood, Victoria, Australia
Penguin Books Canada Ltd, 2801 John Street, Markham, Ontario, Canada L3R 1B4
Penguin Books (NZ) Ltd, 182–190 Wairau Road, Auckland 10, New Zealand

Penguin Books Ltd, Registered Offices: Harmondsworth, Middlesex, England

This translation first published 1970
9 10

Printed and bound in Great Britain by
Cox & Wyman Ltd, Reading
Set in Monotype Garamond

Contents

Part Three: Who Will Gain the Inheritance?

Introduction

BALZAC'S aim was never the simple one of most novelists:
to tell a gripping, convincing story with varying degrees of
skill, complexity and symbolism. Clearly, he wished to write
exciting stories (and no story in the world is more exciting
than *The Black Sheep*, combining as it does the compelling
readability of the blood-and-thunder with the deeper insights
of literary art); but he hoped also to write historical stories.
As a young man, his idol amongst novelists had been Sir
Walter Scott, the historian of England in the Tudor age,
Scotland in the seventeenth and eighteenth centuries and the
Crusades to the Holy Land. In the hard years of his beginnings
as a writer, when a whole series of pseudonymous novels had
laboriously taught him the craft besides keeping the wolf
from the door, Balzac had tried to emulate Scott: stories of
medieval tournaments and robber barons, accounts of the
struggle between Armagnacs and Burgundians in the early
fifteenth century and between the Houses of Valois and Guise
in the sixteenth were either planned or written. Little remains
of this early ambition in the ninety-four novels which now
make up *The Human Comedy*. Luckily for himself, Balzac began
his long series of serious novels with *The Chouans*, a story much
nearer to his own time; it describes the guerrilla warfare
between Royalist and Revolutionary forces in North-West
France about the time he himself was born. From this book
sprang the concept of a vast system of interrelated novels
describing the history of contemporary France in all its facets
– Paris and the provinces, industry and agriculture, upper,
middle and working classes – which would move forward
in time as Balzac proceeded with *The Human Comedy*, and
which was little more than half complete at his death in 1850.
'People are beginning to realize that I am much more of an
historian than a novelist,' he wrote in 1845.

7

Whether or not we agree with his assessment of his own work (and *The Human Comedy* is certainly an immense repository of historical information: French bankruptcy procedure, methods of paper manufacture, styles of dress, the topography of Paris and of numerous provincial towns, fashions in house furnishing, the political attitudes of the aristocracy after 1815 all come into its purview), it is certainly important to bear Balzac's scheme of priorities in mind. The historical material provided in *The Black Sheep* is by no means extraneous to the novel, apart from the long description of Issoudun. Better, perhaps, than in any other novel in *The Human Comedy*, it is intimately interwoven into the fabric of the tale.

At the centre of the novel are two brothers, Joseph and Philippe Bridau, whom Balzac modelled on himself and his scapegrace brother, Henri. The story revolves round the contrasts between their characters, the varying degrees of success which at different times in their careers they obtain in the world, the conflicting views which their mother (Agathe), their great-aunt (Madame Descoings), the townsfolk of Issoudun, etc., have of them . . . and the way in which (generally speaking) both are misunderstood – the virtuous artist, Joseph, being thought of as a shiftless good-for-nothing and Philippe, the cynical, selfish, brutal son, admired for his good looks, bravery and panache. But which of them *is* the black sheep?

The underlying irony of the novel is that the boys' own mother (like, perhaps, Madame Balzac?) is so completely blind as to their true characters. Time and time again, in Part One of the story, circumstances compel her to admit that Philippe is a heartless scoundrel, unworthy to be treated as a son. At one point she even banishes him from the house, but within a few days she has become blind again, yearns to see him, grieves to think that by her own action she has turned him out into the streets of Paris with scarcely enough money to buy shelter. On the other hand, she simply cannot understand Joseph. Her heart does not warm to the way of life he has chosen to lead. Joseph does not even have the satisfaction of being loved unreservedly by his mother.

8

Success comes slowly in art. Joseph's financial outlook is bleak; he has no prospect of promotion; the only exciting things he does are committed to canvas in the silence of his own inspiration; he does not wear the colourful uniform of a colonel in the dragoon guards; and, abomination of abominations, he paints naked women in his studio! It is just possible to understand the reserve which Madame Bridau feels about his choice of career.

But at the opening of the story Philippe is in an even worse financial situation than his younger brother, and with no prospects at all. The brave, dashing young officer who five years before had been Napoleon's aide-de-camp at the Battle of Montereau has no job, and even his half-pay of 300 francs a month* has been taken away from him. After breakfasting at his mother's flat he drifts around Paris in the daytime, bivouacking from one café to another for the inevitable liqueur. Every evening he gambles money he can ill afford . . . and returns home blind drunk in the small hours of the morning. Madame Bridau has even had to get out of bed to help him up the stairs. He, not Joseph, is the black sheep, though their mother will not admit the fact.

When Agathe thinks of Philippe as he was in Napoleon's time and then sees him as he is now, she can always blame 'historical circumstances' for his downfall. If only Napoleon had triumphed at Waterloo, if only the brilliant conquests of the Imperial age had continued, then Philippe would not be as he is today: a down-and-out alcoholic, a dissolute gambler. By now, though still only in his twenties, he would have become a general. She is encouraged in this facile reasoning by the fact that her husband, a middle-ranking civil servant whose devotion to duty led to an early death, had been an intense admirer of Napoleon. The Emperor himself had paid

* The sums of money mentioned by Balzac in *The Black Sheep* have not been converted into their present-day French or English equivalents (though *napoléons, louis, écus* and *livres* have been standardized in terms of the franc). A *sou* was one-twentieth of the value of a franc. Balzac's sums of money can be roughly converted into a modern English equivalent by dividing them by five: thus, 300 francs a month (in Balzac's time) becomes £15 a week in the real terms of today.

the two orphan's fees out of his Privy Purse and, when Philippe decided to become a soldier, had taken a personal interest in his welfare and promotion.

Joseph, on the other hand, can invoke no 'historical circumstances' to justify his imaginary backslidings. He is as he is, and though artists are not the most worldly of men, he understands both Philippe and himself with lucid clarity. The 'historical circumstances' by means of which Philippe's faults of conduct are explained away are themselves imaginary ... as Joseph is quick to point out. No one compelled Philippe to resign his commission. The Bourbons would have been happy if he had remained in the army. A soldier should fight for his country ... not his government. It was Philippe's own stubborn refusal to serve the Bourbons which caused his abrupt retirement at the age of twenty. Expressed in another way, his present purposeless way of life is the result of his undeviating loyalty to Napoleon.

But *The Black Sheep* is much more than a description of two very different brothers, the twists and turns in their fortunes and the undiscerning way in which most people view each of them. During the course of the novel we see Philippe's character transformed beyond recognition, a transformation only indirectly related to the decline in his worldly fortunes from colonel to down-and-out. Philippe develops into one of the supreme monsters of fiction, every inch the equal in wickedness of Heathcliff or Iago – so evil that he seems an incarnation of the devil. Joseph, of course, remains the same: hard-working, devoted to his mother and aunt, unselfish, tolerant, forgiving. The vicissitudes of the story (the thefts he suffers, his failure to assist Madame Descoings over the lottery ticket, the murder charge, his temporary imprisonment) ruffle but do not embitter him.

Selfless, unthinking loyalty to Bonapartism led Philippe to resign his commission and effectively debar himself from a worthwhile career. A second turning-point is reached when he emigrates to America. Balzac makes it plain that the Champ-d'Asile project was a stunt engineered by Liberal Bonapartism, and Philippe is one of the men who were taken in by it. He returns to France downhearted, aggrieved and selfish, but refuses at first to admit that the Texan project was a political contrivance. At this stage in the story, it is just possible to join with Madame Bridau in sympathizing with him. Gradually, however, the venom of calculation enters his soul.

Calculation is one of the key themes in *The Human Comedy*. It is first set out in detail in *Old Goriot*, a novel written seven years earlier than *The Black Sheep*. In order to succeed in the world, a man must be ruthless in exploiting others. Madame de Beauséant, who is herself the disillusioned victim of a man who has jilted her to marry a woman with a large dowry, advises the young hero of *Old Goriot* to treat people as one might treat post-horses on a journey: ride them mercilessly to the next relay, then drop them without compunction, and use each successive horse in a similar way until the goal of one's desires is reached. In this world of predator and prey, where everyone is either exploited or exploiting (or both simultaneously), it is fatal to betray a sentiment. Young dandies will deprive the women who love them of their very last penny and then abandon them. 'If you have any real feeling, hide it like a treasure; never let it be suspected or you will be lost,' Madame de Beauséant also advises Eugène. A mask must be worn, and never put down for a moment, by those who are eager to succeed. 'Where ambition begins, naïve unreflecting actions cease,' Balzac reminds us in *Lost Illusions*. The mask will disguise those feelings on which the potential calculator would exert a stranglehold. Examples of calculation exploiting passion abound in *The Human Comedy* – generally, however, in the Parisian novels, for Paris (as Balzac insists in *Old Goriot*) is a battlefield, on which a man 'must kill to avoid being killed, deceive to avoid being deceived'. It is useless to cavil that Paris could not have been as Balzac describes it: this is the imaginative picture put forward by *The Human Comedy*, and worked out with subtle and ever deepening symbolism.

Philippe becomes a calculator. From war he moves gradually over into politics . . . but this only means that he introduces the principles of war into civilian life. Liberal Bonapartism inveigled him into the Texan project; unwary conspirators prevailed on him to join them in a hopeless act of treason. At the lowest ebb of his fortunes, Philippe has reached the climacteric of his career.

*

Parts Two and Three of *The Black Sheep* transfer the action from Paris to the provinces, a common enough practice in Balzac's novels. *Lost Illusions*, for example, opens at Angoulême; Part Two takes us to Paris; in Part Three, the action reverts to Angoulême. Balzac's ambition to portray the whole of contemporary France in all its aspects is by no means always confined to novels describing either the provinces or the capital.

At Issoudun, about 100 miles south of Paris, lives Agathe's brother, Jean-Jacques Rouget, with a private income of some 60,000 francs (£12,000 a year in present-day terms) and no wife or children to inherit it. Violent contrasts between wealth and poverty are frequently found in Balzac's imaginative universe, and the contrast between Jean-Jacques's and Agathe's situations is by no means incredible. Even nowadays many an unpretentious bourgeois house in France is the home of some very considerable fortune. Besides, Balzac takes good care to explain why the brother should have almost everything and the sister virtually nothing. Their father suspected that, though Jean-Jacques was his son, Agathe was not his daughter and so cut her off with 100,000 francs.

With her husband, a moderately well-paid civil servant, Agathe had lived a comfortable though not luxurious life. His early death had been a devastating blow to her fortunes. But for the Emperor's personal generosity, Philippe and Joseph would have gone without an education. Agathe's aunt, Madame Descoings combined her resources with the modest pension her niece received on the Civil List. Once their education was over, the two boys quickly became self-supporting: Philippe embarked on his brief but glorious career in the army; Joseph's commissions just enabled him to make ends meet. If Philippe had not taken to bad ways, the simple unpretentious cycle of retired life would have gone on unhindered. Admittedly, Madame Descoings had a weakness for backing her favourite numbers in the lottery, and she certainly spent too high a proportion of her income on this foible. Even so, her occasional flutters would never have reduced the little household to penury, or driven Agathe to seek employment. Philippe's theft of the 400 francs is the cause of Madame Descoings's death, which deprives the family of the life interest which was all she obtained from her parents-in-law's estate. Philippe also steals from his brother, pawns his mother's silverware, embezzles money, accumulates debts and launches into a treasonable conspiracy. At each successive crisis, his mother springs to his assistance, but at the opening of Part Two her resources are finally exhausted.

It is against this background of a brother's wealth and a sister's penury that we view Issoudun. Madame Bridau conceives the idea of visiting the town to see her brother, after a separation of thirty years, and to ask him whether he will lend her the money that will obtain Philippe's release from prison. Joseph accompanies her on this errand of mercy, though with his usual clarity of mind he is only too well aware of the hopelessness of the task confronting them.

Money, in Balzac's eyes, is something more than the motive force of a capitalist world. It is power: the power to shape one's life as one pleases, the symbol of the life force itself. Rouget's vast unearned wealth has attracted parasites as a light will attract moths. Flore Brazier, the young woman with whom Jean-Jacques is passionately in love, exploits his attachment. But her master's attentions are rather wearisome, and suddenly – sixteen years after first entering the Rouget household – she falls head over heels in love with Max. Max, too, is a calculator: he exploits Flore just as Flore exploits Jean-Jacques. If for any reason Jean-Jacques's fortune had run dry, Max would have abandoned Flore as surely as she would have abandoned her benefactor. Thus, Flore is an imperfect calculator, a Janus figure at once exploiting and exploited, calculating with regard to the older man but at the mercy of the handsome younger one. (*The Black Sheep* is deliberately lacking in that staple element of most novels, romantic love; and Balzac confessed to Madame Hanska, his mistress and future wife, that writing a novel without this element had proved to be extremely difficult.) However, the situation which confronts us in *The Black Sheep* is by no means unique in *The Human Comedy*. In *Old Goriot*, for instance, Delphine de Nucingen is exploited by de Marsay, but exploits Eugène. All these triangular situations owe much to Racine – except that in Balzac's novels the destructive agent (whether it be erotic passion or maternal love or an addiction to lotteries) is more unambiguously presented as vice.

Flore and Max have no intention of allowing the old man's sister and nephew to come anywhere near the money. For the time being, they can do nothing to regularize their position. Though Flore can impose Max's presence on the household by threats of deserting the old man (thus exploiting his passion for her), she and Max cannot marry, since this would drive Rouget's passion – as with Hermione's, in Racine's *Andromaque* – to relentless fury. Their clear objective must be to ensure that the fortune becomes theirs after his death; and so the family, in the persons of Agathe and Joseph, are the implacable enemies to be eliminated at all costs. Already, Issoudun is taking on the appearance of a battlefield.

First, Flore and Max ensure that the 'Parisians' (a sure means of casting opprobrium!) stay with close friends in the town, not with Jean-Jacques. It is imperative that the brother and sister should never exchange meaningful private conversation: Flore must be a party to everything the old man hears and replies. If Agathe and Joseph stayed at Rouget's house, such private conversation would be unavoidable; and so they stay at the Hochons'. Next, Jean-Jacques sends a message regretting that (a diplomatic) illness prevents him from visiting his sister and nephew at the house where they are staying: again, with the object of ruling out any private conversation between himself and Agathe. The Bridaus are, of course, free to visit the old man whenever they please; but when they are at the house, Flore does not let Rouget out of her sight.

It is during one of Joseph's visits that an incident occurs which Flore and Max later turn to their unexpected advantage. With all Rouget's wealth, it would be unkind (and unwise!) to send the family away empty-handed. They must be fobbed off with something, but what can be given them precious enough to be worth the taking, yet without making any inroads into Rouget's fortune? Max's decision (for he, as the principal calculator, takes all the big decisions in the household) is a sensible one in the circumstances. Jean-Jacques had inherited, from his father, thirty-nine pictures, all of which had hung in churches and monasteries until the French Revolution. These Leonardos, Titians, Rubenses and Bellinis are worth a fortune but, needless to say, no one in Issoudun – not even Max – realizes their true value. Philistines that they are, Jean-Jacques and his companions prize them more for the frames than the canvases. Since Joseph is a painter, what better gift could the old man make than these canvases – minus, of course, the frames? Joseph eagerly accepts the offer – a trifle disingenuously, perhaps, bearing in mind that he was aware of their full value. But, seeing that the war against the predators was irretrievably lost, no doubt he wished to win a battle.

Only a few days after receiving the pictures, he jubilantly announces that Rouget has given him pictures to the value of 150,000 francs. The Hochons are as incredulous as Rouget would have been, had Joseph told him of their value. In most situations of everyday life, such a disclosure would certainly not be described as a false move, but in *The Black Sheep* we have a situation which, whilst faithfully describing everyday life, is so articulated as to stress Balzac's own outlook on human nature and the world. Although Joseph cannot be blamed for not knowing, or suspecting, that Monsieur Hochon's two grandsons are spies, the fact remains that a calculator – never letting the mask fall for a moment – would have *concealed* the pictures' worth until such time as he had sold them. As it is, within twenty minutes Jean-Jacques, Flore and Max are apprised of the enormous and unsuspected treasure which has slipped through their hands.

Thus, besides providing moments of light relief, the Knights of Idleness play an integral part in the development of the action. Such is the novel's perfect economy of means. The nocturnal exploits of this band of carefree young men, led by Max, may seem farcical – and even incredible – to the modern reader. But we should remember that the conditions prevailing in 1822 were indeed vastly different from conditions today. It is quite true that, 150 years ago, young men of good family were brought up without a trade or profession. (Balzac goes out of his way to insist that, for a variety of reasons, there was no new work, trade or prosperity in Issoudun.) It is equally true that the meal the Hochons offer Joseph and his mother on their first arrival would have seemed miserly then, by the bourgeois standards of that area, although it may seem fairly luxurious to us today. And it is a fact, of which Balzac (as a historian) was well aware, that in the eighteenth and early nineteenth centuries young upper-class ruffians, similar to the Knights of Idleness, performed nocturnal pranks both in Paris and in provincial towns.

Max is the Grand Master of the Order of Idleness because to be so fits in with his schemes of calculation. Unlike Philippe, this young officer never does anything for the sheer enjoyment of it. He well knows that, over and above the carousing and horseplay, the Knights can be applied, if necessary, to some severely practical purpose. The most useful purpose which they serve is to relay the value of the pictures to Joseph's uncle, and so lead to his discomfiture when he comes to pay his uncle a farewell visit.

With the Fario episode, however, Max – for the first time in his life – goes too far. Momentarily, the mask of calculation is dropped and we see the naked truth of his ruthlessness and malevolence. Having smashed the Spaniard's cart to pieces, there is no need to infest his granary with vermin. Brilliant as is the speech in which Max decks out his spiritual bankruptcy in humorous trappings, no words can conceal the fact that to let hundreds of rats, mice and pigeons into a well-filled granary is no prank but heartless evil. The action itself is not that of a calculator: it exceeds the bounds of tomfoolery and yet leads to no positive advantage. Significantly, this action discredits Max in the town; and in due time, Philippe plays upon this discredit. Calculators always feign goodness and respectability, though having hearts of stone.

In the long run, therefore, the Fario episode turns to Max's positive disadvantage; but in the short term, it provides him with a first-rate tactical opportunity. Joseph cannot sleep after the final meeting with his uncle: it galls him to think that he, so honest, high-principled and conscientious, should be thought of by the whole town as a confidence trickster. By sheer coincidence (one of those coincidences of which war so largely consists), Joseph's insomnia occurs at the same time as Fario's attempted murder of Max. Perhaps only a soldier would have had the presence of mind, and ruthlessness, to say – immediately on coming round from his coma – that it was Joseph who had tried to kill him. Even if the circumstantial evidence had not played so fully into Max's hands, this pitiless accusation would still have been worthy of Balzac's arch-calculators, Henri de Marsay and Maxime de Trailles.

*

Clearly, the visionary artist is unfit to grapple with men of the calibre of Max; and to give him his due, Joseph had known this even before leaving Paris. The reintroduction of Philippe into the story offers a different configuration of circumstances.

As we watch the ex-prisoner settling down to his five years' detention in Issoudun, all we can predict with certainty is that the struggle between him and Max will be just as remorseless as the earlier struggle, and that Philippe will acquit himself more dishonourably than his brother. But Joseph need feel no shame about his ineffectualness. To begin with, Philippe starts with inherited advantages, the knowledge of most, if not all, of the ways in which his brother went wrong. Who would have suspected, when Agathe and Joseph set foot in the sleepy town, that Max's opposition would be so implacable? But Philippe *knows* that they will stop at nothing, not even a trumped-up murder charge, to discredit and hound out the family. And how did the news get back to Rouget that the pictures were worth 150,000 francs? Evidently, spies are at work; and so Philippe takes care never to discuss matters with Monsieur Hochon except when quite definitely out of earshot. Armed with his foreknowledge, even a second artist would have been incomparably more skilful in his fight for the inheritance.

But, in addition to these advantages, Philippe has two others. Firstly, like Max and unlike Joseph, he is a man of the world. Secondly, he is trained in the use of arms, whereas Joseph would inevitably have lost a duel with Max. And the cruel core of the novel is that in the end everything must turn upon a duel. How else are Flore and Max to be displaced? At the same time, however, the duel which both men welcome as inevitable is the supreme gamble.

Either of the men could win this contest. If it did not take place, Philippe would remain permanently excluded from the inheritance, and Max would endure the ignominy of living alongside an enemy who has ousted and discredited him. But what is to prevent Max from uprooting Rouget and Flore, and moving away from a town in which Philippe is condemned to five years' enforced residence? And so Philippe takes the ultimate risk of provoking his enemy to a duel. Issoudun, no less than Paris, has become a battlefield in civilian life. The ironical outcome of the struggle for the inheritance is that, whereas Joseph had been slanderously accused of attempted murder and hounded out of the town, Philippe commits legalized murder and is praised for it.

Unlike the Texan fiasco and the nightly game of roulette and the embezzlement and the political conspiracy, Philippe's duel is a gamble which pays off – a gamble, moreover, in which public opinion, Fario's thirst for vengeance and Philippe's own native cunning are on his side. But the story does not end with his success in the duel. *Old Goriot* had shown an embryonic calculator, Eugène de Rastignac, whose path to success can be traced only intermittently in other novels (for Balzac's characters frequently move from one novel of *The*

Human Comedy to another). *Lost Illusions* had shown a would-be calculator's failure. But *The Black Sheep* shows something never before portrayed in *The Human Comedy*: a calculator's limited success. The duel was a gamble which came off precisely because, on that morning of 3 December 1822, war and civilian life had momentarily coalesced. For a while Philippe's civilian life reaps the fruits of his military success. Then other gambles beckon, gambles which are of a political and financial, not a military, nature. Philippe backs the wrong side in the political crisis of 1830. It is a supreme irony which makes him, the erstwhile Liberal Bonapartist, support Charles X against Louis-Philippe; and it is an irony which proves to be his undoing. At the same time, he entrusts his already enormous fortune to the shady manoeuvres of the two leading financiers in *The Human Comedy*, Nucingen and du Tillet.

And again, the gamble fails, for somehow Philippe is ill-adapted to the ways of civilian life. So it is that the brave colonel whose military career had enjoyed such a meteoric start never rises above the rank of colonel when he does return into the army. In 1815 he should have been an ardent supporter of the Bourbons. In 1822 he should have backed Villèle, not conspired against him. In 1830 he should have switched his allegiance to the House of Orleans. From the political (as against the military) angle, Giroudeau's career offers him an exemplary lesson.

Thus, Philippe being in the last analysis more of a gambler than a calculator, gambling provides the novel with an intricate pattern of symbolic contrasts. War is pure chance: at any moment the bravest and ablest of soldiers may be killed. All Philippe's military gambles (and this includes the duel) are crowned with success; all his civilian ones meet with failure. But whilst gambling deprives Philippe of both life and honour, it provides his mother with an honourable living, when, after lavishing her money on him, she takes a humdrum job in a lottery office. And the money which Philippe stole from Madame Descoings, only to lose it at roulette, is money which would otherwise have made not only his fortune, but his whole family's. Yet, before Philippe's hubris meets its nemesis, he has selfishly won for himself the very amount (three million francs) that Madame Descoings would have won for the whole family had she taken part in the lottery draw of 25 December 1821! Madame Bridau does not live to see the ultimate collapse of Philippe's ambition; but the letter he sends her at the peak of his wealth and success is enough to convince her that he, not Joseph, is the black sheep of the family.

'Balzac,' wrote Théodore de Banville, 'is the immortal Homer of the modern world.' Of no novel is this truer than *La Rabouilleuse*. A latter-day Hector and Achilles, Max and Philippe brace themselves for the final encounter. The battle-fields of Troy dissolve into those of Paris and Issoudun. The prophetic seer is no longer Calchas, braving the wrath of Agamemnon: it is the lawyer Desroches, who knows the secrets of men and who is not afraid to give unwelcome advice to the epic hero himself. Compared with the novels of Dostoievski or Dickens, *The Human Comedy* often seems void of spiritual content. What goes on within the calculators' souls? Is Philippe entirely heartless? Even the innumerable instances of irony do not, as in *Great Expectations*, for example, probe questioningly into the hero's heart. The valedictory paragraph concerning Max is more of an epitaph than a summation of character and motive. Like Homer, Balzac sees all, but does not judge.

D. A.

Member of the Académie Française,
and Curator of the Bibliothèque de l'Arsenal

HERE, my dear Nodier, is a work full of those circumstances which domestic secrecy hides from the law's reach; facts in which the finger of God, so often entitled Chance, compensates for the shortcomings of human justice, and where the moral code is no less instructive and impressive for being voiced with a mocking laugh. I believe that important lessons result from these facts, both for the Family and Motherhood. Perhaps when it is too late, we shall realize the consequences of this erosion of paternal authority, an authority which in bygone times did not cease until the father's death and which was the one human tribunal before which domestic crimes could be judged; on great occasions, Royalty was ready to put its decisions into effect. However affectionate and kind the Mother is, she can no more replace this patriarchal royalty than a Woman can replace a King upon the throne; wherever such an exception occurs, some monstrous being results. Never more vividly than here, perhaps, have I shown how necessary an indissoluble state of marriage is to European society, how great are the misfortunes resulting from feminine weakness and what dangers are inherent in unbridled personal interest. Any society based solely on the power of money should tremble at the prospect of the law's inability to curb the machinations of a system which aspires after success by permitting all possible means to be used in order to attain it. Such a society should take prompt refuge in Catholicism, which will cleanse the masses of the people both by instilling religious feeling and by teaching a system of education that is not merely secular. Enough fine characters and enough instances of great and noble devotion will shine forth in the *Scenes of Military Life* for it to be possible in this novel to show how much depravity is caused in certain individuals by the demands of war, when in civilian life they are bold enough to act as if they were still on the battlefield. You have looked upon our age with a shrewd eye, and revealed your outlook on the world in a number of bitter reflexions scattered amongst your elegantly written pages; you have appreciated better than anyone the havoc inflicted upon our country's mentality by four successive political systems. For all these reasons it was impossible for me to place this story under the patronage of a more competent authority. Your name will perhaps defend this novel against the accusations it will certainly give rise to: where is the patient who remains silent when the surgeon removes the dressing from his most painful wounds? Not only do I have the pleasure of dedicating this Scene to you; I am proud to make public acknowledgement of the kindness you have always shown

One of your sincere admirers,

DE BALZAC

PART ONE: THE TWO BROTHERS

1. The Descoings and the Rougets

IN the year 1792 the townsfolk of Issoudun were fortunate enough to have a doctor of the name of Rouget who had the reputation of being an extremely wily man. According to what was said by some bold people, he made his wife's life fairly unhappy in spite of the fact that she was the most beautiful woman in the town. Perhaps she was a little stupid. Despite jealous slander, friends' inquisitiveness and the gossip of people who felt indifferent to the Rougets, hardly anything was known of what went on inside the Rouget household. Dr Rouget was one of those men of whom it is colloquially said: 'He's not easy to get on with.' Consequently, people did not discuss him during his lifetime and were always pleasant to his face. His wife, a Mademoiselle Descoings, who even as a girl enjoyed rather poor health (that, it was said, was one of the reasons why the doctor married her), first bore him a son and afterwards a daughter who, by some accident of fate, came into the world ten years later than her brother and whom (so the tale ran) the doctor was not expecting, despite the fact that he was a doctor. The daughter who came so belatedly into the world was called Agathe. These small facts are so simple and commonplace that nothing, it would seem, can justify an historian in placing them at the opening of a story; yet, if they were to remain unknown, a man of Dr Rouget's stamp would be judged a monster and an unnatural father, whereas he was quite simply following his bad inclinations which many people seek to excuse with that terrible axiom: 'Every man has a character of his own!' This masculine proverb has caused much misfortune to many women. The Descoings, the doctor's parents-in-law, who were wool brokers, made it their business to sell the golden fleeces of the province of Berry on the sheep-farmers' behalf and to buy in again for the shopkeepers, thus drawing a commission from both sides. In this career they grew rich and remained miserly: such is the way of many lives. Young Descoings, Madame Rouget's younger brother, did not like Issoudun. He went off to make his fortune in Paris, and set up as a grocer in the Rue Saint-Honoré. This was his undoing. But what can be done about such things? A grocer is attracted towards his trade as powerfully as artists are repelled by it. Insufficient attention has been paid to the social forces which lead people towards different careers. It would be interesting to know what it is that determines a man to become a stationer rather than a baker now that sons are no longer compelled to follow their fathers' trades, as was the custom in ancient Egypt. Love had fostered Descoings' vocation. On seeing the woman who was to employ him, he had said to himself: 'I will become a grocer too!' – besides saying other things to himself at the same time; this woman was a most beautiful creature with whom he fell head over heels in love. With no other aid than patience, and with a little money from his father and mother, he married the widow of his predecessor, Monsieur Bixiou. In 1792 Descoings's business seemed to be thriving. The old Descoings were still alive at this time. Having made their money in wool, they invested it in the purchase of property sequestered by the nation: another golden fleece! Virtually certain that he would soon lose his wife, their son-in-law sent his daughter to stay with his brother-in-law in Paris, not merely so that she could see something of the capital, but also with an ulterior motive in mind. Descoings was childless. Madame Descoings, twelve years older than her husband, was in extremely good health; but she was as plump as a thrush at harvest-time, and the wily old Rouget knew enough about medicine to foresee that – contrary to the way fairy tales end – Monsieur and Madame

24

Descoings would live happily ever after but have no children. The household could become passionately fond of Agathe. It so happened that Dr Rouget was wanting to disinherit his daughter and he flattered himself that he could bring about this result by sending her away from home. This young person, who at that time was the most beautiful girl in Issoudun, did not take after either of her parents. Her birth had led to an eternal quarrel between Dr Rouget and his close friend Monsieur Lousteau, the former Subdelegate who had just left Issoudun. When a family leaves its native district to live elsewhere, the old inhabitants of a locality as delightful as Issoudun are entitled to ponder the reasons for so outrageous an action. According to a few scandalmongers, Monsieur Rouget (a vindictive man) had vowed to kill Lousteau. Coming from a doctor, this threat had all the force of a cannon-ball. When the office of subdelegate was abolished by the National Assembly, Lousteau left Issoudun never to return. After the Lousteaus' departure, Madame Rouget spent all her time with the ex-Subdelegate's own sister, Madame Hochon, who was her daughter's godmother and the only person to whom she would confide her distress. So it came about that what little was known in Issoudun of the beautiful Madame Rouget was disclosed by this good lady, but not until after the doctor was dead.

Madame Rouget's first words, when her husband spoke to her of sending Agathe to Paris, were: 'I shall never see my daughter again!'

'And how right she was, I'm afraid!' the respectable Madame Hochon often remarked.

Poor Madame Rouget grew as yellow as a quince, and her state of health did nothing to contradict the people who claimed that Rouget was gradually killing her. The behaviour of her great booby of a son also contributed to the unhappiness of a mother so unjustly accused of unfaithfulness. Hardly restrained, perhaps even encouraged by his father, this boy, who was stupid in every way, showed her neither the consideration nor the respect which any boy owes his mother. Jean-Jacques Rouget resembled his father, but only in his bad features, and the doctor was by no means good either in physique or character.

The arrival of charming Agathe Rouget brought no happiness to her uncle Descoings. That very week, or rather decade (for the Republic had been proclaimed), he was imprisoned by Fouquier-Tinville on Robespierre's orders. Rash enough to believe that the so-called famine was a trumped-up business, Descoings stupidly voiced his opinions (he thought there was free speech now!) to several of his clients whilst serving them. Citizeness Duplay, a joiner's wife with whom Robespierre lodged and who did the great citizen's housework, honoured Descoings's shop with her custom – much to his misfortune. She considered that the grocer's opinions were offensive towards Maximilien I. Already dissatisfied with the ways of the Descoings household, this illustrious knitting woman of the Jacobin club regarded Citizeness Descoings's beauty as a sort of aristocracy in itself. She exaggerated Descoings's words as she repeated them to her good and gentle master. The grocer was arrested on a vulgar charge of cornering food supplies. After his imprisonment, Descoings's wife strove to secure his release; but she was so clumsy in her endeavours that if any observer had heard her addressing the arbiters of his destiny, he would easily have believed that she wanted to get rid of him in a decent and respectable manner. Madame Descoings knew Bridau, a secretary to the Minister of the Interior, Roland, and the right-hand man of all who succeeded Roland at this Ministry. She enlisted Bridau's help and support in an attempt to save the grocer's life. This most incorruptible Head Clerk, one of those virtuous dupes who are always so admirable in the very extent of their disinterestedness, was most careful not to try and bribe the people on whom Descoings's fate depended; instead, he tried to enlighten them! But as for enlightening people in those times, you might as well have asked them to restore the Bourbons to the throne. The Girondin Minister, who was then engaged in a struggle with Robespierre, asked Bridau: 'Why are you mixed up in this?' Everyone whom the honest official approached repeated the atrocious sentence: 'Why are you mixed up in this?'

Bridau wisely advised Madame Descoings to wait quietly on events. But instead of winning the esteem of Robespierre's housekeeper, she darted fire and flames against the informer: she went to see a member of the National Convention, a man trembling for his own safety, who told her: 'I'll speak to Robespierre about it.' The beautiful grocer's wife slept peacefully after hearing these words; and, naturally, her so-called protector observed the strictest silence. Descoings's life would have been saved if Citizeness Duplay had been given a few sugarloaves or a few bottles of good liqueur. This little episode proves that in revolutionary times it is as dangerous to obtain one's release with the aid of honest people as with the aid of rogues: you must only rely upon yourself. Though Descoings died, he at least had the glory of going to the scaffold in André de Chénier's company. This, no doubt, was the first time that the Grocery Trade and the Craft of Poetry embraced one another in person – for they had secret relationships and always will have. Descoings's death produced far more of a sensation than André de Chénier's. It has taken thirty years to realize that France lost more by Chénier's death than by Descoings's. Robespierre's action had this to be said for it, that until 1830 grocers were too frightened to take any further part in politics. Descoings's shop was a hundred yards from Robespierre's lodgings. The grocer's successor fared badly in the business. He was followed by César Birotteau, the celebrated perfumer. But, as if the scaffold had somehow infected the place with misfortune, the inventor of the *Superfine Oriental Cream* and *Carminative Toilet Water* went bankrupt on the same premises. The key to this problem can only be provided by the occult sciences.

During the Head Clerk's few visits to the unfortunate Descoings's wife, he was struck by Agathe Rouget's cool, artless and tranquil beauty. Coming to console the widow, who was so inconsolable that she would not carry on in the business of her second deceased husband, he ended by marrying this charming girl within ten days, but not until after her father's arrival from Issoudun – which was not long delayed. The doctor was delighted to find things working out better than he had imagined in his wildest expectations, since now his wife became the Descoings' sole heir; he hurried to Paris, not so much to attend Agathe's wedding as to have the marriage settlement drawn up in accordance with his own wishes. Such was Citizen Bridau's disinterestedness and excessive love that he allowed the treacherous doctor a free hand, and the old man exploited his son-in-law's blindness – as subsequent events will show. Madame Rouget, or to be more precise the doctor, therefore became the heir to all the real and personal property that belonged to Monsieur and Madame Descoings, the parents, who died within two years of one another. Rouget eventually got the better of his wife, who died early in 1799. And he owned vineyards, bought farms, acquired forges and had wool to sell! His dearly loved son was incapable of taking up any career; but his father intended him for the condition of Gentleman and allowed him to grow in wealth and stupidity, confident that in any case his son would cope just as easily with the problems of living and dying as the most learned men. As early as 1799, people at Issoudun interested enough to estimate the size of old Rouget's fortune already credited him with a private income of 30,000 francs a year. After his wife's death, the doctor still led a dissipated life; but he regulated it, so to speak, confining his debauchery to the secrecy of the home. The doctor died in 1805 after a life full of idiosyncrasies. Heaven alone knows how much the townsfolk of Issoudun talked about him then, and how many stories were spread around concerning his horrifying private life. Jean-Jacques Rouget, who was kept under firm control by his father after the latter had recognized his stupidity, remained unmarried for reasons of great gravity, whose explanation forms so important an element in this story. As we shall see later, his celibacy was partly the doctor's fault.

It is now necessary to see what were the consequences of the revenge which the father took on a daughter whom he refused to recognize as his own, yet who – please believe this – was his own legitimate child. No one in Issoudun had noticed one of those curious circumstances which make procreation an abyss unfathomable by science. Agathe took after Dr

Rouget's mother. Just as (in the popular phrase) gout jumps a generation from grandfather to grandson, so it is not unusual to find physical resemblances transmitted in an identical manner.

Thus, whilst physically resembling his mother, the elder of Agathe's sons had exactly the same character as Dr Rouget, his grandfather. Let us leave the solution of this problem to the twentieth century, with a fine array of names to describe microscopic animalcules; then, perhaps, our grandchildren and great-grandchildren will write as much nonsense on this mysterious subject as has already been written by our learned societies.

2. *The Bridau family*

AGATHE Rouget deserved general admiration for one of
those faces which, like the Virgin Mary's countenance, are
destined to remain always virginal, even after marriage. Her
portrait, which still exists in Bridau's studio, shows that it was
a perfect oval, and that her white complexion was unblemished
by any trace of redness in spite of the fact that she had golden
hair. Seeing her pure forehead, discreet mouth, fine nose,
pretty ears, long eyelashes and infinitely affectionate dark-blue
eyes, not to mention the placidity which characterizes her
whole face, numerous artists ask our great painter today:
'Is that a copy of a Raphael head?'

Never did any man act on better inspiration than when the
Head Clerk married this young girl. Agathe embodied the
ideal of the housewife brought up in the provinces without
ever leaving her mother's side. Pious, though not fanatical,
she had received no education other than what the Church
makes available to women. She was, therefore, an accomplished wife (in the ordinary sense of that term, for her ignorance
of worldly matters led her into more than one misfortune).
The epitaph of a celebrated Roman lady: 'She worked tapestry
and ran the house', admirably conveys her pure, simple,
tranquil existence. As far back as the time of the Consulate,
Bridau became a fanatical supporter of Napoleon, who
appointed him a Departmental Head in 1804, one year before
Rouget's death. Earning a salary of 12,000 francs a year plus
handsome bonuses, Bridau was most unconcerned about the
shameful results of the winding-up of his father-in-law's
estate at Issoudun, from which Agathe received nothing. Six
months before his death, old Rouget had sold a portion of his
property to his son – allotting the remainder to him both as a
preferential gift and as a legacy to an heir. An advance pay-
ment of 100,000 francs, which Agathe had received in her

marriage settlement, was her share of the inheritance due to her from her parents.

Worshipping the Emperor to idolatry, Bridau served with slavish devotion the powerful conceptions of this modern demi-god, who, finding everything destroyed in France, aimed to reorganize the country. Not once did the Departmental Head say: 'Enough!' Drafts, memoranda, reports, studies – he accepted the heaviest burdens, so happy was he to assist the Emperor; he loved him as a man, adored him as a sovereign and would not allow any criticism either of his actions or plans. From 1804 to 1808, the Departmental Head made his home in a large and beautiful flat on the Quai Voltaire, within close walking distance of his Ministry and the Tuileries. A cook and manservant were the only household staff, even in the days of Madame Bridau's grandeur. Agathe, who always got up first, went with her cook to Les Halles. Whilst the manservant was cleaning the flat, she attended to breakfast. Bridau never left for the Ministry before about eleven. Throughout their married life, his wife never failed to delight in cooking him an exquisite breakfast, the only meal Bridau really enjoyed. At all seasons of the year, and whatever the weather was like when he set out for the office, Agathe would stand at the window watching her husband make his way towards the Ministry, and never turn back into the room until he had disappeared round the corner of the Rue du Bac. She would then clear the table herself and give an eye to everything in the flat, after which she dressed, played with her children, took them out for a walk, or received visitors – whilst awaiting Bridau's return. Whenever the Departmental Head brought urgent work to be done at home, she would settle down beside his table, in his study, sitting as silent as a statue and knitting as she watched him work; she would stay up as long as he stayed up, going to bed just before him. Sometimes the married couple would go out to the theatre, sitting in one of the boxes which were booked permanently by the Ministry. On such occasions they would dine out at a restaurant; and the sight of all that went on in the restaurant always gave Madame Bridau the keenest of pleasures, such as people experience when they have never seen Paris before. Agathe often had to accept invitations to grand formal dinners given in honour of the Departmental Head, who was in charge of a section of the Ministry of the Interior, invitations which Bridau returned in appropriate dignity. She would then dress in the luxurious fashion of the time, but on returning home she was glad to throw off this showy splendour and resume the provincial simplicity that characterized her household. Once a week, on Thursdays, Bridau would entertain his friends. And on Shrove Tuesdays he gave a great ball.

These few words epitomize the whole story of a marriage in which there were only three great events: the births of two children, three years apart, and the death of Bridau, who (worn out by his habit of staying up late at nights) passed away in 1808, just as the Emperor was about to appoint him Director-General, a Count and a Councillor of State. At this period Napoleon gave the domestic affairs of France his particular attention; he overwhelmed Bridau with work and eventually ruined this intrepid official's health. Napoleon, from whom Bridau had never requested anything, had made inquiries about his way of life and private means. Learning that this devoted man had nothing to live on apart from his job, he realized that Bridau was one of those incorruptible souls who enhanced and gave moral tone to his administration, and wished to surprise Bridau by conferring dazzling rewards upon him. The wish to finish off an immense piece of work before the Emperor's departure for Spain killed the Departmental Head, whose death was caused by an inflammatory fever. After his return, the Emperor spent a few days in Paris preparing his 1809 campaign; on learning of this loss, he said: 'There are some men who are irreplaceable!'

. Impressed by an example of loyalty unrewarded by any of those brilliant marks of recognition which he reserved for his soldiers, the Emperor decided to institute an Order for the civilian population, with a substantial pension for its recipients – in just the same way that he had instituted the Legion of Honour for military distinction. The impression produced on his mind by Bridau's death led him to devise the Order of Reunion;

32

but he did not have time to complete his plans for this aristocratic creation, the memory of which has so completely faded
that, on reading the name of this short-lived order, the majority
of my readers will wonder what were its insignia: it had a
blue ribbon. The Emperor named it the Order of Reunion
in the intention of combining the Spanish and Austrian orders
of the Golden Fleece. Providence – as a Prussian diplomat has
said – managed to prevent such a desecration. The Emperor
kept himself informed of Madame Bridau's financial situation.
The two sons were each granted full scholarships to the Lycée
Impérial, and the Emperor paid for their education out of his
Privy Purse. Then, he put Madame Bridau's name down to
receive a pension of 4,000 francs a year, no doubt leaving any
financial provision for the two sons until some future date.

From her marriage to the time of her husband's death,
Madame Bridau had no contact whatsoever with Issoudun.
When her mother died, she was just about to give birth to her
second son. The death of her father, of whose scant affection
towards her she was well aware, coincided with the Emperor's
coronation, which gave Bridau so much work that she was
reluctant to leave her husband. Her brother, Jean-Jacques
Rouget, had never written her a word since she left Issoudun.
Although most upset by her family's tacit repudiation of her,
Agathe eventually gave very little thought to those who never
thought of her. Every year she received a letter from her
godmother, Madame Hochon, to which she would reply with
commonplace remarks, paying no close attention to this
excellent and pious woman's cryptically worded advice. Some
time before Dr Rouget's death, Madame Hochon wrote and
told her goddaughter that she would inherit nothing from her
father's estate unless she empowered Monsieur Hochon to act
as her proxy. Agathe did not wish to be troublesome to her
brother. Whether Bridau realized that her disinheritance was
justified by the provincial laws and customs of Berry, or
whether this pure and just man shared his wife's magnanimity
and worldly indifference in matters of self-interest, he would
not listen to his solicitor Roguin's advice that he should turn
his position to good advantage by disputing the legal docu-

ments on the basis of which Dr Rouget had managed to deprive
his daughter of her lawful share in her father's estate. Husband
and wife gave their approval to the arrangements which were
made in Issoudun.

However, in such circumstances as these, Roguin had made
the Departmental Head think carefully about his wife's
compromised interests. This extremely competent man realized
that, if he were to die, Agathe would be penniless. He then
inquired into the state of his affairs and found that, between
1793 and 1805, he and his wife had had to draw about 30,000
francs of the 50,000 francs cash which old Rouget had given
his daughter; he invested the remaining 20,000 francs in
Government stock. The funds then stood at forty. Consequently, Agathe received a private investment income from
the State of about 2,000 francs a year. With an income of
6,000 francs a year after her widowhood, Madame Bridau could
therefore maintain a respectable standard of living. Still a
provincial at heart, she wanted to dismiss Bridau's manservant,
keeping only her cook, and move to another flat, but Madame
Descoings, her intimate friend who would persist in calling
herself her aunt, sold her furniture, left her own flat and came
to live with Agathe, converting Bridau's study into a bedroom.
The two widows pooled their resources, and found that they
had a joint income of 12,000 francs a year. This course seems
simple and natural enough. But nothing in life demands
closer attention than the things which seem natural; people
are always wary enough of the extraordinary. This is why
you find men of experience, such as attorneys, judges, doctors
and priests, laying enormous stress on the simple things in life:
and people think they are overprecise! The snake hidden
amongst the flowers is one of the finest myths which Antiquity
has handed down to us to guide us in the conduct of our
affairs. How many times do we hear fools exclaim, as they
justify their behaviour in their own eyes or in the eyes of
others: 'It was so simple that anybody would have been taken
in!'

In 1809 Madame Descoings, who would never divulge her
age, was sixty-five years old. Nicknamed the 'beautiful

34

grocer's wife' in her youth, she was one of those few women whom the passage of time leaves unscathed; thanks to her excellent constitution she was fortunate enough to preserve a beauty which, even so, did not stand up to serious examination. Of medium height, and plump and fresh in her appearance, she had beautiful shoulders and a slightly pink complexion. Despite the the catastrophe which had befallen Descoings, her light chestnut-brown hair showed not the slightest change of colour. Exceedingly fond of delicacies, she loved to cook herself tasty little dishes; but, though she gave the impression of thinking a great deal about food, she also adored the theatre and indulged in a vice which she cloaked in the profoundest secrecy: she had her flutters on the lottery! Is not gambling the abyss which mythology represents to us as the leaking barrel endlessly refilled by the Danaides? La Descoings – any woman who gambles on the lottery should be referred to in this way – spent perhaps rather too much money on dress, as do all women fortunate enough to keep their youthful looks into middle age; but, apart from these slight faults of character, she was the easiest of women to live with. Always agreeing with everybody, never upsetting anyone, she delighted people with her sweet, infectious gaiety. Above all, she possessed an eminently Parisian quality which fascinates retired clerks and merchants: she had a sense of humour! The fact that she did not marry for a third time was due, no doubt, to the circumstances of the age. During the wars of the Empire, marriageable men found it much too easy to marry beautiful and wealthy young women to pay any attention to women of sixty.

Madame Descoings tried to cheer Madame Bridau up; she often took her out for drives or to the theatre, she cooked excellent little dinners for her and even tried to marry her to her son Bixiou. Alas! She confessed to Agathe the terrible secret which she, her late husband and her solicitor had kept closely guarded. The young, elegant Madame Descoings, who made out she was thirty-six, had a son aged thirty-five, named Bixiou, who was already a widower; he was an adjutant in the 21st Infantry Regiment, who died at the Battle of Dresden after rising to the rank of colonel, leaving an only son. Madame Descoings, who only ever saw her grandson Bixiou secretly, passed him off as her husband's son by a first wife. She confided in Agathe out of prudence; Colonel Bixiou's son, educated at the Lycée Impérial with the two Bridau boys, was granted an exhibition. This young man, who was both cunning and mischievous even as a schoolboy, later acquired a great reputation both as a cartoonist and wit. Agathe now loved nothing in the world apart from her children, and wished to live only for them. She refused to marry again, out of both common sense and fidelity to her husband. But it is easier for a woman to be a good wife than a good mother. A widow has two tasks, with mutually contradictory obligations: she is a mother, yet must exercise paternal authority. Few women are strong enough to understand and play this dual role. And so, despite her qualities of character, poor Agathe was the innocent cause of many misfortunes.

Because of her limited intelligence and because, too, of that confidence in others which is the habitual attitude of unselfish souls, Agathe fell a victim to Madame Descoings, who plunged her into an appalling misfortune. Madame Descoings gambled on lottery numbers and the lottery would not allow its punters any credit. As she managed the household she could use the housekeeping money as her gambling stakes, in the hope of enriching her grandson Bixiou, her dear Agathe and the young Bridaus; in this way, the household ran gradually into debt. When the debt had mounted to 10,000 francs, she put even more money on the lottery hoping that her favourite number, which had never come out for nine years, would fill the seemingly bottomless deficit. From then on, the debt grew rapidly. Once it had reached the figure of 20,000 francs, Madame Descoings lost her head; and still her lottery number did not win. She then wished to repay her niece by mortgaging her fortune; but Roguin, her solicitor, explained to her that this honest plan was impracticable. On his brother-in-law Descoings's death, the late Dr Rouget had taken over the inheritance, depriving Madame Descoings of any interest in the principal by paying her out of Jean-Jacques Rouget's estate a pension which would lapse at her death. No money-lender would be willing to lend 20,000 francs to a woman of sixty-seven years of age whose only security was a pension of about 4,000 francs a year – at a time when there were 10 per cent investments galore. One morning Madame Descoings went and threw herself at her niece's feet, and between her sobs confessed the state of affairs. Madame Bridau did not breathe a word of blame; she dismissed the manservant and cook, disposed of all unnecessary furniture, sold three-quarters of her Treasury scrip, settled all the debts, and gave notice that she would be leaving her flat.

3. The unfortunate widows

ONE of the most horrible corners of Paris is certainly that portion of the Rue Mazarine which runs from the Rue Guénégaud to the point at which it joins the Rue de Seine, behind the Palais de l'Institut. The tall grey walls of the college and library donated to the City of Paris by Cardinal Mazarin, and which were one day destined to house the Académie Française, cast icy shadows across this part of the street; sunshine is a rare sight, and an icy north wind blows along it. The poor ruined widow took up residence on the third floor of one of the houses in this damp, dark, cold corner.

Facing the house are the Institut buildings, which at that time contained the cells of those wild animals known as 'artists' by middle-class folk and as *rapins* or 'art students' in all the studios. Young men began there as students and could leave on a Government scholarship to Rome. This process was not accomplished without extraordinary commotions, at those times of the year when competitors for the Government scholarships were immured in the cells. To win a scholarship, a sculptor had to produce the clay model of a statue within a given time; a painter, one of the pictures which you can see at the École des Beaux-Arts; a musician would have produced a cantata; an architect, the design for a monument. At the time of writing, this menagerie has been moved from these cold, sombre buildings to the elegant Palais des Beaux-Arts, a few yards away.

Madame Bridau's windows looked down on to the cells, which (with iron bars across their windows) were an exceedingly dismal sight. To the north, the view is blocked by the dome of the Institut. As you walk up the street, the only thing to gladden the eye is the line of cabs waiting at the upper end of the Rue Mazarine. This eventually prompted the widow to put three window boxes outside her windows, in which she

38

tended one of those aerial gardens now threatened by police regulations, and whose greenery rarefies both air and daylight. The house, which backs on to another facing towards the Rue de Seine, is inevitably lacking in depth; it had a spiral staircase. The third floor is at the top of the house. Her flat had three windows and three main rooms: a dining-room, a small drawing-room and a bedroom. Facing these, on the opposite side of the landing, was a small kitchen; above the main rooms are two bachelor bedrooms and an immense loft serving no apparent purpose. Madame Bridau chose this flat for three reasons: the low rent – it was only 400 francs a year, which enabled her to sign a nine years' lease; its closeness to her sons' school – she was only a short distance away from the Lycée Impérial; lastly, she was still living in an area to which she had grown accustomed.

The furnishings matched the flat itself. In the dining-room, which had an unpolished red floor and closely patterned wallpaper with green flowers, there were only the barest essentials in the way of furniture: a table, two sideboards and six chairs – all of which came from the previous flat. The drawing-room had an Aubusson carpet which Bridau had been given when the Ministry was refurnished. There the widow placed one of those ordinary pieces of mahogany furniture with Egyptian heads, which Jacob Desmalter was manufacturing by the hundred in 1806; it was upholstered in a green silk material with white rosettes. Above the sofa, Bridau's portrait – a pastel drawn by a friend – at once commanded attention. Although perhaps the picture lacked artistic finish, the sitter's forehead clearly revealed the strength of character of this great citizen who lived and died in obscurity. The serene expression of his eyes, which were both gentle and proud, was well delineated. The shrewdness, clearly evidenced by his prudent lips, and the frank memory and facial expression of the man whom the Emperor used to refer to with the words: *justum et tenacem*, had been conveyed faithfully, if not brilliantly. Anyone beholding this portrait could see that this man had always done his duty. His face expressed that incorruptibility of character said to have been possessed by several men who spent their lives in the service of the Republic. Opposite, over a card table, shone a coloured reproduction of Vernet's portrait of the Emperor, which shows Napoleon riding rapidly by, followed by his escort. Agathe treated herself to two large birdcages, one of them full of canaries, the other containing parrots. She had indulged in this childish taste since losing her husband – a loss which she found as irreparable as do many other widows. As for Madame Bridau's bedroom, after three months it had become as it was destined to remain until the fateful day when she was compelled to leave it – a jumble which no description could set to rights. Cats sprawled on its easy chairs; when she occasionally let the canaries loose, they left specks of dirt over all the furniture. The poor kind-hearted widow put bird-seed and chickweed for them in various places about the room. Titbits were left out for the cats in chipped saucers. Clothes were strewn around. The bedroom bespoke her provincial origins and conjugal fidelity.

Everything that had been Bridau's was carefully preserved. The equipment he had used in his office was given the same loving attention as in former times would have been given by a paladin's widow to her late husband's weapons. One detail will suffice to indicate her touching worship of her husband. She had wrapped and sealed a pen, writing these words on the envelope: 'The last pen used by my dear husband.' The cup out of which he had drunk his last sip of coffee was preserved on the mantelpiece under a glass cover. Later on, bonnets and hairpieces sat proudly on the glass globes containing her precious relics. After Bridau's death, his young widow of thirty-five showed no trace either of coquetry or feminine vanity. Parted from the one man she had known, respected and loved, and who never caused her any distress, she no longer thought of herself as a woman, nothing mattered to her any more; she no longer paid any attention to dress. Never was there a more simple or more complete abdication of conjugal happiness and coquetry. Love enables some people to lose themselves in another human personality; when they

40

are cut off from that person, life is no longer possible for them. Agathe now lived only for her sons; she grieved to think of all the hardships which her ruin would bring upon them. Ever since her removal to the Rue Mazarine, her face had a tinge of melancholy, distressing to those who saw it. She expected some help to be forthcoming from the Emperor, but the Emperor could do no more for her than he was already doing: each of the boys had been granted 600 francs a year from the Privy Purse, over and above his scholarship.

As for the radiant Madame Descoings, she lived on the second floor in a similar flat to her niece's. She had made over 3,000 francs a year to Madame Bridau, as a preferential charge on her life interest. Roguin, the solicitor, had put everything right for Madame Bridau in this respect, but it would take about seven years for this slow process of repayment to make up the deficit. Having received instructions to build up the 1,500 francs a year investment income, Roguin regularly banked the sums which he recouped. Now reduced to an income of 1,200 francs a year, Madame Descoings lived on a humble scale with her niece. These honest but weak-willed creatures employed a charwoman just for the mornings. The dinner was prepared by Madame Descoings, who liked cooking. In the evenings, a few friends – Ministry clerks whom Bridau had originally appointed – would come for a game of cards with the two widows. Madame Descoings still backed her lottery number, which she said was obstinately determined not to come out in the draws. She was hoping that at a single go she would be able to return all the money she had been compelled to borrow from her niece. She loved the two Bridau boys more than her grandson Bixiou, so strongly did she feel the wrong she had done them, so deeply did she admire the kind-heartedness of her niece, who – even in her moments of greatest suffering – never uttered a word of blame. As you can well believe, Joseph and Philippe were spoiled by Madame Descoings. Like all who wish to have some vice forgiven them, the old punter of the Imperial lottery of France would prepare little dinners for them, laden with dainty morsels. As time went on, Joseph and Philippe had no difficulty at all in wheedling money out of her, with which the younger boy bought sticks of charcoal, pencils, paper and engravings, and the elder, apple turnovers, marbles, pieces of string and knives. Such was her passion for gambling that she became perfectly happy to spend no more than fifty francs a month on housekeeping; then she could gamble the remainder.

Nor would Madame Bridau allow her expenditure to exceed this level – again, out of love for the boys. To punish herself for her overconfidence, she would heroically cut back on her little enjoyments. As is the case with many shy people of limited intelligence, the fact that one single feeling had been hurt and her distrust aroused led her to carry a fault of character to such extreme lengths that that fault took on the stable appearance of a virtue. The Emperor might forget (so she would ponder), or he might perish in some battle, and besides, her pension would cease at her death. She shuddered at the very likely prospect that her sons would be left penniless in the world. Mystified by Roguin's calculations, when he tried to explain how within seven years a deduction of 3,000 francs a year from Madame Descoings's life interest would restore the dilapidated investment income, she believed neither him, nor her aunt, nor the State; she would rely now only upon herself and her self-inflicted hardships. Setting aside 3,000 francs a year from her pension, she would have accumulated 30,000 francs in ten years, which would have yielded at least 1,500 francs a year interest for one of her sons. At thirty-six years of age, she was certainly entitled to expect another twenty years of life; it followed that such a system was bound to provide each of them with the bare minimum.

Thus the two widows had passed from deceptive affluence to self-imposed poverty, one having been brought to this pass by a defect of character, the other by what appeared to be the most unselfish virtue. Not one of these minute details will be irrelevant to the deep moral of this story – a story based upon life's most ordinary interests, but whose scope will perhaps be only the greater for this reason. The sight of the cells, the excited antics of the art students in the street, the fact that it was necessary to look skywards for any consolation from the horrible views that crowd in upon this constantly damp corner, the appearance of his father's portrait so full of soulfulness and grandeur despite the painter's amateurish technique, the sight of rich colours, but colours that had grown mellow and harmonious, inside the flat (it was always so pleasant and tranquil at home!), the greenery of the window boxes, the household's poverty, the mother's preference for her elder son, the difference between his tastes and his younger brother's – in other words, the conjunction of facts and circumstances which is the prelude to this story may perhaps contain the generative causes to which we are indebted for Joseph Bridau, one of the great artists of the contemporary school of French painting.

4. Vocation

PHILIPPE, the elder of the Bridau boys, strikingly resembled his mother. Though he had fair hair and blue eyes, he had a rowdy way with him which easily could be taken for high spirits and even for courage. Twice or three times a month, old Claparon, who had been appointed to the Ministry at the same time as Bridau and who was one of the faithful friends who came in the evenings to play cards with the two widows, would say to Philippe, as he patted him on the cheeks: 'This little fellow will get up to anything!' Spurred on by these words, the boy developed a kind of determination, merely out of bravado. Once this bent had been given to his character, he became skilled in all bodily exercises. Fighting at school filled him with that boldness and scorn for pain from which military valour arises; but naturally, he also contracted the greatest possible aversion to study, for public education will never resolve the difficult problem of simultaneously developing the body and the mind. From the purely physical resemblance between herself and Philippe, Agathe concluded that he must also resemble her in character, firmly believing that one day her delicacy of sentiment would be enhanced by manly strength. Philippe was fifteen years old when his mother came to settle in the dejected flat in the Rue Mazarine, and his sweet ways, which all children have at that age, confirmed her maternal convictions.

Joseph was three years younger than Philippe; he took after his father, but only in the less favourable aspects of his father's nature. To begin with, no matter what one tried to do about it, his thick black hair was always unkempt, whereas his brother was always neat and good-looking, despite his high spirits. Besides this, Joseph could not keep any article of clothing clean (no one could tell what fatality it was which caused this, but too constant a fatality becomes a habit!); if he was given new clothes, he soon had them looking as old as his previous ones. The elder boy looked after his things out of vanity. By slow degrees, the mother grew used to scolding Joseph and holding up his brother to him as an example.

Agathe, therefore, did not always treat her two sons alike; whenever she went off to look for them, she would ask herself apropos of Joseph: 'What state will he have got his clothes into now?' Such trivial details pushed her heart into the abyss of maternal favouritism. Not one of the extremely ordinary-minded people who made up the two widows' circle of acquaintances – old Du Bruel, Claparon, Desroches, not even Agathe's confessor, Abbé Loraux – noticed Joseph's observant ways. Dominated by his inclination, the future colourist paid no attention to anything that concerned himself; this tendency so closely resembled torpor during his years of childhood that his father had felt rather concerned about him. At first, the extraordinary size of his head and the width of his forehead had given rise to fears that the boy might have water on the brain. His restless face, whose originality could be mistaken for ugliness by people unaware of a face's moral significance, had a fairly surly expression during his youth. His features, which filled out later on, looked to be contorted, and the boy's deep attentiveness contorted them even more. Thus, Philippe flattered all his mother's vanities, whereas Joseph never received any compliment from her. Witty remarks fell from Philippe's lips, repartees which induce parents to believe that their children will become remarkable men; Joseph, on the other hand, was always silent and thoughtful. Agathe hoped for wonders from Philippe, but expected nothing from Joseph.

Joseph's leanings towards art were reinforced by a most everyday occurrence: during the Easter holidays of 1812, he was returning with his brother and Madame Descoings from a walk in the Tuileries gardens when he saw an art student sketching a caricature of one of his teachers and he stood rooted to the pavement, lost in admiration of a chalk outline drawing that sparkled with mischievous humour. Next day he stood at the window watching the art students entering the doorway in the Rue Mazarine. He crept downstairs and slipped into the long courtyard of the Institut, where he noticed the statues, busts, unfinished marbles, terracottas and plaster casts, and gazed at them feverishly; for his instinct was making itself felt, a sense of his vocation was stirring within him. A half-open door led him into a low room, where he found ten or a dozen young men drawing a statue; immediately, he became the butt of a thousand jokes.

'Here, little boy!' said one of the young men, noticing him and picking up the inside of a loaf, pieces of which he threw in his direction.

'Whose child is he?'

'God! Isn't he ugly?'

For a quarter of an hour Joseph was subjected to the caricatures of the art students working under the direction of the great sculptor Chaudet; however, after having a good laugh at his expense, the students were struck by his persistence and facial expression, and asked him what he wanted. Joseph replied that he was very eager to learn to draw, whereupon everybody encouraged him. Captivated by their friendliness, the child explained that he was Madame Bridau's son.

'Well! if you are Madame Bridau's son, you can become a great man,' the students exclaimed from every corner of the studio.

'Long live Madame Bridau's son! Is your mother pretty? If your mug's anything to go by, she must look a bit off!'

'So! you want to be an artist,' said the oldest of the art students, leaving his place and walking over towards Joseph to draw him a caricature; 'but do you realize that you have to be brave and put up with great hardships? Yes, there are trials which would knock you for six. There's not one of the fellows here who hasn't had to face these trials. Look, that chap over there went without food for seven days! Let's see whether you have the makings of an artist!'

He seized one of the boy's arms and lifted it straight above his head; then he placed the other arm as if Joseph was about to give a fist blow.

'That's what we call the semaphore trial,' he went on. 'If

you can stay like that, without lowering or changing the position of your arms for a quarter of an hour, well then, you will have proved that you are a plucky little lad!'

'Come on, boy, be brave,' the others said. 'Heavens! You must be ready to suffer if you want to be an artist.'

With all the credulousness of a child of thirteen, Joseph stood stock-still for about five minutes, and all the art students watched him with straight faces.

'No, you're lowering your arms,' one cried.

'Hey! Hold yourself upright, damn you!' said someone else. 'The Emperor himself stood for a whole month in the pose you can see over there,' another added, pointing to Chaudet's fine statue of Napoleon. The Emperor was standing with the Imperial sceptre in his hand. In 1814, this statue was demolished from the column it had so beautifully graced.

Beads of sweat were glistening on Joseph's forehead after ten minutes of this exercise. Just then a small bald-headed man with a pale and sickly-looking face walked into the studio. A deeply respectful silence descended upon the room.

'Well, you rascals, what are you up to now?' he asked, looking at their young victim.

'It's a little fellow who's posing for us,' replied the tall student who had positioned Joseph's arms.

'You ought to feel ashamed of yourselves for torturing a poor child like that,' said Chaudet, lowering Joseph's arms to their normal position. 'How long have you been here?' he asked Joseph, giving him a friendly pat on the cheek.

'For a quarter of an hour.'

'And what brings you here?'

'I would like to become an artist.'

'And where do you come from, which family do you belong to?'

'I come from Mother's.'

'Oh! Mother's!' yelled the students.

'Silence, all of you,' cried Chaudet. 'What does your mother do?'

'She is Madame Bridau. My father, who is dead, was a

47

friend of the Emperor. So, if you will teach me to draw, the Emperor will pay you whatever you ask.'

'His father was a Departmental Head in the Ministry of the Interior,' cried Chaudet, suddenly remembering. 'And you want to become an artist so soon?'

'Yes, sir.'

'Come here as often as you like. We'll find something to amuse you! Give him a portfolio and some paper and pencils, and let him have a try. And bear in mind, you rascals, that his father once did me a good turn. Look here, Well-Rope, go and get some cakes, sweets and dainties,' he added, giving some small change to the student who had played the practical joke on Joseph. 'We'll soon see whether you are an artist from the way you guzzle the grub,' Chaudet continued, stroking Joseph's chin.

Then he walked round examining the work of his pupils, accompanied by Joseph, who watched, listened and tried to understand. The titbits arrived. Everyone ate heartily, including the sculptor himself and the boy. After first being hoaxed, Joseph was now pampered. This scene, so full of the fun and warm-heartedness of the artist's way of life, which Joseph instinctively understood, made a terrific impression on him. The sudden appearance in the room of the sculptor Chaudet, lost to the arts by a premature death and whom the Emperor's patronage destined for a brilliant future, seemed to Joseph to be like a vision. The boy did not tell his mother anything about this escapade, but every Sunday and Thursday he spent three hours in Chaudet's studio. Madame Descoings, who humoured the two darling angels' whims, began to give Joseph pencils, red chalk, engravings and drawing paper. At the Lycée Impérial the future artist sketched his masters, drew his school-friends, daubed charcoal on the dormitory walls and was astonishingly diligent in the drawing lesson. Struck not only by his aptitudes but also by his progress, Lemire, a teacher at the Lycée Impérial, called to inform Madame Bridau of her son's vocation. Being a provincial woman at heart whose knowledge of the arts was as slender as her knowledge of household matters was deep, Agathe was terror-stricken. She burst into tears as soon as Lemire had gone. 'This is the end!' she cried, as Madame Descoings entered the room. 'I wanted Joseph to become a civil servant. His way would already have been made at the Ministry of the Interior; with his father's reputation to help him along, he would have been a Departmental Head by the time he was twenty-five. Instead of that, he wants to become a painter, a really down-and-out job. I felt it in my bones that that child would cause me nothing but worry!'

Madame Descoings confessed that for several months she had been encouraging Joseph's passion for the arts and had cloaked his visits to the Institut every Sunday and Thursday. She had taken him to the Salon, the national exhibition of modern paintings held every other year, and the little fellow's deep interest in the pictures was nothing less than miraculous.

'If he understands the art of painting at thirteen, my dear, your Joseph will turn out to be a genius!'

'Yes, and just look where genius landed his father! Dying of overwork at forty!'

Towards the end of autumn, just as Joseph was entering his fourteenth year, Agathe – defying Madame Descoings's entreaties – went to see Chaudet to object to his taking her son away from her. She found Chaudet wearing a blue smock, moulding his last statue. He was almost discourteous to the widow whose husband had once been so helpful to him at a critical moment. Feeling his life forces already threatened, he was struggling on with that furious intensity which enables you to accomplish in a few moments what is otherwise difficult to execute within a space of months. He was reaching towards a long sought-after solution, wielding his chisel and clay in a staccato fashion which seemed to poor ignorant Agathe to be like the behaviour of a maniac. In any other mood, Chaudet would have burst out laughing; but, hearing Joseph's mother cursing the arts, complaining about the career which was being forced upon her son and asking that he should not be allowed into the studio any more, he worked himself up into a towering rage.

'I feel under some obligation towards your late husband. I

wanted to repay it by giving your son all the encouragement I could, and by watching over your Joseph's first steps in the greatest of all careers! Yes, bear in mind, Madame – if you are not already aware of the fact – that a great artist is a king, in fact even greater than a king: to begin with, he is happier, he is independent, he lives as he feels inclined; better still, he reigns over the world of the imagination. Your son has the finest future ahead of him. Such a natural bent towards painting is very seldom found. Only artists like Giotto, Raphael, Titian, Rubens and Murillo reveal such aptitude so early in life – for I think he ought to become a painter rather than a sculptor. Heavens above! If I had a son like him, I should be as happy as the Emperor is at producing the King of Rome! Anyway, you are in charge of your son's future. Go on, turn him into an imbecile, a man who will just amble through life as a wretched pen-pusher – and you will have committed a murder. I truly hope he will still remain an artist, despite all your efforts. A vocation is stronger than all the obstacles that oppose it! The word vocation means a call – it's a call from God! Only, you will make your son unhappy!' He hurled the clay he no longer needed into a bucket, telling his model: 'That'll do for today.'

Agathe raised her eyes and saw a naked woman sitting on a stool in a corner of the studio where she had not looked before; the sight of this sent her running from the room horrified.

'You must not harbour young Bridau here again, any of you,' Chaudet told his pupils. 'It vexes his mother.'

'Boo!' cried the students as Agathe closed the door behind her.

'And Joseph has been going there!' thought the poor mother, alarmed by what she had seen and heard.

As soon as the students of sculpture and painting learned that Madame Bridau did not want her son to become an artist, they delighted in enticing Joseph into the studio. Despite the promise which his mother forced out of him that he would not go to the Institut again, he often stole into Regnauld's studio, where he was encouraged to daub away at canvases.

When the widow tried to complain, Chaudet's pupils replied that Monsieur Regnauld was not Chaudet; besides, she had not given them her son to look after – and countless other jokes of the same kind. These atrocious students composed and sang a song about Madame Bridau in 137 couplets.

On the evening of this sad day, Agathe would not play her usual game of cards; she sat in her easy chair, overwhelmed by such deep sorrow that tears sometimes glistened in her beautiful eyes.

'What is the matter, Madame Bridau?' asked old Claparon.

'She thinks her son will have to go round begging for his living just because he is cut out to be a painter,' said Madame Descoings, 'but I'm not the slightest bit concerned about my young stepson Bixiou's future, and he too has a passion for drawing. Men will make their way somehow or other.'

'You are right,' said old Desroches, in a harsh tone of voice. (Despite his ability, he had never risen to the position of Deputy Chief Clerk.) 'Fortunately, I have only one son; for with my 1,800 francs a year and a wife who barely earns 1,200 francs a year at her solicitor's stationery office, what would have become of me? I have got my boy into an attorney's office as a junior clerk. He earns 25 francs a month plus his lunches, and I give him an equal amount. He dines and sleeps with us, and that's all! He has his own way to make and he'll manage it! I set the young fellow more work than if he was at school and one day he'll be an attorney; when I give him money to go to the theatre, he is as happy as a lord, he even embraces me. *And* I keep him on a tight rein: I ask him to account for his money afterwards! You are too kind to your children. If your son wants to rough it a little, let him! He'll turn out all right in the end.'

'My boy is only sixteen and his mother worships him,' said Du Bruel, an old Departmental Head who had just retired, 'but I wouldn't take any notice of what he says he wants to be at that early age. It's just a whim, a passing craze. I believe boys must be governed with a firm hand.'

'But you are rich, you are a man and you only have one son,' Agathe interjected.

'Heavens,' Claparon went on, 'children are our tyrants. (I lead with hearts). Mine makes me wild with rage; he has been my ruination. But I've now reached the stage where I have stopped bothering about him. (Trump!) He's much happier for it, too, and so am I. The young rascal has been partly the cause of his poor mother's death. He has taken up commercial travelling, which is really his level; no sooner was he at home than he wanted to go out again, he could never stay in one place for any length of time, he didn't want to learn a thing. All I ask of God is that I should die without seeing him drag my name through the mud! People who haven't got any children miss a lot of pleasures but they also avoid a lot of suffering.'

'That's just typical of fathers!' Agathe thought to herself, bursting into tears again.

'The reason why I'm telling you all this, my dear Madame Bridau, is to persuade you that you must allow your son to become a painter; otherwise, you would be wasting your time.'

'If you were capable of giving him a good dressing-down,' said Desroches bitterly, 'I would advise you to oppose his inclinations; but, knowing how weak you are with them, I think you should let him stick to his paint-brushes and pencils.'

'That's the end!' said Claparon.

'What do you mean, the end?' cried the poor mother.

'I've been trumped in hearts! Desroches's trick card always gets the better of me.'

'Cheer up, Agathe,' said Madame Descoings. 'Joseph will be a great man.'

After this discussion, which went the way of all human discussions, the widow's friends were of the same opinion – an opinion which did not resolve her perplexities. They advised her to let Joseph follow his vocation.

'If he isn't a genius,' said Du Bruel, who was paying court to Agathe, 'you can always find him a job in the Civil Service.'

On the landing Madame Descoings, who saw the three civil servants to the stairs, called them 'the three wise men'.

'She worries too much,' said Du Bruel.

'She is too happy that her son is wanting to do something in life,' Claparon added.

'Besides, if God preserves the Emperor for us,' said Desroches, 'Joseph will have some influence behind him! So what's she worrying about?'

'She's afraid of everything when her sons' well-being is at stake,' Madame Descoings answered. 'Well now, my dear,' she said to Agathe as she came back into the room, 'you see, they all take the same view. Why are you still crying?'

'Ah! If it was Philippe, I shouldn't have any anxiety. You don't know what goes on in those studios! Artists have naked women in them.'

'But they have a fire, I hope,' was Madame Descoings's reply.

5. The great man in the family

A FEW days later came the misfortunes of the retreat from Moscow. Napoleon returned to France to organize a new army and to ask for further sacrifices from the French people. The poor mother was then assailed by very different anxieties. Philippe, who disliked school, absolutely insisted on serving in the Emperor's armies. He had been filled with enthusiasm by a military review he attended at the Tuileries – the last one held there by Napoleon. At that time, military splendour, the sight of the uniforms and the authority conferred by epaulettes held an irresistible attraction for some young men. Philippe believed he had all the aptitude for service in the army which his brother was showing for the arts. Without his mother's knowledge, he sent the Emperor a petition drawn up in the following words: 'Sire. I am the son of your Bridau. I am eighteen, five feet six inches tall, I have good legs, a sturdy constitution, and wish to become one of your soldiers. Under your protection I beg to be admitted into the army,' etc.

Within twenty-four hours the Emperor sent Philippe from the Lycée Impérial to St Cyr; and, six months later, in November 1813, he appointed him a sublieutenant in a cavalry regiment. Philippe remained at regimental headquarters for part of the winter, but as soon as he could ride a horse he set off for the front, full of ardour. During the French campaign, he was appointed a lieutenant after an engagement involving the front line when his impetuosity saved his colonel's life. The Emperor promoted Philippe to captain at the Battle of La Fère-Champenoise, at which he made him an aide-de-camp. Spurred on by such swift advancement, Philippe won the Cross of a Knight of the Legion of Honour at Montereau. Having witnessed Napoleon's farewells at Fontainebleau, and filled with fanatical zeal by this sight, Captain Bridau refused to enlist under the Bourbons. When he came back to his mother's home in July 1814, he found that she was ruined. Joseph's scholarship was withdrawn as from the holidays, and Madame Bridau – whose pension was paid out of the Emperor's Privy Purse – vainly asked for this pension to be charged on the Ministry of the Interior. Joseph, more devoted than ever to his art, and delighted by these events, asked his mother to allow him to go to Monsieur Regnauld's – promising that he would be able to earn his living. He claimed that he was an able enough pupil in the fifth form to be able to miss out the sixth. A captain at nineteen and decorated with the Legion of Honour, Philippe – after serving as aide-de-camp to the Emperor on two battlefields – greatly flattered his mother's vanity; and so, though coarse, rowdy and actually without any merit other than the vulgar bravado of a dashing cavalry officer, he seemed to her a man of genius; whereas Joseph, who was small, thin, sickly, with a wild expression on his face, a child who loved peace and tranquillity, and dreamed of an artist's glory, was bound – in her opinion – to cause her nothing but torments and anxieties. The winter of 1814–15 was propitious to Joseph, who, secretly protected by Madame Descoings and by Bixiou, Gros's pupil, went to work in Gros's celebrated studio, from which so many different kinds of talent emerged, and where he became a close friend of Schinner. Then came the 20th of March. Captain Bridau, who rejoined the Emperor at Lyons and accompanied him back to the Tuileries, was appointed a major in the Dragoon Guards. After the Battle of Waterloo, at which he was wounded, but only slightly, and where he won the Cross of an Officer of the Legion of Honour, he happened to be with Marshal Davoust at Saint-Denis and did not retreat to the Loire Valley with the army. Consequently, thanks to Marshal Davoust's influence, his military rank and the Cross of an Officer of the Legion of Honour were not taken away from him. But he was placed on half-pay. Meanwhile, uneasy about the future, Joseph studied with such intensity that he fell ill several times amidst this hurricane of events.

'It's the smell of paint,' Agathe would remark to Madame

Descoings. 'He really ought to give up a job which is so damaging to his health.'

All Agathe's anxieties were then centred on her son, the lieutenant-colonel. She saw him again in 1816, when he had sunk from the 9,000 francs a year, or thereabouts, which he had been drawing as a major in the Imperial Dragoon Guards, to half-pay of 300 francs a month; she had the attic fitted up for him above the kitchen, spending some of her savings on it. Philippe was one of the Bonapartists most frequently found at the Café Lemblin, a real constitutional backwater. There he adopted the habits, manners and style of life of officers on half-pay; and, as any young man of twenty-one would have done, he carried these attitudes to excess. In all seriousness, he swore an undying hatred of the Bourbons, would not come round to their side and even turned down the various opportunities that cropped up of being appointed to the cavalry of the line with his former rank of lieutenant-colonel. In his mother's eyes, Philippe seemed to be showing great strength of character.

'His father would not have done more than that,' she would say.

The half-pay was enough for Philippe. He did not cost anything at home whereas Joseph was entirely dependent on the two widows. As from this time Agathe's preference for Philippe became noticeable. Until then her favouritism had remained a secret; but the persecution of this loyal soldier of the Emperor, the memory of the wound her darling son had sustained, and his courage in the face of adversity – still a noble adversity in her eyes, even though it was self-imposed – kindled a deeper love in Agathe. The words: 'He is unhappy!' justified everything. Joseph, whose character had that abounding simplicity which is in the heart of every artist at the outset of his career and who in any case had been brought up in some awe of his elder brother, was far from being offended by his mother's preference for Philippe. On the contrary, he agreed with it, sharing her admiration for a courageous man who had carried Napoleon's orders in two battles, a man who had been wounded at Waterloo. How could one doubt the superiority of the elder brother whom he had seen in the fine green and gold uniform of the Dragoon Guards, commanding his squadron at the Champ-de-Mai! Besides, despite her favouritism, Agathe was an excellent mother – she loved Joseph, though she was not infatuated by him; she did not understand him, that was all. Joseph worshipped his mother, whereas Philippe allowed himself to be worshipped by her. Even so, the cavalry officer toned down his soldierly brutality when in her presence; but he scarcely disguised his contempt for Joseph, though expressing it in a friendly way. Seeing his younger brother, a weak and sickly boy of seventeen, engrossed by his powerful intellect and emaciated by hard and continuous work, Philippe used to call him 'Junior'. His invariably protective attitude would have been offensive but for the carefree outlook of the artist, who believed in any case that soldiers concealed a heart of gold beneath their brutal exterior. Joseph, poor boy, had not yet learned that truly talented soldiers are as gentle and polite as any other superior class of people. In all circumstances genius is identical in its expression.

'Poor boy!' Philippe used to say to his mother. 'We mustn't pester him. Let him have his fun.' In his mother's eyes, Philippe's disdain seemed indicative of brotherly affection.

'Philippe will always love his brother and protect him,' she thought.

In 1816 Joseph obtained his mother's permission to convert the loft next door to his attic bedroom into a studio; and Madame Descoings gave him some money to buy the articles essential to his trade as a painter, for in the widows' household painting was nothing more than a trade. With the intelligence and enthusiasm that go hand in hand with any vocation, Joseph arranged everything himself in his dejected-looking studio. At Madame Descoings's request, the landlord opened up the roof and fitted a skylight. The loft became a huge room, which Joseph painted a chocolate colour; he hung a few sketches on the walls. Agathe put a small cast-iron stove in it – not without regret – and Joseph could work at home, without, however, neglecting Gros's and Schinner's studios.

About this time the Constitutional Party, largely supported

by officers on half-pay and Bonapartists, caused riots outside the House of Deputies in support of the Charter, which nobody wanted; it also hatched several conspiracies. Philippe, who became involved in these, was arrested and later released for lack of evidence; but the War Minister discontinued his half-pay, transferring him to what could be called a 'disciplinary list'. France had become impossible for him to live in for he would eventually fall into some trap set for him by *agents provocateurs*. At that time there was much talk of *agents provocateurs*. Whilst Philippe was playing billiards in dubious cafés, wasting his time and contracting the habit of sipping small glasses of various liqueurs, Agathe was in mortal anxiety about the great man of the family. The 'three wise men' had grown too accustomed to making the same journey each evening, too fond of climbing the staircase leading up to the two widows' flat and finding them waiting and ready to ask them about the impressions of the day ever to desert them; they still turned up for their game of cards in the little green drawing-room. Despite the purges of 1816, the Ministry of the Interior had retained Claparon, one of those timid men who whisper news that can be read by anybody in the *Moniteur*, adding however: 'But do not mention my name!' Desroches, who had been placed on the retired list a little later than old Du Bruel, was still arguing about his pension rights. Seeing Agathe's despair, the three friends advised her to send the colonel away on a journey.

'There is talk of conspiracies, and your son – with a character like his – will be implicated in some business or other, for there are always traitors.'

'Damn it! He is the stuff out of which his Emperor created marshals,' Du Bruel said in a low voice, glancing around him, 'and he must not give up his career. Let him go off and serve in the East, in the Indies . . .'

'What about his health?' asked Agathe.

'Why doesn't he get a job?' asked old Desroches. 'So many private companies are being set up! I am going to become head clerk in an insurance office, as soon as my retirement pension has been agreed.'

'Philippe is a soldier. He only likes war,' Agathe retorted, in a bellicose vein.

'Then he ought to be sensible and ask to be re-enlisted.'

'With this lot?' cried the widow. 'Oh! I shan't ever advise him to do that.'

'You are making a mistake,' said Du Bruel. 'My son has just been found a job by the Duc de Navarreins. The Bourbons behave excellently towards those who sincerely come round to their side. Your son would be appointed lieutenant-colonel in some regiment.'

'Only noblemen are required in cavalry regiments and he will never become a colonel,' cried Madame Descoings.

Agathe, terrified, begged Philippe to go abroad and enlist in the service of some foreign power which would still look favourably on a man who had been an aide-de-camp in the Imperial armies.

'Serve a foreign power?' Philippe cried in horror.

Agathe embraced her son warmly, saying: 'He's just like his father.'

'He is right,' said Joseph. 'Frenchmen are too proud of the Column in the Place Vendôme to go and enlist in some foreign army. Besides, perhaps Napoleon will come back again a second time!'

To please his mother, Philippe then had the magnificent idea of joining General Lallemant in the United States and helping in the founding of the Champ-d'Asile, one of the most terrible confidence tricks ever to have been disguised as a 'national appeal'. Agathe gave 10,000 francs out of her savings and spent 1,000 francs taking her son to Le Havre and seeing him set sail. At the end of 1817 Agathe was somehow able to live on the 600 francs a year that still remained from her investment in the Government funds; then, acting on a brainwave, she at once invested the 10,000 francs savings she still possessed and so derived an additional private income of 700 francs a year. Joseph wished to co-operate in this self-sacrifice. He went about dressed like a ragamuffin; he wore heavy boots and blue stockings; he refused to wear gloves and burned coal in his grate; he lived on bread, milk and

Brie cheese. The poor boy's only encouragement came from old Madame Descoings and from Bixiou, his friend both at school and studio, who at this time was drawing his admirable caricatures whilst employed in a humble capacity in one of the ministries.

'How glad I was when the summer of 1818 came round!' Bridau often said, as he related the hardships encountered in those days. 'The sun saved me from having to buy coal.'

Already as gifted as Gros himself in the techniques of colour, he only saw his master now to consult him. He was thinking of challenging the Classical school, of breaking down Greek conventions and doing away with the shackles in which art was immured – art to which Nature belongs as it is, in the omnipotence of her creations and her fantasies. Joseph was preparing himself for his struggle which, from the time when he made his first appearance at the Salon of 1823, was never-ending. It was a terrible year: Roguin, Madame Descoings's and Madame Bridau's solicitor, absconded, taking with him the sums of money set aside over the last seven years from the life interest on capital which already ought to have produced an annual income of 2,000 francs. Three days after this disaster, a bill of exchange arrived from New York; it was for 1,000 francs, and Philippe had drawn it on his mother. Deceived like so many others, the poor young man had lost all his possessions at the Champ-d'Asile. This letter, which caused Agathe, Madame Descoings and Joseph to burst into tears, spoke of debts incurred in New York, where comrades sharing his misfortune stood surety for the colonel.

'But *I* made him go to America,' cried the poor mother, adept in justifying Philippe's faults.

'I do not recommend you,' old Madame Descoings told her niece, 'to send him often on journeys of this kind.'

Madame Descoings was heroic. She still regularly gave 5,000 francs a year to Madame Bridau, but she was equally regular in backing the same lottery number which, ever since 1799, had never come out in the draw. About this time, she began to have her doubts about the management's impartiality. She blamed the government, believing it very

60

capable of suppressing the three numbers in the urn so as to make the punters lay extravagant stakes. After rapidly examining their resources, the two women realized that it was impossible to raise 1,000 francs without selling a portion of their investment income. They spoke of pawning their silver or else perhaps some of their linen or all unnecessary furniture. Frightened by these proposals, Joseph went to see Gérard and explained his position to him; the great painter obtained for him from the Ministry of the Royal Household a commission to produce two copies of his own portrait of Louis XVIII, at a fee of 500 francs per copy. Though seldom generous, Gros took his pupil to the shopkeeper who supplied all his artist's materials, and told him to charge Joseph's requirements to his own account. But the 1,000 francs would be paid only when the copies had been delivered. Joseph then painted four easel paintings in ten days, sold them to art dealers and brought the 1,000 francs to his mother, who was then able to settle the bill of exchange. A week later another letter arrived, in which the colonel informed his mother that he was setting sail aboard a packet-boat, the captain of which had been persuaded to take him on the strength of his own word. Philippe announced that he would need at least another 1,000 francs on his arrival at Le Havre.

'That's all right,' Joseph said to his mother. 'I shall have finished my copies by then. You can give him the 1,000 francs.'

'Dear Joseph!' Agathe cried, bursting into tears and embracing him. 'God will bless you. So you love him, this poor persecuted brother of yours? He is our glory and all our future. So young, so brave and so unfortunate! Everything is against him. At least, let us three take his side!'

'You see that painting does serve some useful purpose, after all,' Joseph replied, happy that he had at last obtained his mother's permission to become a great artist.

Madame Bridau hurried to welcome her darling son, the colonel. Once she had arrived at Le Havre, she walked every day beyond the round tower built by Francis I, looking out for the American packet-boat, her anxiety becoming more and more unbearable every day. Only mothers know how these kinds of suffering revive maternal sentiment. The packet-boat docked one fine morning in October 1819, without damaging itself and without having met with the slightest gust of wind. Even in the most brutal of men, the sight of one's mother and the breath of one's native land always produce some effect, especially after a voyage that has been full of hardships. Philippe, therefore, expressed a warmth of feeling that made Agathe think to herself: 'Ah! How he loves me!'

Alas! the colonel no longer loved anyone in the world except for one person and that person was himself. His misfortunes in Texas, his stay in New York, a place where speculation and individualism are carried to the very highest level, where the brutality of self-interest reaches the point of cynicism and where a man, fundamentally isolated from the rest of mankind, finds himself compelled to rely upon his own strength and at every instant to be the self-appointed judge of his own actions, a city in which politeness does not exist; in other words, the whole voyage, down to its very slightest details, had developed in Philippe the pernicious inclinations of the hardened trooper. He had started to smoke and drink; he had become brutal, impertinent and rude; he had been depraved by hardship and physical suffering. Moreover, the colonel considered himself as having been persecuted. The consequence of such a view is to make unintelligent people hostile and intolerant themselves. In Philippe's eyes, the whole universe began at his head and ended at his feet, and the sun shone only for him. Finally, life in New York – as seen and interpreted by this man of action – had removed all his remaining scruples in matters of morality. With people of this kind only two attitudes towards life are possible: they either believe or disbelieve; they either have all the gentlemanly virtues or they surrender themselves to each and every requirement of necessity. They then get into the habit of exalting into a necessity the slightest self-interest, the most fleeting whim of passion. Such a theory can take a man far. The colonel had preserved – but only in outward appearance – the soldierly qualities of straightforwardness, frankness and unconstraint. For this reason, he was exceedingly dangerous. He seemed as artless as a child; but only having to think of himself, he never did anything without first considering what he ought to do as carefully as a wily lawyer thinks up some scoundrelly trick. Words cost him nothing: he threw out as many of them as people were prepared to believe. If, by a stroke of misfortune, someone took it into his head not to accept the explanations whereby he justified the discrepancies in his behaviour and language, the colonel, who was first-rate with the pistol, who could challenge the ablest of fencing-masters and who had the composure of a man to whom life is of trifling value, was ready to demand satisfaction for the slightest hostile remark. Meanwhile, however, he seemed to be the sort of man who would take the law into his own hands, thus precluding any peaceful settlement of the quarrel. His imposing build had broadened out, his face had become sunburned during his stay in Texas, he still had the laconic manner and peremptory tone of a man who had had to win the respect of the people of New York. With this appearance, simply dressed, his body visibly toughened by recent misfortunes, Philippe seemed a hero to his poor mother; but the long and the short of it was that he had become a scoundrel. Alarmed by her darling son's destitution, Madame Bridau bought him a complete wardrobe of clothes at Le Havre; hearing the tale of his misfortunes, she did not have the heart to stop him from drinking, eating and enjoying himself in the way that a man must drink, eat and enjoy himself who has just come back from the Champ- d'Asile. Certainly, the conquest of Texas by the remnants of the Imperial Army was a fine project; it came to nothing not so much because of circumstances as through the failure of men, because today Texas is a republic with a bright future ahead of it. This incident in the history of Liberalism at the time of the Restoration is decisive proof that its interests were entirely self-centred and in no way patriotic, and only con- cerned with power. There was no lack either of men, places, inspiration or loyalty; but what was not forthcoming was the money and assistance of that hypocritical party which, though having enormous sums of capital at its disposal, gave nothing when the retrieval of a whole empire was at stake. Housewives of Agathe's type have that sound common sense which enables them to see through such political chicanery. The poor mother obtained an inkling of the truth, on hearing her son's account; for, devoted to the interests of her exiled son, she had noted the pompous advertisements of the Constitutional newspapers whilst Philippe was overseas, and had followed the progress of that notorious appeal which barely produced 150,000 francs when five or six million were required. The Liberal leaders were quick to realize that they were doing Louis XVIII's work for him by sending forth from France the glorious remains of the Imperial army, and they abandoned the most loyal, keen and enthusiastic of the men, those who came forward first into the venture. Agathe could never bring herself to explain to her son how he had been much more of a dupe than a persecuted man. Such was her faith in her idol that she reproached herself with ignorance and lamented the misfortune of the times, which were proving so disastrous for Philippe. And indeed, until then, throughout all his misfortunes, he had been less to blame of himself than the victim of his idealistic character, his energy, the Emperor's downfall, the Liberals' double-dealing and the Bourbons' relentless harassment of the Bonapartists. During the week they spent at Le Havre, a horribly expensive week, Madame Bridau did not dare suggest that he should come to terms with the Royal Government and present himself for employment at the War Ministry; she had enough on her hands in getting him away from Le Havre, where the cost of living is exorbitantly high, and in bringing him back to Paris when all she had left was the money for the journey home.

6. Mariette

MADAME Descoings and Joseph, who were awaiting the exile's arrival in the courtyard of the Royal Stage-coach Offices, were struck by the change that had come over Agathe's face.

'Your mother has gone looking ten years older in two months,' Madame Descoings said to Joseph as embraces were being exchanged and the two trunks unloaded.

'Hello, Mère Descoings,' was the colonel's tender greeting for the woman whom Joseph always affectionately called 'Maman Descoings.'

'We haven't got any money for the cab,' Agathe wailed.

'I have,' the young artist replied. 'My brother has a superb complexion,' he added, looking at Philippe.

'Yes, I'm as seasoned as a tobacco-pipe. But *you* haven't changed, youngster.'

Then aged twenty-one, and appreciated by a few friends who supported him in his days of tribulation, Joseph was now feeling his strength and aware of the talent within him. He represented the art of painting at an intellectual club consisting of young men who devoted their lives to the natural sciences, literature, politics and philosophy; he was, therefore, offended by this contemptuous manner, to which Philippe gave further expression by twisting his ear as you would a child's. Agathe noticed the kind of coldness which both Madame Descoings and Joseph showed Philippe after the warm tenderness of their initial greeting; but she put everything right by telling them of the sufferings Philippe had undergone during his self-imposed exile. Madame Descoings, wishing to celebrate the return of a man whom she called the Prodigal Son (but only under her breath), had prepared the best possible dinner, to which old Claparon and Monsieur Desroches senior were invited. All the friends of the family were supposed to call

65

during the evening, and so they did. Joseph had informed
Léon Giraud, D'Arthez, Michel Chrestien, Fulgence Ridal
and Bianchon, his friends from the club. Madame Descoings
told Bixiou, her so-called stepson, that a game of écarté would
be laid on for the young men. Young Desroches, who, thanks
to his father's iron will, had obtained his law degree, was also
invited to the party. Du Bruel, Claparon, Desroches and
Abbé Loraux scrutinized the exile and were frightened by his
coarse manners and behaviour, his voice damaged by indulgence in liqueurs, his vulgar turns of speech and his glance.
Whilst Joseph was arranging the card tables, Agathe's most
devoted friends gathered round her, asking: 'What job are
you intending to put Philippe into?'

'I do not know,' she replied. 'But he still does not want to
serve under the Bourbons.'

'It is very difficult to find him a job in France. If he doesn't
go back into the army, it will be a good while before he finds
himself a niche in the Civil Service,' said old Du Bruel. 'And
certainly, you only have to hear him to realize that he won't
be able to fall back on writing plays to make his fortune like
my son.'

From the glance Agathe gave him in reply, everyone
realized how worried she was over Philippe's future; and,
as none of her friends had any money of their own to offer
her, they all remained silent. Philippe, young Desroches and
Bixiou played écarté, a game which was then all the rage.

'Maman Descoings, my brother hasn't any money to play
with,' Joseph whispered into the ear of this kind and excellent
woman.

The punter of the Royal Lottery went off to fetch twenty
francs and handed it to the artist, who secretly slipped it into
his brother's hand. All the guests arrived. Two tables of
boston were made up and the party became very lively.
Philippe turned out to be a bad card-player. After first winning
a great deal of money, he lost everything; eventually, towards
eleven in the evening, he was fifty francs in debt to young
Desroches and Bixiou. More than once, the noise and arguing
that was going on at the écarté table rang in the ears of the

peaceful boston players, who cast stealthy glances in Philippe's direction. Philippe revealed himself in such an unpleasant light that, in his final quarrel with young Desroches, who also was none too good at the game, the latter's father blamed his son for the disturbance and forbade him to play any more, though Desroches was actually in the right. Madame Descoings did likewise with her grandson, who was beginning to make such witty remarks that Philippe could not understand them – remarks which could imperil this cruel satirist in the event of one of them entering the colonel's thick skull.

'You must be tired,' Agathe whispered to Philippe. 'Go to bed.'

'Travel educates the young,' Bixiou said smilingly, when Philippe and Madame Bridau had left the room.

Joseph, who got up at daybreak and went to bed early, did not stay up till the end of the party. Next morning, as they were getting the breakfast ready in the morning room, Agathe and Madame Descoings could not help thinking that their evening parties would be exceedingly expensive if Philippe went on playing 'that game', as Madame Descoings called it. The old woman, then aged seventy-six, offered to sell her furniture, give up her second-floor flat to the landlord, who would be only too glad to get it back again, turn Agathe's drawing-room into a bedroom for herself and convert the morning room into a drawing-room cum dining-room. In this way they would save 700 francs a year. This reduction in their expenses would enable them to allow Philippe sixty francs a month until such time as he found a job. Agathe agreed to this sacrifice. When the colonel came down to breakfast, his mother asked him if he had found his small bedroom comfortable; then, the widows explained the family's situation to him. Madame Descoings's and Agathe's combined investment income was 5,300 francs a year, of which Madame Descoings's 4,000 francs a year was an annuity. Madame Descoings gave Bixiou (whom for the last six months she had been acknowledging as her grandson) an allowance of 600 francs a year, and an equal allowance to Joseph; the remainder of her income was spent on household expenses and housekeeping, as was Agathe's. They had used up all their savings.

'Don't worry,' said the lieutenant-colonel. 'I am going to look round for a job, I shan't be dependent on you. All I ask for the time being is something to eat and somewhere to sleep.'

Agathe embraced her son, and Madame Descoings slipped 100 francs into Philippe's hand to pay off the debt incurred at cards the evening before. Within ten days the furniture had been sold, the flat vacated and Agathe's home rearranged with a rapidity unequalled, except in Paris. During these ten days, Philippe regularly made off after breakfast, came back for dinner, went off again in the evening, and only came home to sleep about midnight. The habits which this unemployed soldier contracted almost mechanically and which became deep-rooted were as follows: he had his boots polished on the Pont-Neuf for the two sous he would have spent if he had crossed the river by the Pont des Arts. At the Palais-Royal he drank two small glasses of brandy and read the papers – an occupation which took him up to midday. About this time, he trudged along the Rue Vivienne as far as the Café Minerve where Liberal politicians hatched their plots, and here he joined other ex-officers in a game of billiards. Whether he was winning or losing, Philippe always had three or four small glasses of various liqueurs, and he smoked ten cigars of excise tobacco a day on his walks to and from the café and during his strolls along the streets. After smoking a few pipes in the evenings at the Estaminet Hollandais, he went up to the gaming-rooms about ten o'clock. The waiter would give him a card and a pin. He would inquire of one or two practised gamblers how often the red and the black had come up and would stake ten francs at the most opportune moment, without ever playing more than three turns, whether he won or lost. Whenever he had won, which almost invariably happened, he would drink a bowl of punch and then make his way back to his attic; then he would talk of knocking out the extremists and the Life Guards, and he would sing 'Let us look after the safety of the Empire!' as he climbed up the stairs. Hearing him, his poor mother would say to herself:

'Philippe's in a gay mood tonight'; and she would go upstairs to embrace him, without complaining of the fetid smell of punch, liqueurs and tobacco.

'You must be pleased with me, aren't you, my dear mother?' he asked her towards the end of January. 'I'm leading the most regular life.'

Philippe had dined five times at a restaurant with old friends. These ex-soldiers had told one another about the state of their affairs as they discussed the hopes which were held out by the construction of a submarine ship with which it was hoped to rescue the Emperor. Amongst the old friends with whom he had renewed contact, Philippe was particularly fond of an old captain in the Dragoon Guards named Giroudeau, in whose company he had started his military career. This ex-cavalryman was instrumental in adding a fourth vice to Philippe's three existing ones: liqueurs, cigars and gambling – thus causing him to complete what Rabelais would call 'the devil's own retinue'. One evening early in February, Giroudeau took Philippe, after dinner, to the Théâtre de la Gaîté, where they occupied a box allocated to a small theatrical journal belonging to his nephew Finot, whose cashier and accountant he was and for whom he made and checked the newspaper wrappers. As was the fashion amongst Bonapartist officers who belonged to the Constitutional opposition, the two men wore a full frock-coat with a square collar, buttoned up the neck, trailing down to the heels and adorned with the rosette of the Legion of Honour. Each carried a lead-handled Malacca cane attached to a plaited leather strap. To use one of their own expressions, they had 'been on the bottle', and were exchanging mutual confidences as they entered the box. In the hazy excitement produced by a few bottles of wine and some small glasses of various liqueurs, Giroudeau pointed out to Philippe a small, plump and agile ballet-dancer named Florentine, whose favours and affection came his way, as did the theatre box, through the all-powerful influence of the newspaper.

'But how far do her favours extend with an old dapple-grey war-horse like you?' Philippe inquired.

'Thank God I haven't abandoned the ancient doctrines of our glorious uniform!' Giroudeau replied. 'I have never spent a sou on getting a woman.'

'What?' cried Philippe, putting a finger over his left eye.

'Yes,' Giroudeau answered. 'But, between ourselves, the newspaper had a lot to do with it. Tomorrow, in a couple of lines, we will recommend the management to give Mademoiselle Florentine a few steps to dance. Damn it, my dear boy, I am very happy.'

'Hey! If this respectable fellow Giroudeau, forty-eight years old and with a head as bald as my knee, a big belly, a face like a vinegrower's and a potato-shaped nose, is the friend of a ballet-dancer, then I ought to be the friend of the leading actress in Paris,' Philippe thought to himself. 'How did you pick her up?' he asked aloud.

'I'll take you to Florentine's place this evening. Although my bird only gets paid fifty francs a month from her job at the theatre, she is quite well provided for because a retired silk merchant named Cardot gives her 500 francs a month.'

'Eh . . .?' said Philippe, jealously.

'Bah! True love is blind,' came the reply.

After the show, Giroudeau took Philippe to Mademoiselle Florentine's. Her flat was only a few yards away from the theatre, in the Rue de Crussol.

'We'll have to behave decently,' Giroudeau told him. 'Florentine has her mother living with her. As you will realize, I can't afford to pay anyone to keep an eye on her, so that the good lady is her real mother. This woman used to be a concierge, but she is not without intelligence. Her name is Cabirolle. Call her Madame, she likes that.'

That evening Florentine had a friend in to see her, a girl named Marie Godeschal, who was as beautiful as an angel, as frosty in her manner as a ballerina and whose teacher Vestris predicted the most brilliant future for her as a dancer. Mademoiselle Godeschal, who was keen to make her début at the Panorama-Dramatique under the assumed name of Mariette, was relying on the protection of one of the Principal Gentlemen of the Bedchamber, to whom Vestris had been promising to introduce her for a long time. Vestris, who still had an eye for the women, did not think she was knowledgeable enough yet. The ambitious Marie Godeschal brought lustre to her pseudonym of Mariette; but in any case her ambition was a very laudable one.

She had a brother, who was a clerk in Derville's office. Orphans reared to a life of hardship, but loving one another, she and her brother had seen life as it is in Paris. The brother wished to become an attorney, so as to be able to provide for his sister. He lived on ten sous a day. The sister had coolly resolved to become a dancer; and by taking as much advantage of her beauty as of her legs, she intended to buy her brother a practice. Outside the range of their feelings for one another, their mutual self-interest and their life together, everything seemed to them as it did in former times to the Romans and Jews: barbaric, foreign and hostile. To those who knew her well, this most beautiful of friendships (destined always to remain unchanged) was the key to Mariette's character. At that time, brother and sister lived on the eighth floor of a house in the Vieille Rue du Temple. Mariette had begun to study dancing at the age of ten, and was now sixteen. Alas! For want of slightly better clothing, her unassuming beauty – ill-kempt, dressed in printed calico concealed beneath an angora rabbit-skin shawl, and shod in iron pattens – could only be guessed at by those Parisians whose whole lives were given over to the pursuit of young working girls and the tracking down of beauties who had come upon misfortune.

Philippe fell in love with Mariette. Mariette saw him as the major who had served in the Dragoon Guards, the Emperor's aide-de-camp, a young man of twenty-seven; the fact that he was so obviously superior to Giroudeau would give her the satisfaction of proving her own superiority over Florentine. Florentine and Giroudeau (Giroudeau wishing to make his friend a happy man, Florentine seeking to provide Mariette with a protector) urged Mariette and Philippe to celebrate a 'common-law marriage'. The expression 'common-law marriage' is equivalent to the term 'morganatic marriage' used by kings and queens. As he left, Philippe confided his poverty to Giroudeau; the old libertine reassured him warmly.

'I'll mention you to my nephew Finot,' Giroudeau said to him. 'Do you see, Philippe, we now live in a world where civilians lay down the law and speechifying is all that counts, and we'll have to put up with it. The pen is all-powerful today. Ink is taking the place of gunpowder, words are replacing bullets. And, after all, these little editor chaps are very ingenious fellows and quite easy to get on with. Come and see me tomorrow at the newspaper office; I'll have outlined your position to my nephew. Before long, you'll get a job with some newspaper or other. Make no mistake about it, Mariette is accepting you now because she has got nothing else, no contract, no possibility of making a début anywhere, and I have told her that, like me, you are about to get a job in journalism. She will convince you that she loves you for your own sake – and you will believe her! Do as I do, keep her in a walk-on role for as long as you can! I was so in love with Florentine that, as soon as she wanted to dance a few steps, I asked Finot to urge that she should be given her début; but my nephew said to me: "She's talented, isn't she? Well then, the day she dances her first steps on the stage, she'll show you the door." Oh! that's Finot all over. He's got all his chairs at home, you'll see.'

The next day, at about four in the afternoon, Philippe arrived at the Rue du Sentier where, in a tiny mezzanine office, he found Giroudeau caged like some wild animal in a sort of hen-coop complete with hatch, a small stove, a small table, two small chairs and some small logs. The setting was enhanced by the magic words: 'Subscription Office', painted on the door in black lettering, and still further lustre was added by the words 'Cash Desk', handwritten and fastened up over the grille. Along the wall facing the captain's premises was a long bench where a disabled soldier was having a bite to eat. He had one arm amputated, and Giroudeau called him Redskin – no doubt because of the Egyptian swarthiness of his complexion.

'Not bad!' said Philippe, scanning the room. 'What are

you doing here, a man who fought in poor Colonel Chabert's regiment at Eylau? Christ Almighty! Senior officers like you!'

'Well, yes! Hm. Hm. A senior officer turning out subscription receipts for a newspaper,' said Giroudeau, fixing his black silk cap firmly on his head. 'And besides, as the publisher, I am responsible for all that nonsense,' he added, pointing to the newspaper.

'And I went out to Egypt, but now I go to the Stamp Office,' said the disabled soldier.

'Hold your tongue, Redskin,' Giroudeau ordered. 'You are in the presence of a soldier who carried the Emperor's orders at the Battle of Montmirail.'

'I was there too!' was Redskin's reply. 'It was there that I lost my arm.'

'Redskin, look after the till, I'm going up to see my nephew.'

The two ex-officers climbed up to the fourth floor, to an attic at the end of a corridor, where they found a young man with pale, cold eyes, lying on a wretched-looking sofa. The civilian did not move, though he offered cigars to his uncle and his uncle's friend.

'My dear fellow,' Giroudeau said to him in a soft, submissive tone of voice, 'this is the brave major of the Imperial Guards whom I have spoken to you about.'

'Well?' asked Finot, eying Philippe up and down. Philippe, like Giroudeau, lost all his energy in the presence of this diplomat of journalism.

'Dear boy,' Giroudeau went on, trying to act like an uncle, 'the colonel has just got back from Texas.'

'Oh! so you fell into the Texas trap, this Champ-d'Asile business. But you were still quite young to wish to become a "Ploughman soldier".'

The bitterness of this joke can only be understood by those who remember the deluge of engravings, folding-screens, clocks, bronzes and plaster casts to which the idea of the ploughman soldier gave rise – that grandiose image of the fate of Napoleon and his men, which finally gave rise to several vaudevilles. This gimmick made at least one million francs. You can still find ploughman soldiers on wallpaper in the depths of the provinces. If the young man had not been Giroudeau's nephew, Philippe would have slapped him on both cheeks.

'Yes, I fell into that trap. I lost 12,000 francs through it, not counting the waste of time,' Philippe replied, trying to force a smile.

'And you still love the Emperor?' asked Finot.

'He is my God.'

'Are you a Liberal?'

'I shall always belong to the Constitutional Opposition. Foy! Manuel! Laffitte! There are men for you! They'll get rid of those miserable wretches who only came back to France when the Allies had paved the way!'

'Well!' Finot went on, coldly, 'you must make the best you can of your misfortune, for you have been a victim of the Liberals, my dear fellow! Remain a Liberal, if that is the way you are inclined; but threaten the Liberals that you will reveal the blunders that were made in Texas. You didn't get a sou of the money raised in the national appeal, did you? Well then, you are in a strong position; ask to see the appeal's accounts. This is how things will turn out: a new Opposition newspaper is being set up, under the patronage of the left-wing members of parliament. You will become its cashier, at a salary of 3,000 francs a year – a job that will be permanent. All you have to do is to obtain 20,000 francs caution money. Find that, and the job will be yours within a week. I will advise them to silence you by getting you offered the job; but shout for it, and shout hard!'

Philippe was profuse in his thanks. Giroudeau let him go on a few yards ahead, and then said to his nephew: 'Well! You are a fine one, you are! You're paying me 1,200 francs a year here.'

'The paper won't last twelve months,' Finot answered. 'I've got better things in store for you.'

'Good Lord!' Philippe said to Giroudeau. 'He's no booby, your nephew isn't! I had never thought of taking advantage of my position in the way he advises.'

That evening, at the Café Lemblin and at the Café Minerve, Colonel Bridau hurled abuse at the Liberal party which appealed for subscriptions, sent men out to Texas, spoke hypocritically of ploughman soldiers and left brave men helpless and destitute, after misappropriating scores of thousands of francs from them and sending them packing for two whole years.

'I am going to ask to see accounts of the nation-wide appeal,' he remarked to one of the regulars at the Café Minerve, who passed this on to left-wing journalists.

Philippe did not go home to the Rue Mazarine. He went to Mariette's, to tell her about his future co-operation in a newspaper which would have 10,000 subscribers, and where her ambitions as a ballet-dancer would be warmly supported.

Agathe and Madame Descoings waited for Philippe's return in agonies of fear: the Duc de Berry had just been assassinated. Next day, the colonel arrived home a few minutes after breakfast. When his mother told him of the anxiety which his disappearance had caused her, he flew into a temper and asked her whether or not he was grown up.

'Christ! I'm bringing you a piece of good news, and you both look as solemn as a funeral. The Duc de Berry is dead. Well, good riddance to him! That's one of them less. I'm going to be appointed cashier of a newspaper at a salary of 3,000 francs a year, so you've got no need to worry about me any more.'

'Can it be true?' cried Agathe.

'Yes, providing you can put down 20,000 francs caution money. All you have to do is deposit your Treasury bond as security. You'll still draw your 650 francs interest every half-year.'

For nearly two months the widows had been racking their brains to find out what Philippe was doing and what job to put him into. They were so happy with this prospect that they no longer thought about the various catastrophes that were liable to arise from day to day. That evening, the three wise men, old Du Bruel, Claparon (who was dying) and hard-headed old Desroches, were unanimous in advising Agathe to stand surety for her son. The newspaper, which very fortunately had been set up before the Duc de Berry's assassination, avoided the blow which Monsieur Decazes then dealt the Press. Madame Bridau's Treasury bond worth 1,300 francs a year was deposited as caution money and Philippe was officially appointed cashier. This virtuous son immediately promised to pay 100 francs a month for his board and lodging. The widows declared that no son could behave more generously. People who had predicted the worst about him congratulated Agathe.

'We had misjudged him,' they said.

Poor Joseph, not to be outdone by his brother, struggled to become self-supporting – and succeeded. Three months later, the colonel, who ate and drank as much as four men, who was difficult to please and who led the two women into excessive expense, on food, had not yet paid them a sou. Out of politeness, neither his mother nor Madame Descoings wanted to remind him of his promise. The year went by, and still not a single one of those coins so energetically described by Léon Gozlan as a 'tiger with five claws' had passed from Philippe's pocket into the household. Admittedly, the colonel has assuaged his own scruples of conscience on that score: he rarely dined at home.

'Anyway, he's happy,' said his mother. 'His mind's at rest, he has a job!'

Such was the influence of the feuilleton edited by Vernou, a friend of Bixiou, Finot and Giroudeau, that Mariette made her début not at the Panorama-Dramatique, but at the Théâtre de la Porte-Saint-Martin, where she scored a success in partnering Bégrand. One of the directors of this theatre was a rich and showy general who had turned impresario out of love for an actress. In Paris you can always find men who become theatre directors out of love for actresses, dancers or singers. This general knew Philippe and Giroudeau. With the help of Finot's and Philippe's little newspapers, Mariette's début was arranged between the three officers with a rapidity which seems to indicate that all human passions work harmoniously together whenever they are leading to reckless folly. It was not long before Bixiou had mischievously informed his grandmother and pious Agathe that Philippe, the cashier, the bravest of the brave, loved Mariette, the celebrated dancer at the Théâtre de la Porte-Saint-Martin. This stale piece of news hit the two widows with all the violence of a thunderbolt. To begin with, Agathe's religious outlook caused her to look upon actresses as incarnate fiends; besides, they were both under the impression that such women lived on gold, drank pearls and dilapidated even the largest fortunes.

'Well,' Joseph said to his mother, 'do you think my brother is so stupid as to give his Mariette money? Those kind of women only ruin rich men.'

'They're already talking of engaging Mariette at the Opéra,' said Bixiou. 'But don't be afraid, Madame Bridau, the diplomatic corps put in an appearance at the Porte-Saint-Martin, this lovely girl won't be with your son for much longer. It is rumoured that an ambassador is head over heels in love with her. Here's another piece of news! Old Claparon is dead; they're burying him tomorrow, and his son, who has become a banker and is absolutely made of money, has ordered the cheapest kind of funeral. That boy has no manners. They don't behave like that in China!'

Activated by greed, Philippe proposed to the dancer just as she was on the point of beginning her new job at the Opéra; but, either because she had divined his intentions, or else because she had realized how necessary it was for her to keep her independence if she was to make any headway in her career, Mademoiselle Godeschal turned him down. For the remainder of the year, Philippe only visited his mother twice a month at the most. Where was he? Either at his job, at the theatre or with Mariette. No ray of light concerning his goings-on came the way of the little household in the Rue Mazarine. Giroudeau, Finot, Bixiou, Vernou and Lousteau saw him leading a life of dissipation. Philippe went to every party given by Tullia, one of the leading dancers of the Opéra, and also to all Florentine's (who took Mariette's place at the Porte-Saint-Martin), and Matifat's, all Coralie's and Camusot's. From four o'clock in the afternoon, when he left his cashier's office, he enjoyed himself until midnight; for some party or other had always been fixed up the evening before, or else someone was giving a good dinner, or a supper or a gambling party. Philippe was in his element. His carnival life lasted eighteen months, but it was not without its tribulations. At her début at the Opéra in January 1821, Mariette conquered the heart of one of the most dazzling dukes at Louis XVIII's court. Philippe tried to hold his own with the duke; but, despite a certain amount of good fortune at the gaming-tables, his infatuation left him no alternative but to take money from the till of the newspaper, when the time came round for subscriptions to be renewed in April. By May, he was 11,000 francs in debt. During this fatal month Mariette went over to London to exploit the lords, whilst the temporary Opera-house was being built at the Hôtel Choiseul in the Rue Lepelletier. As always happens, Philippe, in his misfortunes, had reached the stage of loving Mariette despite her glaring infidelities; but she had never seen anything more in this young man than a rough soldier, devoid of wit and intelligence, the first rung of a ladder on which she did not wish to remain stationary for too long. For this reason, foreseeing that Philippe would soon be without money, she had gained protectors in the world of journalism, who relieved her of the necessity of retaining Philippe. Nevertheless, she was grateful to Philippe in a way that only such women can be – and even then, such gratitude is always reserved for the man who, as it were, first smoothed out for them the trying difficulties of any theatrical career.

7. Philippe absconds

FORCED by circumstances to allow his terrible mistress to
decamp to London without going after her, Philippe went
back to his winter quarters (as he called them) in his attic in
the Rue Mazarine. His mind dwelt on sombre thoughts
whenever he went to bed or awoke. He felt it impossible to
live otherwise than he had been living for the past year. The
atmosphere of luxury in Mariette's flat, the dinners and suppers,
evenings spent in the wings of the theatre, the verve of wits
and journalists, the noisy bustle which went on around him,
all the seductions of sense and vanity – this life, which is only
to be found in Paris and which offers some new experience
every day, had become more than a habit to Philippe; it was
a necessity, no less than his tobacco or his little glasses of
liqueur. He accepted the fact that it was impossible for him to
live without these continual enjoyments. The idea of committing suicide crossed his mind, not because people would
eventually discover a deficit in his till, but because of his
separation from Mariette and his exclusion from that atmosphere of pleasure in which he had been revelling for a year.
Full of these dark thoughts, he walked into his brother's
studio for the very first time and found him dressed in a blue
smock, copying a picture for an art dealer.

'So that's how pictures are painted?' he said, as a way of
opening the conversation.

'No!' replied Joseph, 'but it's how they're copied.'

'How much do you get paid for that?'

'Never enough; 250 francs. But at the same time I study
the various techniques of the masters. I'm learning from it.
I discover the secrets of my profession. That's one of my
pictures,' he said, pointing with the tip of his brush to a
sketch that was still not dry.

'And how much a year do you manage to earn now?'

'Unfortunately, I'm still only known to my fellow painters. I'm helped along by Schinner, who's going to get me some work at the Château de Presles, where I shall be going around October to paint some arabesques, architraves and ornaments – for which I'll be well paid by the Comte de Sérizy. With odd jobs like that, together with orders from art dealers, I shall be able to earn about 1,800 to 2,000 francs a year from now on, all expenses paid. At the next national exhibition of painting I am going to show that picture over there. If it appeals to the public, then I shall be made. My friends are pleased with it.'

'I'm no expert in all this,' Philippe said in a low voice which made Joseph look at him closely.

'What's the matter?' the artist asked, seeing his brother go pale.

'I'd like to know how long it would take you to do my portrait.'

'Well, working at it all the time, and provided the weather's bright, I'd have it finished within three or four days.'

'That's too long, I could only allow you one day. My poor mother loves me so much that I'd like to leave her a portrait of myself. Don't let's mention it any more.'

'Why, are you going off again?'

'This time, it's for good,' Philippe replied with a false tone of gaiety.

'Philippe, what is the matter? If it's something serious, I'm a man, I'm no fool. I myself am preparing for some hard struggles; and, if discretion is needed, I shall be discreet.'

'Are you sure?'

'On my honour.'

'You won't say anything to anybody?'

'Nobody.'

'Well, I'm going to blow my brains out.'

'What? So you're fighting a duel?'

'I'm going to commit suicide.'

'But why?'

'I took 11,000 francs out of my till, and tomorrow I've got to present my accounts. My caution money will be reduced by half: our poor mother will be reduced to managing on 600 francs a year. That's nothing! Later on, I could repay her with a fortune. But I shall be dishonoured! I don't want to live a life of dishonour.'

'You won't be disgraced if you pay it back, but you'll lose your job. All you'll have is the 500 francs a year pension from the Cross of the Legion of Honour and you can live on 500 francs a year.'

'Farewell!' said Philippe, hurrying down the staircase, not wishing to hear anything more.

Joseph came down from his studio to lunch with his mother, but Philippe's confidential disclosures had robbed him of his appetite. He took Madame Descoings on to one side and told her the dreadful news.

Uttering a terrible cry, the old woman dropped a small saucepan of milk she was holding and threw herself into a chair. Agathe came running up. Punctuated by exclamations, the disastrous truth was revealed to Philippe's mother.

'Him! Dishonoured! Bridau's son stealing from the till he's in charge of!'

The widow trembled from head to toe. Her eyes dilated, staring glassily. She sat down and burst into tears.

'Where is he?' she cried, between her sobs. 'Perhaps he's thrown himself into the Seine!'

'You mustn't lose heart,' Madame Descoings said, 'just because the poor boy has taken up with a bad woman who's caused him to do stupid things. Heavens above! This sort of thing often happens. Until he came back from America, Philippe had had so many misfortunes, and so few opportunities of being happy and loved, that you mustn't be surprised by his passion for this creature. All passions lead to excess! Even I am open to blame for one little excess and still think myself an honest woman! One single fault doesn't amount to vice! And then, after all, people who never do anything wrong never do anything right!'

Agathe's despair so overwhelmed her that Madame Descoings and Joseph had to play down Philippe's misconduct, telling her that something of the kind happened to every family.

'But he's twenty-eight,' Agathe cried. 'He isn't a child.'

This terrible remark revealed how deeply preoccupied the poor woman was with her son's behaviour.

'Mother, I can assure you that he was only thinking of your distress and the wrong he's done you,' Joseph told her.

'Oh God! If only he comes back, if only he's alive, I'll forgive him everything!' the poor mother exclaimed, her mind haunted by the terrible picture of Philippe's body being dragged lifeless from the water.

For a few moments, a gloomy silence reigned. The day went by, torn between the cruellest alternatives. All three would dash to the drawing-room window whenever there was the slightest noise outside. Their minds were absorbed in a host of conjectures. During this time, whilst the family were in agonies of despair, Philippe was calmly tidying everything up in his office. He had the effrontery to present his accounts, saying that – fearing some misfortune – he had kept the 11,000 francs at home. The rascal left the office at four, taking another 500 francs from the till, and calmly went over to the gaming-rooms, which he had never visited during his time at the newspaper – for he had astutely realized that a cashier cannot haunt the gaming-tables. The young man, subtle in his selfishness, as his behaviour later in the story will reveal, was much more like his grandfather Rouget than his virtuous father. Perhaps he would have made a good general; but, in private life, he was one of those thoroughgoing rascals who mask their contrivances with a veneer of legality and conceal their disreputable actions beneath the face-saving reticence of the family circle. In this supreme undertaking, Philippe kept all his steadiness of mind. At first he was on the winning side and even amassed 6,000 francs in stake money; but he allowed himself to be dazzled by the desire to put a sudden and decisive end to all his uncertainties. He left the game of *trente-et-quarante* on learning that at the roulette table the black had just passed sixteen times. He walked over and staked 5,000 francs on the red, and the black came up again a seventeenth time. The colonel then put his thousand-franc note on the black and won. Despite this astonishing stroke of luck, his brain was tired. Although he knew this, he still wanted to play on; but that sixth sense which gamblers need and which comes in sudden flashes of illumination had already dimmed. Moments of listlessness followed, the gambler's undoing. Lucidity of mind, like the sun's rays, is only effective when it goes straight to its target; it can only guess accurately when it looks things steadily in the face; it grows murky if confronted by the oscillations of chance. Philippe lost everything. After an experience as painful as this, even the most light-hearted of men would break down, as would the boldest. On the way home, Philippe did not think of his threat of suicide, however; he had never intended to take his own life. He no longer considered the job he had lost, or the sadly reduced caution money, or his mother, or Mariette who had brought him to this ruin. He walked like an automaton. When he reached home, his weeping mother, Madame Descoings and his brother leapt to greet him, kissed him and joyfully carried him to the fireside.

'Good!' he thought, 'the threat has had its effect.'

This monstrous son put on an appropriately tragic look, all the more readily in that he had been deeply shaken by his experience at the gaming-table. Seeing her darling son pale and dishevelled, the poor mother knelt at his feet, kissed his hands, placed them on her own heart and gazed and gazed at him, with tears welling to her eyes.

'Philippe,' she said in a choking voice, 'promise me that you won't ever do away with yourself. We'll overlook everything!'

Philippe looked at his sorrowing brother and at Madame Descoings struggling against her tears, and said to himself: 'They're good-folk!' Then he took his mother in his arms, lifted her up, seated her on his lap, pressed her against his heart and, embracing her, whispered into her ear: 'You have given me life a second time!'

Madame Descoings was somehow able to serve an excellent dinner, to which she contributed a couple of bottles of mature wine and a small quantity of rum – the rum was a treasure from her old stock.

'Agathe, we must let him smoke cigars!' she said over dessert. And she offered Philippe cigars.

The two poor creatures had imagined that, by allowing this young man every comfort, he would love their home and would want to stay there. Both tried to get used to the cigar smoke which they detested. Philippe did not even notice their immense sacrifice. Next day, Agathe looked ten years older. Once her anxieties had been allayed, reflexion followed, and the poor woman could not get a moment's sleep during that terrible night. She would be brought down to the level of 600 francs a year. Like all plump and gormandizing women, Madame Descoings, who was plagued with a stubborn catarrhal cough, was becoming sluggish in her movements; her footsteps resounded on the staircase like blows at a log. She could die at any time, and with her would go 4,000 francs a year. Was it not ridiculous to rely on this additional income? What was Agathe to do? What would become of her? Firmly resolved that she would become an old people's nurse rather than be a burden on her sons, Agathe did not think of herself. But what would Philippe do, with only the 500 francs a year from his Cross as an officer of the Legion of Honour? During the past eleven years, Madame Descoings's annual contribution of 3,000 francs had very nearly paid off her debt twice over; she still sacrificed her grandson's interests to those of the Bridau family. Though Agathe's honesty and rectitude were severely offended by this appalling disaster, she kept on saying to herself: 'Poor boy! Is it his fault? He is loyal to his oath. I was wrong not to get him married. If I had found him a wife, he wouldn't have got mixed up with this dancing woman. He has such a strong constitution!'

The old tradeswoman had also been thinking, during the night, how she could rescue the family honour. At daybreak she got out of bed and went into Agathe's bedroom.

'It's neither your place nor Philippe's to deal with such a delicate matter,' she told her friend. 'Even though our two old friends, Claparon and Du Bruel, are dead, we still have old Desroches, who is so level-headed, and I'm going to go and see him this morning. Desroches will then tell people that Philippe's misfortune is due to his misplaced confidence in a friend, that his weakness in this kind of direction makes him quite unsuitable to look after a cash-desk. What has happened to him now could happen again. Philippe will choose to resign, rather than be dismissed.'

Seeing that this white lie would preserve her son's honour, at least so far as strangers were concerned, Agathe embraced Madame Descoings, who went off to arrange this horrible business. Philippe had slept like a log.

'She's a cunning old girl!' he said smiling, when Agathe told him why their breakfast was being delayed.

Old Desroches, the last remaining friend of these two poor women, a man who – despite all his sternness – had never forgotten how Bridau had found him a job, carried out the delicate mission which Madame Descoings had entrusted to him with all the astuteness of an accomplished diplomat. He came to dine with the family, to remind Agathe that she had to go next day to the Treasury, in the Rue Vivienne, to sign the transfer certificate for the portion of the interest she had sold, and to draw the dividend warrant for the 600 francs a year which was still hers. The old civil servant did not leave this despairing house without first getting Philippe to sign a petition to the War Minister, requesting his readmission into the army. Desroches promised the two women that he would keep an eye on the petition's progress through the War Ministry and, by taking advantage of the Duke's triumph over Philippe in the matter of Mariette, gain this great lord's protection.

'In three months' time he will be a lieutenant-colonel in the Duc de Maufrigneuse's regiment, and you won't have him on your hands any more.'

Desroches left the house, with Joseph and the two women showering him with their blessings. Two months later, as Finot had predicted, the newspaper ceased publication, and so Philippe's misconduct had no repercussions in the outside world. But Agathe's maternal feelings had been most deeply wounded. Now that her confidence in Philippe had been shaken, she lived from day to day in perpetual qualms, qualms that were tinged with a peculiar satisfaction whenever her sinister forebodings proved to be mistaken.

When men such as Philippe who are endowed with physical courage, but whose moral characters are cowardly and ignoble, find that their world is falling back into its old pattern again after a catastrophe in which such moral scruples as they had have been more or less destroyed, the friendly indulgence of family or friends is an encouraging bonus. They count on always being able to get away with wrongdoing; their warped minds and sated pasions cause them to ponder how it was that they succeeded in circumventing the laws of society. And from that moment forward they become horribly cunning.

So a fortnight later Philippe, who once more had lapsed into boredom and idleness, returned inevitably to his café routine, going the rounds of the bars and drinking a little liqueur at each, playing lengthy games of billiards with bowls of punch as his refreshment, and spending his evenings at the gaming-tables, where whenever the opportunity arose he would venture small sums of money and make trifling gains that were just large enough to keep up his disorderly way of life. Ostensibly thrifty (so as to be the more successful in deluding his mother and Madame Descoings), he wore a hat that was almost filthy and which was threadbare over the crown and round the brim, boots that had been repaired, a worn-out coat, once red but now brown with age, and marked with liqueur and coffee stains, in whose buttonhole the rosette of the Legion of Honour was barely visible. His greenish doeskin gloves had to last him a long time. He wore his satin neckerchief until it was like a rag. Mariette was the young man's only love; her betrayal of him greatly hardened his heart. Whenever he happened to have unexpected wins, or whenever he had supper with his old friend Giroudeau, he would resort to the 'Venus of the crossroads', in a gesture of brutal disdain for the whole of the feminine sex. Regular in his habits, he would breakfast and dine at home, to which he returned every night about one o'clock. Three months of this terrible existence filled poor Agathe with renewed confidence.

As for Joseph, he was working on the magnificent picture which made him his reputation; and he lived in his studio. Sharing her grandson's faith in him, Madame Descoings believed in Joseph's triumphant future and showered motherly comforts upon him. She brought him his breakfast in the morning, ran his errands and cleaned his boots for him. The painter scarcely put in an appearance before dinner-time, and his evenings belonged to his friends in the Club. Moreover, he was reading a great deal, and giving himself that deep and serious education which can only be had from within oneself, and to which all talented men have devoted themselves between twenty and thirty years of age. Seeing little of Joseph, and feeling no anxiety about him, Agathe lived only for Philippe, who alone provided her with the alternatives of allayed fears and appeased terrors which to some extent constitute the life of the heart and are as necessary to motherhood as they are to love. Desroches, who came about once a week to see the widow of his former principal and friend, inspired her with hope: the Duc de Maufrigneuse had asked for Philippe to be admitted to his regiment; the War Minister was having a report drawn up about him; and, as Bridau's name was not to be found on any police list or legal file, Philippe would receive his service letter, readmitting him into the army, early in the following year. To obtain this success, Desroches had brought all his knowledge of the administrative machine into play. Information derived from police headquarters revealed that Philippe went gambling every evening, and he thought it necessary to confide this secret to Madame Descoings, but only to her, making her promise to keep a close eye on the future lieutenant-colonel; everything could be lost if there was any scandal. For the time being, the War Minister would not be investigating whether Philippe was a gambler. And once back in active military service, the lieutenant-colonel would give up a passion that had only come into being because he was unemployed. Agathe no longer had any evening visitors; she would read

87

prayers by the fireside whilst Madame Descoings told her own
fortune by cards, seeking an explanation of her dreams and
applying the principles of the cabbala to her own gambling.
This obstinate woman never missed a draw: she kept on
backing her combination of lottery numbers, which had still
not come up. Her numbers were about to become twenty-one
years of age, they were approaching adulthood. The old
punter set much store by this childish circumstance. One of
the numbers had never been thrown up on any wheel ever
since the lottery began; consequently, Madame Descoings
laid enormous sums of money on this particular number and
all the combinations of the three figures. The lower mattress
of her bed served as a storing place for the poor woman's
savings. She would unsew it, tuck a gold coin inside, well
wrapped up in wool, money she could ill afford, and then sew
the mattress up again. At the last Paris draw of the year, she
wished to risk all her savings on the combinations of her
favourite numbers. The passion for lotteries, so universally
condemned, has never been studied. No one has realized that
it was the opium of poverty. The lottery was the most powerful fairy in the world: did it not nurture magical hopes? The
spin of the roulette wheel which flashed mountains of gold
and enjoyment before the gamblers' eyes was as rapid as
lightning; but the lottery gave five whole days of existence
to this splendid lightning flash. Where is there today a social
power that, for a mere forty sous, can keep you happy for
five days and provide you with all the delights of civilization
in an ideal form? Tobacco, an addiction that is a thousand
times more immoral than gambling, destroys the body, attacks
the mind and stupefies a nation; whereas the lottery did not
cause the slightest misfortune of this kind. Moreover, the
passion for lotteries was compelled to discipline itself, not
only because of the distance in time between the draws but
also because each gambler had his favourite wheel. In the
hope that the numbers she had backed for twenty years would
eventually win their reward, she had undergone enormous
hardships so as to have complete freedom to lay her stake at
the last draw of the year. Whenever she had cabbalistic

dreams, for not all her dreams corresponded to the lottery numbers, she would go and tell Joseph about them: he was the only person who would listen to her, not only without scolding her, but delighting her with some of those sweet words by which artists console the follies of the mind. All great talents respect and understand true passions: they are able to account for them and find their roots either in the heart or in the head. According to Joseph, his brother loved tobacco and liqueurs, his old aunt Descoings loved lottery numbers, his mother loved God, young Desroches loved litigation, old Desroches loved fishing – everybody, he said, had some passion or other. His own passion was ideal beauty in all its manifestations: he loved Byron's poetry, Géricault's painting, Rossini's music and Sir Walter Scott's novels.

'Everybody to his own taste, aunt,' he cried. 'Only your lottery numbers are a long time turning up.'

'They'll come up eventually. You'll be rich, and so will my grandson Bixiou!'

'Give it all to your grandson,' Joseph would reply. 'Anyway, it's up to you to do as you wish!'

'Ah! if they do turn up, I'll have enough money for everybody. To begin with, you'll have a fine studio, you won't have to give up the Théâtre des Italiens to pay for your models and artist's materials. Do you know, my dear boy,' she told him, 'you haven't given me a very pretty role in that picture?'

Out of economy, Joseph had asked Madame Descoings to pose for him in his magnificent picture of a young courtesan brought by an old woman to a Venetian senator. This picture, one of the masterpieces of modern painting, a work which even Gros imagined was a Titian, was marvellously successful in preparing young artists to recognize and proclaim Joseph's superiority at the Salon of 1823.

'The people who know you are well aware who you are,' he replied gaily, 'and why should you be worried about those who don't know you?'

In the last ten years or so, Madame Descoings's complexion had taken on the mellow tones of a pippin at Easter. Her wrinkles had moulded the fullness of her flesh, which had become soft and cold. Her lively eyes seemed to sparkle with thoughts that were still young and vivacious; but they closely resembled the eyes of a greedy woman, the more so as there is always something greedy in the gambler's mentality. Her chubby face showed traces of profound duplicity – ulterior motives buried deep within the heart. Her passion necessitated secrecy. The movements of her lips showed some indication of gluttony. Although, therefore, she was the honest and excellent woman you have already seen, the eye could easily be mistaken about her character. For this reason, she was an admirable model for the old woman whom Bridau wished to paint. The inspiration for this picture had come from Coralie, a young actress of sublime beauty, who died in the flower of youth and who had been the mistress of a young poet, Lucien de Rubempré (who himself had been a friend of Bridau). This fine canvas was accused of being a pastiche – though it was, in fact, a splendid combination of three portraits. Michel Chrestien, a young member of the Club, had allowed his Republican's head to be portrayed as the senator's; Joseph added a few touches of maturity to his features, just as he exaggerated Madame Descoings's expression.

This great picture, which was destined to cause such a stir, and which earned Joseph so much hatred, jealousy and also admiration, was already sketched out. But, compelled to interrupt his work on it in order to attend to commissions that would bring him his daily bread, he copied the paintings of the old masters, saturating himself with their techniques; this is why he is one of the ablest of painters. His artist's common sense had prompted him to conceal from Madame Descoings and his mother the money he was beginning to make from his paintings, seeing in his mother's love for Philippe and his aunt's passion for the lottery the ruin of each. The composure which Philippe had shown at the moment of catastrophe, the calculation concealed beneath the trumped-up threat of suicide but which Joseph had discerned, the memory of the misconduct in a career which he ought not to have given up – everything down to the very slightest details of his brother's behaviour had finally opened Joseph's eyes. Such astuteness is rarely lacking in painters who for whole days work in the silence of their studios on paintings which to a certain extent leave the mind free. They bear some resemblance to women: their minds can revolve round the small details of life, penetrating their hidden meanings.

Joseph had bought one of those magnificent chests, which at that time had not yet become fashionable, to decorate a well-lit corner of his studio where the light glittered on the shallow carving, giving back all its lustre to this masterpiece of sixteenth-century workmanship. In it he found a secret drawer where he was saving up a nest-egg. With the trusting simplicity of all true artists, he regularly put the money intended for his monthly expenses into a death's-head which stood in one of the compartments of the chest. Since his brother's return to the fold, he was constantly discovering a discrepancy between his total monthly expenses and the money remaining in the death's-head. The 100 francs he had allocated for the month was disappearing at an incredible rate. Finding nothing left in the skull, when he had only spent forty or fifty francs that month, he said the first time: 'It looks as if my money has gone for a walk!' When it happened a second time, he kept note of his expenditure; but even though (like Robert-Macaire) he added 16 and 5 together and made 23, he still could not make head or tail of it. When, on a third occasion, he discovered a still graver discrepancy, he disclosed this distressing matter to old Madame Descoings, who loved him with a motherly, tender, confident, credulous and enthusiastic love so lacking in his own mother – however kindly the latter might be; that love which is just as necessary to an artist at the beginning of his career as is the hen's care for her chicks until they themselves have grown feathers. Only to her could he confide his terrible suspicions. He was as sure of his friends as he was of himself, and certainly Madame Descoings was not taking anything from him to stake it on the lottery. When he told her his idea, the poor woman wrung her hands; only Philippe could have committed this trifling domestic theft.

'Why doesn't he ask me for anything he needs?' Joseph cried, putting some paint on to his palette and muddling up all the colours without even noticing it. 'Would I refuse him money?'

'But it's robbing a child,' Madame Descoings exclaimed, her face stricken with the deepest horror.

'No,' said Joseph. 'I'll let him do it, he is my brother. My purse is his. But he ought to tell me.'

'Put a fixed amount of money there this morning, and don't touch it,' Madame Descoings told him. 'I'll take note of who comes to your studio; and, if only he comes, then you will know for certain.'

So, the very next day Joseph obtained certain knowledge of the forced loans which his brother was extorting. Philippe would enter the studio when Joseph was out, and take whatever small sums he needed. The artist trembled for his small treasure.

'Wait!' he said to Madame Descoings, laughingly. 'I'll catch you out, my fine fellow.'

'And quite right too. We must teach him a lesson, because I too sometimes find money missing out of my purse. But, poor boy, he must have his tobacco, he's so used to it.'

'Poor boy, poor boy!' the artist replied. 'I rather agree with Fulgence and Bixiou: Philippe is constantly pulling our legs. First, he gets mixed up in riots and has to be sent over to America, which costs mother 12,000 francs. He can't find anything in the forests of the New World, and his return costs as much again as his outward voyage. On the pretext of having passed on to some general a couple of words spoken by Napoleon, Philippe has ideas of himself as a great soldier, whose duty it is to pull faces at the Bourbons; meanwhile, he enjoys himself, travels around and sees the country. I'm not going to be taken in by his so-called misfortunes. He looks to me like a man who gets the best of things wherever he is! This joker is found an excellent job; he lives it up with a dancing girl from the Opéra, embezzles money from a newspaper, and once again mother is 12,000 francs out of pocket. As far as I'm concerned, I'm certainly prepared to overlook it; but Philippe will eventually ruin the poor woman. He thinks I'm a nonentity – because I wasn't in the Dragoon Guards!

Yet perhaps I'll have to provide for our dear, good mother in her old age, whereas, if he carries on the way he's going, this ruffian will come to no good. Bixiou was saying to me: "Your brother's a real devil!" Well, your grandson is right: Philippe will end up in some escapade where the family's honour will be jeopardized, and once again we'll have to fork out 10,000 or 12,000 francs! He gambles every evening; when he comes home as drunk as a lord, he drops pricked cards on the staircase, which he's been using to keep count of the red and the black. Old Desroches is trying hard to get Philippe back into the army, but I think he would simply hate having to go back into military service again, believe you me! Would you ever have thought that a lad with such beautifully clear blue eyes and such a look of the chivalrous young knight would have turned out a real scoundrel?'

Despite the wisdom and coolness of mind with which Philippe used to play his stakes each evening, from time to time he would lose everything. Impelled by an irresistible desire for the initial stake of the evening, ten francs, he would lay his hands on any money that was available in the household – his brother's, any left lying around by Madame Descoings, or Agathe's. Once already the poor widow, as she was just falling into a deeper sleep, had experienced a terrifying sight: Philippe had come into her bedroom and had taken all the money he could find from the pockets of her dress. Agathe had pretended to be asleep, but the rest of the night she spent weeping. She now saw things clearly. One instance of misconduct doesn't amount to vice, Madame Descoings had said; but, after constant repetitions, vice it clearly was. Agathe was no longer in any doubt: her dearest son had neither delicacy nor honour. The morning after she had had this terrible experience, after breakfast and before Philippe left the house, she had taken him into her bedroom to beseech him to ask her for any money he might need. But then Philippe's requests for money became so frequent that Agathe had soon parted with all her savings. For the last fortnight she had been penniless and was thinking of finding employment; she had spent several evenings discussing with

Madame Descoings the various ways in which she could earn some money. Already the poor mother had been to ask the *Père de Famille* for some tapestry to work, for which she would be paid about twenty sous a day. Despite her niece's profound discretion, Madame Descoings had clearly guessed the reason for this desire to earn money in a job open to women. Besides, the changes that had come over Agathe's face spoke volumes: her fresh complexion was drying up, her skin was tight over her temples and cheekbones, and her forehead was becoming wrinkled. Her eyes were losing their clearness. Obviously, she was being consumed by some fire within herself; she wept during the nights. But what caused the greatest ravages in her personality was the fact that she could not speak of her sorrows, sufferings and forebodings. She never fell asleep before Philippe's return. She waited to hear his footsteps in the street; she had grown to understand the variations in his voice and gait, the very language of the cane which he dragged along the pavement. There was nothing which these did not reveal; she always knew to what depth of drunkenness Philippe had fallen. She trembled whenever she heard him stumble on the staircase; one night she had got out of bed to pick up the gold coins from the spot where he had floundered. When he had been drinking and had won money, his voice was hoarse, his cane dragged along. But when he had lost money, his footsteps were somehow dry, precise, replete with fury; he would hum in a clear voice, holding his cane in the air, over his shoulder. When he had won, his face was gay and very nearly affectionate at breakfast time; he would joke with coarse vulgarity – but the great thing was that he was joking with Madame Descoings, Joseph and his mother. When he had lost, on the other hand, he was gloomy; his curt, staccato voice, his harsh look, his very sadness were frightening to behold. Each day his life of debauchery and the constant round of liqueurs made further changes in a face that had once been so handsome. The veins of his face were bloodshot, his features were becoming coarse, his eyes were losing their lashes and were dry and dull. Finally, careless about his personal appearance, Philippe exhaled the fetid odours of the drinkshop, a smell of muddy boots which, to any stranger, would have seemed to set the seal on his debauchery.

'You really ought to get yourself a complete new set of clothes made,' Madame Descoings said to Philippe one day early in December.

'And who'll pay for them?' he replied in a bitter voice. 'My poor mother hasn't got a sou left; I draw 500 francs a year. I should have to spend a year's pension to buy some new clothes, and I have mortgaged my pension for three years.'

'Why?' asked Joseph.

'A debt of honour. Giroudeau took 1,000 francs from Florentine to lend them to me. . . . Things are pretty rough, admittedly, but when you think that Napoleon is at St Helena and is selling his silverware to make ends meet, soldiers who are loyal to him can easily walk ill-shod,' he said, pointing to his down-at-heel boots. And he left the room.

'He isn't a bad boy,' said Agathe, 'and he means well.'

'You can admire the Emperor and still look after your personal appearance,' Joseph replied. 'If only he looked after himself and his clothes, he wouldn't look like a ragamuffin!'

'Joseph, you must make allowances for your brother,' Agathe said. 'You are doing what you are happy to do whereas he certainly isn't in his rightful place in the world!'

'Why did he leave the army?' Joseph asked. 'What does it matter if Louis XVIII's beetles or Napoleon's cuckoo are on the regimental colours, as long as they're French colours? France is France! I'd paint for the devil. A soldier must fight, if he's a soldier, for the love of the thing. And if he had remained peacefully in the army, he would be a general today.'

'You are both unfair towards him,' Agathe protested. 'Your father, who worshipped the Emperor, would have approved of him. Still, he has agreed to go back into the army. God only knows the grief which your brother feels over what he regards as a sort of treachery.'

Joseph rose to go upstairs to his studio; but Agathe took hold of his hand, saying to him: 'Be kind to your brother, he is so unhappy!'

Madame Descoings followed the artist to his studio, telling him that he should take care not to offend his mother's feelings and pointing out how much she had changed and how deep her private grief must be. To their great surprise, they found Philippe in the studio.

'Joseph, dear boy,' he said in an offhand way, 'I'm awfully hard up. Christ! I owe my tobacco shop thirty francs for cigars, and I daren't go past that damned shop until I pay. I've already promised them the money ten times.'

'Well, I much prefer that way of asking,' Joseph replied. 'Take the money out of the death's-head.'

'But I took all that last night, after dinner.'

'But there was forty-five francs.'

'Yes, that's what I made it. I found it there. Did I do wrong?'

'No, Philippe,' the artist replied. 'If you were rich, I'd do the same; only, before taking it, I'd ask if you agreed.'

'It's so humiliating to have to ask,' Philippe continued. 'I'd much prefer you to take money without asking, as I do: that shows there's more confidence between us. In the army, if a comrade dies, and he's got a good pair of boots on and you've got a shoddy pair, you exchange.'

'Yes, but you don't take the good pair of boots if he's still alive.'

'Oh, that's quibbling!' Philippe snapped back, shrugging his shoulders. 'So, you haven't got any more money?'

'No,' said Joseph, unwilling to disclose his secret drawer.

'In a few days' time we shall all be rolling in money,' Madame Descoings said.

'Yes, you believe your lottery numbers are going to come up on the 25th, when the Paris draw takes place. But you'll have to put an awful lot of money down if you want to make all our fortunes.'

'A stake of 200 francs could win three million, without counting the "doubles" and "predetermined selections".'

'Yes, 15,000 to 1, you just need 200 francs to put down,' Philippe cried.

8. *How a mother's love can change for the worse*

MADAME Descoings bit her lip; she had made an imprudent remark. And, indeed, Philippe asked himself as he went downstairs: 'Where has the old hag hidden her gambling stakes? It's money wasted. I could use it so well! With four stakes of fifty francs a time, you can win 200,000 francs! And it's more likely than winning on the lottery!'

He racked his brains to think where Madame Descoings had probably hidden it. The day before religious festivals, Agathe would go to church and remain there a long time; no doubt, she would make confession and prepare herself for the communion service. It was Christmas Eve; Madame Descoings had to go out to buy a few delicacies for the Christmas morning party, after they had got back from church; at the same time, she would perhaps go and stake her money on the lottery. The lottery draws were every five days, on the wheels of Bordeaux, Lyons, Lille, Strasbourg and Paris. The Paris lottery had its draw on the 25th of each month and its books closed at midnight on the 24th. The colonel studied all the circumstances and kept his eyes open. About midday he came back to the house when Madame Descoings had gone out; but she had taken the key with her. That was no problem. Philippe pretended he had forgotten something, and asked the doorkeeper to go and find the locksmith, who lived only a short distance away in the Rue Guénégaud, and who came and opened the door. The soldier's first thought was to ransack her bed: he unmade it and felt the mattresses before the frame; in the lower mattress, he found the gold coins, wrapped up in paper. He had soon unpicked the canvas and taken out the 400 francs; then, without going to the trouble of sewing the canvas up again, he remade the bed neatly enough for Madame Descoings not to notice anything.

Philippe made off hurriedly, planning to gamble the money

97

in three separate stakes, at three-hourly intervals and each time for only ten minutes at a stretch. Since 1786, when public gaming-houses were introduced, this has always been the procedure of true gamblers – men who played for high odds, whom the management feared and who (as the saying goes) often broke the bank. But, before gaining this expertise, such men had lost fortunes. The bankers' whole outlook, and the way they made their profits, depended upon two factors: the impassiveness of the bank and of the equal stakes known as the *refait*, half of which it retained; and the notorious bad faith – at which the Government connived – whereby gamblers' stakes were only accepted and paid at the bank's discretion. In other words, gambling, which refused to allow the rich, cool-minded gambler to play, devoured the substance of men stupid and obstinate enough to lose their heads at the sight of the rapid movement of the wheel. The bankers at *trente-et-quarante* performed almost as quickly as at roulette.

Philippe had finally attained the self-possession of the field-marshal whose clear eye and lucid intellect are untroubled by the maelstrom of events. He had gained a mastery of the finer points of gambling, which by the way provides a livelihood for a thousand or so Parisians strong-minded enough to confront the abyss of failure every evening of their lives without ever feeling dizzy. With his 400 francs, Philippe made up his mind that he would make a fortune that very day. Keeping a reserve of 200 francs in his boots, he put the other 200 francs into his pocket. At three o'clock he arrived at the gaming-house which is now the site of the Théâtre du Palais-Royal, and where the stakes were highest. Half an hour later, he left with 7,000 francs. He went straight to Florentine, to whom he owed 500 francs, repaid her the money and suggested that they ought to dine at the Rocher de Cancale after the theatre. On his way back he went to the Rue du Sentier and called in at the newspaper office to tell his friend Giroudeau about the party they were planning. At six, Philippe won 25,000 francs and left again after ten minutes, as it had been his intention to do. By ten in the evening, he had won 75,000 francs. After a magnificent supper, he returned to the gaming-table about midnight, drunk and full of self-confidence. Defying his self-imposed resolution, he played for a further hour and doubled his fortune. The bankers from whom he had wrested 150,000 francs (by his sheer skill at the game) watched him attentively.

'Will he leave now or will he stay?' they asked one another with a glance. 'If he stays, he is done for.'

Philippe, thinking he was in luck, stayed on. Towards three in the morning, the 150,000 francs had been recovered by the bank. Having drunk considerable quantities of grog whilst at the gaming-table, the officer left the room in a state of intoxication that was made all the more severe by the cold night air which met him outside; but a waiter followed him out, picked him up and took him to one of those horrible houses where the following words are written up over a lamp at the entrance: 'Bed and Breakfast'. The waiter paid in advance for the ruined gambler who was laid fully clothed on a bed, where he remained until the evening of Christmas Day. The management of the gaming-house showed consideration for their regulars and for gamblers who played for high stakes. Philippe did not wake until seven o'clock on Christmas evening. His mouth felt clammy, his face was swollen and he was shivering with nervous fever. The strength of his constitution enabled him to walk all the way home, a home on which – without so wishing – he had brought mourning, grief, misery and death.

The previous evening, having got his dinner ready, Madame Descoings and Agathe had sat waiting for Philippe for about two hours. They did not begin their meal before seven. Agathe almost always went to bed at ten, but as she wished to go to the midnight mass she went to bed that evening as soon as the meal was over. Madame Descoings and Joseph remained alone by the fireside, in the little sitting-room which served every purpose; and the old woman asked Joseph to work out for her her notorious bet, her gigantic bet on the famous lottery numbers. She wished to play both 'doubles' and 'predetermined selections', in other words to go for every possible permutation. When she had fully relished the beauty of this plan, and had emptied two cornucopias at the feet of her favourite, telling him of her dreams of fortune and even proving to him that she was absolutely certain to win (she was only worried about the difficulty of bearing such good fortune, and she could hardly wait from midnight until ten the following morning), Joseph, who could not see any sign of the 400 francs she was intending to put down, ventured to mention this to her. The old woman smiled and took him into her bedroom, which had once been the drawing-room.

'You'll see!' she said.

Madame Descoings unmade her bed as quickly as she could and looked for her scissors with which to unpick the mattress. She put her glasses on, looked carefully at the canvas, noticed that it had been undone and dropped the mattress. Hearing the old woman sigh from the depths of her heart, and almost overcome himself by the sudden rush of blood through his veins, Joseph instinctively stretched out his arms towards the veteran punter, caught her as she fainted and laid her in an armchair, calling to his mother to come. Agathe got out of bed, put her dressing-gown on and hurried in. By the light of a candle she applied the usual remedies for fainting, putting eau-de-Cologne on her aunt's temples, cold water on her forehead and a burnt feather beneath her nostrils. Madame Descoings finally came round.

'They were here this morning; but *he* has taken them, the monster!'

'What?' asked Joseph.

'I had 400 francs sewn into my mattress, two years' savings. Only Philippe can have taken them . . .'

'But when?' cried the poor mother, overwhelmed with dismay. 'He hasn't been home since breakfast.'

'I only wish I could be mistaken,' replied old Madame Descoings. 'But this morning, in Joseph's studio, when I was talking about my bet, I had a funny feeling this would happen. I ought to have gone with my little nest-egg straight away and put it on the lottery. That's what I was wanting to do and I can't imagine why I didn't! Oh, I remember now! I went to buy him some cigars!'

'But the flat was locked,' said Joseph. 'And it's so beastly

I just can't believe it! You mean that Philippe was spying on you and undid your mattress. You mean that he planned all this. No, I can't believe it!'

'I felt the money there this morning when I was making my bed after breakfast,' Madame Descoings insisted.

Terror-stricken, Agathe went downstairs and inquired whether Philippe had been back during the day; the door-keeper told her the whole story about Philippe. Chilled to the heart, the mother came back upstairs looking completely shattered. As white as the cambric of her nightdress, she walked as one imagines spectres to walk, noiselessly, slowly and with superhuman effort – yet almost mechanically. In her hand was a candlestick, and the taper cast its light full on her face, revealing eyes that were glazed with horror. Without being aware of it, she had dishevelled her hair by rubbing her hands across her forehead, which lent such beauty to this horrifying sight that Joseph stood transfixed by this ghostly apparition of remorse, by the vision of this statue of Terror and Despair.

'Aunt,' said Agathe, 'you must take my cutlery. I have got six place-settings. That will repay the money I owe you. I took the money for Philippe. I thought I should be able to put it back again before you noticed it. Oh! How I have suffered!' She sat down. Her dry, staring eyes trembled a little.

'Philippe's the one who did this trick,' Madame Descoings whispered to Joseph.

'No, no,' Agathe went on. 'Take my table-ware, sell it, it's no use to me. We eat with yours.'

She went into her bedroom, picked up the canteen of cutlery, thought it felt light, opened it and found a pawn-ticket. The poor mother uttered a terrible cry. Joseph and Madame Descoings came running in, looked inside the box – and the mother's sublime lie was exposed. All three stood silently, not daring to look at one another. Then, with an almost insane motion of the hand, Agathe put her finger to her lips as if to urge that no one should divulge this secret. All three returned to the sitting-room and stood by the fire-side.

'Look, my dears,' said Madame Descoings, 'it's a terrible blow. I feel sure I would have been lucky this time. But I'm no longer concerned about myself, I'm only thinking of you both! Philippe,' she said, addressing her niece, 'is a monster; he hasn't got one scrap of love for you, in spite of everything you've done for him. Unless you're on your guard as far as he's concerned, the wretch will see you turned out into the street. Promise me that you'll sell your investments and buy an annuity with the capital. Joseph has a good job which will keep him from want. If you do this, my dear, you'll never have to be dependent on Joseph. Monsieur Desroches is wanting to set his son up in a lawyer's office. Young Desroches (he was then twenty-six years old!) has found a practice. He'll pay you an annuity in return for your 12,000 francs.'

Joseph seized his mother's candle and ran upstairs to his studio. He came back into the room with 300 francs. 'Here, aunt,' he said, offering her his small savings, 'it's no business of ours what you do with your money. We owe you the sum of money that's missing, and here is most of it!'

'Do you think I'd take the poor little bit that you've put by, with all your scrimping and saving that it distresses me to see! Have you gone out of your mind, Joseph?' cried the old punter of the Royal Lottery of France, visibly hestitating between her unshakable faith in her lottery numbers and Joseph's action which seemed to her to be a sacrilege.

'Oh! Do whatever you want with it,' said Agathe, driven to tears by her true son's spontaneous impulse.

Madame Descoings took Joseph's head in her hands and kissed him on the forehead. 'My dear boy, please don't tempt me. Look, I should only lose more money. It's all nonsense, this lottery business!'

Never was there a more heroic word spoken in the hidden dramas of private life. Is not that a case of affection triumphing over a deeply ingrained vice? Just at this moment, the church bells began to toll for the midnight mass.

'And then, there isn't time, in any case,' Madame Descoings went on.

'Ah! Here are your fiendishly complicated calculations,'

exclaimed Joseph; and the warm-hearted artist seized the numbers, dashed down the stairs and ran to place the money on the lottery. When he had gone, both Agathe and Madame Descoings burst into tears.

'There he goes, the darling boy,' cried the old lady. 'But they'll all be his winnings, because it's his money he's putting on!'

Unfortunately, Joseph had no idea where the lottery offices actually were; the regulars knew their whereabouts in Paris as well as any smoker knows the tobacconist's shops today. The artist ran like a madman, peering at all the lanterns. On asking passers-by where the nearest lottery office was, he was told that they had shut, but that the office on the steps of the Palais-Royal sometimes stayed open for a few minutes longer. He rushed immediately to the Palais-Royal, only to find that the office had just closed.

'If you'd been two minutes earlier, you could have placed your bet,' said one of the ticket-hawkers who used to stand at the foot of the steps, yelling those strange words: '1,200 francs for forty sous', and offering tickets that had already been filled in.

By the glimmer of the street-lamp and the indoor lights of the Café de la Rotonde, Joseph looked to see if, by any chance, these tickets contained any of Madame Descoings's numbers. But, not seeing any, he walked back home with sorrow in his heart, knowing that he had failed in his self-appointed task of fulfilling the old lady's wishes. He told her of his misfortunes. Agathe and her aunt went off together to the midnight mass at Saint-Germain-des-Prés. Joseph went to bed. The Christmas Eve supper did not take place as it usually does after midnight mass. Madame Descoings was completely beside herself, and Agathe's heart was aching with an eternal grief. The two women got up late. It was striking ten o'clock when Madame Descoings tried to bestir herself to get breakfast ready, which, in fact, was not served until half past eleven. About this time, oblong boards announcing the winning numbers used to be hung up over the doors of the lottery offices. If Madame Descoings had had her ticket, she would have gone out at half past nine to the Rue Neuve-des-Petits-Champs to learn her fate, which was always decided in a house adjacent to the Finance Ministry, and on the site of which the Théâtre Ventadour and the Place Ventadour now stand. Whenever there was a draw, the inquisitive could stand at the doors of this house and, gazing at the throng of old women, cooks and dotards, behold as interesting a sight as that of the stock-holders queuing up outside the Treasury to draw their dividends.

'Congratulations on your fortune!' cried old Monsieur Desroches, who came in just as Madame Descoings was lingering over her last sip of coffee.

'What?' choked poor Agathe.

'Her numbers have come up in the draw,' he replied, showing the list of winning numbers written on a small piece of paper, one of the pieces of paper which lottery officials used to put out by the hundred in a wooden bowl on their counters.

Joseph read the list. So did Agathe. But not Madame Descoings who was stricken as if by lightning. Seeing the sudden change in her features, and hearing her cry, old Monsieur Desroches and Joseph carried her to her bed. Agathe ran to get a doctor. The old woman had had a stroke and did not regain consciousness until four o'clock, or thereabouts, on Christmas afternoon. Despite this improvement in her condition, old Dr Haudry, her physician, advised her to put her affairs in order and to think of the next world. She had only uttered a single phrase: 'Three million francs ...!'

Informed of these circumstances by Joseph (though with suitable reticence), old Desroches cited several examples of gamblers whom a fortune had eluded on the very day when, by some fatal stroke of chance, they had forgotten to put down their stakes; but he realized how such a blow was bound to be fatal, coming as it did after twenty years' perseverance. At five, a deep hush lay over the little flat. Watched over by Joseph and his mother, one seated at the foot and the other at the head of the bed, the sick woman was awaiting the arrival of her grandson, whom Desroches had gone to bring.

Suddenly the sound of Philippe's footsteps and cane was heard on the staircase.

'Here he is! Here he is!' cried Madame Descoings, sitting bolt upright in bed and despite her paralysis now able to speak.

Agathe and Joseph were profoundly moved by the attitude of horror which gripped the sick woman so violently. Their painful suspense was entirely justified by the spectacle of Philippe's drawn face, bluish-white in colour, and his tottering gait and the horrible state of his eyes, deeply ringed, dull yet nevertheless haggard. He was shivering violently with fever and his teeth were chattering.

'Hell fire and damnation!' he cried. 'There's neither crust nor crumb, and my throat is parched. Well, what's the matter? The devil is always interfering in our affairs. Old mother Descoings is in bed, staring at me with eyes as big as saucers...'

'Silence, sir,' Agathe said to him, raising herself to her feet, 'and at least show some respect for the misfortune you have brought upon us.'

'Ah, ah, sir, is it now?' he replied, looking his mother full in the face. 'My dear little Mother, that's not very polite. So you don't love your boy any more?'

'Are you worthy of love? Have you already forgotten what you did yesterday? Now, think about finding yourself a flat, you won't live here any longer with us. Move out as from tomorrow, for, in the condition you're in at the moment, it's very difficult...'

'... To throw me out, isn't it? Ah! So you're playing the melodrama of the "Banished Son". Well, well, so that's your attitude? Just let me tell you this: you're all of you fine specimens. What have I done wrong? I performed a little emergency operation on the old girl's mattress. Money shouldn't be tucked away in wool, for Christ's sake! And where's the crime in that? Didn't she take 20,000 francs from you? Aren't we all her creditors? I took my share of the debt. So there!'

'Oh God! Oh God!' cried the dying woman, joining her hands in prayer.

'Shut up, cried Joseph, jumping at his brother and putting his hand over his mouth.

'Wheel through ninety degrees, by the left, painter's apprentice,' replied Philippe, putting his hand on Joseph's shoulder, spinning him round and throwing him on to an easy chair. 'You mustn't lay hands like that on the moustache of a major in the Imperial Dragoon Guards.'

'But she repaid me everything she owed me,' cried Agathe, jumping up and looking at her son flushed with vexation. 'In any case, that's my business, not yours. You're killing her with your talk. Get out,' she ordered, with a gesture that used up all her remaining energy, 'and never darken my doors again. You are a monster.'

'I, killing her?'

'But her lottery numbers came out in the draw,' yelled Joseph, 'and you stole the money she was going to have put down.'

'If she kicks the bucket because of missing her lottery numbers, it doesn't mean to say I've killed her,' the drunkard replied.

'Get outside this instant,' screamed Agathe, 'you horrify me. You have every conceivable vice. Oh God! Can it be my son?'

A dull rattling sound, coming from Madame Descoings's throat, had increased Agathe's irritation.

'I love you still, Mother, even though you are the cause of all my misfortunes,' Philippe said. 'You're throwing me out, on Christmas Day, the day when – what's his name?... Jesus – was born. What did you do to Grandfather Rouget, your father, for him to have chased you out of his house and disinherited you? If you hadn't upset him, we would have been rich and I shouldn't have been brought down to the lowest level of poverty. What did you do to your father, you who are such a good woman? Now you see how I can be such a good son, and even so thrown out of the house; I, the glory of my family.'

'The shame of it!' cried Madame Descoings.

'You will either get out or kill me,' roared Joseph, throwing himself at his brother with the fury of a lion.

'My God! My God!' wept Agathe, standing up and trying to separate the two brothers.

At this moment Bixiou and Dr Haudry entered the room; Joseph had knocked his brother to the ground and laid him out.

'He's a real wild beast,' he said. 'Just one word and I'll . . .'

'I won't forget this!' bellowed Philippe.

'A family discussion?' asked Bixiou.

'Pick him up,' said the doctor. 'He's just as sick as the poor woman; undress him, pull off his boots and put him to bed.'

'That's easier said than done,' cried Bixiou. 'We'll have to cut his boots off him. His legs are too swollen.'

Agathe found a pair of scissors. When she had cut the boots, which at that time were worn over tight-fitting trousers, ten gold coins rolled out on to the floor.

'There's her money,' Philippe murmured. 'Damned fool that I am! I forgot the reserve. I too have missed a fortune!'

The delirium of extreme fever gripped Philippe, who now began to talk wildly. Helped by old Desroches, who came up at this moment, and also by Bixiou, Joseph carried the wretched man to his bedroom. Dr Haudry had to write a note asking the Hôpital de la Charité to send a straitjacket, for the delirium was now so far advanced that he was afraid Philippe might commit suicide: he had reached the pitch of frenzy. At nine, calm was restored in the household. Abbé Loraux and Desroches were trying to console Agathe, who never stopped weeping beside her aunt's bed. She listened, shaking her head, and maintained a stubborn silence. Only Joseph and Madame Descoings knew the depth and extent of the wound within her.

'He'll mend his ways, mother,' Joseph finally said when old Desroches and Bixiou had left.

'No! Philippe is right: my father laid a curse upon me. I haven't got any right to. . . . There's your money,' she said to Madame Descoings, gathering together Joseph's 300 francs and the 200 francs that had been found on Philippe. 'Go and see if your brother needs anything to drink,' she added, speaking to Joseph.

'Will you keep a promise made at my death-bed?' asked Madame Descoings, feeling her mental faculties about to escape her.

'Yes, aunt.'

'Well, swear to me that you will put your capital into a life annuity with young Desroches. You're going to miss my pension now, and from what I hear you say, you would allow this wretch to fleece you of your very last sou.'

'I promise, aunt.'

The old grocer woman died on 31 December, five days after receiving the dreadful blow which old Desroches had so innocently dealt her. The 500 francs, which was the only money in the household, was barely sufficient to pay her funeral expenses. All she left in the way of property was a small amount of silverware and some furniture which Madame Bridau bought back from her aunt's grandson. Agathe was reduced to living on an annuity of 500 francs a year, paid by young Desroches who negotiated the outright purchase of 'absolute title-deeds', in other words, a practice without clients, and who took her capital of 12,000 francs in exchange for the annuity. She surrendered her third-floor flat to the landlord and sold all surplus furniture. When, a month later, Philippe began his convalescence, Agathe explained to him coldly that the expense occasioned by his illness had used up all their ready money. From now on she would have to work for her living. She therefore implored him, in the most affectionate manner, to go back into the army and fend for himself.

'You could have spared me the sermon,' Philippe replied, looking at his mother with the cold eyes of indifference. 'I can well see that neither you nor my brother love me any more. I'm now alone in the world; but I prefer it!'

'Make yourself worthy of affection,' replied the poor mother, chilled to the depths of her heart, 'and we shall give you ours.'

'Nonsense!' he cried, interrupting her.

He picked up his old hat which was fraying at the edges, and also his cane, cocked his hat over one ear and went whistling down the stairs.

'Philippe! Where are you going, without any money?' cried his mother, unable to keep back her tears. 'Here . . .'

She handed him 100 francs in gold coins, wrapped in a piece of paper. Philippe came back up the stairs and took the money.

'Well! You're not even going to kiss me?' she said, bursting into tears.

He hugged his mother to his heart, but without that spontaneous outpouring of emotion which alone gives meaning to an embrace.

'Where are you going now?' asked Agathe.

'To Florentine, Giroudeau's mistress. There are friends for you!' he snapped back.

Philippe descended the staircase. Agathe went back indoors, her legs trembling, her eyes veiled with tears, her heart grief-stricken. She knelt in prayer beseeching God to take into His protection this unnatural son – and so renounced the heavy burden of her motherhood.

9. Philippe's last acts of misconduct

BY February 1822, Madame Bridau was installed in the bed-room which Philippe had occupied and which was situated over the kitchen of her former flat. On the opposite side of the staircase were the artist's studio and bedroom. Seeing his mother reduced to such penury, Joseph at least wanted to see her as comfortable as possible. After his brother's departure, he took a hand in furnishing the garret, stamping it with the unmistakable character of an artist. He laid a carpet. The bed, simply arranged but in exquisite taste, had all the appearance of monastic simplicity. The walls, hung with a none too expensive percale, which was well chosen and harmonizing in colour with the reupholstered furniture, gave the interior a clean, elegant look. Joseph made a double door opening out on to the landing, and on the inside of the door he hung a curtain. The window was concealed by a blind, which softened the glare of the daylight. Even if the poor mother's way of life had now assumed the simplest expression that a woman's life can take in Paris, at least Agathe was better off than anyone else could have been in similar circumstances – thanks to her son. To save his mother from the cruellest hardships of a Parisian household, Joseph took her each day to dine at a table d'hôte in the Rue de Beaune, where fashionable women, Members of Parliament and titled people ate, and for which each customer paid ninety francs a month. Having only to prepare lunch for herself and Joseph, Agathe fell into the way of life she had formerly shared with her husband. Despite Joseph's white lies, she eventually found out that her dinners were costing him about 100 francs a month. Shocked by the enormity of this expense and unable to imagine how her son could earn much money by painting naked women, she obtained a job in a lottery office, with the help of her confessor, Abbé Loraux. This office belonged to the Comtesse de Bauvan, the widow of one of the leaders of the Royalist rebellion in Brittany; the pay was 700 francs a year. Lottery offices, a type of appointment reserved for influential widows, quite often provided the family who looked after them with a living. But, during the Restoration, the difficulty of rewarding – within the limits of constitutional government – all the services which government had received, meant that impecunious titled women were given not one but two lottery offices, with receipts amounting to some 6,000 to 10,000 francs a year. In these circumstances, the widow of the general or nobleman who had been fortunate enough to receive such protection did not look after her offices herself but let them out to managers. Where the managers were men, they were able to do without a clerk; for the office always had to remain open from morning until midnight and there was a considerable amount of paperwork for the Finance Ministry. The Comtesse de Bauvan, to whom Abbé Loraux explained Madame Bridau's position, promised that when her manager left, Agathe should take his place; meanwhile, she stipulated that the widow should receive a salary of 600 francs a year. As she had to be at the office from ten o'clock in the morning, poor Agathe scarcely had time for dinner: she had to be back at the office by seven in the evening, and did not get away before midnight. In two years, Joseph never once failed to turn up in the evening to escort his mother to their home in the Rue Mazarine, and he often met her to take her out to dinner. His friends saw him leave the Opéra, the Italiens and the most brilliant parties to be at the Rue Vivienne before midnight.

Agathe soon contracted that monotonous regularity of life in which people who have been stricken by violent grief find some centre of support. Every morning, after tidying her bedroom, where there were no longer either cats or birds, and preparing breakfast by the fireside, she would carry it into Joseph's studio and eat it with her son. She would tidy up Joseph's bedroom, put out her own fire, and come and work in the studio by the little cast-iron stove – leaving the room whenever a friend or models came. Although she did not understand anything about art or its techniques, the deep silence of the studio suited her mood. From the point of view of art, she made no progress and did not even try to conceal the fact. She would express artless astonishment at the importance attached to colour, composition and draughtsmanship. Whenever one of his friends from the Club or some painter friend of his, such as Schinner, Pierre Grassou, Léon de Lora (a very young art student who was then nicknamed Mistigris), launched into a discussion, she would come and look at them attentively and could never understand what had given rise to these grand words and heated arguments. She did her son's washing, mended his socks and stockings; she even went so far as to clean his palette for him, collect rags to clean his brushes with and get everything tidy in the studio. Seeing his mother take charge of these details so intelligently, Joseph loaded her with attention. If mother and son were not in complete harmony on the question of art, they were at least admirably united in mutual tenderness.

Agathe had a plan in mind. After coaxing Joseph one morning, as he was sketching an immense painting, completed later on and which was never understood, she made so bold as to say aloud:

'Oh dear! I wonder what he's doing.'

'Who?'

'Philippe!'

'Oh yes! That lad is having to rough it now. He'll mend his ways.'

'But he has already experienced poverty and misfortune, and perhaps it was that which changed him. If he was happy he would be good.'

'Do you really believe, dear Mother, that he suffered during his voyage? If so, you're mistaken. He painted the town red in New York, just as he's doing here now.'

'If he was suffering somewhere near by our house, it would be terrible.'

'Yes, as far as I am concerned, I would gladly give him money, but I don't want to see him. He killed poor aunt Descoings.'

'So you wouldn't paint his portrait?'

'For you, Mother, I would suffer martyrdom itself. I cannot forget one thing: that he is my brother.'

'Would you do his portrait in the uniform of a captain of the horse dragoons?'

'Yes, over there is a fine horse, modelled on Gros, and I don't know how to use it.'

'Well! Go over there to his friend's and see how he is getting on.'

'All right.'

Agathe stood up, dropping her scissors and everything, and came over to kiss Joseph's head, hiding her tears in his hair.

'That's your passion, that boy!' he said. 'And we all have our fatal passion.'

The very same afternoon Joseph went to the Rue du Sentier, where at about four o'clock he found his brother taking Giroudeau's place in the office. The ex-captain of dragoons had become a cashier for a weekly journal run by his nephew. Although Finot still remained the proprietor of the small journal which he had made into a private company with all its shares registered in his own name, the ostensible owner and editor was a friend of his called Lousteau, the son of the same Subdelegate in Issoudun on whom Bridau's grandfather had wished to take revenge – and consequently, Madame Hochon's nephew. To please his uncle, Finot had appointed Philippe as a replacement, nevertheless cutting his salary by half. Then, every day at five, Giroudeau would check the accounts and take away the day's takings. Redskin, the disabled soldier who acted as office clerk and ran errands, kept a bit of an eye on Captain Philippe. But Philippe behaved well. A salary of 600 francs a year plus 500 francs pension from his Cross of the Legion of Honour enabled him to live comfortably, because with free heating during the day, and spending his evenings at theatres to which he was admitted free of charge, he had only to think about his board and lodging. As Joseph entered the room, Redskin was just going out carrying some stamped documents on his head and Philippe was brushing his green linen oversleeves.

'Hello, here's the nipper,' said Philippe. 'Well, let's go and dine somewhere together. Then you can come with me to the Opéra. Florine and Florentine have a box. I go with Giroudeau. You can be one of the party, and you'll meet Nathan!'

He picked up his lead-headed cane and moistened his cigar.

'I can't accept your invitation. I've got to go and take Mother home. We dine at a table d'hôte.'

'Pity! How's she getting on, the old dear?'

'Oh, not too badly. I've repainted father's portrait and also aunt Descoings's. I've finished my own and I would like to give mother your portrait, dressed in the uniform of the Imperial Dragoon Guards.'

'Good!'

'But you'll have to come and pose.'

'Every day, from nine to five, I have to be in this chicken-coop.'

'Two Sundays will be enough.'

'Agreed, little chap,' Napoleon's former aide-de-camp replied, lighting his cigar at the porter's lamp.

When Joseph explained Philippe's situation to his mother, as they were on their way to dine in the Rue de Beaune, he felt her arm tremble within his, and her jaded countenance shone with joy; the poor woman breathed a sigh of relief, like a person relieved of some enormous burden. Next day she loaded Joseph with attention, so great were her happiness and gratitude: she decorated his studio with flowers and bought him two flower-stands. On the first Sunday when Philippe was due to come and pose, Agathe made a point of preparing a delicious lunch in the studio. She put everything on the table, not forgetting a bottle of eau-de-vie now only half full. She then concealed herself behind a screen, in which she had cut a hole. The previous evening, when the ex-dragoons officer had sent his uniform over, she could not help kissing it. When Philippe posed, fully dressed, on one of those stuffed horses which saddle-makers have and which Joseph had hired, Agathe – not to give herself away – had to conceal her gentle sobs under the two brothers' conversation. Philippe posed for two hours before lunch and for two hours afterwards. At three in the afternoon the dragoons officer put on his ordinary clothes again and, smoking a cigar, suggested a second time to his brother that they should go and dine together at the Palais-Royal. He jingled gold coins in his waist pocket.

'No,' Joseph replied, 'you frighten me when I see you with gold.'

'Bah! So you here will always have a bad opinion of me?' cried the lieutenant-colonel in a thundering voice. 'So you're not allowed to have any savings!'

'No, no,' replied Agathe, coming out of her hiding-place and embracing her son. 'Let's go and have dinner with him, Joseph.'

Joseph did not like to scold his mother. He got changed and Philippe took them for a meal at the Rocher de Cancale, in the Rue Montorgueil, where he gave them a sumptuous dinner, the bill for which amounted to 100 francs.

'Hang it!' Joseph said uneasily. 'On an income of 1,100 francs a year, like Ponchard in *The White Lady*, you're saving up enough money to buy yourself a gentleman's estate!'

'Ah! I'm on to a good thing,' the dragoons officer replied. He had drunk an enormous quantity of wine.

Hearing these words on the threshold of the restaurant, and just as they were about to get into a carriage to go to the theatre, for Philippe was taking his mother to the Cirque-Olympique, the one theatre to which her confessor had given her permission to go, Joseph grasped his mother's arm and she immediately pretended to be feeling unwell and so declined his invitation to the theatre. Then Philippe took his mother and brother back to the Rue Mazarine, where, when she was on her own again with Joseph in his attic, she remained profoundly silent.

Next Sunday, Philippe came to pose again. This time their mother was visibly present at the sitting. She served lunch and was able to put questions to the officer. She then learned that the nephew of old Madame Hochon, her mother's friend, occupied a certain position in the literary world. Philippe and his friend Giroudeau moved in a world of journalists, actresses and booksellers, and were thought of as cashiers. Philippe, who always drank kirsch whilst posing after lunch, let his tongue run away with him. He boasted that he would be somebody important again before very long. But, when Joseph asked him about his financial resources, he made no reply. As it happened, there was no newspaper the following day on account of a religious festival, and Philippe, to have done with the portrait, suggested that he might come again then for a final sitting. Joseph pointed out to him that the national exhibition of painting would soon be round again; he did not have enough money to buy frames for his two pictures and could only obtain the money by finishing the copy of Rubens which an art dealer called Magus had asked him to produce. The original belonged to a wealthy Swiss banker who had only lent it for ten days, and tomorrow was the last day; it was therefore imperative to postpone the sitting till the following Sunday.

'Is that it?' Philippe asked, looking at the Rubens, which stood propped up on an easel.

'Yes,' Joseph replied. 'It's worth 20,000 francs. That's what genius can do. Some bits of canvas are worth hundreds of thousands of francs.'

'I prefer your copy.'

'It's newer,' said Joseph laughing, 'but my copy is only worth 1,000 francs. I need to work on it tomorrow to give it the same tones as the original and age it so that people can't distinguish between them.'

'Good-bye, Mother,' Philippe said, embracing Agathe. 'Till next Sunday.'

The following day, Élie Magus was due to come and pick up his copy. A friend of Joseph's, Pierre Grassou, who worked for this dealer, wanted to see the finished copy. On hearing him knock at the door, Joseph – to play a trick on him – put his copy, which he had varnished with a special preparation, in the original's place, standing the original on his easel. He completely hoaxed Pierre Grassou de Fougères, who was amazed by his achievement.

'Would it deceive old Élie Magus?' Pierre Grassou asked him.

'Let's see,' said Joseph.

The picture dealer did not come; it was late. Agathe was dining with Madame Desroches, who had just lost her husband. So Joseph suggested to Pierre Grassou that he should join him at his table d'hôte. Downstairs he left the key of his studio with the doorkeeper, as was his custom.

'I have to pose this evening,' Philippe told the doorkeeper an hour after his brother's departure. 'Joseph will soon be back and I'll wait for him in the studio.'

The doorkeeper gave him the key. Philippe went upstairs, took the copy, thinking it was the original, came downstairs again, gave the key back to the doorkeeper, pretending he had forgotten something and went off to sell the Rubens for 3,000 francs. He had taken the precaution of giving Élie Magus a message from his brother, telling him to postpone his visit until the following day. That evening, when Joseph returned escorting his mother home from Madame Desroches's, the porter told him of his brother's whim; Philippe had no sooner come than he was gone again.

'I'm sunk if he hasn't had the decency to take just the copy,' the painter exclaimed, guessing that there had been a theft. He ran up to the third floor, rushed into his studio and said: 'Thank God! He has been what he always will be, a dirty rascal!'

Agathe, who had followed Joseph, could not make any sense of this remark; but when her son explained it to her, she remained standing without tears in her eyes.

'So I have only one son left,' she said in a feeble voice.

'We didn't wish to show him up in front of strangers,' Joseph continued, 'but now we must tell the porter not to admit him. Tomorrow we will keep our keys on us. I'll finish his blasted face from memory, it's almost complete.'

'Leave it as it is; it would be too painful for me to see it,' Agathe replied, hurt to the depths of her heart and stupefied by the extent of Philippe's cowardice.

Philippe knew what the money from the sale of this copy would be used for, he knew the abyss into which he was plunging his brother, yet he had respected nothing. After this ultimate crime, Agathe never mentioned his name again. Her face took on an expression of bitter, cold and concentrated despair. One thought was killing her.

'Some day,' she kept on repeating to herself, 'we shall see Bridau in court.'

*

Two months later, just as Agathe was about to set off for her lottery office one morning, there was a visitor for Madame Bridau, who was breakfasting with Joseph. It was an old soldier who said he was a friend of Philippe's and who had apparently come on urgent business.

When Giroudeau introduced himself, both mother and son trembled, particularly as the ex-dragoons officer had the disquieting expression of an old sea-wolf. His dull grey eyes and greying moustache and the wisps of untidy hair encircling a skull that was the colour of fresh butter had something of a decrepit, lustful appearance. He was wearing an old charcoal grey coat which was adorned with the rosette of an officer of the Legion of Honour, and would hardly button across a pot belly that was in perfect harmony with a mouth stretching from ear to ear and powerful shoulders. His torso was supported by frail little legs. His complexion, flushed at the cheekbones, indicated that he led a gay life. The pouches of his cheeks, deeply lined, sagged over a shabby black velvet collar. Amongst other adornments, the ex-dragoons officer wore an enormous pair of gold ear-rings.

'What a rip!' thought Joseph, using a popular expression that had now caught on in the studios.

'Madame,' said Finot's uncle and cashier, 'your son is in such an unfortunate position that it is impossible for his friends not to beg you to share with them the fairly onerous burdens he is imposing upon them. He is no longer able to carry out his duties with the newspaper, and Mademoiselle Florentine of the Théâtre de la Porte-Saint-Martin is lodging him at her home in the Rue de Vendôme, in a poverty-stricken attic. Philippe is dying. If you and his brother are unable to pay for a doctor and medicines, we shall be forced – in the interests of his recovery – to have him transferred to the Hôpital des Capucins; whereas for 300 francs we would look after him ourselves. He absolutely needs a sick-nurse. He goes out in the evenings whilst Mademoiselle Florentine is at the theatre and takes irritating things which are harmful to his illness and treatment; and, as we love him, it makes us really unhappy. This poor young man has mortgaged his pension for three years. He has been temporarily replaced at the newspaper office and has nothing left in the world. He will commit suicide, Madame, unless we put him in Dr Dubois's nursing-home. This respectable institution will cost ten francs a day. Florentine and I will pay half the monthly bill, will you pay the other? Come on! He won't be in for much more than a couple of months!'

'Monsieur, it is difficult for a mother not to be eternally grateful to you for what you are doing for my son,' Agathe replied, 'but this son has been cut out of my heart; and, as for giving you any money, I simply haven't got any. Not to be dependent on my son here, who is killing himself with working day and night and who is worthy of a mother's love, I'm starting the day after tomorrow as deputy manageress of a lottery office. At my age!'

'And what about you, young man?' the ex-dragoons officer asked Joseph. 'Come on! Won't you do for your brother the same as a poor ballet-dancer from the Porte-Saint-Martin and an old soldier are doing?'

'Look,' said Joseph, growing impatient, 'do you want me to tell you in artists' language why you have come here? You're trying to have us on!'

'Well then, tomorrow your brother will go to the Hôpital du Midi.'

'He'll be quite all right there,' Joseph replied. 'If ever I was in his position, I'd go there!'

Giroudeau left the room very crestfallen, but also very seriously humiliated at having to send to the Hôpital des

Capucins a man who had carried the Emperor's orders at the Battle of Montereau.

Three months later, one morning towards the end of July, as she was on her way to her lottery office, Agathe, who went by the Pont-Neuf to avoid paying a sou at the Pont-des-Arts, noticed a man by the shops on the embankment of the École des Beaux-Arts as she herself was walking along the parapet of the embankment. At the sight of this man, who wore the dress of what might be termed a 'second-class pauper', her heart turned over; she thought he bore some resemblance to Philippe. In Paris, there are in fact three classes of pauperdom. First, there is the poverty of the man who keeps up appearances now but whose future is secure: the poverty of young men, artists and society people who are temporarily embarrassed. The signs of this poverty are only visible to the most practised observer and even then a microscope is required. These people make up the equestrian class of paupers, they still go around in cabs. In the second class of the order are old men who have ceased to care about anything, and who wear the cross of the Legion of Honour over an alpaca coat in June. Theirs is the poverty of old retired people, ageing clerks whose home is at Sainte-Périne, people who are hardly concerned any more about how they dress. Finally, there is the poverty that goes about in rags, the pauperdom of the working class; this is poverty in its most poetical form, admired and painted (especially at carnival time) by Callot, Hogarth, Murillo, Charlet, Raffet, Gavarni, Meissonier and artists generally. The man whom Agathe thought she recognized as her son was midway between the two lower classes of the order. She noticed his badly worn collar, filthy hat, boots that were down at heel and patched together, and a threadbare coat with shapeless buttons whose gaping and bent centres perfectly matched the worn-out pockets and grimy collar. Wisps of down showed that, if the coat contained anything at all, it could only be dust. The man took his hands – as black as any workman's – out of a pair of charcoal grey trousers whose stitching was coming undone. Across his chest he wore a knitted woollen waistcoat which was brown with use, peeped out from under his sleeves and hung loosely over his trousers; in fact, it seemed to be everywhere and no doubt was a substitute for linen. Philippe was wearing an eye shield made of green taffeta and brass wire. The colour of his complexion, his nearly bald head and haggard face indicated clearly enough that he had just been released from the terrible Hôpital du Midi. His blue coat, now white at the edges, was still decorated with his rosette, and because of this passers-by looked at this war veteran – no doubt, some victim of the government – with mingled curiosity and pity; for the rosette was disturbing to look at and inspired even the fiercest extremist with honourable doubts concerning the Legion of Honour. At this time, although government policy had been to discredit the Order by unlimited conferment, still there were fewer than 53,000 people in France on whom it had been bestowed. Agathe shuddered to the depths of her very being. Even though it was now impossible for her to love this son, he could still cause her great suffering. Yielding for the last time to a maternal impulse, she wept on seeing the Emperor's dazzling aide-de-camp make as if to enter a tobacconist's to buy a cigar, but halt on the threshold; he had fumbled in his pockets and there was nothing there. Agathe hurried across the embankment, got her purse out, put it into Philippe's hand and disappeared as quickly as if she had committed a crime. For two days she was unable to eat or drink anything. Still before her eyes was the horrible vision of her son dying in Paris of starvation.

'After he's used up all the money in my purse, who else will give him any?' she thought. 'Giroudeau was not lying: Philippe has just come out of hospital.'

No longer did she see in him the murderer of her poor aunt, the scourge of his family, the domestic thief, the gambler, the drunkard, the lowest of debauchees; he was a convalescent dying of hunger, a man who enjoyed smoking but had no tobacco. At forty-seven, she looked as old as a woman of seventy. Her eyes grew dim in weeping and in prayer.

But this was not the last of the deadly blows which her son was to deal her; her most horrible foreboding became a reality. An officers' conspiracy was discovered within the army and an extract from the *Moniteur* was proclaimed in the streets, containing details about the arrests that had been made.

As she sat in her little lottery office in the Rue Vivienne, Agathe heard them shouting the name of Philippe Bridau. She fainted, and the manager, realizing her distress and how she would need to take action on her son's behalf, gave her a fortnight's holiday.

'Ah! We have driven him to this with our harshness,' she told Joseph, as she went to bed.

'I'll go and see Desroches,' Joseph answered.

Whilst the artist was entrusting his brother's case to Desroches, who had the reputation of being the wiliest and most astute of all Parisian attorneys and who also acted for several people of note, including Des Lupeaulx (who was at that time Secretary-General of a Ministry), Giroudeau called on the widow, who this time believed him.

'Madame, find 12,000 francs and your son will be released for lack of evidence. It's a matter of buying off two witnesses.'

'I shall find you the money,' the poor mother said, knowing neither where nor how.

Spurred on by the impending danger, she wrote to her godmother, old Madame Hochon, asking her whether Jean-Jacques Rouget would provide the money needed to save Philippe. If Rouget refused, she begged Madame Hochon to lend it to her, undertaking to repay it to her within two years. By return of post, she received the following letter:

My Dear Girl,

Though your brother has a clear 40,000 francs a year investment income, without counting the money he has put by over the last seventeen years, which Monsieur Hochon estimates at more than 600,000 francs, he won't give a sou to nephews whom he has never seen. As for me, you are unaware of the fact that I shan't have six francs to call my own, so long as my husband remains alive. Hochon is the greatest miser in Issoudun. I simply don't know what he does with his money. He doesn't even give his grandchildren twenty francs a year. If I wanted to borrow money, I should need to have his consent which he would not give. I haven't even tried to get anyone to speak to your brother about this matter; living with him is a mistress who completely rules the roost. It's a downright shame to see how the poor man is treated at home, when he has a sister and nephews. I have several times hinted to you that, if you came to Issoudun, you could perhaps save your brother and snatch for your sons, from the claws of this parasite, a fortune of 40,000 francs – perhaps even 60,000 francs a year; but either you haven't answered my letters, or you seem not to have understood me. And so I have no alternative now but to write to you with absolute frankness. I really do sympathize with you in your misfortune, but I can't do anything except feel sorry for you, my dear girl. The reason why I can't do anything to help you is as follows: at eighty-five years of age, Hochon has four meals a day, eats a salad with hard-boiled eggs every evening, and can run like a rabbit. I've spent my whole life (he'll write my epitaph!) without ever having had twenty francs in my purse. If you do wish to come down to Issoudun, to combat this woman's influence over your brother, Rouget would not invite you to his house for the reasons mentioned. I shall find it a hard enough job to get my husband's permission to invite you here. But you can come to our home. He will respect my wishes in this matter. I know a way of getting him to do what I want . . . and that is to talk to him about my will. It seems such a horrible method that I never resort to it; but I'll do the impossible for you. I hope that your boy Philippe will get out of this mess, especially if you find a good barrister. But come as soon as you can to Issoudun. Remember that, at fifty-seven, your idiotic brother is older and more infirm than Monsieur Hochon. So it's urgent. People are already talking about a will which would deprive you of the inheritance; but, according to what Monsieur Hochon says, there is still time to get it revoked. Good-bye, dear Agathe, and God be with you! You can always depend on your loving godmother.

MAXIMILIENNE HOCHON, née LOUSTEAU

PS. Has my nephew Étienne, who writes in the newspapers and who is said to be friendly with your son Philippe, been to pay you his compliments? But come down here . . . and we'll chat about him.

This letter greatly preoccupied Agathe. She felt herself obliged to show it to Joseph, to whom she had had to relate Giroudeau's proposal. The artist, who became a prudent man wherever his brother was involved, remarked to his mother that she ought to tell Desroches everything.

Struck by the good sense of this remark, mother and son went to call on Desroches, in the Rue de Bussy, the following morning at six. The attorney, as spare in build as his late father, with a shrill voice, a rough complexion, implacable eyes and the face of a weasel licking the blood of chickens from his lips, leapt like a tiger on learning of Giroudeau's visit and the proposal he had made.

'Ah! Madame Bridau,' he cried, in his broken voice, 'when will you stop being taken in by your damned rogue of a son? Don't pay a penny for him! I'll take responsibility for Philippe. It's to save his future that I want to get him tried by the House of Peers. You're afraid to see him convicted – but may God allow his barrister to get him convicted! Off you go to Issoudun and rescue your son's fortune. If you don't succeed, if your brother has made a will in this woman's favour and you can't get it revoked ... well, at least get the facts together in support of an *ad captandum* appeal accusing her of wrongfully obtaining the inheritance! I'll take charge of that case. But you're too honest a woman to find the grounds for a court case of this kind! I'll run down to Issoudun during my holidays ... if I'm able.'

These words: 'I'll run down to Issoudun' made the artist tremble with delight. Desroches winked to Joseph, indicating that he should let his mother go on a little ahead of him, and kept him behind for a moment.

'Your brother is a terrible wretch. Either by accident or design he has caused this conspiracy to be discovered. He's such a cunning devil that you can never really weigh him up! Call him fool or traitor, as you please! No doubt, he will be put under police supervision, but nothing more. Don't worry, only I know this secret. Hurry to Issoudun with your mother. You've got your wits about you; try to rescue this inheritance.'

'Come on, Mother darling. Desroches is right,' Joseph said, catching up with his mother on the staircase; 'I've sold my two pictures; let's go down to the Berry district, since you've got a fortnight's holiday.'

After writing to her godmother to inform her of their

arrival, Agathe and Joseph set off the following evening for Issoudun, leaving Philippe to his fate. The coach passed by the Rue d'Enfer on its way to the Orleans road. When Agathe saw the Luxembourg prison to which Philippe had been transferred, she could not help saying: 'If it wasn't for the Allies, he wouldn't be there today!'

Many sons would have shown impatience at this remark, or would have smiled in pity; but the artist, alone with his mother inside the coach, seized her and pressed her against his heart, saying: 'Oh! Mother, you are a mother in the way Raphael was a painter! And you'll always be a foolish mother!'

PART TWO: A BACHELOR'S HOUSEHOLD IN THE PROVINCES

10. Issoudun

Soon distracted from her grief by the various sights along the road, Madame Bridau was obliged to think ahead to the goal of her journey. Naturally, she re-read Madame Hochon's letter, which had made so powerful an impression on the attorney Desroches. Struck by the words 'mistress' and 'parasite' which had been used by a seventy-two-year-old woman, as pious as she was respectable, to describe the person who was devouring Jean-Jacques Rouget's fortune, and seeing him described as 'idiotic', she asked herself how the fact of her presence at Issoudun could rescue an inheritance. Joseph, a poor and utterly unselfish artist, did not know much about the law, and his mother's exclamation worried him.

'Before sending us to rescue an inheritance, our friend Desroches ought to have told us how to go about it,' he cried.

'As far as my memory goes (I've been so bothered about Philippe being in prison, perhaps without any tobacco, and waiting to stand trial before the Court of Peers), I seem to remember that young Desroches told us to get together the grounds for an *ad captandum* appeal, in the event of my brother having made a will in this . . . this . . . woman's favour.'

'It's all very well for Desroches to say that,' was Joseph's answer. 'Anyway, if we don't know how to go about it, I'll ask him to come down.'

'Don't let's worry our heads needlessly,' Agathe replied. 'When we get to Issoudun, my godmother will advise us.'

This conversation took place just as Madame Bridau and Joseph were entering the Sologne district, after changing coaches at Orleans; it gives a clear indication of the unfitness of the artist and his mother to play the part allocated to them by their terrible master, Desroches. But, returning to Issoudun after thirty years' absence, Agathe was about to discover such changes in the way of life there that it is necessary to give an outline of the town in a few paragraphs. Without such an outline, it would be difficult to understand the heroism shown by Madame Hochon in backing up her goddaughter, and equally difficult to understand Jean-Jacques Rouget's strange position. Although the doctor had always given his son to understand that Agathe was no relation of theirs, even so it was a little too extraordinary for a brother not to have shown his sister any sign of life for thirty years. Obviously, this silence was due to peculiar circumstances which any relations other than Joseph and Agathe would have long since inquired into. In a word, between the position of Issoudun at this time and the interests of the Bridau family there were certain links which will transpire in the course of the story.

With all due respect to Paris, Issoudun is one of the most historic towns in France. Despite the historical prejudice which claims that the Emperor Probus is the Noah of the Gauls, Caesar has spoken of the excellent wine of Champ-Fort (*de Campo Forti*), one of Issoudun's best vineyards. Rigord writes of this town in words which leave no doubt as to its large population and immense volume of trade. But it would seem that the evidence of these two men ascribes too recent a foundation to Issoudun, in relation to the town's great antiquity. In fact, excavations recently conducted by a learned local archaeologist, Monsieur Armand Pérémet, have discovered a fifth-century basilica (probably the only remaining one in France) beneath the famous tower of Issoudun. The very materials out of which this church was constructed bear the marks of an ancient civilization, for its stones come from a Roman temple which it replaced. Thus, according to Monsieur Pérémet's researches, the very name of Issoudun – like that of all French towns whose ancient or modern suffix ends in 'dun' (*dunum*) – points to an autochthonous origin. This word 'dun', solely applied to hills consecrated by the Druidic cult, seems to indicate some military and religious establishment of the Celts. It is said that beneath the Dun built by the Gauls the Romans erected a temple to Isis. This, according to Chaumeau, is how the town's name 'Is-sous-Dun' is derived, 'Is' being the abbreviation of Isis.

Richard the Lionheart undoubtedly built the famous tower (where he minted money) over a fifth-century basilica, which was the third monument of the third religion in this ancient town. He used this church as a necessary support when raising the height of the town walls, and preserved it by mantling it over with feudal fortifications. At that time, the transitory power of the Routiers and the Cottereaux, *condottieri* whom Henry II of England set up in opposition to his son Richard, when the latter revolted against him in his capacity of Comte de Poitou, was centred on Issoudun. The history of Aquitaine, which the Benedictine Order left unchronicled, will undoubtedly never be written now, when there are no longer any Benedictines to write it. For this reason one can never probe too deeply into these mysteries of archaeology whenever the occasion arises; they are gaps in the history of our civilization.

There is another indication of Issoudun's former power: the fact that over a great area of land the Tournemine was converted into a canal, this small river being raised several yards above the level of the Théols, the river which encircles the town. This canal is undoutedly a product of Roman genius. Finally, the suburb extending from the castle in a northerly direction is crossed by a road which for more than two thousand years has been known as the Rue de Rome. The suburb itself is called the 'Faubourg de Rome'. The inhabitants of this suburb, who have something specially distinctive about their race, blood and facial appearance, claim to be descended from the Romans. Almost all are wine-growers, and they lead remarkably moral and upright lives, no doubt because of their origins and perhaps also because of their victory over the Cottereaux and Routiers, whom they wiped out on the plain of Charost in the twelfth century.

After the Revolution of 1830, France was in too much of a turmoil to pay any attention to the revolt of the Issoudun wine-growers, a terrible event whose details, by the way, have never yet been made known – and with good reason. At first, the townsfolk of Issoudun would not allow the troops to enter their town. They themselves wished to be responsible for their own safety, according to the custom of burgesses in the Middle Ages. The government were forced to give in to people backed up by 6,000 or 7,000 wine-growers who had burned down all the archives and offices of the Inland Revenue and who dragged one of the clerks from the City Dues Office through the streets, halting at each lamp-post and crying: 'String him up there!' The poor man was rescued from these furious men by the National Guard, who saved his life by taking him off to prison on the pretext that they were going to prosecute him. Only when the general had surrendered to the wine-growers could he enter the town, and he needed courage to penetrate their serried ranks; for, just as he appeared at the Town Hall, a man from the Faubourg de Rome raised his *volant* to the general's neck (the *volant* is a large bill-hook attached to a pole, used for trimming trees). The man shouted: 'Get rid of the tax-collectors, or else!' This wine-grower would have beheaded a man whom sixteeen years of warfare had left unscathed, but for the speedy intervention of one of the leaders of the revolt, who obtained the promise that the Houses of Parliament would be asked to suppress 'house rats' . . .!

In the fourteenth century, Issoudun still had 16,000 or 17,000 inhabitants, all that remained of a population which had been twice that size in Rigord's time. Charles VII had a mansion there; it is still standing today and until the eighteenth century was known as the King's House. At that time the town was the centre of the wool trade and supplied part of Europe with this commodity, manufacturing blankets, hats and also excellent kid gloves on a large scale. In Louis XIV's reign, Issoudun, which produced both Baron and Bourdaloue, was also spoken of as a town of elegance, fine language and good society. In his history of Sancerre, Abbé Poupart claimed that the inhabitants of Issoudun excelled all other inhabitants of Berry in their subtlety and native wit. Today, the splendour and wit of former times have disappeared without trace. Issoudun, covering an area that indicates its former importance, has no more than 12,000 inhabitants – and this includes the wine-growers of four enormous suburbs, Saint-Paterne, Vilatte, Rome and Les Alouettes, small towns in themselves. The middle class, like the middle class of Versailles, have spacious streets to walk around in. Issoudun is still the centre of the Berry wool trade, but this trade is threatened by the improvements in the breed of sheep which are taking over everywhere, but which Berry will not adopt. The Issoudun vineyards produce a wine that is drunk in two *départements* and which, if only it was produced in the same way as Burgundy and Gascony produce theirs, would become one of the best French wines. Alas! Do as we have always done, avoid innovations – such is the law of this particular area. For this reason, the wine-growers continue to leave the grape stalks in the wine whilst it is fermenting, with the result that their wine becomes detestable, whereas otherwise it could be the source of new wealth and work in the region. Owing to the bitter taste which the grape stalks give the wine, a taste which is said to change with age, Issoudun wine lasts a century. This reason given by the wine-growing industry is sufficiently important in the science of wines to be worthy of publication. Indeed, Guillaume Le Breton has celebrated this property of Issoudun wines in a few verses of his *Philippide*.

Thus, Issoudun's decline is due to a spirit of reactionary conservatism driven to insensate lengths. A single fact will illustrate this attitude of mind. When the road from Paris to Toulouse was being built, it was natural enough to take it from Vierzon to Châteauroux via Issoudun. The road would have been shorter than if it went via Vatan, which is what eventually happened. But the local notabilities and the town council, the minutes of whose discussions are said to exist, asked that the road should be diverted via Vatan, on the grounds that, if the main road went through their town, food would go up in price and chickens would cost thirty sous each. No parallel can be found for such an action except in the wildest regions of Sardinia, a country so densely populated, so prosperous in former centuries, and nowadays so deserted. When, in a laudable intention of civilizing the country, King Charles Albert tried to link up Sassari, the island's second capital, with Cagliari by means of a beautiful and magnificent road, the only road that exists in that Mediterranean savanna, the direct route would have been through Bonorva, a district inhabited by turbulent tribes – all the more similar to our own Arab tribes in that both descend from the Moors. Seeing that they were about to be linked up with civilization, the wild inhabitants of Bonorva – without even taking the trouble of discussing the matter – declared their opposition to the projected route. The government ignored their objections. The first engineer who came to plant the first landmark was struck in the head by a bullet and died on the spot. No police inquiries were made in this matter, and the road is now twenty miles longer than was originally intended.

At Issoudun, the steady decline in the cost of wine consumed on the spot, whilst satisfying the middle classes' desire to keep down the cost of living, is ruining the wine-growers, who are increasingly hit by production costs and taxation; in exactly the same way, the wool trade and indeed the whole locality are being ruined by a reluctance to improve the breed of sheep. Country people thoroughly detest any form of change, even when they can see that it is in their own interests to accept it. A Parisian comes across a workman in the countryside who has eaten a huge quantity of bread, cheese and vegetables for his dinner; he proves to him that, if he were to substitute a portion of meat for this diet, he would eat more healthily and cheaply, work better and not use up his life energy so quickly. The inhabitant of Berry acknowledges the accuracy of these calculations. 'But the tittle-tattle, sir!' he replies. 'What do you mean, the tittle-tattle?' 'Well, yes, what would people say?' 'He would be the talk of the whole countryside,' remarked the landowner on whose property this scene took place, 'people would think he was as well off as a town-dweller. In other words, he's afraid of public opinion, afraid of being pointed at, of being called weak or sickly. . . . That's how things are round here!' Many middle-class people say this last sentence with pride.

But, if ignorance and routine are unchangeable in the country areas where peasants are left to fend for themselves, the town of Issoudun has also reached a point of complete social stagnation. Needing to resist the dwindling-away of private fortunes by sordid economy, each family keeps itself to itself. Furthermore, local society is for ever deprived of that antagonism which gives distinction to a way of life. The town no longer contains those opposing forces which animated the Italian states of the Middle Ages. Issoudun no longer has an aristocracy. The Cottereaux, Routiers, Jacquerie, Wars of Religion and Revolution have completely wiped out the nobility. And the town is very proud of this triumph. Issoudun has invariably refused to quarter a garrison – and always for the same reason of keeping down the cost of food. It has lost its means of communication with the century in which it lives, as well as losing the profits which the presence of a body of troops entails. Until 1756, Issoudun was one of the most pleasant of garrison towns. It was deprived of its garrison after a judicial scandal which caught the attention of the whole of France, involving Lieutenant-General au Bailliage and the Marquis de Chapt, whose son, a dragoons officer, was put to death because of some love affair – justly perhaps, but treacherously even so. The quartering of the forty-fourth half-brigade, imposed upon Issoudun at the time of the Civil War, was not calculated to reconcile the local inhabitants to the military. Bourges, whose population declines every decade, is stricken with the same social malady. The life force is ebbing away from these great bodies.

Admittedly, the government has been responsible for these misfortunes. A government's duty is to look out for such blotches upon the 'body politic', and to put them right by sending out energetic men to these sickly localities, men who will rectify the face of things. Alas! Far from that happening, people congratulate themselves on the fatal and funereal calm. Besides, how can one send out new administrators or skilled magistrates? Who nowadays is keen to go and bury himself in an area where there is much good to be done but no glory to be achieved? If, by some chance, ambitious men are appointed to those towns who are not natives of the area, they are soon overcome by the prevailing force of inertia, and settle down into the rhythm of this atrocious provincial life. Issoudun would have paralysed Napoleon.

On account of its peculair situation, the administrative subdivision of Issoudun was administered in 1822 by men who all came from Berry. Thus, authority was either non-existent or weak, except in those cases – which naturally are very rare – where justice is forced into action by the blatant gravity of the case. The Crown Attorney, Monsieur Mouilleron, was everybody's cousin, and his Deputy Public Prosecutor belonged to one of the families of the town. The Chief Judge, before attaining this high position, had distinguished himself by one of those witticisms which, in the provinces, set a dunce's cap upon a man's head for the term of his natural life. After concluding the preliminary judicial investigation in a criminal case involving the death penalty, he said to the accused: 'My dear Pierre, the affair is clear, you'll have your head chopped off. Let that be a lesson to you.' The Police Superintendent, who had held his post since the Restoration, had relations in the whole administrative area. And the influence exerted by religion was not only nil, but the priest enjoyed no respect whatsoever. The bourgeoisie, liberal-minded, scoffing and ignorant, used to tell more or less comic stories about the poor man's relations with his housekeeper. But this did not prevent the children from going to Sunday school, or making their first communion; and there was still a church school in the town. Mass was said at Issoudun and people always observed the religious festivals. They paid their taxes, the one thing which Paris requires from the provinces; and the mayor passed decrees. But these acts of social life were accomplished out of routine. Thus, the weakness of the civil service was in perfect harmony with the district's intellectual and moral condition. The events of this story will, moreover, depict the consequences of this state of affairs – a state of affairs which is by no means as unusual as you might think. Many French towns especially in the south are like Issoudun. The situation into which the triumph of the middle class has thrown this subprefecture is the same as awaits the whole of France and even Paris itself, if the middle class continues to direct the external and internal politics of our country.

Now, a word about the town's topographical features. Issoudun spreads out from north to south along a hillside which curves round towards the Châteauroux road. At the foot of this hill, a canal was built long ago to serve the requirements of small factories or to flood the moats surrounding the town walls at a time when the town was in a state of flourishing prosperity. This canal is now called the 'Rivière Forcée', or artificial river, and its waters flow into the River Théols. The Rivière Forcée forms an artificial arm which discharges its waters into the natural river, beyond the Faubourg de Rome, at the point where the Théols is joined by the Tournemine and certain other streams. These small streams of flowing water, together with the two rivers, irrigate the fairly extensive meadows which are encircled on all sides by white or yellowish hills dotted about with black specks. Such is the appearance of the vineyards of Issoudun for seven months of the year. The vine-growers cut back the vine-stocks annually, leaving only a hideous stump, inside the funnel, without any stake to support it. So, when you approach the town from Vierzon, Vatan or Châteauroux, eyes that have been saddened by monotonous stretches of plain are pleasantly surprised at the sight of Issoudun's meadows, the oasis of this area of Berry, which supplies the surrounding districts with vegetables within a radius of twenty-five miles. Below the Faubourg de Rome is a vast marshy area, the whole of which is cultivated as kitchen gardens and divided up into two regions known as Bas and Haut Baltan. A long, huge avenue with two smaller side avenues of poplars leads out of the town across the meadows to an ancient monastery called

Frapesle, whose English-style gardens – the only ones of their kind in the administrative subdivision – have been given the high-sounding name of Tivoli. On Sundays, courting couples exchange sweet confidences there.

Inevitably, the marks of Issoudun's former grandeur are evident to the attentive observer, and the most striking of all these are the divisions into which the town conveniently falls. The Castle, which once upon a time – what with its walls and moats – was a town in itself, now forms a distinct area into which you can only penetrate today by means of the ancient gateways and from which the only exits are three bridges traversing the arms of the two rivers. It is the only area in Issoudun which looks like an ancient town. In places the town walls still reveal their enormous layers of stone on which houses are built. Above the Castle is the Tower, which at one time was the fortress. Whoever wished to become master of the town which sprawled around these two fortified points had to capture both the Tower and the Castle. Possession of the Castle did not automatically ensure possession of the Tower. The Faubourg de Saint-Paterne, which stretches out palette-like beyond the Tower in the direction of the meadows, is too large not to have been in very distant times the town itself. From the Middle Ages onwards Issoudun, like Paris, seems to have climbed up the hill on which it was originally built and clustered beyond the tower and the Castle. In 1822 this theory was virtually confirmed by the existence of the charming church of Saint-Paterne, recently demolished by the heir of the man who bought it from the nation. This church, one of the finest specimens of Romanesque architecture in France, was destroyed without one person having drawn the West Door, which was still in a state of perfect preservation. The one voice which attempted to save the monument found no echo anywhere, neither in the town nor in the department. Although the Castle of Issoudun had all the appearance of an ancient town, with its narrow streets and old houses, the town proper – which was captured and burned down several times in different centuries, especially during the period of the Fronde when it was completely destroyed by fire – has a modern look.

Spacious streets, spacious at least in relation to other towns, and well-built houses form quite a striking contrast with the appearance of the Castle, so that in some geography books Issoudun is described as 'beautiful'.

11. The Knights of Idleness

IN a town formed after this pattern, without any activity at all, not even commercial activity, without any taste for the arts, without any learned societies, and where everybody remains at home, it was bound to happen – and did happen, after the Restoration, in 1816, when the war had ceased – that, amongst the young men of the town, several had no career to follow and had no idea what to do with themselves until such time as they got married or came into their parents' fortunes. Bored at home, these young men found nothing to amuse them in the town; and since, according to the proverbial expression, youth must sow its wild oats, they had their practical jokes at the expense of the town itself. It was very difficult for them to operate in broad daylight when they would have been recognized and, once the cup of their crimes had been filled to the brim, they would eventually have appeared before the court of summary jurisdiction, at the first slightly extravagant peccadillo; consequently, they prudently chose to stage their practical jokes at night. Thus, in these ancient remains of so many various civilizations, all of them gone beyond recall, a vestige of that ancient spirit of waggishness that distinguished bygone times flickered like an expiring flame. These young men found their amusement in the ways that Charles IX and his courtiers, Henry V and his boon companions formerly did – and as people once used to in many of our provincial towns. Once they had become confederates by the very fact that they had to help and defend one another, and think up amusing pranks, the collision of ideas increased that store of mischievousness which youth always has and which is even to be found in the animal world. Their unholy alliance gave them, moreover, the trivial pleasures which the mystery of a never-ending conspiracy confers. They nicknamed themselves the 'Knights of Idleness'.

During the daytime these monkeys were little saints; they all pretended to be extremely peaceful souls and, of course, they slept fairly late into the morning whenever they had performed some mischievous prank the previous night. The Knights of Idleness began their operations with vulgar practical jokes, such as unhooking and changing round shop signs, ringing doorbells, hurling some barrel which its owner had inadvertently left outside his door down into the cellar of his neighbour, who was then woken out of his sleep by a noise so loud that you would have thought a mine had exploded. In Issoudun, as in many towns, you go down to your cellar by a trap-door whose covering, placed near the entry to the house, is covered over with a stout hinged plank, with a big padlock to lock it with. These latter-day Mohocks had still not graduated, by the end of 1816, from the jokes that all scamps and young men play in all provincial towns. But, in January 1817, the Order of Idleness obtained a Grand Master, and now distinguished itself by tricks which, until 1823, spread a kind of terror throughout Issoudun or at least kept its craftsmen and middle-class people in a state of perpetual alarm.

Its chief was a certain Maxence Gilet, known more simply as Max, whose antecedents, no less than his physical strength and youth, destined him to fill this role. Maxence Gilet was thought in Issoudun to be the illegitimate son of the Sub-delegate, Monsieur Lousteau, whose attentions to the female sex left many memories – Madame Hochon's brother, the man who, as we have seen, had called down upon himself old Dr Rouget's wrath on the occasion of Agathe's birth. But the friendship between the two men, until the time of their quarrel, was so close that, in a phrase that was current in the region at that time, they willingly walked along the same roads. And so people claimed that Max could just as easily be the doctor's son as the Subdelegate's; but he was neither's, for his father was a charming dragoons officer garrisoned at Bourges. Nevertheless, on account of their enmity, the doctor and the Subdelegate each claimed constantly to have fathered Max – very luckily for him. Max's mother, the wife of a poor clog-maker in the Faubourg de Rome, was – for her soul's damnation – a dazzling beauty, with the beauty of a woman of Trastevere, the one benefit she transmitted to her son. Madame Gilet, who was expecting Max in 1788, had for a long time been hoping for this blessing from Heaven, which people were nasty enough to attribute to the attentions of the two friends – no doubt to set each of them against the other. Old Gilet, who was a habitual drunkard, encouraged his wife's waywardness with a collusion and indulgence that are not without parallels in the lower orders. To obtain protectors for her son, Madame Gilet took good care not to disabuse the spurious fathers. In Paris she would have made millions of francs; in Issoudun, she sometimes lived comfortably, sometimes wretchedly, and in the long run was despised.

Madame Hochon, Monsieur Lousteau's sister, gave about thirty francs a year to enable Max to go to school. This liberality which Madame Hochon was really unable to afford, on account of her husband's miserliness, was naturally attributed to her brother, who was then at Sancerre. When Dr Rouget, who was not happy living alone, noticed Max's handsome good looks, he paid for the boy – whom he called the young rascal – to board at a church school until 1805. As the Subdelegate died in 1800, and as the doctor's offer of five years' boarding-school education to Max seemed dictated by a feeling of vanity, the question of who was his father remained for ever unsolved. Maxence Gilet, the butt of thousands of jokes, was also quickly forgotten. This is why. In 1806, a year after Dr Rouget's death, the young man, who seemed to have been born to a life of adventure and who, furthermore, was endowed with remarkable strength and agility, was freely committing hosts of misdemeanours that involved him in greater or lesser degrees of danger. He was already on friendly terms with Monsieur Hochon's grandsons, helping them to annoy every grocer in town; he would pick people's fruit before they could get at it themselves, thinking nothing of scaling the orchard walls. There was no one to beat this devil in violent exercise; he played prisoners' base to perfection, he could run as fast as a hare. Gifted with eyesight as keen as Leather-Stocking's, he was already passionately fond of hunting and shooting. Instead of doing his lessons, he spent his time shooting at targets. He used the money which he managed to wangle out of the old doctor to buy bullets and gunpowder for a second-rate pistol which old Gilet, the clog-maker, had given him. During the autumn of 1806, Max – then aged seventeen – committed an involuntary murder when, at nightfall, he terrified a young pregnant woman whom he surprised in her garden, where he was intending to steal fruit. Threatened with the guillotine by his father, the clog-maker, who no doubt wanted to get rid of him, Max escaped in a single journey to Bourges, where he met with a regiment on its way to Spain, and joined up in the army. The affair of the young woman's death had no repercussions.

A boy of Max's disposition was bound to distinguish himself, and he distinguished himself so well that in three campaigns he was promoted captain – the little schooling which he had been willing to pick up was of great benefit to him. In 1809, in Portugal, he was abandoned presumed dead in an English battery, into which his company had penetrated without being able to hold it. Max, captured by the English, was transported to the Spanish hulks at Cabrera which were the most horrible of all. He was certainly recommended for the cross of the Legion of Honour and the rank of major; but the Emperor was in Austria at the time and was reserving his decorations for those soldiers whose brilliant exploits he witnessed with his own eyes. He had no liking for men who allowed themselves to be captured, and moreover he was fairly dissatisfied with the way things were going in Portugal. Max remained on the hulks from 1810 to 1814. During these four years he went completely to seed, for the hulks were tantamount to a convict prison, minus the element of crime and infamy. To begin with, to preserve his full freedom of action and resist the corruption prevailing in these ignoble prisons unworthy of a civilized people, the young, handsome captain killed seven swashbuckling tyrants in duels (these duels took place in an area six feet square), and the victims of these men were overjoyed to see the hulks rid of their presence. Max dominated his prison-ship, thanks to the prodigious skill he acquired in the use of arms, bodily strength and dexterity. But, in his turn, he committed arbitrary acts; he had various weak characters to do his work for him, who toadied him. In this school of suffering, where embittered characters dreamed only of revenge and where sophistries hatched in the minds of men living in such close confinement legitimized evil intentions, Max became thoroughly depraved. He listened to those whose one dream was to make a fortune at any cost, who did not even shrink from criminal actions providing these actions were accomplished without leaving evidence of guilt. When peace came at last, he was released from the prison-ship, perverted and yet innocent, capable in a high sphere of action of becoming a great statesman but a miserable wretch in private life, according to the circumstances of his destiny.

Back at Issoudun, he learned the sad end of his father and mother. Like all those who give way to passion and who, in the words of the proverb, live a short life but a merry one, the Gilets had died at the workhouse in the most terrible poverty. Almost immediately the news of Napoleon's landing at Cannes spread across France. Max had nothing better to do than go to Paris to request his Cross and promotion to the rank of major. The Marshal who then held the portfolio of the War Ministry remembered Captain Gilet's brave conduct in Portugal and appointed him to a captaincy in the Guards, a rank which was equivalent in an infantry regiment to that of major; but he was unable to get him the Cross. 'The Emperor has said that you would be well able to win yourself the Cross, at our first engagement,' the Marshal told him. And, indeed, on the evening after the Battle of Fleurus, in which Gilet distinguished himself, the Emperor noted that the brave captain should be decorated with the Cross. After Waterloo, Gilet withdrew to the Loire district. At demobilization, Marshal Feltre would neither promote Gilet to a higher rank nor grant him his Cross. Max returned to Issoudun in a mood of exasperation that is easy to imagine; he did not wish to enlist again without his Cross and the rank of major. The Ministry considered that these conditions were unreasonable, coming as they did from a young man of twenty-five who was unknown and could well be promoted colonel by the age of thirty. Max consequently resigned his commission. The major, for the ranks obtained in 1815 were mutually acknowledged by Bonapartists, forfeited his small income, known as half-pay, granted to officers of the Loire army. Seeing this handsome young man, who had only 400 francs in the world, people took pity on him in Issoudun and the mayor appointed him to a clerkship at the Town Hall, at a salary of 600 francs a year. Max occupied this post for about six months but then left it of his own accord, and his place was taken by a captain named Carpentier, who like him had remained loyal to Napoleon.

Already Grand Master of the Order of Idleness, Gilet had assumed a style of life which caused him to lose the respect of the leading families in the town, though they did not make their disfavour obvious to him; for he was of a violent temperament and everybody feared him, even the officers of the Napoleonic army, who had also refused to serve the Bourbons and had come back to Berry to vegetate. In view of the outline of Issoudun sketched a few pages back, the inhabitants' coldness towards the Bourbons is in no way surprising. It was for this reason that Issoudun had more Bonapartists (in relation to its small size) than any other town. As is well known, almost all the Bonapartists became Liberals. In Issoudun and the surrounding district there were about a dozen officers in Maxence's position, and Max became their leader, he was so popular with them all – except, however, with this Captain Carpentier, his successor, and a certain Monsieur Mignonnet, a former artillery captain in the Guards.

Carpentier, a cavalry officer who had risen from the ranks, was not long in marrying; his wife allied him with one of the leading families in the town, the Borniche-Héreaus. Mignonnet who had studied at the École Polytechnique, had served in a regiment which believes itself in some way superior to all others. In the Imperial army there were two shades of superiority amongst officers. Many of them had no less contempt for the bourgeois, mere civilians, than noblemen had for serfs, or conquerors for the vanquished. At times these men were none too observant of the laws of honour in their relations with the civil power, or were very reluctant to criticize anyone who maltreated civilians. Others, especially the artillery (perhaps because of their republicanism), did not adopt this attitude, the logical extension of which was quite simple — to create two nations within France: a military nation and a civilian one. Whereas, therefore, Major Potel and Captain Renard, two officers living in the Faubourg de Rome, and whose opinions concerning the civilian population never varied, were Maxence Gilet's friends in spite of everything, Major Mignonnet and Captain Carpentier took the side of the bourgeoisie, declaring that Max's behaviour was unworthy of the honour of a soldier. Major Mignonnet, a small, shrivelled-up man full of a sense of his own importance, occupied his time with studying the problems posed by the advent of the steam-engine, and lived in a modest sort of way, confining his social activity to visiting Monsieur and Madame Carpentier. His inoffensive habits and scholarly pursuits earned him the respect of the whole town. And it was said that Monsieur Mignonnet and Monsieur Carpentier were quite different people from Major Potel, Captain Renard, Captain Gilet and other regulars of the Café Militaire, where the old soldierly ways and procedures of the Empire were still observed.

At the time of Madame Bridau's return to Issoudun, Max, therefore, was excluded from middle-class society. Moreover, he did himself credit by not turning up at the club, called the Circle, and by never uttering a word of complaint about people's grave disapproval of him — though he was the most elegant and best dressed man in the whole of Issoudun, spent a great deal of money in the town and was exceptional enough to own a horse, something as unfamiliar in Issoudun as Lord Byron's horse was in Venice. We shall soon see how Maxence, an impoverished soldier with no family resources, was able to act the dandy in Issoudun; for the scandalous behaviour which earned him the contempt of the town's timid or religious inhabitants is closely bound up with the reasons which were bringing Agathe and Joseph to Issoudun. In his facial expression and cocksure bearing, Max seemed to care very little indeed about public opinion; no doubt, he intended to get his revenge one day and dominate those very people who now despised him. Moreover, if Max was underestimated by people of the middle class, this unfavourable opinion was counterbalanced by the working class's admiration for his character. His fine presence, courage and resoluteness were bound to appeal to the masses, to whom in any case his depravity was unknown – for not even the middle classes suspected its full extent. At Issoudun, Max played a role rather similar to the Blacksmith's in *The Fair Maid of Perth*: he was the champion of Bonapartism and the Opposition. People relied upon him in the same way as the townspeople of Perth relied upon Smith in dire emergencies. One episode in particular brought into prominence the man who was both the hero and victim of the Hundred Days.

In 1819 a battalion commanded by Royalist officers, young men who had graduated at the Maison Rouge, was passing through Issoudun on its way to Bourges, where it was due to be garrisoned. Not knowing what to do in a town as 'constitutional' as Issoudun, the officers went to spend their time at the Café Militaire. In every provincial town there is a Café Militaire. The one in Issoudun, built in a corner of the town walls looking out over the Place d'Armes and run by an officer's widow, naturally served as a club for the town's Bonapartists, the officers on half-pay and those who shared Max's opinions and were able to voice their admiration of the Emperor, thanks to the prevailing spirit within the town. From 1816 onwards, a banquet was held every year at Issoudun, to celebrate the anniversary of Napoleon's coronation. The first three Royalist officers to enter the café asked for the newspapers, including *La Quotidienne* and *Le Drapeau Blanc*. The state of opinion in Issoudun, and above all in the Café Militaire, did not approve of Royalist newspapers. The café only had *Le Commerce*, the name which *Le Constitutionnel* was forced to take for some years after it had been suppressed by an official decree. But, on the first day of its publication under the new title, it began its Paris news column with the words: 'Trade is essentially constitutional' ('Le commerce est essentiellement constitutionnel'), and so people still called it by its old name. Every reader understood the pun, so full of malice and hostility, by means of which they were requested to take no notice of the shop-sign, the wine that was sold at the shop still being the same.

The fat café proprietress replied to the Royalist officers from behind her counter that she did not have the newspapers they required.

'What papers do you have, then?' asked one of the officers, a captain. The waiter, a small young man dressed in a short jacket of blue cloth, and wearing a coarse linen apron, brought them *Le Commerce*. 'Oh! so that's your paper. Do you have another?'

'No,' the waiter replied. 'That's the only one.'

The captain tore up the organ of the Opposition, and scattered the shreds over the floor, spitting on them and crying: 'Get me some dominoes!' Within ten minutes the news of the insult which had just been inflicted upon the Constitutional Opposition and Liberalism itself, in the person of the sacrosanct newspaper which attacked the Church with the courage and wit with which everyone was familiar, had spread through the streets and struck like lightning into every home; people were discussing it everywhere. And everywhere everyone was saying the same thing simultaneously: 'Let's tell Max!' Max was soon informed. The officers had not finished their game of dominoes before Max entered the café, accompanied by Major Potel and Captain Renard, and followed by thirty young men eager to see how the episode would end – almost all of whom remained standing around in groups in the Place d'Armes. The café was soon filled to the doors.

'Waiter, will you get me my paper, please?' Max asked in a quiet voice. A little comedy was being enacted.

The fat woman, in a timid and conciliating way, replied: 'Captain, I've lent it to someone.'

'Then go and get it,' cried one of Max's friends.

'Can't you do without your newspaper today?' the waiter asked. 'We haven't got it now.' The young officers started to laugh, and threw sneaking glances at the townsfolk.

'Somebody has torn it up!' cried a young man from the town, looking towards the feet of the young Royalist captain.

'Who took it upon himself to tear up my newspaper?' Max asked in a thundering voice, his eyes burning with anger and folding his arms.

'And we spat on it,' the three young officers replied, getting up and staring Max in the face.

'You have insulted the whole town,' said Max, white with anger.

'Well, so what?' asked the youngest of the three officers.

With a skill, audacity and smartness that none of these young men could have foreseen, Max slapped the cheeks of the first officer in the row, saying to him: 'Do you understand French?' They went out to fight a duel in the Allée de Frapesle, three against three. Potel and Renard would never allow Maxence Gilet to stand up on his own against three officers. Max killed his man. Major Potel wounded his so seriously that the unfortunate fellow, the son of a wealthy family, died the following day at the hospital to which he had been transferred. As for the third, he got away with a sword blow and in fact wounded Captain Renard, his opponent. The battalion left for Bourges during the night. This affair, which was much talked about in the Berry district, set the final seal on Maxence Gilet's heroism.

The Knights of Idleness, all of them young (the oldest was not yet twenty-five), admired Maxence. A few of them – far from sharing their families' prudishness and narrow-minded severity with respect to him – envied his position and thought him very fortunate. Under such leadership the Order performed wonders. From January 1817 onwards, not a week passed without some new trick having caused a commotion in the town. On a point of honour, Max stipulated that the Knights should fulfil certain conditions. Statutes were promulgated. The young rascals became as alert as pupils of Amoros, as bold as brass, adept at all physical exercises, as strong and adroit as criminals. They perfected the art of climbing over roofs, of scaling houses, of jumping, of walking noiselessly, of mixing plaster and blocking up doors. They had a whole arsenal of ropes, ladders, tools and disguises. Thus the Knights of Idleness attained the very peak of mischievousness, not only in the execution but also in the conception of their practical jokes. They finally achieved that genius in wrong-doing which so delighted Panurge, and which causes laughter and makes the victim look so ridiculous that he dare not even complain. Moreover, these young men from the best families had means of obtaining information from people's homes which was useful to them in their outrageous behaviour.

In very cold weather these devils incarnate would easily carry a stove into the yard and load it with wood so that the fire was still burning the next morning. Then the news was circulated around the town that Mr so and so (a notorious miser!) had been trying to heat his yard.

Sometimes they all lay in ambush in the Grand 'Rue or the Rue Basse, streets which are, as it were, the two arteries of the town and which lead off at right angles into many narrow streets. They would each crouch at the corner of a wall, at the end of one of these small streets, keeping themselves on the alert. Just when each family was halfway through its first sleep, the young rascals would cry out in frightened voices 'Well, what is it? What is it?' from door to door across the town. These repeated questions would wake up the towns-folk, who would come out in their night shirts and cotton nightcaps, with candles in their hands, everybody asking each other questions and making the strangest remarks and the funniest faces imaginable.

There was a poor bookbinder, a very old man who believed in devils. Like nearly all provincial craftsmen, he worked in a small low shop. The Knights, dressed up as devils, would invade his shop at night and put him in the chest where he kept his trimmings, leaving him shouting as loudly as three burning men. The poor man would wake up his neighbours and tell them about the appearance of Lucifer, and the neighbours could scarcely convince him otherwise. The book-binder narrowly escaped madness.

During a harsh winter, the Knights demolished the fireplace of the income tax inspector's office and rebuilt it in a single night to look exactly the same as before, without making any noise or leaving the slightest trace of their activity. Inside, the chimney was so arranged as to blow smoke into the room. The tax inspector put up with this state of affairs for two months before discovering why his chimney, which had been working so well and with which he had been so satisfied, was playing him such tricks. He had to have the chimney rebuilt.

One day the Knights placed some paper that had been soaked in oil and three boots containing straw treated with sulphur in the fireplace of an old over-religious woman – a friend of Madame Hochon's. The next morning, when she lit her fire, the poor woman, a peaceful, sweet-tempered woman, thought she had lit a volcano. The fire brigade arrived, the whole town came running up and, as several of the firemen were Knights of Idleness, they flooded the poor woman's house, frightening her with the prospect of a drowning after already terrifying her with fire. The shock made her ill.

Whenever they wanted to make someone stay up all night, armed and in a state of mortal anxiety, they would write him an anonymous letter warning him that he was about to be burgled; then, they would creep one by one along his walls or beneath his windows, whistling to one another.

One of their funniest tricks, which provided the town with amusement for a very long time and which is still told there, was to send a note to all the relations of an old lady well known for her miserliness and who would leave a considerable fortune, informing them of her death and asking them all to turn up punctually to witness the affixing of seals to the deceased's property. About eighty people arrived, from Vatan, Saint-Florent, Vierzon and the surrounding districts, all dressed in deep mourning, but all fairly glad at heart, some with their wives, widows with their sons, children with their fathers, some in covered two-wheel carts, some in wickerwork gigs and others in shabby farm-carts. Just imagine the scenes that took place between the old woman's servant and the first arrivals! Not to mention the consultations with solicitors! It was almost a riot in Issoudun.

Finally, one day the Subprefect decided that this state of affairs was quite intolerable – all the more so as it was impossible to discover who was playing these tricks. Of course suspicion fell upon the young men; but, as the National Guard had a purely nominal presence in Issoudun at that time, as there was no garrison, and the lieutenant in charge of the gendarmerie had no more than eight gendarmes under his command and there were no patrols, it was impossible to obtain firm proof. The Subprefect was then put on to the Knights' black list and immediately considered an object of aversion. This civil servant was in the habit of eating two fresh eggs for breakfast. He kept hens in his yard, and added to the custom of eating fresh eggs that of wishing to cook them for himself. Neither his wife, nor his maid, nor anybody at all, in his opinion, had any idea how to boil an egg properly; he would look at his watch and pride himself on surpassing everybody in this particular. He had been boiling his eggs for two years with a success which earned him a thousand teasings. For a whole month the knights collected his hens' eggs every night, putting hard-boiled eggs in their place. The Subprefect could make neither head nor tail of it, and also lost his reputation of being the 'Subprefect with the passion for eggs'. In the end, he began to eat something else for breakfast. But he never suspected the Knights of Idleness, whose practical joke had been too perfectly conceived. Max thought up the idea of greasing the pipes of his stove every night with an oil saturated with such fetid smells that it was impossible to remain within doors. And, as if that was not enough, one day his wife, wishing to go to mass, found the inside of her shawl stuck together with such a strong glue that she had to go to church without it. The Subprefect asked for a transfer. His cowardice and abject surrender finally established the comic and mysterious authority of the Knights of Idleness.

12. At La Cognette's

BETWEEN the Rue des Minimes and the Place Misère there was in those days a small area enclosed towards its lower end by an arm of the Rivière Forcée and above by the town wall, from the Place d'Armes as far as the Marché à la Poterie. This sort of misshapen square was filled with houses of poverty-stricken appearance, huddled closely together and divided by such narrow streets that it is impossible for two people to walk along them abreast. This part of the town, a sort of Cour des Miracles, was inhabited by poor people or people with badly paid jobs, who lived either in these hovels or in even more disreputable dwellings. No doubt it was an infamous area in every age, the haunt of low-living people, for one of the roads is called 'Rue du Bourriau' (Hangman's Street). It is an established fact that for more than five centuries the public executioner had his house there, with a red front door. The man who assists the executioner at Châteauroux still lives there, if public rumour is to be believed, for middle-class people never actually see him. Only the vine-growers are in touch with this mysterious being, who has inherited from his predecessors the gift of curious fractures and wounds. Once upon a time the prostitutes held court there – in the days when Issoudun behaved as if it was a capital. There were people hawking second-hand articles which did not seem likely to find any buyers; dealers in old clothes whose stalls gave off the most fearful stench. In other words, the same dubious population which is to be found in such areas in almost every town, and which is dominated by one or two Jews. On the corner of one of these dark streets, in the liveliest part of the district, a tavern existed between 1815 and 1823, and perhaps even later still. It was kept by a woman known as La Cognette. This tavern was a fairly well-built house, with pieces of white stone filled in with rubble and mortar; there was an upper storey with a loft above. Above the doorway gleamed an enormous pine branch resembling Florentine bronze. As if this symbol was not eloquent enough in itself, the eye was struck by the blue poster glued to the door-casing, below which the words 'Good March Ale' were written: it showed a soldier pouring out beer for a woman wearing a very low-necked dress; a stream of frothy liquid curved steeply from his jug to the glass she was holding out, and the whole thing was painted in a colour which would have made even Delacroix faint. The ground floor of the tavern consisted of a huge room which did service both as a kitchen and dining-room, with the provisions that are needed in the pursuit of this trade hanging from nails driven into its rafters. Behind this room a steep, narrow staircase led upstairs; but at the foot of this staircase, there was a door which opened into a small, long room, looking out on to one of those provincial courtyards that resemble a chimney-flue, they are so narrow, dark and tall. Hidden away behind a lean-to shed and concealed from general view by high walls, this small room was where the Rascals of Issoudun held their plenary court. To all outward appearances, old Cognet used it to put up country people on market days; but secretly, he acted as host to the Knights of Idleness. Cognet, at one time a stableman in a wealthy household, had eventually married La Cognette, who earlier in her life had been employed as a cook by some respectable family. The Faubourg de Rome, like Italy and Poland, still continues – in the Latin manner – to use a feminine form of the husband's name to describe the wife. Putting their savings together, old Cognet and his wife had bought this house to set up an inn there. La Cognette was aged about forty. She was tall, plump, with a nose like Roxelane's, and had swarthy skin, jet-black hair, brown eyes both round and bright, and an intelligent and humorous look; by virtue of her character and culinary skill, she was selected by Maxence Gilet as the Order's official cook. Old Cognet was probably about fifty-six. He was thickset, dominated by his wife and – as she was always humorously saying – he could not help looking on things with a favourable eye, because he only had one eye. For seven years, from 1816 to 1823, neither husband nor wife let the slightest remark slip as to what took place every night at their premises and what was plotted there; they always had the warmest affection for all the Knights. Their loyalty was undeviating. But perhaps it will seem rather less praiseworthy when one remembers that their own self-interest demanded both silence and affection. However late the Knights turned up at the inn, old Cognet would get out of bed on being roused by a signal of knocking, open the door, light the fire and candles and go down to the cellar to bring wines that had been specially bought for the Order. Meanwhile, La Cognette would cook them an exquisite supper, either before or after expeditions on which they had sometimes decided the previous evening and sometimes the same day.

Whilst Madame Bridau was travelling down from Orleans to Issoudun, the Knights of Idleness were preparing one of their best tricks. An old Spaniard, a former prisoner of war, had remained in the area when peace came, carrying on a small business as a corn merchant. He came to the market early, and left his empty cart below the Tower of Issoudun. Maxence was the first to arrive at the meeting-place agreed for that evening, which was by the Tower.

'What are we going to do tonight?' he was asked in a whisper.

'Old Fario's cart is there,' he answered. 'I nearly broke my neck over it. First of all, let's get it up on to the hill by the Tower. Then we'll see.'

When Richard the Lionheart built the Tower of Issoudun, he placed it – as has already been said – over the ruins of the basilica on whose site the Roman temple and Celtic Dun had formerly stood. These ruins, each of which represented a long period of centuries, formed a mountain replete with the archaeological remains of three eras. Richard's tower stands, therefore, on a cone which slopes equally steeply on all sides and whose summit can only be reached by clambering up the slopes. To give a brief but adequate description of this tower, it can be compared to the Obelisk of Luxor standing on its pedestal. The Tower's pedestal, which at that time concealed so many unknown archaeological treasures, rises to a height of eighty feet above the town. Within an hour, the cart had been taken to pieces and hoisted bit by bit on to the mound at the foot of the Tower in an operation similar to that by which soldiers carried the artillery during the crossing of the Mont Saint-Bernard. The cart was then put together again and all traces of the operation so carefully removed that it seemed to have been raised aloft by the devil or some fairy wand. After this exploit the Knights all returned hungry and thirsty to La Cognette's and were soon seated round the table in the little low room, laughing in advance at the faces Fario would pull when, about ten o'clock the next day, he came to pick up his cart.

Naturally the young men did not play these pranks every night. The combined genius of Sganarelle, Mascarille and Scapin would not have sufficed to think up 365 practical jokes a year. For one thing, circumstances were not always favourable to them: perhaps there was too much moonlight, or perhaps respectable people had been too much put out by the last trick; or else, some member of the Order might refuse to take part if a relation of his was involved. But, even though the rascals did not forgather every night at La Cognette's, they met during the day and shared in the lawful delights of shooting and grape-gathering during the autumn, or skating in winter. In this group of twenty young men who chose this manner of protesting against the town's social stagnation, some were on closer terms of friendship with Max than others; some idolized him. A man of his character often inspires youth with fanatical enthusiasm. Madame Hochon's two grandsons, François Hochon and Baruch Borniche, were Max's most devoted supporters. These two lads more or less considered Max as their cousin, giving credence to the local opinion that he was related to the Lousteaus by the bar sinister. Moreover, Max generously lent these two young men money which their grandfather Hochon refused to allow them for their amusements; he took them shooting with him, he trained them in his ways. In other words, his influence over them was far greater than their own family's. They were both orphans and, though they were now of age, still remained under the guardianship of Monsieur Hochon, their grandfather, owing to circumstances which will be explained when the notorious Monsieur Hochon makes his appearance in our story.

At this moment, François and Baruch (let us call them by their Christian names, for the sake of clarity) were sitting on either side of Max at the head of the table dimly lit by the smoky light of four two-ounce candles. The party had drunk some twelve or fifteen bottles of various wines, for there were no more than eleven Knights present. When the wine had loosened everybody's tongues Baruch (whose Christian name in itself points to a vestige of Calvinism in Issoudun) remarked to Max: 'You're going to find yourself vitally threatened.'

'What do you mean?' asked Max.

'My grandmother has had a letter from Madame Bridau, her goddaughter, announcing her arrival and also her son's. Yesterday my grandmother had two bedrooms got ready for their stay.'

'And what's that got to do with me?' said Max, picking up his glass, draining it at a gulp and putting it back again on to the table with a comical gesture.

Max was thirty-four. One of the candles placed by his side cast a glow on his martial countenance, illuminating his forehead and admirably bringing out his white complexion, fiery eyes and black, slightly frizzy hair, which was as glossy as jet. His hair rose steeply above his forehead and temples, clearly forming five tonguelike masses which our ancestors used to call 'the five points.' Despite these sharp contrasts of black and white, Max had a very sweet face which derived its charm from the fact that it was similar in shape to the faces of Raphael's Madonnas, with their firm mouths and graceful smiles straying upon their lips; this was the sort of expression which Max had finally assumed. The rich colouring which gives the faces of people from Berry such variety, heightened his good-humoured expression. When he laughed heartily, he showed a set of thirty-two teeth fit to adorn the mouth of any society belle. Five foot four in height, Max was admirably proportioned, neither fat nor thin. Whereas his manicured hands were white and fairly beautiful, his feet recalled the Faubourg de Rome and the Imperial infantry. He would undoubtedly have made a magnificent general; he had shoulders that would have borne the destiny of a Marshal of France and a chest broad enough to wear all the decorations in Europe. Intelligence enlivened his every movement. He was born graceful, as are almost all love children, and his true father's noble blood was dazzlingly evident.

'So you don't know, Max,' shouted young Goddet from the other end of the table (his father, formerly a surgeon-major, was the best doctor in town), 'that Madame Hochon's goddaughter is Rouget's sister? She's on her way down with her artist son because she's wanting to get her hands on the old chap's fortune – and then goodbye to your rake-off.'

Max frowned. Then, scrutinizing every face in turn around the table, he noted the effect this harangue had produced on everybody, and replied: 'What has that got to do with me?'

'But surely,' François continued, 'if old Rouget revoked his will, assuming he's already made one benefiting the Fisherwoman . . .'

At this point Max interrupted his henchman with the words: 'When, on arriving in this town, I heard you called 'one of the five Hochons,' playing on the pun about your names* which has been going the rounds for the last thirty years, I silenced the man who called you that, my dear François, and I did it so sharply that since then no one in Issoudun has repeated that stupid nickname, not in front of me, at least! And now that's how you repay me: you use a contemptuous nickname to describe a woman to whom everyone knows I am attached.'

Never before had Max said so much about his relations with the woman to whom François had just applied the nickname by which she was known in Issoudun. Having been imprisoned on the hulks, he had enough experience of the world, and as a major in the Grenadier Guards he was well enough aware of the meaning of honour, to guess how the townspeople's

*'Un des cinq Hochons' (one of the five Hochons) is pronounced in exactly the same way as 'un des saints cochons' (one of the holy pigs).

disrespect for her originated. This was why he had never allowed anybody to say one word to him about Mademoiselle Flore Brazier, Jean-Jacques Rouget's housekeeper-mistress whom the respectable Madame Hochon had so energetically described as a parasite. Moreover, everyone knew that Max was too touchy to discuss this subject unless he first introduced it himself – and he had never spoken of it. And it was too dangerous to incur Max's anger or vex him, for his best friends ever to have teased him about Flore. When anyone talked about Max's liaison with this girl in the presence of Major Potel or Captain Renard, the two officers with whom he was on an equal footing, Potel had replied: 'If he's the illegitimate brother of Jean-Jacques Rouget, why shouldn't he live in the same house with him?'

'In any case,' Captain Renard had continued, 'that girl is a real gem, after all; and if he loves her, where's the harm in that? Hasn't young Goddet become Madame Fichet's lover so as to get the daughter as a reward for the drudgery of loving the mother?'

After this well-merited rebuke, François completely lost the thread of his ideas; but he was still more confused when Max said to him gently: 'Go on.'

'No!' cried François.

'You oughtn't to lose your temper, Max,' cried young Goddet. 'Haven't we agreed that we can say anything and everything round this table? Wouldn't we all become the mortal enemies of any one of our number who repeated outside these four walls anything that is said, thought or done in this room? The whole town nicknames Flore Brazier the Fisherwoman. Because François accidentally let this name slip, is it a crime against the Order of Idleness?'

'No,' said Max, 'it merely concerns our personal friendship. On second thoughts, I realized that we were all Knights together, and so I said to him: "Go on. . . ."'

There was a profound silence. The pause became so embarrassing to everybody that Max cried: 'I'm going to go on on his behalf,' (It was a sensation!) 'indeed, on behalf of all of you!' (There was amazement!) 'And I'm going to tell you what's passing through your minds.' (The excitement was unbelievable!) 'You are thinking that Flore, the Fisherwoman, the Brazier woman, old Daddy Rouget's housekeeper – for he's known as Daddy Rouget, this old boy who'll never have any children! – you're thinking, I say, that this woman has been providing for all my needs, since I came back to Issoudun. Because I can throw 300 francs a month down the drain, often entertain you sumptuously, like this evening, and lend all of you money, you think I'm taking the money out of Mademoiselle Brazier's pocket? Well, yes I am!' (There was uproar!) 'Yes, confound him, Mademoiselle Brazier has set her sights on the old man's fortune.'

'She has certainly earned it, what with the father and the son,' said young Goddet, speaking up from his corner.

Max smiled at young Goddet's joke. 'You probably imagine that I plan to marry Flore after old Rouget's death, because the old man's sister and nephew, whom I've just heard mentioned for the first time, are going to jeopardize my future?'

'That's right!' cried François.

'That's the opinion of everyone sitting round this table,' Baruch said.

'Now, now, be calm, my friends,' Max replied. 'Forewarned is forearmed! I'm speaking to the Knights of Idleness! If I need the Order's help to send these Parisians scuttling home again, can I rely on it? Oh! Only within the limits of our practical jokes,' he added hastily, noticing a general revulsion. 'Do you imagine I want to kill or poison them? Thank God, I'm no fool. And, in any case, supposing the Bridaus did succeed and Flore was only left with what she already has, I shouldn't mind, do you understand? I love her so much that I prefer her to Mademoiselle Fichet, even assuming Mademoiselle Fichet was interested in me.'

Mademoiselle Fichet was the wealthiest heiress in Issoudun, and the prospect of marrying her was a big factor in determining young Goddet's attentions to her mother. Frankness is so admirable a quality that the whole body of eleven knights stood up as one man.

'You are a fine fellow, Max!'

'That's talking, Max, we'll rechristen ourselves the Knights of Deliverance.'

'To hell with the Bridaus!'

'We'll bridle them, the Bridaus!'

'After all, three of the Order have got married!'

'Hang it! Old Lousteau was very fond of Madame Rouget; isn't it less bad to love a housekeeper, who's fancy-free and unattached?'

'And if old Rouget, who's dead now, was Max's father, it's all one family!'

'It's a free country!'

'Three cheers for Max!'

'Down with the hypocrites!'

'Let's drink to the beautiful Mademoiselle Brazier's health!'

Such were the eleven replies, acclamations or toasts yelled by the Knights of Idleness – and inspired, let it be admitted, by their exceedingly lax morals. You can see what was Max's purpose when he made himself Grand Master of the Order of Idleness. By thinking up these pranks and putting young men from the best families in Issoudun under an obligation to him, Max wished to acquire supporters for the day of his rehabilitation. He rose gracefully, brandishing a glassful of claret, and everyone waited for him to speak.

'For the evil I wish you, I wish you all a wife who is the equal of beautiful Mademoiselle Brazier! As for the relations from Paris who are about to invade our town, I have nothing to fear from them; we'll see what the future holds!'

'We mustn't forget Fario's cart!'

'Heavens! It's safe enough,' young Goddet said.

'Oh! Leave that to me. I'll round off that joke all right!' Max cried. 'Be at the market place early tomorrow and let me know when the old chap starts looking for his barrow.'

The clocks were striking half past three. The Knights filed silently out of the room, each to return to his own home, keeping close to the walls and walking noiselessly – they wore list slippers. Max walked slowly back to the Place Saint-Jean which was in the upper part of the town between the Porte Saint-Jean and the Porte Villate; it was the area where wealthy middle-class people lived. Major Gilet had managed to conceal his fears, but the news chilled him to the heart. Since his time on or beneath the hulks he had developed a capacity for dissimulation every inch as deep as his corruptness. His passion for Flore Brazier was primarily motivated by old Rouget's 40,000 francs a year from landed property, as you can well imagine. From the manner in which he had been conducting himself, it is easy to see how self-confident Flore had made him feel concerning the financial prospects for which she depended on the old bachelor's affection. Even so, the news of the lawful heirs' arrival was of such a kind as to shake Max's faith in Flore's power. The savings accumulated over a period of seventeen years were still in Rouget's name. Even if he revoked the will, which Flore claimed had been drawn up in her favour long ago, at least these savings could be rescued by having them transferred to Mademoiselle Brazier's name.

'The stupid girl has never breathed a word to me about the nephews and sister in seven years!' Max cried turning from the Rue Marmouse into the Rue l'Avenier. '750,000 francs invested in ten or a dozen lawyers' offices at Bourges, Vierzon and Châteauroux, can't be changed into ready money and invested in Government securities within a week, without news of it getting out in a place where there is so much tittle-tattle! First, we must get rid of the relatives; but once we have got rid of them, we must hurry up and convert this fortune into cash. Anyway, I'll think it over . . .'

Max was tired. With his master-key, he entered old Rouget's house and went to bed noiselessly, saying to himself: 'To-morrow I shall be able to think more clearly.'

13. *Flore Brazier*

IT is not, perhaps, irrelevant to explain how the queen of the Place Saint-Jean obtained her nickname, the Fisherwoman, and how she had established her position within the Rouget household.

As he grew older, the old doctor, Jean-Jacques's and Madame Bridau's father, realized his son's worthlessness. He kept him under fairly strict check, so as to drill him into a routine that would guide him through life; but, without being aware of it, he was in fact preparing him to accept the yoke of whatever tyranny first managed to put a halter over his head. One day, as he was on his way back from his rounds, the malicious, depraved old man noticed a ravishingly beautiful little girl sitting beside the meadows in the Avenue de Tivoli. On hearing the clatter of the horse's hoofs, the child jumped up out of one of the streams which, looked at from above Issoudun, resemble silvery ribbons against the background of a green dress. Like some water-nymph, the little girl suddenly revealed one of the most beautiful, virginal faces ever imagined by a painter, Old Rouget, who knew everything there was to know about the district, had never come across such miraculous beauty. The girl was almost naked. She wore a shoddy short skirt full of holes and all torn, made out of a poor-quality woollen material with brown and white stripes. A leaf of coarse paper, kept in place by a willow twig, was all she had in the way of a head-covering. Beneath this piece of paper, which was covered with penstrokes and letter Os, and which fully deserved its name of school exercise paper, the most beautiful blond hair ever hoped for by a daughter of Eve was twisted and bunched up by a comb ordinarily used for combing horses' tails. Her pretty sunburnt chest showed patches of white beneath the sunburn, as did her neck which was covered by a tattered scarf that had

161

once been a Madras handkerchief. Her skirt was fastened between her legs, and clipped up and attached to her waistline by a large pin; it reminded you of a swimming-costume. Her feet and legs could be seen in the clear water, and their delicate outline was worthy of the sculpture of medieval times. Her charming body, exposed to the sun, had a reddish tone by no means lacking in grace. Her neck and chest were fit to be clothed in silk and cashmere. Finally, the look in the little nymph's blue eyes, with their attractive lashes, would have brought any painter or poet to his knees. The doctor, who knew enough about anatomy to know that she had a delightful figure, realized how much would be lost to the arts if this charming model were to destroy her beauty by labouring in the fields.

'Where do you come from, my dear? I have never seen you before,' said the old doctor, who was then seventy years old.

This scene took place in September 1799.

'I come from Vatan,' the girl replied.

Hearing a middle-class voice, an evil-looking man, who was sitting about two hundred yards away higher up the stream, raised his head and shouted: 'Hey! What's the matter, Flore? You're chattering instead of fishing; we'll lose all our catch!'

'And what have you come from Vatan to do here?' the doctor asked, paying no attention to the man's cry.

'I'm fishing for my uncle Brazier over there.'

With the help of a stout branch whose twigs were splayed out in the shape of a racket, she was stirring and muddying the water of the stream. Frightened by an operation they did not understand, the crayfish quickly swam upstream, and in their confusion got caught up in nets which the fisherman had placed a convenient distance away. Flore Brazier was holding her branch in her hand, with all the grace of innocence.

'But has your uncle got permission to catch crayfish?'

'What! Aren't we living under the united and indivisible Republic?' Uncle Brazier shouted from the place where he was sitting.

'We are under the Directory,' the doctor replied, 'and I know of no law which allows a man from Vatan to come and fish on land belonging to the Commune of Issoudun. Have you a mother, my dear?'

'No, sir, and my father is at the workhouse in Bourges. He went mad after catching sunstroke in the fields.'

'How much do you earn?'

'A shilling a day during the season. I goes fishing as far as Braisne. I glean at harvest time. In the winter, I spin.'

'You must be nearly twelve.'

'Yes, Sir.'

'Do you want to come home with me? You'll be well fed and clothed, and you'll have pretty shoes to wear.'

'No, no. My niece must stay with me. I'm responsible for her before God and *mean*,' said Uncle Brazier, who had walked over towards his niece and the doctor. 'I'm her guardian, do you understand?'

The doctor could hardly refrain from smiling; but he kept his serious look which would certainly have vanished from anyone else's face at the sight of Uncle Brazier. This so-called 'guardian' was wearing a peasant's hat dilapidated by rain and sunshine, as jagged in outline as a cabbage leaf on which several caterpillars had been living, and patched together with white thread. Beneath the hat was a black, lined face, whose mouth, nose and eyes formed four dark points. His short, shabby jacket looked like a piece of tapestry, and his trousers were made out of the coarse material from which floor-cloths are made.

'I am Dr Rouget,' the doctor said; 'and since you are this child's guardian, bring her over to me, in the Place Saint-Jean. You won't have done a bad day's work, nor will she.'

Without giving him the time to reply, confident that uncle Brazier would turn up bringing the pretty young fisherwoman with him, Dr Rouget galloped off towards Issoudun. And indeed, just as the doctor was sitting down to his meal, the cook announced that Citizen and Citizeness Brazier were waiting to see him.

'Please be seated,' the doctor said to the uncle and niece.

Flore and her guardian, still barefoot, looked round at the doctor's sitting-room with amazement. This is why.

The house which Rouget had inherited from the Descoings occupies a central position in the Place Saint-Jean, which is a sort of long and very narrow quadrangle lined with a few sickly-looking lime-trees. Its houses are better built than anywhere else in the town, and the Descoings' home is one of the finest. This house, which is opposite Monsieur Hochon's, has three casement windows on the first floor facing the square and, on the ground floor, a carriage gateway leading into a courtyard, beyond which is a garden. Beneath the archway of the main entrance is a door which gives access to a vast room lit by two windows opening out on to the road. The kitchen is behind this room, but separated from it by a staircase leading up to the first floor and the attics above. At right angles to the kitchen are a wood-store, an open shed where the laundrywork was done, a stable for two horses and a coach-house, and above these are small lofts housing oats, hay and straw, in one of which the doctor's manservant slept.

The drawing-room so keenly admired by the little peasant girl and her uncle was panelled with the sort of grey-painted sculpted wainscoting common in Louis XV's reign. It had a fine marble fireplace, over which was a huge mirror with a gilded frame and no additional looking-glass above it; here Flore gazed at her own reflection. A few pictures hung at intervals along the wainscoting. They had been confiscated from the abbeys of Déols, Issoudun, Saint-Gildas, La Prée, Le Chezal-Benoît and Saint-Sulpice, and from the monasteries of Bourges and Issoudun, which the liberality of our kings and faithful worshippers had enriched with precious gifts and some of the finest works of art of the Renaissance. Thus, amongst the pictures that had been preserved by the Descoings and which later had passed by inheritance to the Rougets were a 'Holy Family' by Albani, a 'St Jerome' by Domenichino, an 'Ecce Homo' by Giovanni Bellini, a 'Madonna' by Leonardo da Vinci, a 'Christ Bearing His Cross' by Titian which came from the Marquis de Bélâbre, the one who withstood a siege and who was beheaded in Louis XIII's reign, a 'Lazarus' by Paolo Veronese, a 'Marriage Of The

Virgin' by Domenico Strozzi, two church pictures by Rubens and a copy of a picture by Perugino made either by Perugino or Raphael; finally, two Correggios and an Andrea del Sarto. The Descoings had chosen these treasures from three hundred religious paintings, without having any idea of their value, and with the paintings' state of preservation as their one criterion. Not only did several have magnificent frames; a few were even protected by glass. It was because of the beauty of the frames and the value which the panes seemed to indicate that the Descoings had kept these canvases. The furniture in the room had, therefore, much of the luxury so highly prized nowadays, but which people did not appreciate then in Issoudun. The clock which stood on the mantelpiece between two superb silver candelabra, each with six branches, clearly foreshadowed Boulle in its monastic splendour. The carved oak armchairs, each covered in a piece of tapestry devotedly worked by aristocratic ladies, would have been greatly sought after today, for they were all surmounted with coronets and coats of arms. Between the two windows was a richly carved side-table that had come from some castle, with a huge Chinese vase (where the doctor used to keep his tobacco) standing on its marble top. Neither the doctor, nor his son, nor the cook, nor the manservant took any particular care of these priceless treasures. By the hearth, people spat on an exquisitely delicate surround whose gilded mouldings were mottled with verdigris. A handsome chandelier, made partly of crystal and partly of porcelain flowers, was riddled (as was the ceiling from which it hung) by black specks that betrayed the extreme liberty enjoyed by flies. The Descoings had draped the windows with coarse brocade curtains that had been stolen from the bed of some commendatory abbot. To the left of the doorway an ancient chest, worth a few thousand francs, was used as a sideboard.

'Now, Fanchette,' said the doctor to his cook, 'we need two glasses. And fetch us some old wine.'

Fanchette, a plump servant from the Berry district whose reputation as the best cook in Issoudun surpassed La Cognette's, came running up with a promptness that revealed the doctor's despotic authority, besides of course a certain amount of personal inquisitiveness.

'What is an acre of vineyard worth in your district?' the doctor asked, pouring Brazier a glass of wine.

'300 francs in ready money.'

'Well, you leave me your neice as a servant-girl, her wages will be 300 francs a year, and as her guardian you'll draw the 300 francs.'

'Every year?' asked Brazier, opening his eyes as wide as saucers.

'I leave that to your own conscience,' the doctor replied. 'She is an orphan. Until she is eighteen, Flore has got nothing to do with drawing money.'

'Seeing that she's twelve, that would mean six acres of vineyard,' the uncle said. 'But she's a lovely girl, as gentle as a lamb, well built, very agile and very obedient. . . . Poor little thing, she was the apple of my poor brother's eye.'

'And I'll pay you a year in advance,' the doctor went on.

'Look here, pay me two years in advance and I'll leave her with you, for she'll be better off with you than at my house because my wife beats her; she can't stand her. There's only me stands up for her, this dear little creature who's as innocent as a new-born child.'

On hearing this last sentence, the doctor was struck by the word 'innocent'. He beckoned to uncle Brazier and walked outside with him into the courtyard and thence into the garden. Flore was left standing beside the table with its bottle and glasses, whilst Fanchette and Jean-Jacques plied her with questions and she artlessly told them of her chance encounter with the doctor.

'Well, good-bye, my little sweetheart,' uncle Brazier said, coming back in again to kiss Flore on the forehead. 'You can certainly say that I've looked after your happiness in putting you here with this good and worthy father of the poor. You must obey him like you obey me, be very well behaved, very good and do everything he tells you.'

'Get the bedroom ready above mine,' the doctor told Fanchette. 'Little Flore, who's certainly got the right name,

will sleep there tonight. Tomorrow we'll get the shoemaker
and the seamstress to come round and have a look at her. Lay
her a place at the table straight away; she is going to eat with
us.'

That evening, there was only one subject of conversation
throughout Issoudun; the fact that a little 'Fisherwoman'
had come to live in Dr Rouget's house. This nickname
remained with Flore Brazier – in a region noted for its mockery
– before, during and after her good fortune.

No doubt the doctor wished to do on a much smaller
scale for Flore Brazier what Louis XV did on a large scale
for Mademoiselle de Romans: but he set about it too late!
Louis XV was still young, whereas the doctor was in the prime
of old age. From twelve to fourteen years of age, the charming
little Fisherwoman experienced unalloyed happiness. Well
dressed and with a much better wardrobe than the richest girl
in Issoudun, she wore a gold watch and jewels which the
doctor gave her to encourage her in her studies; for she had
a teacher employed to teach her reading, writing and arith-
metic. But the almost animal-like life she had led as a country
girl had instilled in Flore such a deep repugnance for the
bitter cup of knowledge that the doctor could not get her to
make any headway in her education. His intentions with
regard to this girl, whom he was cleaning up, educating and
bringing out with the most touching concern for her welfare,
the more so as people had thought him incapable of showing
any affection, were variously interpreted by the gossiping
bourgeoisie in the town, whose tittle-tattle was apt – as in the
case of Max's and Agathe's parentage – to perpetrate fatal
inaccuracies. It is no easy task for people in small towns to
get to the bottom of things when faced with the innumerable
conjectures, contradictory reports and suppositions to which a
particular fact gives rise. Provincial people – like the politicians of Petite Provence, at the Tuileries, in former times –
are determined to find an explanation for everything, and
eventually do find out the truth. But everybody sticks to the
particular side of the story which he himself likes best; he
sees the true side of his own tale, expounds this to other people

and maintains that his version is the only correct one. Thus, despite the fact that everyone lives in the public eye and in spite of all the prying that goes on in small towns, truth is frequently obscured; and before it does come to light, it is either so long in doing so that the truth or falsehood of the story has become a matter of indifference or else calls for the impartiality of a historian or other superior intellect, who view things from an elevated standpoint.

'What do you expect the old devil to do with a little girl of fifteen – at his age?' people were asking two years after Flore's arrival.

'You are right,' would be the reply, 'his high days and holidays were over a good long time ago.'

'My dear fellow,' someone shrewdly remarked, 'the doctor is disgusted with his son's stupidity, and he still hates his daughter Agathe; in this difficult situation, perhaps the only reason why he has lived so prudently for the last two years is to marry the little girl, if she can give him a fine strapping boy, as agile and lively as Max.'

'Come off it! Do you really believe that, after leading the sort of life which Lousteau and Rouget led from 1770 to 1787, they could have children at turned seventy-two? Look, the old rascal has been reading the Old Testament, if only from a medical point of view, and he's seen how King David kept warm in his old age. . . . That's all, my friend.'

'People say that when Brazier gets drunk in Vatan, he boasts that the doctor was seen coming!' cried one of those people who are particularly inclined to see the gloomy side of things.

'Ah! Heavens, my friend! What don't people say at Issoudun?'

For five years, from 1800 to 1805, the doctor enjoyed supervising Flore's education, without experiencing any of the annoyances which Mademoiselle de Romans's ambition and pretensions are said to have given Louis XV.

Comparing her life at the doctor's house with the life she would have been leading with her uncle Brazier, the little girl was so happy that she no doubt complied with her master's demands, just as any Oriental slave would have done. Without wishing to offend philanthropists and writers of idylls, it must be said that country people have the haziest conceptions of some virtues. Their scruples arise from self-interest, not from any feeling of what is good or beautiful. The prospect of a life of poverty, unremitting work and destitution causes them to regard as legitimate anything that can release them from their hellish round of hunger and ceaseless toil, especially if the law has nothing to say against it. There are few exceptions to this generalization. From the social point of view, virtue is an adjunct of prosperity and is rooted in education. For this reason Flore was an object of envy to every girl within a radius of thirty miles, although in the eyes of the Church her way of life was thoroughly reprehensible. Born in 1787, she was brought up amidst the saturnalian levels of 1793–1798, whose repercussions extended as far as these country districts, in which there were no priests, no religion, no altars and no religious ceremonies, where marriage was legalized mating and where Revolutionary maxims made a profound impact, above all at Issoudun, with its rebellious tradition. By 1802 Catholic forms of worship had barely been re-established. The Emperor had great difficulty in finding priests. As late as 1806 many parishes throughout France were still without religious ministrations, so slow was the clergy's return after their decimation on the scaffold and their violent dispersals. In 1802, therefore, nobody could have blamed Flore, unless it was her own conscience. And, in any child who had uncle Brazier as guardian, would not conscience be much weaker than self-interest? If, as all the circumstances indicated, the cynical doctor's advanced age finally compelled him to respect the virtue of a fifteen-year-old child, Flore was nevertheless considered a very 'wide-awake' girl (to use a local expression). Be this as it may, some saw conclusive proof of her innocence in the fact that the doctor's cares and attentions ceased: during the last two years of his life, his attitude towards her was more than cold.

Old Rouget had killed enough people in his career not to know when his end was approaching; finding himself swathed, as he lay dying, in the mantle of one of the philosophers of the encyclopedist movement, his solicitor urged him to make some bequest to this young girl, who was then seventeen.

'Well then, let us emancipate her,' he said.

This witticism sums up the old man's character. He never failed to derive sarcastic remarks from the very professions of those to whom he was speaking. By cloaking his disreputable actions with a veneer of wit, he obtained people's forbearance, in a part of the world where wit always won the day, especially when grounded in shrewd self-interest. The solicitor realized that the doctor's remark was a cry of concentrated hatred coming from a man whose plan of debauchery had been defeated by nature; it was an act of vengeance against the unwitting object of an impotent desire. His opinion was, to some extent, confirmed by the doctor's obstinacy in refusing to leave the girl anything. 'Her beauty is wealth enough!' he said with a bitter smile, when the solicitor again tried to change his mind on this score.

Jean-Jacques Rouget did not lament his father, as Flore did. The old doctor had made his son very unhappy, especially since he had come of age (Jean-Jacques attained his majority in 1791), whereas he had provided the little peasant girl with the material comforts which country people consider the ideal of happiness. When Fanchette asked Flore after the doctor's funeral: 'Well, what are you going to do now that Master's gone?', Jean-Jacques's eyes really sparkled. His expressionless face lit up for the first time; it seemed to glow in the radiance of one thought, and actually revealed emotion.

'Leave us alone,' he told Fanchette, who was clearing the table.

At seventeen, Flore still had that delicacy of figure and feature, that distinguished kind of beauty which attracted the doctor and which society women know how to preserve, but which fades with peasant women as quickly as the wild flowers in the meadows. Even so, that tendency towards stoutness which afflicts all beautiful peasant women who do not lead a life of labour and deprivation in the fields and sunshine was already noticeable in her. Her breasts had filled out. The curves of her plump white shoulders blended harmoniously with her rich neck, in which wrinkles were already developing. But her face still kept its purity of outline and her chin was still exquisitely slender.

'Flore,' Jean-Jacques said in a trembling voice, 'you have really grown used to this house, haven't you?'

'Yes, Mr Jean . . .'

On the very verge of making his proposal, the young master felt his tongue paralysed by the memory of the dead man whom they had so recently buried, and he wondered to what lengths his father's benevolence had actually gone. Flore, who sat looking at her new employer without being able to divine his simplicity of mind, sat for some time waiting for Jean-Jacques to resume the thread of his conversation; eventually, she left him, not knowing what to make of his obstinate silence. Whatever education Flore had received from the doctor, it took her some considerable time to understand Jean-Jacques, whose life story is briefly as follows.

At his father's death, Jean-Jacques was aged thirty-seven, and as timid and submissive to paternal discipline as a child of twelve. For those who are not prepared to believe in his character, or in the facts of this story, this timidity is the key to his childhood, youth and indeed his whole life. But alas! it is a common enough situation everywhere, even in princely households, for when Sophie Dawes was taken up by the last prince of the Condé family she was in even worse circumstances than Flore Brazier. There are two kinds of timidity: timidity of mind and timidity of the nerves, physical and moral timidity. Each is independent of the other. The body can be afraid and tremble, whilst the mind remains calm and brave; the opposite is also true. This accounts for many strange acts of behaviour. When both kinds of timidity are found in one and the same individual, that man will be worthless throughout his life. *Complete* timidity of this kind is found in the people whom we call idiots.

These idiots often have great qualities of character, except that these qualities are repressed. Some of the monks who have lived lives of ecstasy may perhaps have derived their experiences from this combination of infirmities. This unfortunate physical and moral condition is produced just as easily by perfection of the bodily organs and the soul as by faults hitherto undetected. Jean-Jacques's timidity sprang from a kind of mental sluggishness which a great teacher, or surgeon like Desplein, could have awakened into activity. With him, as with cretins, the urge to love had taken over all the strength and agility which was lacking in the mind – though he had just enough control of his faculties to be able to organize his own life. Devoid of that idealism into which it is sublimated with most young men, the violence of his passionate instinct increased his bashfulness still further. He could never make up his mind to pay court (as the saying goes) to any Issoudun woman. Neither the young girls nor the middle-class women could bring themselves to make advances to a young man of medium build and shamefaced and ungainly expression, whose mediocre-looking face, with its two large, protruding pale-green eyes would have been ugly enough in itself, even if his decayed features and pallid complexion had not already prematurely aged him. In fact, the presence of a woman completely annihilated this lamentable creature, who felt as eagerly urged on by passion as he was held back by the paucity of ideas due to his education. Motionless between two equal forces, he did not know what to say and trembled lest he should be asked any questions – he was so afraid of having to reply to anybody! Desire, which loosens so many tongues, used to freeze his. This was why Jean-Jacques remained aloof, welcoming loneliness because it did not make him feel uncomfortable. The doctor noted the psychological damage which his son's temperament and character had produced, but only when it was too late to do anything about it. He would very much have liked to get his son married; but, as it would have involved handing him over to a domination that would have become absolute, he felt bound to hesitate. Would it not have amounted to handing over the management of his fortune to some strange, unknown woman? From his observation and knowledge of young girls, he well knew how difficult it is to make exact forecasts about women's characters. And so, whilst looking around for a woman whose education and character would have offered firm guarantees, he tried to train his son in the ways of avarice. He hoped in this way to give the simpleton a sort of instinct, even though he was lacking in intelligence. First of all, he accustomed him to a mechanical sort of life, impressing upon him fixed stereotyped ideas as to how his income should be invested. Then, he spared him the chief difficulties of administering landed property by leaving him an estate that was in good order and let out on long leases. Even so, the fact that was destined to dominate the poor creature's life escaped the subtle old man's notice, despite his shrewdness.

Bashfulness is like deceit, it is just as unfathomable. Jean-Jacques fell passionately in love with Flore. But this was only to be expected, incidentally. Flore was the only woman who lived in close proximity to this man, the only one whom he could see without difficulty, gazing at her secretly and studying her at every hour of the day. She brightened his life in the old family home and, although unaware of the fact, provided him with the only pleasures that it was his lot to enjoy during youth. Far from being jealous of the older man, he was delighted by the fact that his father was giving Flore an education; did he not need an easily conquered woman, one who did not even require him to woo her? Passion which, let it be noted, has a wit entirely of its own, can confer a kind of intelligence upon idiots, fools and imbeciles, particularly when they are young. Even in the most brutish man, there is always some animal instinct whose very persistence is akin to thought.

The next day Flore, who had been given food for reflexion by her master's silence, waited for him to make some important declaration; but, though he kept on walking round and round her chair, stealing sly glances at her, with lustful expressions on his face, Jean-Jacques could not think of anything to say. Finally, when the dessert was being served, the master again embarked on the previous evening's scene.

'Are you all right here?' he asked Flore.

'Yes, Mr Jean.'

'Well then, you must stay here.'

'Thank you, Mr Jean.'

This odd state of affairs continued for three weeks. One night when no sound disturbed the silence, Flore, who happened to wake up by accident, heard the sound of regular human breathing outside her bedroom door, and was startled to discover Jean-Jacques lying like a dog on the landing; no doubt, he himself had made the hole at the bottom of her door so as to be able to see into the bedroom.

'He loves me,' she thought; 'but he'll catch rheumatism if he goes on like that.'

Next day, Flore gave her master a peculiar look. She had been touched by this silent and almost instinctive love; she no longer found the poor idiot quite so ugly, with his temples and forehead covered with spots as purulent as ulcers, the sure sign of a diseased blood supply.

'You wouldn't like to go back to the fields, would you?' Jean-Jacques asked when they were alone.

'Why are you asking me that?' she said, looking up at him.

'Just to find out,' Rouget replied, blushing the colour of a lobster.

'Do you want to send me back there?' she asked.

'No, Mademoiselle.'

'Well then, what do you want to know? You must have a reason . . .'

'Yes, I have. I wanted to ask . . .'

'What?' asked Flore.

'But you wouldn't tell me!' said Rouget.

'Yes, of course I would! God's honour!'

'Ah, well,' Rouget continued in frightened tones, 'you are a good girl . . .'

'I'll say I am!'

'Aren't you?'

'Well, what have I said?'

'Well then, are you the same as when you first arrived here, barefoot, when your uncle brought you?'

'That's a fine question! Good Heavens!' Flore replied, blushing.

The terror-stricken young master lowered his head and

never raised it again. Flore, stupefied by the fact that a reply so flattering to any man could be greeted by an attitude of such consternation, withdrew from the room. Three days later, at the same time of day, for both seemed to assign the time of dessert to be their battlefield, Flore spoke up first to her master:

'Have you got something against me?'

'No, Mademoiselle,' he replied. 'No'. (There was a pause.) 'Quite the opposite.'

'You seemed annoyed the other day when I told you that I was a respectable girl.'

'No, I only wanted to know. . . .' (Another pause followed.) 'But you wouldn't tell me . . .'

'Good Heavens,' she went on. 'I'll tell you the whole truth.'

'The whole truth about . . . my father . . .?' he asked in a choking voice.

'Your father,' she said, looking deep into her master's eyes, 'was a good man. . . . He loved a joke. . . . He was a gay old soul. . . . Poor fellow! It wasn't the intention which was lacking. . . . Anyway, concerning something or other in connexion with you, he had ideas of his own. . . . Oh, very bad ideas! Often he used to make me laugh, I'll say . . .! Now there . . .! What are you going to ask me next?'

'Well, Flore,' the young master said, taking hold of her hand, 'since my father meant nothing to you . . .'

'Why, what should he have meant to me?' she cried, like a young girl upset by some hurtful supposition.

'Come on, now listen to me.'

'He was my benefactor, but nothing more. Ah! He would have very much liked me to be his wife but . . .'

'But,' Rouget said, seizing Flore's hand again, which she had withdrawn from his, 'since he meant nothing to you, then could you stay here with me?'

'If you want me to,' she replied, lowering her eyes.

'No, no, if *you* want to,' Rouget continued. 'Yes! You can be . . . the mistress here. Everything that's here will be yours. You will look after my fortune; it will be more or less yours . . . for I love you, and I have always loved you ever since the time when you first came here, barefoot.'

Flore did not reply. When the silence had become almost unbearable, Jean-Jacques thought up this appalling argument: 'Look here, surely it's better than going back to the fields?' he asked her in unmistakable eagerness.

'Heavens, Mr Jean. It's up to you,' she replied.

Nevertheless, even in spite of her remark: 'It's up to you,' poor Rouget was no further forward. Men of his stamp require certainties. The effort it takes them to confess their love is so great and demanding that they are unable to begin their confession all over again. Hence their attachment to the first woman who accepts them. One can only judge events by their results. Ten months after his father's death, Jean-Jacques was a changed man: his pale, leaden face, vitiated by pimples on his temples and forehead, became clear and clean and tinged with pinkish hues. In other words, his face exhaled happiness. Flore insisted that her master should take good care of his personal appearance; she took pride in seeing him smartly dressed; she watched him going off on his walks, standing on the doorstep until he was completely out of sight. Everybody in the town noted these changes, as a result of which Jean-Jacques became a completely different man.

'Have you heard the news?' people asked each other in Issoudun.

'No, what?'

'Jean-Jacques has inherited everything from his father, even the Fisherwoman.'

'Don't you see that the old doctor was cunning enough to leave his son with a housekeeper?'

'She's a real treasure for Rouget, that's true,' was the general cry.

'She's a crafty one, and really lovely too! He'll end up marrying her.'

'Hasn't that girl been lucky?'

'Only beautiful girls have that kind of luck.'

'Ah! That's what you think, but I had my Uncle Borniche-Héreau. Well, you must have heard about Mademoiselle Ganivet. She was as ugly as the Seven Deadly Sins, but even so he left her 3,000 francs a year.'

'Yes! But that was in 1778!'

'It's all the same. Rouget's making a big mistake. He's inherited a cool 40,000 francs a year from his father. He could have married Mademoiselle Héreau.'

'The doctor tried that, but she didn't want him; and Rouget is too much of a fool.'

'Too much of a fool! Women are very happy with people like him.'

'Is your wife happy, then?'

Such was the talk of Issoudun. Although people made fun of this semi-marriage at first, as always happens in the provinces, they eventually praised Flore for devoting her life to the poor old bachelor. Thus, 'what with the father and the son' (to use young Goddet's phrase), Flore Brazier achieved the dominant position within Rouget's household. At this point it will be appropriate to outline the story of her rise to dominance – if only for the edification of bachelors.

14. A horrible and vulgar story

OLD Fanchette was the only person in Issoudun who disliked the fact that Flore Brazier had become all-powerful in her master's household. She protested against the immorality of this union, taking the side of outraged morality. The fact is that, at her age, she felt humiliated that the 'Fisherwoman', once a little girl who had come barefoot into the house, was now her mistress. Fanchette had 300 francs a year invested in Government stock; this was how the doctor had advised her to invest her savings. As her late master had left her an annuity of 300 francs, she could live quite comfortably, and so, on 15 April 1806, she left the house, nine months after her old master's funeral. Does not this date indicate to shrewd people the precise moment at which Flore ceased to be an honest woman?

Flore was clever enough to have foreseen Fanchette's defection, for there is nothing like the exercise of power for teaching you the art of politics; she had decided to do without a maid. Without giving any indication of the fact, she had spent the last six months studying the culinary skills which earned Fanchette the status of a Cordon Bleu cook fit to be employed by a doctor. Doctors are just as appreciative of good food as bishops. Dr Rouget had perfected Fanchette. In the provinces, the lack of anything much to do and the monotony of life there direct the attention of the mind to good food. Although you do not dine as luxuriously in the provinces as you do in Paris, you dine better; the dishes are carefully thought out and planned in detail. In the depths of the countryside there are female cooks as brilliant as Carême himself, unsung geniuses who have the skill of turning a plain dish of beans into something worthy of the nods of approval which Rossini bestows on a perfectly executed piece of music. Whilst studying for his degree in Paris, the doctor had attended

178

Rouelle's chemistry lectures, and from them he had obtained ideas which he applied to the benefit of culinary science. He is famous in Issoudun for certain improvements that are scarcely known outside Berry. He discovered that omelettes were much lighter when the yolks and whites of the eggs were not beaten together in the brutal manner cooks generally adopt. In his view, the whites should be beaten up until stiff and the yolks folded in; a frying-pan should not be used, but instead a porcelain or earthenware *cagnard*. A *cagnard* is a sort of thick four-legged dish which does not crack when placed over the fire, because of the air circulating around it. In Touraine, a *cagnard* is called a *cauquemarre*. Rabelais, I think, speaks of *cauquemarres* being used for cooking those imaginary animals *coquecigrues* – which proves that this utensil is of great antiquity. The doctor had also discovered a way of preventing brown sauces from developing a bitter taste: but this secret, which unfortunately he confined to the limits of his own kitchen, has been lost. Flore had a natural gift for frying and roasting, two skills which cannot be acquired either by observation or hard work, and she quickly surpassed Fanchette. Although she became a Cordon Bleu to please Jean-Jacques, it must be admitted that she, too, was fairly fond of good food. Incapable, as are all uneducated people, of occupying her mind, she devoted her energy to running the household. She polished the furniture, giving it its old shine again, and kept everything in the house as clean as any home in Holland. She supervised the 'laundering' of those deluges, or avalanches, of dirty linen – an event which takes place only three times a year in the provinces. Like a good housewife, she kept an eye on the linen and mended it. Then, eager to wheedle her way into the secrets of Rouget's fortune, she assimilated what little business knowledge he possessed and added to it by conversing with Monsieur Héron, the late doctor's solicitor. By these means she was able to offer excellent advice to her little Jean-Jacques. Confident of remaining the mistress of the household, she showed as much affection and concern in looking after his interests as she would have shown in looking after her own.

She had nothing to fear from her uncle's demands. Two

months before the doctor's death, Brazier had died after falling as he was leaving the inn where he had spent his whole life since his sudden rise to fortune. Flore had also lost her father. She therefore served her master with an orphan's affection, happy to have found a family to belong to and something to interest her in life. To poor Jean-Jacques, this period of his existence seemed like paradise: he fell into the pleasant habits of an animal-like existence, habits which became even pleasanter when combined with a sort of monastic regularity. He always got up late. Flore, who rose much earlier to do the shopping and attend to the housework, would waken her master just early enough for him to find breakfast waiting for him as soon as he had dressed. Towards eleven o'clock, after he had finished his breakfast, Jean-Jacques would go out for a walk and chat with passers-by; returning about three, he would read the newspapers, the county one and a Paris newspaper, both of which he received three days after publication, greasy with passing through thirty hands, dirty with having snuffy noses burying themselves behind them and brown with trailing across so many table tops. In this way Jean-Jacques reached dinner time, on which meal he spent as long as he possibly could. Flore would regale him with the tales of the town and such new gossip as she had been able to glean. The lights were out by about eight o'clock. Going to bed early is a way of economizing on candles and fire that is much practised in the provinces, but it helps to make people stupid by causing them to spend too much time in bed. Too much sleep dulls and befogs the mind.

Such was the way of life which these two people led for nine years. As a way of life, it was both full and empty; its highlights were a few journeys to Bourges, Vierzon and Châteauroux – or even further afield, if neither Monsieur Héron nor any of the solicitors in the other towns had any mortgages to offer as an investment. Rouget lent at 5 per cent on first mortgages, with attornment to the mortgagee's wife in the event of his being married. He never allowed more than a third of the property's real value and arranged for promissory notes to be signed guaranteeing an extra $2\frac{1}{2}$ per cent interest spaced out over the period of the loan. Such were the rules which his father had told him he must always observe. Usury, the blight of every peasant's ambition, is ruining the countryside. A $7\frac{1}{2}$ per cent interest rate seemed so reasonable that Jean-Jacques Rouget could pick and choose as to whom he would lend money to; needless to say, the solicitors, who drew handsome commissions from the clients for whom they obtained such favourable loans, kept the old man informed of all the mortgages that were going. During these nine years Flore obtained complete control over her master – gradually, imperceptibly and without even wishing to do so. At first she treated Jean-Jacques in a very familiar manner. Then, without ever showing him disrespect, she impressed him with such superiority, intelligence and strength of mind that he became his servant's servant. This grown-up child actually welcomed her domination, by allowing her to do him so many services – so much so that Flore treated him as a mother treats her son. Jean-Jacques eventually became so dependent on Flore that he needed a mother's protective love. But besides this, there were other extremely close ties as well! To begin with, Flore looked after the house and all Jean-Jacques's business. Jean-Jacques relied upon her so much in all business matters that, without her, life would have seemed to him not merely difficult but impossible. Besides, this woman had become a necessary part of his existence; she flattered all his whims, she knew them so well! He loved to see her happy face always smiling at him: the only face that would have smiled at him, the only one in which he would ever see a smile intended for himself! Her happiness was of a purely material kind, voiced in everyday words that are the pith and marrow of people's speech in the Berry district. It shone forth in her splendid countenance and was (as it were) a reflexion of his own happiness.

The agitation which Jean-Jacques experienced whenever he noticed that Flore's face was clouded with some annoyance or other indicated the extent of her power; to make quite certain of this power, she wished to use it. With women of this kind, use always amounts to abuse. No doubt she treated her master to some of those scenes which are the unfathomable mysteries of domestic life, and never better described than by Otway in the scene between the Senator and Aquilina – halfway through his tragedy *Venice Preserved* – a scene which magnificently embodies the utmost depths of horror. Flore had by now become so certain of her power that, unfortunately both for herself and for him, she never considered the prospect of marrying him.

Late in 1815, by which time she was aged twenty-seven, she had reached full development of her beauty. Plump and fresh-complexioned, and as white as a farmer's wife from Bessin in Normandy, she certainly resembled that ideal of womanhood which our ancestors used to call a fine figure of a woman. Her beauty, which was very like that of a handsome barmaid (a well-fed, buxom barmaid!), bore some resemblance to that of Mademoiselle Georges in her prime – except for the latter's stately nobility. Flore had the same fine arms with their dazzling roundness, the same opulence of figure and the same satin-like flesh and attractive lines – but the lines of her figure were less harsh than the actress's. Her expression was affection and gentleness itself. Her look did not command respect, as did the most handsome Agrippine to have trodden the stage of the Théâtre-Français since Racine's time; instead it invited hearty joy.

In 1816 Flore saw Maxence Gilet and fell in love with him at first sight. Her heart was pierced by that mythological arrow which so admirably describes a physical sensation and which was thus represented by the Greeks, who had no conception of chivalrous love, the ideal, melancholy love created by Christianity. Flore was too beautiful at that time for Max to disdain such a conquest. And so, at twenty-eight, she experienced true love, idolatrous infinite love, the love which comprises every form of loving, from Gulnare's to Medora's. Once the impecunious officer had learned of Flore's situation with regard to Jean-Jacques Rouget, he viewed his liaison with her as something more than a passing affair. Consequently, to make quite certain of his future prospects, he could think of nothing better than lodging in Rouget's house – he realized the old man's feebleness of character. Flore's passion necessarily made its impact on Jean-Jacques's life and way of living. For a whole month the bachelor – who had grown exceptionally timid – saw a dark, sullen, terrifying expression on Flore's face, which was usually so gay and friendly. He experienced bursts of intentional ill-humour, in the way that a married man does when his wife is thinking of being unfaithful to him. When, during the cruellest on-slaughts, the poor man plucked up enough courage to ask Flore the reason for her change of attitude, she glared at him with eyes flaming with hatred and replied in a voice harsh with scorn and aggression, the like of which Jean-Jacques had never before heard or seen.

'Good Lord! You are really inhuman. For sixteen years I have given you my life and youth, and I never realized until now that you are as cold as stone,' she cried, beating her heart. 'For two months now you have been receiving visits from that brave major, a victim of the Bourbons, who ought to have become a general, and who's stony-broke and stuck in this wretched little town where there's no money to be had. All day long he has to sit on his backside at the Town Hall, earning ... how much? ... a miserable 600 francs a year! A fine sum of money, that is! Whereas you've got investments of 660,000 francs, an unearned income of 60,000 francs a year and, thanks to me, you only spend 3,000 francs a year all told, even including my skirts, in fact including everything! But you never think of offering him a home here, although all the second floor is empty! You prefer mice and rats to dance around up there rather than put a human being there, a boy whom your father always acknowledged as his own son! ... Do you want to know what you are? I'll tell you what you are, a murderer! And I know why! You have seen that I was show-ing an interest in him, and that annoys you! You may seem stupid but you've got more malice in you than the nastiest men.... Anyway! I am interested in him, yes, very interested...'

'But Flore ...'

'Oh! Don't Flore me! You can go and get another Flore (if you can find one!), for let me be poisoned with this glass of wine if I don't leave your shabby little house immediately! I haven't cost you a penny during the twelve years I've been here, thank God, and you have had quite a lot of fun on the cheap. Anywhere else I'd have been well paid for doing what I've done here: washing everything, ironing, looking after the laundry, doing the shopping, cooking, looking after your interests in every possible way and this is my reward!'

'But Flore . . .'

'Yes, Flore; you'll get Flores, at your age, fifty-one, and in your bad state of health which is getting steadily worse at an alarming rate, as I know only too well! And besides, you're not even amusing to live with!'

'But Flore . . .'

'Leave me alone!'

She left the room, slamming the door so violently that the house re-echoed with the noise and seemed to shake on its foundations. Jean-Jacques Rouget gingerly opened the door and walked even more gingerly into the kitchen, where Flore was still grumbling.

'Flore,' he said sheepishly, 'this is the first time you've ever mentioned your wish. How do you know whether I agree with it or not?'

'To begin with, we need a man in the house. People know that you keep some 10,000, 15,000 or 20,000 francs here; if any burglars came to steal it, we should be done in. I have no particular desire to wake up one fine morning cut up into four pieces, like they did with that poor servant who was stupid enough to defend her master! But if they know that there's a man in the house who's as brave as a lion, and who's no fool either, because Max would eat three burglars in no time, then I would sleep a happier woman. People may tell you a lot of nonsense: that I love him, adore him, etc. etc. Do you know what your reply will be? Well, you'll tell them that you know all about that but your father told you on his deathbed not to forget poor Max. Nobody will breathe another word, because everybody knows that your father used to pay for him to go to the church boarding-school! For nine years now I've been eating your bread . . .'

'Flore, Flore.'

'More than one fellow has courted me in that time, so there! I have been offered gold chains, watches, etc. etc. Dear little Flore, why not leave that silly old fool Rouget – that's what they call you! Me leave him? No thank you! I couldn't leave a good innocent man like him! What would become of him? That's what I've always replied. No, I know where I belong.'

'Yes, Flore, I've only got you in the whole world, and I'm so happy with you. If it would please you, my dear, well then! we'll have Maxence Gilet here. He can eat at our table.'

'Lord! I should hope so.'

'Now, now, don't fly into a temper.'

'If there's food enough for one, there's enough for two,' she said laughingly. 'But if you wanted to be nice, do you know what you'd do, my little lambkin? You'd take a walk in the direction of the Town Hall, about four o'clock, and you'd make a point of seeing Major Gilet and invite him to dinner. If he refuses, you will say that it would give me great pleasure. He's too fond of the ladies to refuse then. Then, towards the end of the meal, if he starts telling you about his misfortunes in life, the hulks and all that, which you'll be clever enough to bring round into the conversation, then you'll invite him to come and live with us here! If he objects, don't worry, I'll manage to persuade him.'

As he walked slowly along the Boulevard Baron, the old bachelor thought this scene over as carefully as he could. If Flore left him . . . (the very thought of it caused his mind to go blank), what other woman would he find . . .? Would he be able to get married . . .? At his age, he would only be married for his money, and even more cruelly exploited by his legitimate wife than by Flore. Besides, the thought of being deprived of her affection caused him terrible anguish, even though her affection was illusory. He was as charming as he could be to Major Gilet. As Flore had desired, the invitation was extended to him in the presence of other people – so as to save Maxence's honour.

Flore and her master were reconciled; but as from that day, Jean-Jacques noticed small ways in her behaviour which indicated that there had been a complete change in her affections. For a whole fortnight Flore Brazier complained of Monsieur Rouget's tyrannical authority to tradesmen, people in the market place and the old cronies with whom she used to gossip; he had now taken it into his head to invite his so-called illegitimate brother into the house! But nobody was deceived by all these histrionics, and the general opinion of Flore was that she was exceptionally subtle and crafty.

Old Rouget was very happy to have Max installed in a position of some authority in his house, for now he had some-one who loaded him with attentions without being servile. Gilet would chat and discuss politics and sometimes would go out for a stroll with the old man. As soon as the officer had settled in, Flore no longer wanted to do the cooking. Cooking, she said, ruined her hands. Asked to do so by the Grand Master of the Order of Idleness, La Cognette recommended one of her relations, an old woman whose master, a parish priest, had just died without leaving her a legacy; she was an excellent cook who would be eternally devoted to Flore and Max. Moreover, on the authority of these two influential people, La Cognette promised her relation a pension of 300 francs a year after ten years' good, faithful, discreet and honest service. Aged sixty, Védie was remarkable for a face that had been disfigured by smallpox and was of an appropriate degree of ugliness. Once Védie had begun her service, Flore became 'Madame Brazier'. She took to wearing corsets and bought silk gowns and gowns in fine woollen and cotton materials (according to the season)! She had lawn collars, very expensive shawls, embroidered bonnets and lace tuckers; she wore half-boots and kept up a style of elegance and a richness of dress which made her more youthful in appearance. She was like a rough diamond, cut and mounted by the jeweller so as to enhance its value. She wanted to be a credit to Max. In 1817, after the first year had gone by, she obtained a horse from Bourges for the poor major's use (it was said to be an English horse); Max was tired of going about on foot. He had recruited from somewhere in the neighbourhood a Pole named Kouski, formerly a lancer of the Imperial Guards, a man in such reduced circumstances that he was delighted to enter the Rouget household as the major's manservant. Max was Kouski's idol, especially after the duel with the three Royalists. From 1817, therefore, old Rouget's household consisted of five people, three of whom were masters, and the household expenses rose to about 3,000 francs a year.

*

By the time Madame Bridau was on her way back to Issoudun, intending (in Maître Desroches's words) to rescue an inheritance that had been so gravely compromised, old Rouget had gradually arrived at an almost vegetative existence. For one thing, Mademoiselle Brazier raised the standard of cooking to an episcopal level as soon as Max had assumed a position of some authority within the household. Thoroughly accustomed to good food, Rouget ate more and more copiously, carried away by Védie's delicious dishes. In spite of this exquisite and abundant food, he put on very little weight. Every day he deteriorated in health, like a sick man; his eyes had large rings around them; perhaps he was overstraining his digestion. But when the townspeople asked him about his health, as he was on his walks, he would reply that he had never felt better. And because he had always been known for his extremely limited intelligence, no one noticed the constant degeneration of his mental faculties. His love for Flore was the one feeling which kept him alive. He lived only for her. His weakness towards her knew no bounds. He obeyed her slightest look, watching her movements as a dog watches its master's slightest gestures. To quote Madame Hochon's words, old Rouget (aged fifty-seven) seemed older than Monsieur Hochon who was then in his eighties.

15. Old Fario's cart

As you can imagine, Max's apartment was worthy of this charming young man. In fact, during the last six years the major had increased its comfort year by year, improving even its smallest details both for his own sake and Flore's. Even so it was merely the Issoudun style of comfort: painted floors, quite elegant wallpapers, mahogany furniture, mirrors with gilded frames, muslin curtains with red stripes and a bed whose canopy and curtains were arranged in the way provincial upholsterers arrange them for some wealthy bride. To them it seems the very height of magnificence, but such beds are pictured in vulgar fashion engravings – and they are so commonplace that Parisian retailers no longer stock them for newly-married couples. In addition (and this was a terrible innovation, which was the talk of Issoudun), there was rush matting on the staircase, no doubt to deaden the sound of footsteps; this meant that, whenever he came home about daybreak, Max did not disturb anybody. Rouget never suspected his guest's involvement in the nocturnal pranks played by the Knights of Idleness.

About eight in the morning Flore, wearing a pretty cotton dressing-gown with hundreds of pink stripes, and a lace bonnet and fur-lined slippers, gently opened Max's bedroom door. Seeing that he was asleep, she remained standing beside his bed.

'He got back so late,' she thought, 'half past three. You have to have a strong constitution to stand up to those kind of amusements. He *is* strong, the darling. . . . I wonder what they were doing last night?'

'Ah! There you are, my dear Flore,' said Max, waking up in the way soldiers do who, because of their experience of war, immediately recover their composure and organize their ideas, however suddenly they wake up.

'You're sleepy, I'll go.'

'No, stay. There are serious things. . .'

'Have you all been doing something silly in the night?'

'Oh yes! But it's about us and that old beast. Why did you never tell me about his family? Well anyway, they're on their way here, the family: no doubt to create difficulties for us.'

'What! I'll go and give him a good dressing-down,' Flore said.

'Mademoiselle Brazier,' Max said gravely, 'this is too serious a matter to go about it thoughtlessly. Send me my coffee upstairs. I'll drink it in bed whilst I think what attitude we must adopt. . . . Come back at nine, we'll talk it over then. Meanwhile, pretend you know nothing.'

Startled by this news, Flore left Max and went off to prepare him his coffee. But, a quarter of an hour later, Baruch came rushing into the room, saying to the Grand Master: 'Fario is looking for his wheelbarrow!'

Within five minutes Max dressed, came downstairs and, apparently out for a stroll, walked as far as the foot of the Tower, where he found that quite a considerable number of people had gathered.

'What's up?' Max asked, making his way through the crowd towards the Spaniard.

Fario was a shrivelled little man, as ugly as any Spanish grandee. His fiery eyes were as beady as if they had been drilled with a gimlet, and they were very close to his nose; in Naples, they would have given him the appearance of a fortune-teller. This little man seemed gentle because he was serious, calm and slow in his movements. For this reason he was known as 'good old Fario'. But his gingerbread complexion and gentle manner concealed from ignorant people (though revealing it to the watchful observer) the semi-Mauritanian character of a Granada peasant who until now had never been stung out of his coolness and indolence.

'Are you sure,' Max asked him, after listening to the corn merchant's complaints, 'that you brought your cart with you? There are no thieves at Issoudun, thank God.'

'But it was here.'

'If the horse was still harnessed to the cart, couldn't it have walked off with it?'

'But my horse is over there,' Fario replied, pointing to his horse, which stood harnessed about thirty yards away.

Keeping a serious face, Max walked up to the spot where the horse was standing, so as to be able to see the foot of the Tower when he looked up, for the throng of people were beneath. Everybody followed Max, which was just what the rascal wanted.

'Could someone have absent-mindedly put the cart into his pocket?' cried François.

'Come on, have a look in your pockets!' Baruch said.

On all sides, people burst into peals of laughter. Fario started swearing. When a Spaniard does this, he has reached the highest peak of anger.

'Is your cart light?' asked Max.

'Light?' said Fario. 'If the people who are laughing at me had it on their feet, their corns wouldn't be hurting them any more.'

'But your cart must be awfully light,' Max replied, pointing towards the Tower, 'because it has flown on to the hill.'

On hearing these words, everyone looked up, and within an instant the market place was in a state of riot. Everybody was pointing this fairy cart out to everybody else. Everyone was talking about it.

'The devil protects inn-keepers, who all end up in Hell,' young Goddet told the dumbfounded corn merchant. 'He wanted to teach you not to leave carts lying around in the streets, instead of putting them up at the inn.'

At this, hoots of laughter rang out from the crowd, for Fario had the reputation of being miserly.

'Come on, my good fellow,' said Max. 'You mustn't lose heart. We'll climb up to the Tower to find out how your barrow got there. God Almighty! We'll even lend you a hand. Are you coming, Baruch?' 'You,' he whispered into François's ear, 'move everybody away, so that there's nobody at the foot of the hill by the time we get up there.'

Fario, Max, Baruch and three other Knights climbed up to

the Tower. During this fairly dangerous ascent, Max pointed out to Fario that there were no signs or damage indicating that any cart had gone up that way. Fario believed it was some kind of spell, he was thoroughly bewildered. When they had reached the top they studied the matter carefully, and the fact seemed to them quite impossible.

'How am I going to get it down?' asked the Spaniard, his small black eyes showing terror for the first time, and his gaunt yellow face, which seemed as if it ought never to change colour, growing suddenly pale.

'How?' Max said. 'But that doesn't seem difficult to me.'

And, taking advantage of the corn merchant's amazement, he seized the cart with his sturdy arms, manipulating it by its shafts so as to hurl it to the ground; then, just as it was about to fall from his hands, he cried in a thundering voice:

'Stand clear down below!'

But there was no difficulty there; the throng of people, warned by Baruch and tense with curiosity, had withdrawn to the square, from where it was possible to see what was going on on the hill. The cart was shattered in the most exquisite manner into an infinite number of bits and pieces.

'We've got it down,' said Baruch.

'Ah, you devils, you wretches!' Fario cried. 'Perhaps it was you who carried it up here!'

Max, Baruch and their three companions started to laugh at the Spaniard's insults.

'We wanted to lend you a hand,' Max answered coldly. 'I nearly got pulled down myself with the weight when I was grappling with your blasted cart, and that's all the thanks we get! What part of the world do you come from?'

'I come from a part of the world where people never forgive,' Fario replied, trembling with rage. 'My cart will be the cab in which you'll go to the devil . . .! Unless,' he went on, becoming as gentle as a lamb, 'you perhaps want to buy me a new one as a replacement?'

'We'll have to see about that,' Max said, walking back down the hill.

When they reached the foot of the Tower and had rejoined

the nearest clusters of laughing people, Max took hold of Fario by one of the buttons of his jacket, saying: 'Yes, my dear Fario, I'll make you a present of a magnificent cart, if you'll give me 250 francs first; but I can't guarantee that it will be able to cope with towers, any more than this one.'

On hearing this joke Fario became as cold in his manner as if he had been concluding a deal.

'Heavens!' he replied. 'You'd never have used old Rouget's money more wisely than by giving me some for a new cart.'

Max went pale and lifted his terrible fist to Fario's face; but Baruch, realizing that any blow struck at Fario would not merely involve the Spaniard, picked Fario up as if he had been a feather, whispering to Max: 'Don't do anything silly!'

This brought the major to his senses. He started to laugh, and replied to Fario: 'I accidentally smashed your cart up. You have been trying to say nasty things about me. So we're quits.'

'Not quite,' Fario murmured. 'But I'm very happy to know how much my cart was worth.'

'Ah! Max, you have found your match!' said a witness of the scene who did not himself belong to the Order of Idleness.

'Good-bye, Monsieur Gilet, I haven't thanked you yet for all the help you've given me this morning,' said the corn merchant, jumping astride his horse and riding off amid general acclamation.

'We'll look after the iron off the wheels for you!' shouted a wheelwright who had come along to look at the results of the fall.

One of the shafts was sticking up out of the ground as straight as a tree. Max stood pale and thoughtful, chilled to the heart by the Spaniard's parting words. For five days Fario's cart was the talk of Issoudun. And, as young Goddet said, it was destined to go on a long journey, for it eventually made its way round the whole of the Berry district, where Max's and Baruch's pranks were a staple of conversation.

What hurt the Spaniard most was that a week after the event he was still the laughing-stock of three *départements* and the subject of everybody's gossip. As a result of the vindictive Spaniard's terrifying replies, Max and Flore were also the talking-point of immense discussions, discussions that were whispered in Issoudun, but spoken aloud at Bourges, Vatan, Vierzon and Châteauroux. Maxence Gilet knew the district well enough to guess how venomous this tittle-tattle would be.

'You can't stop them from gossiping,' he thought. 'Ah! I slipped up there.'

'Well, Max,' said François, taking him by the arm, 'they're due this evening.'

'Who are?'

'The Bridaus! My grandmother has just received a letter from her goddaughter.'

'Listen, my lad,' Max whispered to him, 'I've thought this whole business over very carefully. It mustn't look as if either Flore or I have anything against the Bridaus. If the old man's relatives leave Issoudun, it must be you, the Hochons, who drive them out. Watch these Parisians carefully; and, after I I have had a look at them, we'll meet tomorrow at La Cognette's and see what we can do about them and how we can get them into your grandfather's bad books.'

'The Spaniard has found the chink in Max's armour,' Baruch said to his cousin François, as they went back to Monsieur Hochon's house and watched their friend returning to his.

Whilst Max was having his joke, Flore – defying her fellow-boarder's instructions – had been unable to contain her anger; and regardless of whether she was assisting or upsetting his plans, she railed against the poor bachelor. Whenever Jean-Jacques incurred his servant's anger, he was immediately deprived of the attentions and blandishments which were the joy of his life. In other words, Flore was punishing her master as one would punish a child. And so, there was an end to those affectionate little greetings with which she used to lard her conversation: words such as 'my darling', 'my dear', 'my lambkin', 'my pet', 'my sweetheart', etc. spoken in different tones of voice and with varying degrees of tenderness in her expression. She addressed him, bluntly and coldly, as 'vous', in an ironically respectful way; and it cut the unfortunate old bachelor to the quick, no less than if it had been a sword blade.

The 'vous' was tantamount to a declaration of war. And then, instead of being around when the old man got up, and finding him his things, anticipating his wishes, looking at him with the kind of admiration every woman can show and which is all the more charming if crudely expressed: 'You are as fresh as a rose.' 'Good Heavens! You're in wonderful health.' 'How handsome you are, old Jean!' Instead of regaling him as he was getting up with the jokes and spicy stories that amused him, Flore left him to get dressed on his own. If he called her, she would shout from the foot of the stairs: 'I can't do everything for you at once, get your breakfast ready and wait on you hand and foot in your bedroom. Aren't you big enough to get dressed all on your own?'

'Heavens! What have I done to her?' the old man wondered, receiving one of these rebuffs on asking for shaving-water.

'Védie, take Monsieur some warm water,' Flore ordered.

'Védie,' the old man asked, dazed with dread of Flore's impending anger, 'what is the matter with Madame this morning?'

Flore Brazier insisted on being called 'Madame' by her master, Védie, Kouski and Max.

'It seems she's learned something about you that's not very nice,' Védie answered, putting on an extremely prim expression. 'You're in the wrong, sir. I know I'm only a poor servant woman and you may well say it's no concern of mine to stick my nose into your affairs; but even if you looked at all the women in the world, like that king did in the Holy Scriptures, you wouldn't find Madame's equal anywhere. You ought to kiss her footsteps as she goes by. ... Yes! if you cause her any anxiety, it's like stabbing at your own heart!' She continued in this vein until tears welled to her eyes.

Védie left the poor man thunderstruck. He fell back into an armchair, staring into space like a melancholy fool; he even forgot to shave. Such alternations of affection and coldness wrought in this feeble being – who was only kept alive by the experience of love – the morbid results that a body sustains on passing suddenly from tropical heat to polar cold. These alternations produced a kind of moral pleurisy, as devastating in its effects as any physical illness. Flore was the only person in the world who could have this effect on him; for to her, and to her alone, he was as kind as he was stupid.

'Well now! Why haven't you shaved your beard?' she said, coming through the doorway.

She gave old Rouget the most violent shock. Pale and drawn, he blushed all over for a moment without daring to complain of this onslaught.

'Your breakfast is waiting for you! But you may as well come down in your slippers and dressing-gown; you'll be breakfasting on your own.'

And, without waiting for his reply, she disappeared from the room. Leaving the old man to breakfast on his own was, of all the penances she inflicted on him, the one that most grieved him: he loved to talk as he ate. On reaching the bottom of the stairs, Rouget was seized by a fit of coughing, for all this emotion had brought on his catarrh.

'Carry on! Carry on with your coughing!' Flore shouted from the kitchen, not caring whether her master heard her or not. 'Lord! The old rascal is strong enough to get over that without us getting worked up about it. If he ever does cough his soul up, it won't be till we're dead and buried.'

Such were the complimentary remarks she used to aim at Rouget when she was angry. In a mood of profound sadness the poor man sat down at the corner of the table, in the middle of the room, and despairingly surveyed his antique furniture and ancient pictures.

'You might have put a neck-tie on,' Flore said, entering the room. 'Do you think it's pleasant to have to look at a neck like yours, which is redder and more wrinkled than a turkey-cock's?'

'But what have I done?' he asked, raising his large light green eyes, which were brimming with tears, whilst Flore stared coldly at him.

'What have you done?' she said. 'You don't know? You're a hypocrite if ever there was one! Your sister Agathe, who's as much your sister as I am sister to the tower of Issoudun (according to what your father used to tell me), and in fact who's no relation to you at all, is coming down from Paris with her son, this wretched cheapjack painter, and they're going to call and see you.'

'My sister and nephews are coming to Issoudun?' he asked, completely amazed.

'Oh yes! Pretend you know nothing about it; make me imagine you didn't write asking them to come. There's deceitfulness for you! But don't worry, we shan't disturb your Parisians, because before ever they set foot in here, we'll have shaken the dust of this house off our feet. Max and I will leave you, never to return. As for your will, I'll tear it up into pieces before your very eyes, do you hear? *You* leave your money to your family, since we're no relations of yours. And then you'll see whether you will be loved for your own sake by people who've never been to see you these thirty years, people who have never even seen you at all! Your sister won't be able to take my place! That mealy-mouthed religious maniac!'

'Is that all it is, darling little Flore? Well then, I shan't see my sister or nephews. I swear that this is the first I've heard of their arrival. It's some trick thought up by Madame Hochon, the old pious hypocrite.'

Max, who came within earshot of old Rouget's words, suddenly appeared in the room, asking in a master's tone of voice: 'What's the matter?'

'My friend,' the old man went on, happy to buy the soldier's protection (by an arrangement with Flore, Max always took the old man's side), 'I swear to you in God's name that this is the first I've heard of this. I've never written to my sister. My father made me promise never to leave her any of my property; even to give it to the Church rather than leave it to her. Anyway, I shan't see either my sister Agathe or her sons.'

'Your father was wrong, my dear Jean-Jacques, and Madame is even more in the wrong,' Max replied. 'Your father had his good reasons, no doubt, but he's dead now, and his hatred should die with him. ... Your sister is your sister, your nephews are your nephews. You owe it to yourself to give them a good reception, and you owe it to us as well. What would people say in Issoudun...? By thunder! I've got enough on my plate already. The final straw would be to have people telling me we keep you all to ourselves, that you're not free to do as you like, that we have set you against your family and are trying to get hold of your money. ... But I'll be hanged if I don't walk out on you if ever that's said! The other insult's enough! Come on, let's have lunch.'

Flore, who had become as meek as a lamb, helped Védie to set the table. Old Rouget, filled with admiration for Max, took hold of his hands and led him into a window-recess, whispering to him: 'Ah, Max! If I had a son, I wouldn't love him as much as I love you. Flore was right! You two are my family. ... You're a man of honour, Max, and everything you've just said is right.'

'You must entertain your sister and nephew, but without making any change in your will,' Max replied, interrupting him. 'In this way you'll satisfy both your father and the world at large.'

'Well, my dears,' Flore cried gaily, 'the game ragout will be going cold. Come on, old boy, have a wing,' she added, smiling at Jean-Jacques Rouget.

On hearing this, the old man's horse-like face lost its cadaverous tints; his sagging lips took on an opium-eater's smile. But he began coughing again, for this happiness of regaining her favour caused him as violent an emotion as the penance itself. Flore stood up, snatched a little cashmere shawl from off her shoulders and tied it round the old man's neck, saying: 'It's so stupid to get worked up like that, all for nothing. Come on, you silly old thing, it'll do you good to wear the shawl; it's been next to my heart.'

'What a kind creature she is!' Rouget said to Max, whilst Flore went off to fetch a black velvet skull-cap for the bachelor's almost bald head.

'As beautiful as she is kind,' Max replied, 'but she is quick-tempered like everybody who is openly affectionate.'

Perhaps my readers will accuse me of painting too crude a picture; perhaps they will say that Flore's outbursts are so close to the truth of human nature that the painter should leave them in the shadow? Well, this scene, which has been rehearsed a hundred times with the most terrifying variations, is typical – in its crude form and horrible truthfulness – of the scenes played by all women, at whatever point in the social scale they happen to be, when some self-interest or other has turned them away from the path of obedience and they have seized power into their own hands. Like great politicians, they consider that the end justifies the means. Between Flore Brazier and a duchess, between a duchess and the wealthiest middle-class woman and between the middle-class housewife and the most brilliant of kept women the only differences that can be discerned are those which are attributable to their education and differing environments. Instead of Flore's violent outbursts, we have the sulky moods of aristocratic women. At every point in the social scale, bitter jokes, witty ridicule, cold disdain, hypocritical complaints and trumped-up quarrels obtain the same success as the plebeian words of this scheming housekeeper.

Max started to tell the Fario story so amusingly that the old man began to laugh. Outside in the corridor Védie and Kouski, who had come to hear the story, added to the amusement. Flore could not control her laughter. After lunch, whilst Jean-Jacques was reading the newspapers, for they now subscribed to the *Constitutionnel* and the *Pandore*, Max took Flore upstairs to his own room.

'Are you sure that he hasn't made any other will since he left you all his property?'

'He hasn't got anything to write with,' she replied.

'He could have dictated one to some solicitor or other,' Max said. 'If he hasn't done so already, we must be prepared for that to happen. So, let's give the Bridaus a marvellous welcome, but at the same time let's also try to convert all the mortgage investments into ready money – and without any delay either! Our solicitors will be only too happy to arrange some transfers: that's how they get their living. Government funds are rising every day. We are about to conquer Spain and release Ferdinand VII from his Cortes; so next year, perhaps, the funds will exceed par. That's why it would be a good thing to invest the old man's 750,000 francs in Government stock whilst it's still only at 89! Only, see if you can get them put down in your name. Then, we'd always have that amount put by!'

'That's a marvellous idea,' Flore said.

'And, as we'll have 50,000 francs a year interest on capital of 890,000 francs we ought to get him to borrow 140,000 francs over two years, repayable in two equal instalments. Then, two years from now we'll have drawn 100,000 francs in Paris and 90,000 francs here, so we're not risking anything.'

'But for you, darling handsome Max, whatever would have become of us?' she replied.

'Oh! Tomorrow evening, at La Cognette's, after I've had a look at these Parisians, I'll find some way of getting rid of them through the Hochons themselves.'

'Aren't you clever, my sweetheart! You certainly are a darling.'

16. The five Hochons

THE Place Saint-Jean is situated halfway along a street which at its upper end is known as the Rue Grande-Narette and as the Rue Petite-Narette at its lower end. In Berry, the word *narette* describes the same geographical feature as the Genoese word *salita* – in other words, a street with a steep incline. Between the Place Saint-Jean and the Porte Vilatte the *narette* is very steep indeed. Old Monsieur Hochon's house faces Jean-Jacques Rouget's. Often from the window in the living-room, at which Madame Hochon used to sit, you could see what was going on in old Rouget's house, and vice versa, when the curtains were drawn or the doors open. Monsieur Hochon's house is so like Rouget's that the two buildings were no doubt built by the same architect. Hochon, who at one time had been the tax-collector at Selles in Berry and who, moreover, was born at Issoudun, had returned to his native town to marry the Subdelegate's sister (the Subdelegate Lousteau, who was so attentive to women); he thus exchanged his post at Selles for the corresponding one at Issoudun. Having retired from business by 1786, he escaped the turmoils of the Revolution, with whose principles, by the way, he was fully in agreement – as were all 'respectable people' who take the winning side. Monsieur Hochon's reputation for extreme avarice was not unfounded. But would it not be repeating the story to give a description of him here? One example of avarice for which he became famous will no doubt suffice to give you a complete understanding of Monsieur Hochon.

At the time of his daughter's marriage to a Borniche (this daughter had since died), a dinner had to be given for the Borniche family. The young bridegroom, who was heir to an enormous fortune, died of grief as a result of some bad business speculations and, above all, his parents' refusal to help him in his difficulties. These old Borniches were still living at the time of our story, happy in the thought that Monsieur Hochon had taken on the guardianship (he had done so because of his daughter's dowry which he was at great pains to rescue). On the day of the signature of the marriage settlement, the grandparents of both families were assembled in the room with the Hochons on one side and the Borniches on the other, all dressed in their Sunday best. Whilst the marriage settlement was being read, a duty solemnly performed by the young solicitor Héron, the cook came in and asked Monsieur Hochon for some string to truss a turkey, an essential feature of the meal. The former tax-collector got out of his coat pocket a piece of string which had no doubt already been used for some packet or other. He gave it to her, but before the servant had reached the door, cried out: 'Gritte, mind you give it me back!' (Gritte is the common abbreviation in Berry for Marguerite.) You will now understand both Monsieur Hochon's character and the joke which the town had thought up apropos of his family, which consisted of father, mother and three children: they were known as *les cinq Hochon*!

With each passing year old Hochon became more cranky and more particular, and at the time of our story he was eighty-five years old! He belonged to that category of men who, as they are walking along a road engaged in lively conversation, stoop to pick up a pin, saying: 'There's a day's work for a woman!' and then stick this pin into the cuff of their sleeve. He complained forcefully about the shoddy manufacture of modern cloth, pointing out that his coat had only lasted him ten years. Tall, dry, thin, with a yellow complexion, saying and reading little, never tiring himself and as punctilious as any Oriental, he ran his household along the most austere lines, even measuring out his family's food and drink. (His family, by the way, were fairly numerous, and consisted of his wife, a Lousteau before marriage, his grandson Baruch and Baruch's sister Adolphine, who were the old Borniches' heirs, and finally his other grandson François Hochon).

Hochon, his elder son, was called up in 1813 following the conscription of young men of good family who hitherto had escaped enlistment and who became known as *les gardes d'honneur*; he had been killed at the Battle of Hanau. Whilst still a very young man, this heir presumptive had married a wealthy woman, so as not to be compelled into military service; but he dilapidated her whole fortune, foreseeing his end. His wife, who followed some distance behind the French army, died at Strasburg in 1814, leaving debts there which were never paid by old Hochon, who confronted her creditors with that axiom of ancient jurisprudence: *Women are minors.*

So people could still say *les cinq Hochon*, since the household still consisted of three grandchildren and the two grandparents. And so the joke still persisted, for no joke grows stale in the provinces. Gritte, who was then aged sixty, was their maid of all work.

Though very large, the house had little furniture. Even so, it was very easy to accommodate Joseph and Madame Bridau in two bedrooms on the second floor. This made old Hochon regret that he had kept two beds up there, each with its old armchair of unvarnished wood, upholstered with tapestry, and its walnut table on which a water-jug of the kind known as a *Gueulard* stood in a blue-rimmed wash-basin. The old man used to lay out his harvest of apples, winter pears, medlars and quinces on a bed of straw in the two rooms, where rats and mice reigned supreme; not surprisingly, these rooms smelt of fruit and mice. Madame Hochon had everything cleaned and tidied there: the wallpaper, which in places had been peeling off the walls, was stuck on again with sealing wafers; she decorated the windows with little curtains which she herself cut out of some old muslin covers which belonged to her. Then, when her husband refused to buy any small list carpets, she lent Agathe her own bedroom rug, calling this forty-seven-year-old mother of two sons her 'poor little dear!' Madame Hochon borrowed two bedside tables from the Borniches and very daringly rented from a secondhand dealer next to La Cognette's two old chests of drawers with copper handles. She still had two pairs of candlesticks, made of precious woods and turned on a lathe by her own father, who was passionately fond of this work. Between 1770 and 1780, it was fashionable for wealthy people to learn some trade or other, and old Monsieur Lousteau, who at one time had been Head Clerk to the Board of Excise, became a turner just as Louis XVI became a locksmith. These candlesticks were decorated with roots of rosewood, peach and apricot, arranged in rings. Madame Hochon ventured to put out these precious relics! Such preparations and so great an act of sacrifice increased Monsieur Hochon's solemnity; he still could not believe that the Bridaus were about to descend upon him.

On the morning of the never-to-be-forgotten day when Fario was hoaxed, Madame Hochon remarked to her husband after breakfast: 'I hope, Hochon, that you will welcome my goddaughter Madame Bridau in an appropriate manner.' Then, after making sure that her grandchildren had left the room, she added: 'I am the mistress of my own wealth. Do not make it necessary for me to mention Agathe in my will as a requital for our ungracious welcome.'

'Do you really believe, Madame,' Hochon replied in a low voice, 'that at my age I cannot show puerile and honest civility?'

'You know very well what I am trying to say, you crafty old fellow. Be gracious to our guests and remember how very fond I am of Agathe.'

'You were also fond of Maxence Gilet, who is now going to devour an inheritance that rightfully belongs to your dear Agathe! Yes! In him you nourished a serpent within your bosom; but, after all, the Rougets' money had to go to some Lousteau or other.'

After this reference to Agathe's and Max's presumed parentage, Hochon made as if to leave the room; but old Madame Hochon, a woman who was still upright and precise in manner, who powdered her face and wore a round bonnet with looped ribbons, a tight-sleeved dress of dove-coloured taffeta, and heelless slippers, placed her snuff box on her little table and said to her husband: 'Really, how can an intelligent man like you, Monsieur Hochon, repeat stupid notions which, unfortunately, deprived my poor friend of her peace of mind and my poor goddaughter of her father's fortune? Max Gilet is no son of my brother, whom I strongly advised at that time to look after his money. In any case, you know as well as I do that Madame Rouget was virtue itself.'

'And the daughter is worthy of the mother, for she seems very stupid to me. After losing all her fortune, she has brought her sons up so well that one of them is in prison awaiting trial before the Court of Peers on a criminal indictment, a charge of some Berton-like conspiracy. As for the other, he is in an even worse mess; he is an artist! We shall have eaten more than one peck of salt with your protégés before they rescue idiotic old Rouget from the claws of Gilet and his Fisher-woman.'

'That is enough, Monsieur Hochon. Let us hope that they will get something out of this business.'

Monsieur Hochon picked up his hat and ivory-headed cane and left the room, appalled by this terrible sentence. He had not expected to find his wife so determined. Madame Hochon picked up her prayer book to read the Ordinary of the Mass, for at her advanced age she could not go to Church every day: it was difficult enough for her to attend services on Sundays and religious festivals. Since receiving Agathe's reply, she included with her normal prayers a prayer beseeching God to open Jean-Jacques Rouget's eyes, bless Agathe and prosper the enterprise on which she herself had encouraged her god-daughter to embark. Concealing her feelings from her two grandsons (whom she accused of being 'Calvinist heretics'!), she had asked the parish priest to help in bringing about this success by saying masses during a novena undertaken by her granddaughter Adolphine Borniche, who was responsible for the prayers at Church by proxy.

Adolphine, who was then aged eighteen and who for seven years had been working alongside her grandmother in this cold house with its methodical and monotonous ways, gladly undertook the novena, particularly as she herself was hoping to inspire some feeling in Joseph Bridau, the artist whom Monsieur Hochon had misunderstood and in whom she took the keenest interest on account of those very enormities of conduct which her grandfather laid at the young Parisian's door.

Moreover, the old people, the respectable folk, the leading lights of Issoudun, the fathers of families fully agreed with Madame Hochon's attitude; their good wishes for her goddaughter and *her* sons accorded with the well concealed contempt they had long felt for Maxence Gilet's behaviour. Thus the news of the arrival of old Rouget's sister and nephew created two opposing camps in Issoudun: on the one hand, the old-established and important bourgeoisie who could do no more than express pious wishes and observe events they were unable to influence; and on the other hand, the Knights of Idleness and Max's followers who unfortunately were in a position to do the Parisians much harm.

*

So it was that Agathe and Joseph alighted from the coach in the Place Misère, outside the coach office, at three o'clock in the afternoon. Although she was tired, Madame Bridau felt a new lease of life on seeing her birthplace again, as each step brought back to her memories and impressions of her youth. In the conditions prevailing in Issoudun at that time, the Parisians' arrival became common knowledge within ten minutes. Madame Hochon came to the doorstep to greet her goddaughter, embracing her as if she had been her own child. After living for seventy-two years a life that was both empty and monotonous, in which (on looking back) she could count the coffins of her three children, all of whom died unhappy deaths, she had developed feelings of maternal attachment towards a young woman whom, as she put it, she 'had had in her pockets' for sixteen years. In the depths of the provinces she had cherished this longstanding friendship, this childhood and its memories, as if Agathe had actually been present in the flesh; it was for this reason that she was passionately interested in the Bridaus' welfare. Agathe was led triumphantly into the room where Monsieur Hochon sat stately and unconcerned.

'Here is Monsieur Hochon. How do you think he looks?' the godmother asked her goddaughter.

'Why! Exactly the same as when I last saw him.'

'Ah! It's obvious that you come from Paris, you are so complimentary,' Monsieur Hochon said.

Then introductions took place: young Baruch Borniche, a tall youth of twenty-two; young François Hochon, who was twenty-four; and young Adolphine, who blushed and did not know what to do with her arms and especially her eyes, for she did not wish to give the impression of looking at Joseph Bridau, who was inquisitively examined – but from different standpoints – by both the two young men and their grandfather. The miser was thinking to himself: 'He's just out of hospital, he must be as hungry as a convalescent.' The two young men were thinking: 'What a rogue! What a face! We'll have our work cut out with him!'

'This is my son, the painter, my kind-hearted Joseph!' Agathe finally said, pointing to the artist.

In the accents of the word 'kind-hearted' an effort was discernible, through which Agathe's whole heart betrayed itself: she was thinking of the Luxembourg prison.

'He doesn't look well,' Madame Hochon cried, 'and he doesn't take after you.'

'No, Madame,' Joseph answered with an artist's unaffected frankness, 'I take after my father, even in his ugliness!'

Madame Hochon squeezed Agathe's hand, which she was holding in hers, and looked her in the face. Her gesture and glance implied: 'Yes! I quite understand, my dear, why you prefer that rascal Philippe.'

'I never saw your father, my dear boy,' Madame Hochon replied aloud; 'but you only need to be your mother's son for me to love you. Besides, you are very gifted, according to what the late Madame Descoings used to write to me, who was the only person in your household to give me news of you all latterly.'

'Gifted!' said the artist. 'Not yet; but with time and patience perhaps I shall succeed in winning both a reputation and a fortune.'

'At painting?' asked Monsieur Hochon, with deep irony.

'Now, Adolphine,' Madame Hochon interrupted, 'go and see whether dinner is ready.'

'Mother,' Joseph said, 'I'll go and see to our trunks, which have just arrived.'

'Hochon, show Monsieur Bridau the rooms,' the grandmother said to François.

As dinner was to be served at four and it was still only half past three, Baruch went out into the town to spread the news about the Bridau family and describe Agathe's dress and (still more important) Joseph's appearance, with his haggard, sickly and quite unique face so like people's ideal mental picture of a bandit. Joseph was the principal subject of conversation in every household that day.

'Old Rouget's sister must have had a monkey looking at her during her pregnancy,' people said, 'her son looks like a macaque.' 'His face is like a bandit's, and he has an evil eye.' 'They say he's really peculiar to look at, quite terrifying.' 'Every artist is like that in Paris.' 'They are as nasty as wild asses and as spiteful as monkeys.' 'It's their job.' 'I have just seen Monsieur Beaussier, who says he would not like to meet him at night in a dark wood; he saw him in the coach.' 'He has deep eye-sockets like a horse, and he gesticulates like a madman.' 'That young man seems to be capable of anything; perhaps it was because of him that his brother, who was a tall handsome man, has turned out so badly.' 'Poor Madame Bridau doesn't look very happy in his company. Supposing we made use of him whilst he's here and had our portraits painted?'

These opinions, which spread like wildfire across the town, gave rise to an extraordinary degree of curiosity. Everyone who was on visiting terms with the Hochons vowed to pay them a visit that evening so as to have a look at the Parisians. In a stagnant town like Issoudun, the Bridaus' arrival was like the rafter that fell amongst frogs.

After putting his mother's and his own things in their respective attic bedrooms, and after looking round the rooms, Joseph studied the silent house whose bare walls, staircase and wood panelling seemed to distil cold, and where only the very strictest necessities were to be had. He was struck by the sudden transition from Paris, with its poetical atmosphere, to the silent and inhospitable provinces. But when, on going downstairs, he noticed that Monsieur Hochon himself was cutting everyone's portion of bread, he understood Molière's Harpagon for the first time in his life.

'We would have done better at the inn,' he thought. His fears were confirmed when he saw the dinner. After a soup whose thin stock indicated that quantity was a more important factor than quality came some boiled beef, triumphantly garnished with parsley. The vegetables, in a separate dish, counted as one course on the menu. This boiled beef was given pride of place at the centre of the table and three other dishes placed round it: hard-boiled eggs on sorrel, which stood opposite the vegetables, a salad tossed in nut oil and, by the salad, small pots of cream where burned oats took the place of vanilla and which tasted as much like vanilla as chicory coffee tastes like mocha. This course was rounded off by radishes and butter, which were set out in two dishes at either end of the table, alongside black radishes and gherkins; and it had Madame Hochon's approval. The kind old lady nodded with pleasure on seeing that, on the first day at least, her husband had arranged things handsomely. The old man glanced back at her and shrugged his shoulders, as if to say: 'Just look at the expense you are putting me to!'

As soon as it had been dissected by Monsieur Hochon into slices as thin as the soles of dancing-shoes, the boiled beef was followed by three pigeons. The local wine was of the 1811 vintage. On her grandmother's advice, Adolphine had decorated both ends of the table with flowers.

'We'll have to rough it here,' the artist thought, as he surveyed the table.

And he began to eat with the appetite of a man who had breakfasted at Vierzon at six in the morning on an abominable cup of coffee. When Joseph had swallowed his bread and asked for more, Monsieur Hochon rose from the table, slowly fumbled in his coat pocket for a key, unlocked a cupboard behind his chair, brandished a hunk off a twelve-pound loaf, ceremoniously cut another round, sliced it into two halves, put it on to a plate and passed the plate across the table to the young painter with the silent stoicism of an old soldier who says to himself before a battle: 'Anyway, today I may be killed.' Joseph took half of this round, realizing that he must not ask for any more bread. No member of the family expressed any astonishment at a scene which to Joseph seemed so heartrending. The conversation went on apace. Agathe discovered that the house in which she had been born, which was her father's house until he had inherited the Descoings' had been purchased by the Borniches. She expressed a wish to revisit it.

'No doubt,' her godmother replied, 'the Borniches will be coming this evening, for we shall be having the whole town in to have a look at you' (turning towards Joseph), 'and then they will invite you to call on them.'

As a dessert the maid brought in some of the soft goat's milk cheese for which Touraine and Berry are famous, and which so faithfully reproduces in a niello pattern the outline of the vine leaves on which it is served that it ought to have led to the invention of engraving in Touraine. With some ceremony, Gritte placed nuts and time-hallowed biscuits on either side of these small cheeses.

'Come on, Gritte, what about some fruit?' asked Madame Hochon.

'But, Madame, there's no rotten fruit left,' Gritte replied.

Joseph burst out laughing as if he had been in his studio with his friends, for he suddenly realized that the precaution of starting with fruit that was already beginning to go bad had by now degenerated into a habit.

'Never mind! We can still eat the good fruit,' he replied with the verve and gaiety of a man who has decided the attitude he will adopt.

'Well, go on then, Monsieur Hochon,' the old lady cried.

Very offended by the artist's joke, Monsieur Hochon brought back some yellow peaches, pears and St Catherine plums.

'Adolphine, go and pick us some grapes,' Madame Hochon said to her granddaughter.

Joseph looked at the two young men questioningly: 'How do you get such flourishing faces on a diet like this?' Baruch understood his incisive glance and started to smile, for his cousin Hochon and he had always behaved with discretion. The standard of living at home was fairly immaterial to people who dined three nights a week at La Cognette's. Besides, before dinner Baruch had received word that the Grand Master was summoning a plenary session of the Order at midnight, to offer it a magnificent meal and also ask it for some help. This welcoming meal which old Hochon had laid on for his guests is indication enough how necessary the nocturnal banquetings at La Cognette's were for the health of these two big young men, who – blessed with such hearty appetites – never missed a single one.

'We will take our liqueur in the drawing-room,' said Madame Hochon, rising from her seat and motioning to Joseph to take her arm. As she was the first to leave the room, she had an opportunity of saying to the painter: 'Well, my poor boy! That dinner won't give you indigestion; even so, it was as much as I could do to get you that. You will have to fast here. You'll just about eat enough to keep alive, but that's all. So, be patient about the food.'

The artist was delighted by the simple good-heartedness of this excellent old woman who was actually condemning herself out of her own mouth.

'I shall have lived fifty years with that man, without ever having had as much as sixty francs jingling in my purse! Oh! If it wasn't a matter of rescuing your fortune, I would never have dragged you and your mother here into my prison.'

'But how have you managed to keep alive?' the painter asked ingenuously, with the gaiety that never deserts French artists.

'Well, I pray.'

Joseph shivered slightly on hearing these words, which made the old woman seem so grandiose a figure that he stepped back three paces to contemplate her face; he thought she looked radiant and imbued with so tender a serenity that he exclaimed: 'I will paint your portrait!'

'No, no,' she said. 'I have been too wearied by the world to want to stay on in it in a painting!'

Cheerfully saying these sad words, she took out of a cupboard a flask containing some blackcurrant liqueur which she had made herself in her own kitchen, for she had obtained the recipe for it from those famous nuns to whom we are indebted for the gâteau d'Issoudun, one of the greatest creations of French confectionery and one which no chef, cook, pastrycook or confectioner has been able to imitate. Monsieur de Rivière, our ambassador at Constantinople, used to order enormous quantities of it every year for Mahmud II's seraglio. Adolphine held a lacquer plate laden with those little old glasses with engraved sides and gilded rims; then, as her grandmother filled each one, she would hand it to one of the party.

'Pass them round, my father will have one!' Agathe cried gaily, reminded by this changeless ceremony of her own youth.

'Hochon is going off in a few minutes to his club to read the newspapers. We shall have a little time to ourselves,' the old lady whispered to her.

And indeed, ten minutes later, the three women and Joseph were sitting alone in the drawing-room where the wood-block floor was never polished but only swept, and whose tapestries, framed in grooved and moulded oak, and indeed whose whole furniture – so simple and yet almost sombre – seemed to Madame Bridau to have remained exactly as she had left it. The Monarchy, Revolution, Empire and Restoration, which showed so little regard for anything, had respected this room in which their splendours and disasters had left not the slightest trace.

'Ah! My dear godmother, my life has been so full of cruel ups and downs compared with yours,' Madame Bridau cried, surprised to note that even a stuffed canary, which she had known when it was alive, stood on the mantelpiece between the old clock, the old copper candelabra and some silver candlesticks.

'My dear child,' the old woman answered, 'the trials of life are in the heart. The greater and the more necessary our attitude of resignation is, the more struggles we have within ourselves. Let us not talk about me, let us talk about your concerns. You are staying just opposite the enemy,' she went on, pointing across to the sitting-room in Rouget's house.

'They are sitting down to their meal,' said Adolphine.

This young girl, who was very nearly a recluse, was always looking out of the windows, hoping to obtain some inkling of the enormities attributed to Maxence Gilet, Flore Brazier and Jean-Jacques, some account of which reached her ears whenever she was sent out of the room so that the others could discuss them. The old lady told her granddaughter to leave her alone with Monsieur and Madame Bridau until any visitors called.

'I know Issoudun inside out,' she added, looking at the two Parisians. 'This evening we shall have ten or a dozen batches of inquisitive visitors.'

Hardly had Madame Hochon had time to relate to the two Parisians the events and details concerning the astonishing power that Flore Brazier and Maxence Gilet had obtained over Jean-Jacques Rouget – without adopting the synthetic method of narration with which this story has presented the facts, but spicing her account with the innumerable commentaries, descriptions and hypotheses with which the story was garnished by both good-natured and ill-natured gossips – than Adolphine entered the room announcing the arrival of the Borniches, the Beaussiers, and Lousteau-Prangins, the Fichets, the Goddet-Héreaus, fourteen people altogether, all of whom could be seen hovering in the background.

'You see, my dear,' the old lady concluded, 'it's no easy matter to snatch this fortune from out of the lion's mouth.'

'With a scoundrel like the one you've just described and a woman as brazen as that hussy, it looks to me so difficult as to be impossible,' was Joseph's answer. 'We should have to spend at least a year at Issoudun fighting their influence and counteracting their hold on my uncle. ... The fortune isn't worth all the bother, quite apart from the fact that you have to dishonour yourself with innumerable unworthy actions. My mother only has a fortnight's holiday. Her job is safe; she must not put it at risk. I have some important work in October which Schinner has obtained for me from a peer of France. . . . You see, Madame, my own fortune is in my brushes!'

These remarks were received with profound bewilderment. Although superior in outlook to the townsfolk amongst whom she lived, Madame Hochon set no faith in painting. She looked at her goddaughter, and again squeezed her hand.

'This Maxence is a second edition of Philippe,' Joseph whispered to his mother, 'but with more political shrewdness and more tactical sense than Philippe. Well, Madame!' he said aloud. 'We shan't overstay our welcome with Monsieur Hochon!'

'Ah! You are a young man, you don't know anything about the world! If you use a little common sense and astuteness, you can obtain results within a fortnight. Listen to my advice and go about things the way I recommend.'

'Yes, it's quite true, I feel I'm exceptionally useless in matters of domestic politics,' Joseph replied. 'For example, I have no idea what Desroches himself would advise us to do if my uncle refuses to see us tomorrow.'

Madame Borniche, Madame Goddet-Héreau, Madame Beaussier, Madame Lousteau-Prangin and Madame Fichet, all of them furnished with their husbands, now entered the room. After the usual compliments, the fourteen guests sat down and Madame Hochon could not avoid introducing her goddaughter Agathe and Joseph to them. Joseph sat in an armchair, slyly studying the sixty faces which, as he put it when talking to his mother, posed for him gratis from half past five to nine o'clock. Joseph's attitude that evening towards the patricians of Issoudun did not in any way modify the small town's opinion of him; everyone retained an impression of his mocking glances, everyone was made uneasy by his smiles, or frightened by his face which seemed so sinister to people unable to recognize the strangeness of genius.

At ten o'clock, when everybody went to bed, Madame Hochon kept her goddaughter in her bedroom until midnight. Sure of being left to themselves, the two women confided the griefs of their lives to one another and exchanged their sadnesses. Recognizing the immensity of the desert in which the strength of a beautiful unknown soul had been wasted, hearing the last resonances of a mind whose destiny had remained unfulfilled, and learning the sufferings of a heart which was essentially generous and charitable and whose generosity and charity had never found scope for action, Agathe no longer thought of herself as the more unfortunate of the two women, realizing how many distractions and small delights life in Paris had brought to mitigate the bitternesses sent down from Heaven.

'You, who are so very religious, dear godmother, tell me what I have done wrong and why God is punishing me.'

'He is preparing us for the next life, my child,' the old lady replied as it was striking midnight.

17. Maxence-Machiavelli

At midnight, the Knights of Idleness crept one by one like shadows to the tree-lined Boulevard Baron, where they walked up and down talking in whispers.

'What will it be tonight?' was the first thing everyone said on meeting another member of the Order.

'I think that all Max intends to do tonight is stand us a jolly good meal,' François said.

'No, Flore and he are in serious difficulties. No doubt he will have thought up some joke to play on the Parisians.'

'It would be wonderful to send them packing.'

'My grandfather, who is already very frightened that there are two more mouths to feed in his house, would welcome any pretext . . .' Baruch remarked.

'Well, my Knights!' Max declared in a low voice as he came up. 'Why are you all looking at the stars? They won't distil any kirsch! Come on! To La Cognette's! To La Cognette's!'

'To La Cognette's!'

Shouting as with one voice, the young men produced a horrible din that passed over the town like the hurrah troops make when charging to the assault; then, a deep silence reigned. The next day, a number of people said to their neighbours: 'Did you hear some terrible shouting last night, about one o'clock? I thought there must have been a fire somewhere.'

A dinner worthy of La Cognette's culinary skill delighted the eyes of the twenty-two guests, for the Order was at its maximum strength. At two o'clock, just as they were beginning to sip, one of the words in the Order's private jargon, which describes fairly well the action of drinking in small mouthfuls whilst savouring the full delicacy of the wine, Max began to speak.

'My dear friends, this morning, apropos of the unforgettable trick we played on Fario's cart, your Grand Master's honour was so deeply wounded by that vile corn merchant, a Spaniard into the bargain,' ('Oh! The hulks!' all cried) 'that I have resolved to let this rascal feel the full weight of my vengeance – whilst not exceeding the usual limits of our amusements. After thinking about it all day, I have found a way of carrying out a most excellent joke, a joke which might even drive him out of his senses. Whilst avenging the Order, which has been attacked in my own person, we shall also be giving sustenance to animals venerated by the ancient Egyptians, small beasts which after all are amongst God's creatures, yet which are so unjustly persecuted by men. Good flows from evil actions, and evil actions from good! Such is the law of life! I order each and every one of you therefore, on pain of your most humble Grand-Master's displeasure, to obtain as secretly as possible twenty male rats or, God willing, twenty pregnant rats! Have your contingents ready within three days. If you are able to obtain a greater number, the surplus will be most welcome. Keep these interesting rodents without giving them anything at all to eat, for it is essential that these dear little animals should have a ravenous hunger. Note that I include in the category of rats both mice and field-mice. Multiply twenty-two by twenty, and we shall have four hundred odd accomplices which, when they are let loose in the old Capucin church where Fario has stored all the corn he has just bought, will consume a certain quantity of this corn. But let us make haste! Fario must deliver a good proportion of his corn in a week's time; now I wish our Spaniard, who at present is travelling somewhere in the locality on business, to find that terrible damage has been done. Gentlemen, I cannot claim any merit for this invention,' he said, noticing signs of general admiration. 'Let us render unto Caesar the things which are Caesar's, and unto God the things that are God's. This idea is merely an imitation of Samson's foxes in the old Bible story. But Samson was an incendiary and so hardly deserving of the name of a philanthropist; whereas we, like the Brahmans, protect persecuted races. Mademoiselle Flore

Brazier has already put out all her mouse-traps and my right-hand man, Kouski, is on the look-out for field-mice. I have spoken.'

'I know where I can get an animal that will be the equivalent of forty rats,' said young Goddet.

'What?'

'A squirrel.'

'And *I* can let you have a little monkey who will get drunk on corn,' said a novice.

'No good!' said Max. 'People would know where these animals came from.'

'During the night,' said young Beaussier, 'we could bring a pigeon each from each of the pigeon-cotes on the surrounding farms and push them through a hole we could make in the roof. Soon there would be several thousand pigeons.'

'So, for a week, Fario's corn store is subject to the Order of the Night,' Gilet cried, smiling at Beaussier, a big young man. 'You know people get up early at Saint-Paterne. No one must go there without first having turned the soles of his list slippers inside out. Knight Beaussier, the inventor of the pigeons, shall take charge of this operation. *I* will make a point of signing my name in the heap of corn. *You* will be the sergeant-majors in charge of our friends the rats. If the warehouseman sleeps in the Capucin church, we shall have to get him tipsy after a drinking bout with his friends, but we must do it adroitly so as to be able to remove him far away from the scene of this orgy we are offering to rodent animals.'

'You haven't said a word about the Parisians,' young Goddet said.

'We must study them. Nevertheless, I offer my fine sporting-gun which came from the Emperor himself, a masterpiece from the Versailles gunmakers, worth 2,000 francs, to whoever can think up some way of playing a trick on these Parisians, which will put them in such bad odour with Monsieur and Madame Hochon that they are immediately sent packing by the two old people, or else leave of their own accord without, of course, causing too much harm or inconvenience to the ancestors of my two friends Baruch and François.'

'All right! I'll think about it,' said young Goddet, who was passionately fond of hunting.

'If the inventor of this prank does not want my gun, then he can have my horse!' Max added.

After this midnight supper, twenty brains tortured themselves trying to think up some plot that would embarrass Agathe and her son whilst still keeping within the bounds of the programme Max had laid down. But only the devil himself, or else blind chance, could succeed in this enterprise, so difficult were the conditions that had been imposed.

Next morning, Agathe and Joseph came downstairs just before the second breakfast, which was at ten. The title of 'first breakfast' was given to a cup of milk accompanied by a slice of bread and butter, which was eaten either in bed or just after getting up. Whilst awaiting Madame Hochon who, despite her age, minutely performed all the ceremonies that duchesses in Louis XV's reign applied to their dress and appearance, Joseph noticed Jean-Jacques Rouget standing on the doorstep of the house opposite. He naturally pointed him out to his mother, who could not recognize her brother, he had changed so much since she had last seen him.

'That's your brother,' said Adolphine, linking arms with her grandmother.

'What a cretin!' cried Joseph.

Agathe joined her hands and raised her eyes to Heaven: 'What a state they've brought him to! My God, can that be a man of fifty-seven?'

She scrutinized her brother carefully and saw Flore Brazier standing behind the old man. Flore was hatless; beneath her fine lace shawl her snow-white back and dazzlingly clear chest could be seen. She was as well dressed as any rich courtesan, wearing a dress made of grenadine (a silk material then in fashion), which had a whalebone bodice and leg-of-mutton sleeves; she had superb bracelets on her wrists. A gold chain shimmered against her bodice. Flore Brazier was bringing Jean-Jacques his black silk skull-cap so that he would not catch cold. Evidently, this was a calculated scene.

'Ah! There's a beautiful woman!' Joseph cried, 'and it's a

rare enough sight! She was born to be painted, as people say!
What gorgeous flesh tints! Just look at those warm tones,
those boldly chiselled features, those full curves and those
shoulders! She'd make a magnificent caryatid, or a splendid
model for one of Titian's Venuses.'

Adolphine and Madame Hochon thought he must be
speaking Greek; but Agathe, who was standing behind her
son, motioned to them that she was used to this kind of
idiom.

'Do you think a woman's beautiful when she's robbing
you of a fortune?' asked Madame Hochon.

'That doesn't prevent her from being a splendid model; just
plump enough, without spoiling the hips and figure.'

'My dear boy, you're not in your studio now,' said Agathe,
'and Adolphine is present.'

'That's true, I'm sorry; but I must say that all the way from
Paris to here, I have seen nothing but plain women.'

'My dear godmother,' Agathe said, 'how can I see my
brother? For if he is with that creature . . .'

'Don't worry!' said Joseph, 'I'll go and see him! I don't
think he's anywhere near so cretinous now I know that he has
had the good sense to feast his eyes on a Titian-like Venus.'

'If he hadn't been stupid,' said Monsieur Hochon, happening to come into the room at this moment, 'he would have
got married in the usual way and had children, and you
wouldn't be in a position to inherit his fortune. It's an ill wind
that blows nobody any good.'

'Your son's idea is a good one,' said Madame Hochon.
'The first time, he can go all on his own to call on his uncle;
and he can impress upon him that he must be alone if you
come to see him.'

'So you want to upset Mademoiselle Brazier?' said Monsieur Hochon. 'No, no, Madame, you must put up with this
misfortune. . . . Even if you don't get the inheritance, at least
try to obtain a little legacy.'

The Hochons were no match for Maxence Gilet. Whilst
they were having breakfast, Kouski brought a letter from his
master Monsieur Rouget, addressed to his master's sister,

Madame Bridau. This is the text of the letter, which at Madame Hochon's wish was read aloud to her husband:

My Dear Sister,

Strangers have informed me of your arrival in Issoudun. I well understand the motives which lead you to prefer Monsieur and Madame Hochon's house to my own; but, if you do come to see me, you will be received in my home as you deserve to be. I would have come over and visited you first if my health did not compel me to stay indoors at the moment. Please accept my affectionate apologies. I shall be delighted to see my nephew and should be pleased if he could dine with me tomorrow; young men are less particular about company than women are! He will give me great pleasure if he brings Monsieur Baruch Borniche and Monsieur François Hochon along with him.

Your affectionate brother,
J.-J. ROUGET

'Say that we are having breakfast, that Madame Bridau will reply shortly and that the invitations are accepted,' Monsieur Hochon told the maid.

And the old man raised a finger to his lips, instructing everyone to be silent. When the front door had closed, Monsieur Hochon – who had no reason to suspect his two grandsons' friendship with Maxence – glanced at his wife and Agathe in his subtlest manner: 'He as much wrote that letter as I am capable of giving away 500 francs. . . . It's the soldier with whom we'll be corresponding.'

'What do you mean?' asked Madame Hochon. 'Never mind, we'll reply. As for you, Monsieur,' she added, turning to the painter, 'go and dine over there by all means; but if . . .'

The old lady was silenced by a look from her husband. Realizing how close his wife's friendship with Agathe was, old Hochon was afraid she might bequeath some legacy to her goddaughter in the event of the latter's forfeiting the whole of Rouget's fortune. Although fifteen years older than his wife, the miser hoped to inherit her money, and one day be in control of their combined fortunes. This hope had become an obsession with him. It was because of this that Madame Hochon had discovered a way of obtaining some concessions from her husband, by threatening to make a will. And so Monsieur Hochon took his guests' side. Besides, an enormous inheritance was at stake; and, in a spirit of social justice, he wanted to see it go to the rightful heirs rather than be snatched out of their hands by unworthy strangers. In any case, the sooner this matter was settled, the sooner his guests would leave. Since the outset of the struggle for the inheritance, which until just recently had been a mere project of his wife's, Monsieur Hochon's mental activity, deadened by the monotony of provincial life, had regained new vigour. From a few affectionate words which old Hochon said apropos of her goddaughter that very morning, Madame Hochon was quite agreeably surprised to note that this most competent and subtle auxiliary was supporting the Bridaus.

By midday, the combined intelligence of Monsieur and Madame Hochon, Agathe and Joseph (both the latter were quite astonished to find the two old people so careful in their choice of words), had produced the following reply, drawn up solely with Flore and Maxence in mind.

My Dear Brother,
The fact that I have not been to Issoudun for thirty years and have not kept in touch with anyone here, not even with you, is due not only to the strange and false ideas which my father harboured against me, but also to the misfortunes *and* happiness of my life in Paris; for, though God made me happy as a wife, He has made me unhappy as a mother. You are not unaware that my son, your nephew Philippe, is awaiting trial on a charge that carries with it the death penalty, and all because of his loyalty to the Emperor. Bearing this in mind, you will not be surprised that a widow who has to earn her living by taking a lowly paid job in a lottery office should have come to seek consolation and help from those who are closest to her in the town of her birth. The son who has accompanied me on my journey has chosen to follow one of those careers that demand the greatest talent, hardest sacrifices and longest study before leading to any results. In his career fame precedes fortune. In other words, even when Joseph has made our family's name illustrious, he will still be poor. Your sister, my dear Jean-Jacques, would have borne the consequences of a father's injustice without complaint; but forgive a mother for reminding you that you have

two nephews, one of whom carried the Emperor's orders at the
Battle of Montereau and served in the Imperial Guards at Waterloo,
and is now in prison; whilst, from the age of thirteen, the other
nephew has been absorbed in his vocation to a difficult but glorious
career. Both Joseph and I thank you most warmly for your letter,
my dear brother, and Joseph will certainly accept your invitation.
Illness excuses everything, Jean-Jacques, and I shall come and
visit you. A sister is always happy to be with her brother, whatever
way of life he has adopted.

With fond love,
AGATHE ROUGET

'Now things are under way! When you go over, you can
speak to him bluntly about his nephews,' Monsieur Hochon
said to Agathe.

The letter was taken across by Gritte, who returned ten
minutes later to give her master and mistress an account of
everything she had learned or been able to see – as is the way
in the provinces.

'Madame, since yesterday evening,' she said, 'the whole
house has been tidied up by Madame, who . . .'

'Who do you mean, Madame?' old Hochon asked.

'But that's how the Fisherwoman is called over there,'
Gritte replied. 'She used to leave the living-room and all
Monsieur Rouget's rooms in an awful mess; but since
yesterday the house has become just as it used to be before
Monsieur Maxence's arrival. You could admire yourself in
the polish! Védie told me that Kouski went off on horseback
this morning at five o'clock; he came back with groceries
about nine. It'll be the most splendid dinner, just like a dinner
for the Archbishop of Bourges. The little jugs are being
placed inside the big ones, and everything is in its rightful
place in the kitchen: "I want to entertain my nephew well,"
the old man keeps on saying, as he makes inquiries about
everything! It seems that the Rougets were delighted with the
letter. Madame came to tell me that. Oh! She really is dressed
up! She really is! I've never seen anything nicer, ever! She
has two diamond ear-rings, worth 3,000 francs apiece, Védie
told me, and lace, and rings on her fingers, and so many

bracelets you'd almost think they were a shrine, and a beautiful silk gown like an altar frontal! Then she said to me: "Monsieur is very pleased to know that his sister is so good-natured, and I hope she will allow us to entertain her as she deserves. We hope she will have a good opinion of us after the welcome we mean to give her son. . . . Monsieur is most eager to see his nephew." She was wearing little black satin shoes and stockings. Oh! They were marvellous. There were sort of flowers in the silk and little holes; you'd almost have thought it was lace, you could see her pink flesh through them. *And* she's about fifty-one! With such a pretty little apron, which Védie told me cost as much as two years of our wages.'

'Well, I must go and get changed,' the artist said smilingly.

'What are you thinking about, Monsieur Hochon?' asked the old lady when Gritte had left the room.

Madame Hochon drew her goddaughter's attention to her husband who sat deep in thought, with his head in his hand and his elbow leaning against the arm of his armchair.

'You're up against a wily rascal!' said the old man. 'With your outlook on life, young man,' he added, looking at Joseph, 'you're no match for a fellow who's as tough as Maxence. You will commit blunders, whatever advice I give you; but at least let me have a clear account of everything you see, hear and do this evening. Now! We must trust in God! Try to get a little time alone with your uncle. If, despite your intelligence, you can't manage to speak to him privately, we shall already have some insight into their plan. But if you can obtain a moment with him on his own without anybody listening, then you must get him to tell you as much as he will about his position there, which is by no means a happy one, and you must plead your mother's cause with him.'

At four o'clock, Joseph crossed the narrow street separating the Hochons' house from Rouget's, a sort of avenue of sickly-looking lime-trees, 200 feet long and as wide as the Grande Narette. On the nephew's arrival, Kouski – wearing polished boots, black trousers, a white waistcoat and a black coat – walked ahead of him to announce his name. The table was already laid in the dining-room and Joseph, who easily recognized his uncle, went straight up to him and embraced him, and then greeted Flore and Maxence.

'We've never met in all these years since I was born, my dear uncle,' he said gaily; 'but better late than never.'

'You are very welcome, dear boy,' replied the old man, looking at his nephew in a bewildered manner.

'Madame,' Joseph said, addressing Flore with an artist's verve, 'this morning I was envying my uncle the pleasure of admiring you every day.'

'Yes, isn't she beautiful?' the old man said, his dull eyes becoming almost bright.

'Beautiful enough for an artist's model.'

'Nephew,' old Rouget went on, prompted by a nudge from Flore, 'this is Monsieur Maxence Gilet, a man who has served in the Imperial Guards, just like your brother.'

Joseph stood up and bowed.

'Your brother, I believe, was in the dragoons. I was an infantryman,' said Maxence.

'On horseback or on foot,' said Flore, 'you were all risking your lives!'

Joseph was scrutinizing Max as intently as Max scrutinized him. Max was dressed in the way young dandies used to dress at that time: he bought his clothes in Paris. A pair of sky-blue trousers, with large pleats that were very full, set his feet off to advantage by revealing only the tips of his boots, on which he wore spurs. His waist was held in by a white waistcoat with carved gold buttons, which was laced up the back so as to serve as a belt. This waistcoat which buttoned up to the neck, fitted closely to his broad chest whilst his black satin collar forced him to keep his head up in military fashion. He wore a short black coat with a superb cut. An elegant gold chain dangled from his waistcoat pocket, inside which a flat gold watch was just barely visible. He was fingering a 'locust' key, a kind of key which Bréguet had just invented.

'He's a very good-looking fellow,' thought Joseph, admiring with a painter's eye the lively expression, the appearance of bodily strength and the intelligent grey eyes that Max had derived from his aristocratic father. 'My uncle must be very tiresome. This pretty girl has looked for compensations elsewhere, and it's a threesome in this household. That's quite obvious!'

At this moment Baruch and François arrived.

'Have you been to see the Tower of Issoudun yet?' Flore asked Joseph.

'If you feel like going for a little stroll before dinner, which won't be ready for another hour, we could show you this great attraction.'

'I should love to!' replied the artist, unable to see any objections to this proposal.

Whilst Flore went off to put on her hat, gloves and cashmere shawl, Joseph – noticing the pictures – jumped up suddenly as if some wizard had touched him with his wand.

'So! you have got some pictures, uncle?' he said, studying the one that had caught his attention.

'Yes, they came from the Descoings, who bought up the furniture that had been discarded from monasteries and churches in this area at the time of the Revolution.'

Joseph was no longer listening; he was admiring every painting. 'That's magnificent!' he cried. 'Ah, but there's a picture for you! That one doesn't spoil the collection! Ah, each one gets better and better, like at Nicolet's.'

'There are seven or eight very large ones in the attic, which we kept because of the frames,' said Gilet.

'Let's go and see them!' cried the artist whom Maxence took upstairs to the attic.

Joseph came down again full of enthusiasm. Max whispered to Flore, who then took old Rouget into the window-recess. Joseph heard her say in a low voice, but just loud enough to be audible: 'Your nephew is a painter. Those pictures are no use to you. Be nice to him and give him them.'

'I gather you're a painter,' the old man said, leaning on Flore's arm and walking up towards his nephew who was ecstatically admiring an Albani.

'I'm only a fresher at the moment.'

'What's that?' asked Flore.

'A beginner.'

'Well,' said Jean-Jacques, 'if these pictures can be of any use to you in your career, I'll give you them. But I must keep the frames. You see, the frames are gilded, and in any case they're so funny; I'll put . . .'

'Heavens, uncle, you can use them for copies which I'll send you – they'll be the same size,' Joseph said delightedly.

'But that'll take you time and you'll need canvases and colours,' said Flore. 'It will cost you money. Look here, old man, pay your nephew 100 francs per copy – you've got twenty-seven pictures down here. . . . And I think there are eleven in the attic; they are enormous and you must pay double the price for them. . . . Let's say they cost 4,000 francs altogether. . . . Yes, your uncle can certainly pay you 4,000 francs for the copies, as he's keeping the frames! And then you'll need frames, and apparently the frames cost more than the pictures: it'll cost you a fortune! Well, Monsieur?' Flore went on, nudging the old man's arm. 'Well? It's not dear; your nephew will charge you 4,000 francs for brand-new pictures in place of your old ones.' She whispered into his ear: 'It's an acceptable way of giving him 4,000 francs, he doesn't seem up to much to me.'

'Very well, nephew, I will pay you 4,000 francs for the copies.'

'No,' replied the honest artist, '4,000 francs plus the pictures is too much; you see, the pictures are worth something in themselves.'

'Accept his offer, you ninny,' Flore said to him, 'as it's your uncle.'

'All right then, I accept,' replied Joseph, overcome by the bargain he had just made, for he recognized a Perugino.

This explains the joyful expression on the artist's face as he came out of the house offering Flore his arm – all of which fitted admirably into Maxence's plans. Neither Flore, nor Rouget, nor Max, nor anyone in Issoudun could have any idea of the pictures' value, and the wily officer thought that a mere trifle had secured this triumph, as Flore walked proudly along on the arm of her master's nephew, on the best terms with him, and with the whole town looking on in amazement. People came running to their doors to witness her triumph over the family. The exorbitant episode caused a profound sensation, as Max hoped and expected. When the uncle and nephew returned home again about five, there was only one subject of conversation in every household: the fact that old Rouget's nephew, Max and Flore were in perfect harmony. And the story of the gift of the pictures and the 4,000 francs was already going the rounds. The dinner, at which Lousteau, Mayor of Issoudun and one of the judges, was also present, was magnificent. It was one of those provincial dinners that last for five hours. The choicest wines enlivened the conversation. Over dessert, about nine o'clock, the artist, sitting between Flore and Max and opposite his uncle, had got on to almost friendly terms with the officer, whom he thought the finest fellow in the world. He returned home about eleven, the worse for drink. As for old Rouget, Kouski carried him to bed unconscious: he had eaten as much as a travelling actor and drunk like the sands of the desert.

'Well,' said Max, when he and Flore were alone together about midnight, 'isn't that better than behaving sulkily towards them? The Bridaus will be made to feel welcome, they'll be given little presents and loaded with kindness, they can't help singing our praises; and they'll go off quite peacefully, leaving us peacefully to ourselves. Tomorrow morning Kouski and I between us will take out all these canvases and send them over to the artist so that he has them when he wakes up. We'll put the frames in the attic and redecorate the dining-room wall with those glossy wallpapers which have scenes from *Télémaque* painted on them, like I've seen at Monsieur Mouilleron's.'

'Yes, that'll be much prettier,' said Flore.

The following day, Joseph did not wake up until noon. Lying in bed, he could see the canvases stacked one on top of another; they had been brought into the room so silently that he had not heard anything. Whilst he was examining the pictures once again and recognizing masterpieces, studying the painters' various styles and looking for their signatures, his mother had gone across to see her brother and thank him.

She had been prompted to do this by old Monsieur Hochon who, realizing all the stupidities which the artist had committed the previous evening, despaired of the Bridaus' cause.

'You're up against some sly devils. In the whole of my life I've never seen anything to beat that soldier's behaviour: it does seem as if war educates young men. He ran rings round Joseph! Joseph actually went out for a stroll with the Fisher-woman on his arm! No doubt they have shut his mouth for him with wine, some second-rate pictures and 4,000 francs. Your artist hasn't caused Maxence much expense!'

The shrewd old man had outlined the attitudes which his wife's goddaughter should adopt, telling her to fall in with Maxence's ideas and to cajole Flore, so as to reach a sort of intimacy with her and obtain a few minutes' conversation with Jean-Jacques. Madame Bridau was given a marvellous reception by her brother, who had been suitably schooled by Flore. The old man was in bed, ill with the previous evening's excesses. Since Agathe could not immediately plunge into a serious discussion, Max had thought that it would be both fitting and magnanimous to leave the brother and sister alone. His calculation proved to be justified. Poor Agathe thought that her brother looked so ill that she did not wish to deprive him of Madame Brazier's care and attention.

'Besides,' she told the old bachelor, 'I wish to make the acquaintance of someone to whom I am indebted for my brother's happiness.'

These words visibly pleased the old man, who rang for Madame Brazier to come upstairs. As you can imagine, Flore was not far away. The two female adversaries exchanged greetings. Flore displayed most servile and attentive affection. She thought that Monsieur's head was a little too low, shook the pillows up and behaved like a bride of yesterday. Not unnaturally, the old bachelor warmed in his expressions of feeling.

'We owe you, Mademoiselle, much gratitude for the devotion you have shown my brother for so long, and for the way you are so attentive to his welfare,' Agathe said.

'That's true, dear Agathe,' the old man answered. 'Thanks

to her I have known what happiness is, and besides she is a woman with many excellent qualities.'

'And because you cannot reward Mademoiselle enough, you ought to have made her your wife. Yes! I am too devoted to my religion not to hope that you will obey its precepts. You would both enjoy much more peace of mind if you were not at variance with the laws and our moral code. Dear brother, I came to ask you for help in my terrible distress, but please do not think that we wished to make any comment as to how you should leave your fortune.'

'Madame,' said Flore, 'we well know that your father was unjust towards you. Your brother can vouch for it;' (she glared at her victim) 'the only quarrels we have had have been about you. I have argued with him that he owes you the share of his fortune of which you were so unjustly deprived by my poor dear benefactor, for your father was my benefactor' (here, sobs came into her voice). 'I shall never forget him. . . . But your brother has finally listened to reason.'

'Yes,' old Rouget said. 'When I make my will, you will not be forgotten.'

'Let's not talk about all this, my dear brother. You still don't understand my true character.'

From this initial contact, you can easily imagine how Madame Bridau's first visit passed off. Rouget invited his sister to come to dinner the next day but one.

During these three days, the Knights of Idleness caught an immense quantity of rats, mice and field-mice which, one fine night when they were dying with hunger, were let loose in the heaps of grain; altogether, there were 436 of them, including several pregnant animals. Not content with finding Fario these lodgers, the Knights made a hole in the roof of the Capucin church, through which they pushed ten or a dozen pigeons from ten different farms. These animals peacefully regaled themselves, all the more peacefully because Fario's warehouse boy was led astray by a young rascal with whom he went drinking from morning to night, without paying any attention to his master's grain.

Madame Bridau believed, contrary to old Hochon's opinion,

that her brother had not yet made his will; she was intending to ask him what were his intentions with respect to Mademoiselle Brazier, the first time she happened to be alone with him, for Flore and Maxence were always deluding her with this hope, which was invariably disappointed in the end.

Although the Knights all racked their brains for some way of putting the two Parisians to flight, they could only think up impossible absurdities.

18. A stab in the chest

AFTER a week – half the period of time Agathe and Joseph were supposed to be staying at Issoudun – they were, therefore, no further forward than on the first day.

'Your attorney doesn't understand the provinces,' old Hochon told Madame Bridau. 'What you are coming to do here can't be done in a fortnight or even fourteen months; you ought never to leave your brother alone, and you must fill his head with religious ideas. The only way you will countermine Flore's and Maxence's fortifications is by involving a priest in this business. That's what I think, and it's time you set about things.'

'You have got strange ideas about the clergy,' Madame Hochon remarked to her husband.

'Oh, you're all the same, you old religious fanatics!' cried the old man.

'God would never bless an enterprise founded on sacrilege,' said Madame Bridau. 'To harness religion to such. . . . Oh, but we would be even more criminal than Flore!'

This conversation took place over breakfast and both François and Baruch were listening with ears wide open.

'Sacrilege!' was old Hochon's reply. 'But if some good priest, as holy as some of the priests I've known, knew the difficulties you are in, he would not think it sacrilege to bring back to God's mercy your brother's erring soul, fill him with a true feeling of repentance for all his faults and get him to dismiss the woman who is causing the scandal, besides assuring him of an eternal destiny; explaining to him that his conscience would be at rest if he gave a few thousand francs a year to the Archbishop's little seminary, bequeathing his fortune to his natural heirs.'

Such was the passive obedience which the old miser had obtained within his household from his own children, and subsequently transmitted to his grandchildren who were in any case under his guardianship and for whom he was amassing a handsome fortune, only doing (as he put it) the same for them as he did for himself, that Baruch and François did not express the slightest astonishment or disapproval at these words; but they exchanged meaningful glances, conveying how harmful and fatal to Max's interests they thought this idea would be.

'The fact is, Madame,' said Baruch, 'that if you wish to have your brother's inheritance, that is the only proper way of obtaining it; you must remain at Issoudun long enough to carry out this plan.'

'Mother,' Joseph said, 'you would do well to write to Desroches about all this. I myself do not expect anything further from my uncle, after what he has already been kind enough to give me.'

After realizing how very valuable the thirty-nine pictures were, Joseph had carefully removed the nails from them, laid paper across them (sticking it to the canvases with ordinary glue), placed the pictures one on top of another and crammed this bulky consignment into an immense box, which he had sent (by carrier) to Desroches, whom he would notify in advance. The precious cargo had been despatched the previous day.

'It doesn't take much to make you happy,' Monsieur Hochon told him.

'But it wouldn't be difficult to get 150,000 francs for the pictures.'

'So you painters think!' snorted Monsieur Hochon, looking at Joseph in a peculiar way.

'Listen,' Joseph replied, addressing his mother, 'I'm going to write to Desroches, explaining the state of affairs here. If Desroches advises you to stay, you'll stay. As far as your job is concerned, we can always find a similar one later.'

'My dear boy,' said Madame Hochon to Joseph, as she left the table, 'I don't know what your uncle's pictures are, but they must be good ones, judging from where they came from. If they were only worth 40,000 francs, that's 1,000 francs apiece, don't breathe a word of it to anybody. Though my grandsons are discreet and well mannered, they might well gossip about this so-called find, without meaning any harm. Then the whole of Issoudun would know about it, and we mustn't let our opponents suspect it. You go about things like a child!'

And indeed, by midday many people in Issoudun, and most important of all Maxence Gilet, had been informed of Joseph's opinion, which resulted in people unearthing old pictures they had forgotten about and displaying hideous daubs in prominent positions. Max regretted that he had urged the old man to give away the pictures, and his anger against the family, on hearing of old Hochon's plan of action, was all the greater because of what he called Jean-Jacques's idiocy. The only thing he had to fear was the influence religion could exert upon a weak-minded individual. This information from his two friends had the effect of confirming Maxence Gilet's decision to capitalize all Rouget's contracts, and borrow money on his landed property so as to invest in Government funds as quickly as possible; but it was even more urgent to send the Parisians packing. However, even the genius of Mascarille and Scapin would not have found it easy to solve this problem. On Max's advice, Flore put it about that Monsieur was now finding walking too much of an effort: at his age he needed to go by carriage. This pretext was necessitated by the fact that Rouget, Flore and Max would need to go to Bourges, Vierzon, Châteauroux and Vatan to realize the old man's investments, without anyone in the district being any the wiser. At the end of the same week, the whole of Issoudun was astonished to learn that old Rouget had been over to Bourges to buy a carriage – an action which was defended by the Knights of Idleness in terms very favourable to Mademoiselle Brazier. Flore and Rouget bought a horrible four-wheeled covered carriage with darkened windows and cracked leather curtains. It was twenty-two years old, with nine military campaigns to its credit, and came from the sale that had taken place following the death of a colonel who was friendly with Grand-Marshal Bertrand, and who, during the absence of the Emperor's faithful companion, had undertaken to look after Bertrand's estates in Berry. This carriage, painted a glaring green, looked rather like a landau, but the shaft had been modified so that only one horse need be harnessed to it. It belonged, therefore, to that category of carriages which the diminution of fortunes has made so very popular, and which at that time were candidly known as 'demi-fortunes', for their original name had been *seringues*. The upholstery of this 'demi-fortune', termed a landau at the auction sale, was worm-eaten; its braiding resembled a disabled soldier's chevrons; it rattled like a heap of scrap metal; but it only cost 450 francs. And Max bought from the regiment then garrisoned at Bourges a good strapping mare which they no longer required and which could be used to pull the carriage. He had it repainted dark brown, picked up quite a good set of harness second-hand, and the whole of Issoudun was agog with excitement, as it waited expectantly to see old Rouget's horse and carriage! The first time the old man went out in his carriage, it made so much noise that everyone came running to their doors, and there was not one window which did not have its inquisitive on-lookers. The second time, the old bachelor drove as far as Bourges, where, to save himself the tiresome details of the operation advised or, if you prefer, ordered by Flore Brazier, he conferred powers of attorney on Maxence Gilet at a lawyer's office, with the purpose of making over to him all the contracts named in the proxy. All Flore did was to assist Monsieur Rouget, in converting into ready money his invest-ments in Issoudun and the surrounding districts. The leading solicitor at Bourges received a visit from Rouget, who asked him to obtain a mortgage of 140,000 francs on his landed properties. No one in Issoudun knew anything about these proceedings, so discreetly and intelligently were they carried out. Maxence, who was a good horseman, could easily ride over to Bourges and back between five in the morning and five in the evening, and Flore no longer let the old man out of her sight. Old Rouget had not objected to the operation which Flore had imposed upon him; but he insisted that Mademoiselle Brazier should only be given a life interest in the scrip for 50,000 francs a year investment income and that the ownership without usufruct should be in his name. The obstinacy displayed by the old man in this domestic struggle caused Max much anxiety; he already suspected that the sight of the family had inspired Rouget with ulterior motives.

Amidst these great developments, which Max wished to conceal from the townsfolk, he completely forgot about the corn merchant. Fario set about delivering his corn, after various manoeuvres and journeys whose object was to push up the price of cereals. The day after his return to Issoudun, he noticed that the roof of the Capucin church was black with the dense gathering of pigeons, for he lived opposite. He cursed himself for not having had the roof attended to, and immediately rushed over to his warehouse, where he found that half his grain had been devoured. Thousands of mouse and rat droppings, scattered about everywhere, revealed a contributory cause of the ruin. The church was a Noah's ark. But in his fury the Spaniard went as white as a sheet when, on trying to discover the extent of his losses and the damage, he observed that all the corn below was almost sprouting, owing to a number of water-pots which Max had thought of inserting into the heap of corn by means of a tin tube. The pigeons and rats were acting out of purely animal instinct; but the hand of man was visible in this last stroke of perversity. Fario sat down on the altar steps of one of the side chapels, and buried his face in his hands. After a full half-hour of Spanish meditation, he noticed the squirrel which young Goddet had been so eager to give him as a lodger, playing with its tail on one of the cross beams on the middle of which the roof-tree rested. The Spaniard rose coldly, his calm face seeming to his warehouse boy to all the world like an Arab's; Fario did not complain; he returned to his house; he went off to hire a few workmen to put the good corn into sacks and spread the wet corn to dry in the sun, so as to preserve as much of it as possible; then he busied himself with his deliveries after assessing his losses at three-fifths of the whole. But his manoeuvres during the last few days had caused a rise in the price of grain, and he lost even more money by having to buy in the three-fifths of his stock that were missing; consequently, his losses were much more than half the whole. The Spaniard had no enemies; he rightly attributed this act of revenge to Gilet. People proved to him that Max and a few others were the sole originators of the nightly farces and that they had quite definitely hoisted his cart on top of the Tower, and taken such delight in ruining him! In fact, the loss was 3,000 francs, almost all the capital which Fario had laboriously amassed since peace had been concluded. Eager for revenge, he showed all the persistence and cunning of a spy who has been promised a large reward. By lying in hiding at nights in Issoudun, he eventually obtained proof of the Knights' dissolute excesses; he saw the young men, counted them, spied their meeting-places and their banquets at La Cognette's; then he hid himself to witness one of their pranks, and became thoroughly acquainted with their goings-on during the night.

Despite all his errands and preoccupations, Maxence did not wish to neglect these nightly amusements, first of all so as not to let the secret leak out of the big operation that was being carried out with regard to old Rouget's fortune and, secondly, so as always to keep his friends in training. The Knights had agreed to play one of the pranks they had been talking about for years. In a single night, they were going to distribute poisoned pellets to all the watchdogs in the town and suburbs. Fario heard them coming out of La Cognette's tavern, congratulating themselves in advance on the success which this prank would obtain, and the general dismay that would be caused by this latter-day Massacre of the Innocents. Besides, what apprehension it would give rise to, implying sinister designs on the homes of the poor animals' masters!

'Perhaps it will make everybody forget about Fario's cart!' said young Goddet.

Fario no longer needed to hear these words to confirm his own suspicions; and in any case, his mind was made up.

After staying three weeks in Issoudun, Agathe acknowledged – as did Madame Hochon – that the old miser had been right in his opinion; it would take several years to destroy the influence which Flore and Max had acquired over her brother. Agathe had made no progress in securing Jean-Jacques's confidence and had never been able to obtain any conversation alone with him. On the contrary, Mademoiselle Brazier was triumphantly outmanoeuvring the heirs by taking Agathe with her for drives in the carriage, with Agathe sitting beside her and Monsieur Rouget and his nephew up above. Mother and son were impatiently expecting a reply to the confidential letter they had sent Desroches. The day before the one when the dogs were to be poisoned, Joseph, who was bored stiff in Issoudun, received two letters. The first was from the great painter Schinner, whose age allowed of a closer and more intimate friendship than was possible with Gros, their master. The second letter came from Desroches.

Here is the text of the first, postmarked Beaumont-sur-Oise:

My Dear Joseph,

I have finished the main paintings in the Château de Presles for the Comte de Sérizy. I have left the frames and the paintings of ornaments; and I have spoken so well of you, both to the Comte and Grindot, the architect, that you have only to pack up your brushes and come down. You will be very satisfied with the pay. I am off to Italy with my wife, so you can take Mistigris to help you. This young monkey is very talented, I have put him at your disposal. He is already fidgeting like a clown, at the thought of all the fun he will have at the Château de Presles. Good-bye, my dear Joseph; if I am away and don't exhibit anything at the next Salon, you will take my place! Yes, dear Jo, I am convinced your picture is a masterpiece; but it's a masterpiece which will get the word 'Romanticism' slung at it, and you're going to have a very awkward and unpleasant time of it! But after all, as our joker Mistigris says, the fellow who's always playing around with all our proverbs and turning them all into puns, life *isn't all cheer and victuals.* How are you getting on at Issoudun? Farewell,

Your friend,
SCHINNER

And here is Desroches's letter:

My Dear Joseph,

This Monsieur Hochon seems to me a very wise old man, and you've given me the highest idea of his capacities: he is completely right. And so my advice (since you ask me for it) is that your mother should stay on at Issoudun with Madame Hochon, paying them a modest sum of money (say, 400 francs a year) to compensate her hosts for the cost of her board. In my view, Madame Bridau should comply fully with Monsieur Hochon's advice. But your excellent mother will have many qualms of conscience, and she is up against people who have no scruples at all and whose conduct is a political masterpiece. Maxence is dangerous, and you are quite right: I think he is just as able a man as Philippe, in a different way. This rascal uses his very vices to further his fortune, and never indulges in any amusement that won't assist his own ends, whereas your brother's follies were actually to his detriment. Everything you tell me appals me, for I wouldn't be able to do very much if I came down to Issoudun. If Monsieur Hochon assists your mother behind the scenes, he will be more useful to you than I could be. You may as well come back again, you are no use at all in a business which demands constant attention, minute observation, slave-like dedication, and discretion in words and a deceitfulness in actions that are quite repugnant to an artist's character. Even though you've been told that there's no will yet, believe me, one was drawn up a very long time ago. But wills can be revoked, and so long as your stupid uncle is alive, he is certainly capable of being worked on by remorse and religion. Your fortune will be gained after a struggle between Flore Brazier and the Church. A time will undoubtedly come when this woman will be powerless to influence the old man, and then religion will be all-powerful. So long as your uncle hasn't made any gifts *inter vivos*, nor changed the nature of his property, all will be possible at such time as religion gains the upper hand. You must therefore ask Monsieur Hochon to keep as close an eye as he can on your uncle's fortune. We must find out whether his landed property is mortgaged, and where he has invested his money and in whose name. It is so easy a matter to fill an old man with fears concerning his own safety, once he parts with his property and gives it to strangers, that with only the very slightest amount of cunning an heir can nip in the bud any attempt to expropriate an inheritance. But is your mother, with her ignorance of the world, her disinterestedness and her religious ideas, able to manage such an operation? Anyway, all I can do is point these things out to you. Everything you have done up to now must have caused them alarm, and perhaps your opponents will now toe the line!

'That's what I call advice,' cried Monsieur Hochon, proud of being appreciated by a Parisian attorney.

'Oh! Desroches is a splendid fellow,' Joseph replied.

'It would not be without value to have our two ladies read this letter,' the old miser went on.

'Here it is,' said the artist, handing the letter over to the old man. 'I myself shall be leaving tomorrow, and so I'll go and say good bye to my uncle.'

'Ah!' said Monsieur Hochon. 'Monsieur Desroches asks you in a postscript to burn the letter.'

'Burn it after showing it to my mother,' replied the artist.

Joseph Bridau dressed, crossed the little square and called at his uncle's house. Rouget was just finishing breakfast, and Max and Flore were sitting at the table.

'Don't bother to get up, uncle. I am coming to bid you good bye.'

'So you are leaving us?' asked Max, exchanging glances with Flore.

'Yes, I have some work to do at Monsieur de Sérizy's country house. I'm very eager to go down there, especially as he's influential enough to help my poor brother when his case comes up before the Court of Peers.'

'Oh well! Work hard,' the old man said in a stupid sort of way. Joseph thought Rouget looked awfully changed. 'Yes, you must work hard . . . I'm sorry you are going.'

'Oh! But my mother is staying on for a little while,' Joseph continued.

Flore noticed Max's lips twitch, as if to say: 'They're following the plan of action Baruch has told me about.'

'I am very happy to have been down here,' said Joseph, 'for I have had the pleasure of making your acquaintance, and you have enriched my studio.'

'Yes,' said Flore, 'instead of enlightening your uncle as to the value of his pictures, which are said to be worth over 100,000 francs you have very smartly sent them off to Paris. . . . This dear old man is just like a child! Somebody has just been telling me that at Bourges Cathedral there was a little Pussy. . . . No! What's his name? Poussin, that used to hang in the choir until the Revolution, and it's worth 30,000 francs all by itself.'

'That's not a very nice thing to have done, nephew,' the old man said, prompted by a sign from Max which Joseph was unable to see.

'Yes, frankly, on your word of honour, what do you think the pictures are worth?' the soldier laughed. 'Good Lord! You've certainly diddled your uncle, but you are only within your rights: that's what an uncle is there for, to be diddled! Nature refused to endow me with any uncles; otherwise, damn it, if I had had any, I wouldn't have shown them any mercy.'

'Did you know, Monsieur, Flore asked Rouget, 'how much *your* pictures were worth? How much did you say, Monsieur Joseph?'

'Well,' replied the artist, blushing as red as a beetroot, 'the pictures are worth something.'

'I have heard that you told Monsieur Hochon they were worth 150,000 francs,' Flore said. 'Is that so?'

'Yes,' replied the artist, who was as honest as a child.

'And did you intend to give your nephew 150,000 francs?' she asked the old man.

'Never! Never!' replied Rouget, after Flore had glared at him.

'Well, there's one way of sorting this out, and that's to give you them back, uncle!'

'No, no, you must keep them,' the old man replied.

'I will send them back to you, uncle,' said Joseph, wounded by Maxence Gilet's and Flore Brazier's offensive silence. 'My own brushes will earn me a fortune, without having to depend on anyone, not even my uncle. . . . Good bye, Mademoiselle. Good bye, Monsieur.'

And Joseph walked back across the square in a state of irritation which all artists will imagine. The whole Hochon family were sitting in the drawing-room. When they saw Joseph gesticulating and talking to himself, they asked him what was the matter. The artist was as open as it was possible for anyone to be. In the presence of Baruch and François, he related the scene he had just experienced. Within two hours it had become the talk of the whole town, enlivened each time it was told with more or less comic details. Some people maintained that the artist had been given a rough handling by Max, others that he had behaved badly towards Mademoiselle Brazier and Max had shown him the door.

'What a child your son is!' Hochon told Madame Bridau. 'The simpleton has been duped by a scene they were keeping in store for him for the day when he came to say good bye. Max and Flore knew the value of the pictures a fortnight ago, when he was stupid enough to mention it here in front of my grandsons, who had nothing better to do than broadcast it to all and sundry. Your artist should have left the town without giving any warning.'

'My son is quite right to return the pictures, if they are so valuable,' Agathe remarked.

'If, as he thinks, they *are* worth 200,000 francs, it's absolute stupidity to have put oneself into a position where they have to be handed back,' old Hochon retorted. 'At least you would have obtained that much money out of the estate, whereas the way things are going at the moment, you'll get nothing! And now this business has almost provided your brother with a reason for not seeing you again!'

Between midnight and one in the morning, the Knights of Idleness began their free distribution of food to all the dogs in town. This memorable expedition was not accomplished until three in the morning, when the young rascals went off for supper at La Cognette's. At half past four, as dawn was breaking, they returned to their homes. Just as Max was turning the corner of the Rue de l'Avenier into the Grand'rue, Fario, lying in wait in a doorway, stabbed him right in the chest, withdrew the knife blade and escaped across the ditches to Vilatte, where he wiped his knife on his handkerchief. The Spaniard went off to wash his handkerchief in the Rivière Forcée and walked peacefully back to Saint-Paterne, where he went back to bed after scaling up to a window which he had left ajar. His new warehouse boy found him fast asleep when he came to waken him.

19. *A criminal matter*

As he fell, Max uttered a terrible cry, which no one could mistake. Accompanied by young Goddet, who lived at the lower end of the Grand'rue, Lousteau-Prangin, a judge's son who was distantly related to the former Subdelegate's family, came running up crying: 'Max has been killed! Help!' But not one dog barked in the town, and no one got out of bed – everybody was so used to the pranks that went on at night. By the time the two Knights reached him, Max had fainted. They had to wake old Monsieur Goddet. Max had clearly recognized Fario; but when he came round at five in the morning, and found himself surrounded by a number of people, he sensed that his wound was not fatal and suddenly thought of turning this attempted assassination to his own advantage by crying out in a doleful voice: 'I do believe I saw the eyes and face of that damned painter!'

Thereupon, Lousteau-Prangin ran to his father, the examining magistrate. Max was carried home by Cognet, young Goddet and two other men who were roused from their beds. La Cognette and old Goddet stood beside Max as he lay on a mattress supported by two pieces of wood. Monsieur Goddet did not wish to do anything until Max was in bed. The people who were carrying the wounded man home naturally looked across towards Monsieur Hochon's house whilst waiting for Kouski to get up; they saw Monsieur Hochon's maid sweeping the doorstep. At Monsieur Hochon's, as in most houses in the provinces, the front door used to be opened very early. Max's one remark had aroused everybody's suspicions, and old Monsieur Goddet shouted:

'Gritte, is Monsieur Joseph Bridau in bed?'

'Ah!' she replied, 'he went out about half past four. He was pacing up and down his bedroom all night. I don't know what was the matter with him.'

This artless reply caused murmurs of horror and exclamations which made the old girl come running over, quite eager to know what was being carried into Rouget's house.

'Well! He's a fine one, your painter!' everybody told her.

And the procession passed by, leaving the maid speechless: she had seen Max lying stretched out on the mattress with his shirt covered in blood – a dying man.

The reason for Joseph's agitation throughout the night will easily be guessed by artists: he was the talk of all the townsfolk of Issoudun, people thought of him as an unscrupulous robber, as something quite different from what he always wanted to be, an honest fellow, a hard-working artist! He would even have given his painting away to have been able to fly like the wind to Paris and hurl his uncle's pictures in Max's face. To be thought of as the plunderer, when in fact it was he who was being plundered! What an absurd state of affairs! This prompted him at daybreak to go pacing up and down the avenue of poplar trees that leads to Tivoli; it was an outlet for his agitation. Whilst the innocent young man was consoling himself with the vow that he would never set foot in that part of the world again, Max was dealing him a blow that was so horribly unbearable for any sensitive soul. When old Monsieur Goddet had felt the wound and made sure that the knife, which had been diverted from its path by a small wallet, had fortunately missed the heart, though it had still caused a terrible wound, he did what all doctors do, especially provincial surgeons: puffing himself up with self-importance, he said that he still could not be sure that Max would pull through; and then left the house after dressing the malicious soldier's injury. The pronouncements of medical opinion were communicated by old Goddet to Flore, Jean-Jacques Rouget, Kouski and Védie. Flore returned to dear Max's bedside, overcome with tears, whilst Kouski and Védie informed the people who had gathered outside the door that the major's condition was virtually hopeless. This news resulted in about two hundred people gathering in the Place Saint-Jean and the two Rues Narette.

'I shan't be more than a month in bed and I know who did

it,' Max told his mistress. 'But we'll turn this to our advantage, and get rid of the Parisians. I've already said I thought I recognized the painter; so pretend I'm going to die, and try to get Joseph Bridau arrested. We'll have him thrown into prison for a couple of days. I think I know the mother well enough to predict that she'll leave for Paris on the spot, taking her painter with her. Then we shan't have any more reason to fear the priests they were intending to set loose on our old imbecile.'

When Flore Brazier came downstairs, she found that the crowd were very ready to believe the assumptions she wished them to believe; with tears in her eyes, she appeared on the doorstep, remarking between her sobs that the artist who looked as if he was that sort of man in any case, had become involved in a heated argument with Max the previous day apropos of the pictures he had 'stolen' from old Rouget.

'This rascal – you only have to look at him to see he's that – imagined that if Max was no longer alive his uncle would leave him his fortune; as if', she added, 'a brother isn't a closer relation than a nephew! Max is old Dr Rouget's son. The old man told me so afore he died!'

'Ah! No doubt he wanted to fire this parting shot. He's got things organized very nicely. He's leaving today,' said one of the Knights of Idleness.

'Max hasn't a single enemy in Issoudun,' someone else said.

'In any case, Max recognized the painter,' said Flore.

'Where is that damned Parisian? Let's find him!' they cried.

'Find him? But he went out of Monsieur Hochon's house at daybreak,' others answered.

One of the Knights of Idleness immediately ran to Monsieur Mouilleron's. The crowd was still gathering, and the sound of people's voices grew threatening.

Excited groups of people could be seen all over the Grande-Narette. Others were standing outside the Église Saint-Jean. A throng of people had gathered by the Porte Villate, at its junction with the Petite-Narette. It was impossible to cross the Place Saint-Jean either at its upper or lower end. You would have thought it was the tail end of a religious procession.

Monsieur Lousteau-Prangin, Monsieur Mouilleron, the Superintendent of Police, the lieutenant commanding the gendarmerie and his brigadier accompanied by two gendarmes had some difficulty in making their way to the Place Saint-Jean, which they reached by walking between two rows of people whose shouts and cries could and did prejudice them against the Parisian whom they so unjustly accused, but against whom the circumstantial evidence seemed overwhelming.

After a conference between Max and the magistrates, Monsieur Mouilleron instructed the police superintendent and the brigadier, together with one gendarme, to inspect what in the language of the Public Prosecutor is known as the scene of the crime. Then, Monsieur Mouilleron and Monsieur Lousteau-Prangin, accompanied by the lieutenant of the gendarmerie, crossed over from old Rouget's house to Monsieur Hochon's, which was guarded by two gendarmes at the bottom end of the garden and by two others at the front door. The crowd was still growing. In the Grand'rue, the whole town was in a state of commotion.

Gritte had already rushed upstairs scared out of her wits and crying to her master: 'Monsieur, we're going to be robbed! The whole town is in a revolution. Monsieur Maxence Gilet has been assassinated; he's going to die! And people say it's Monsieur Joseph that did it!'

Monsieur Hochon dressed quickly and came downstairs; but, confronted by a furious mass of people, he quickly went indoors again, bolting his door. After questioning Gritte, he discovered that his guest had left the house at daybreak, after pacing up and down in his bedroom all night in great agitation; and he had not come back. Frightened by this news, he went into Madame Hochon's room and found that she had just been awakened by the noise. He informed her of the terrible rumour which, whether it was true or false, was driving the whole of Issoudun into a frenzy outside in the Place Saint-Jean.

'There can be no question of his innocence!' cried Madame Hochon.

'But, before his innocence has been established, they may

break into this house and rob us,' said Monsieur Hochon, suddenly going pale (he had some gold in his cellar).

'And what about Agathe?'

'She's sleeping like a log!'

'Ah! It's just as well,' Madame Hochon said. 'I wish she would stay asleep the whole time this affair is being sorted out. A blow like this is enough to kill the poor dear woman!'

But Agathe did wake up, and came downstairs only half dressed: for Gritte's hesitation when she had tried to question her had completely disorientated her. She found Madame Hochon pale, her eyes brimming with tears, standing beside her husband by one of the living-room windows.

'Be brave, my dear little girl, God sends us these tribulations,' the old woman said. 'Joseph is being accused!'

'What of?'

'Of a bad action he cannot have committed,' Madame Hochon replied.

Hearing these words, and seeing Monsieur Mouilleron, Monsieur Lousteau-Prangin and the lieutenant of the gendarmerie walk into the room, Agathe fainted.

'Look here,' Monsieur Hochon said to his wife and Gritte, 'take Madame Bridau away, women can only be an encumbrance in such circumstances. Both of you take her into your bedroom. Please be seated, gentlemen,' continued the old man. 'The misunderstanding which has led to your visit will, I hope, soon be cleared up.'

'Even if there is a misunderstanding,' Monsieur Mouilleron replied, 'the crowd are so exasperated, and their tempers are so high, that I fear for the accused's safety. . . . I would like to keep him at the court and satisfy people's minds.'

'Who would have thought Monsieur Maxence Gilet would have inspired such affection?' said Lousteau-Prangin.

'At this very moment twelve hundred people are pouring in from the Faubourg de Rome: one of my men has just come to tell me,' the lieutenant of the gendarmerie observed, 'and they are crying out for his death.'

'Where is your guest?' Monsieur Mouilleron asked Monsieur Hochon.

'He has gone out for a walk into the country, I think.'

'Call Gritte,' the examining magistrate said, with a serious expression on his face. 'I was hoping that Monsieur Bridau had not left the house. You are not unaware of the fact that the crime was committed a few yards from here, at daybreak?'

Whilst Monsieur Hochon went off to find Gritte, the three officials exchanged meaningful glances.

'I never did like the painter's face,' the lieutenant said to Monsieur Mouilleron.

'Now, my dear,' the magistrate asked Gritte, on seeing her come into the room, 'apparently you saw Monsieur Joseph Bridau leave the house this morning?'

'Yes, sir,' she replied, trembling like a leaf.

'At what time?'

'As soon as I got up; for he was pacing up and down his bedroom all night, and he was dressed when I came downstairs.'

'Was it light?'

'Daybreak.'

'Did he look agitated?'

'I should say so! He looked all out of sorts to me.'

'Ask one of your men to go and get me my clerk of the court,' Lousteau-Prangin told the lieutenant, 'and tell him to bring warrants to . . .'

'Good heavens! Don't be in such a hurry!' said Monsieur Hochon. 'There could be other reasons for this young man's excitement besides premeditated crime: he's leaving for Paris today, after an episode in which Gilet and Mademoiselle Flore Brazier doubted his integrity.'

'Oh yes! That business with the pictures,' Monsieur Mouilleron said. 'Yesterday that was the cause of a violent quarrel, and artists are said to be very hot-headed.'

'Who in the whole of Issoudun had any reason to kill Maxence?' Lousteau asked. 'Nobody, no jealous husband, absolutely nobody. This young fellow has never done anybody any harm.'

'But what was Monsieur Gilet doing in the streets of Issoudun at half past four in the morning?' Monsieur Hochon retorted.

'Look here, Monsieur Hochon, let us get on with our own job,' Mouilleron replied; 'you don't know everything; Max recognized your painter.'

At this very moment, a hubbub of voices was heard at one end of the town; the noise grew louder, like a thunder-clap, as it moved along the Grande-Narette.

'There he is! There he is! He has been arrested!'

These words could clearly be heard against the low-pitched baritone sound of terrifying public uproar. And indeed, on reaching the Place Misère poor Joseph Bridau, who was peacefully walking past the Landrôle mill to be home in time for breakfast, was sighted by every group simultaneously. Fortunately for him, two gendarmes came running up to snatch him away from the inhabitants of the Faubourg de Rome, who had already seized him unceremoniously by the arms, shouting that he ought to be put to death.

'Make way! Make way!' the gendarmes cried, shouting to two of their companions so that one could stand in front of, and the other behind, Bridau.

'Look, Monsieur,' one of those who were holding Joseph said to him, 'our lives are at stake at the moment, just as much as yours. Whether you're innocent or guilty, we must protect you against the riot which Major Gilet's assassination has caused; not content with accusing you of the crime, this rabble actually believes you are the murderer, a man as hard as iron. Monsieur Gilet is worshipped by these people, who seem to want to take justice into their own hands – just look at them! Ah! We saw them in 1830, belabouring the officials of the taxation office, and it was no fun for them, I can assure you!'

Joseph Bridau went as pale as a dying man and had to gather all his strength together to walk at all.

'Well, after all,' he said, 'I'm innocent, so let's walk on!'

He had his cross to bear, this poor artist! He had jeers, insults and death threats thrown at him, as he walked the horrible distance from the Place Misère to the Place Saint-Jean. The gendarmes had to draw their sabres against the

248

infuriated crowd, who threw stones at them. The gendarmes were nearly wounded, and a few missiles struck Joseph's legs, shoulders and hat.

'Here we are!' one of the gendarmes said, entering Monsieur Hochon's drawing-room, 'and it hasn't been too easy, lieutenant.'

'Now, we have to break up the crowd outside, and I see only one way of doing this, gentlemen,' the officer told the magistrates. 'This would be to take Monsieur Bridau to the Law Court, making him walk amongst yourselves; I and all my gendarmes will surround you. You can't be sure of anything when you're up against six thousand madmen.'

'You are right,' Monsieur Hochon said, still trembling for his gold.

'If that is the best way of protecting innocence in Issoudun,' replied Joseph, 'then I must compliment you on it. I have nearly been stoned already.'

'Do you want your host's house to be taken by siege and plundered?' asked the lieutenant. 'Could we, with our sabres, withstand a huge influx of people urged on from behind by a group of impassioned folk who don't understand legal procedures?'

'Well, shall we go now, gentlemen? We can have all this out later,' said Joseph, recovering his usual calm.

'Make way, my friends!' cried the lieutenant. '*He* has been arrested, we're taking him to the Law Court!'

'Have respect for justice, my friends!' said Monsieur Mouilleron.

'Wouldn't you prefer to see him guillotined?' one of the gendarmes asked a threatening group of people.

'Yes, yes!' shouted a man wild with rage. 'We'll guillotine him.'

'He's going to be guillotined,' women echoed.

At the lower end of the Grande-Narette, people were saying: 'They're taking him off to guillotine him; they found the knife on him! . . . Oh! The scoundrel! . . . There's Parisians for you. . . . That fellow had the look of a criminal, you only had to see his face.'

Although Joseph's head was spinning, he walked over to the Law Court from the Place Saint-Jean, maintaining remarkable calm and aplomb. Even so, he was quite relieved to reach Monsieur Lousteau-Prangin's office.

'I don't think I need tell you, gentlemen, that I'm innocent,' he said, addressing Monsieur Mouilleron, Monsieur Lousteau-Prangin and the clerk of the court. 'All I can do is beg you to help me prove my innocence. I don't know anything about this affair.'

When the judge had explained to Joseph all the circumstantial evidence against him, ending up with Max's own evidence, Joseph was utterly dismayed.

'But I left the house after five o'clock; I walked along the High Street, and at half past five I was looking at the façade of your parish church of Saint-Cyr. I had a talk with the bell ringer there, who was coming to ring the angelus, and I asked him for some information about the building, which has a strange, unfinished look about it. Then I walked across the vegetable market, where some women had already gathered. From there, I went to the Place Misère, and the Pont aux Anes, as far as Landrôle mill, where I stood peacefully watching some ducks for five or six minutes, and the mill-hands must have seen me. I saw some women going to the washing-board by the river, they must still be there. They started to laugh at me, saying that I wasn't much to look at; I replied that ugly faces conceal hidden treasures. From there I walked along the big avenue as far as Tivoli, where I had a chat with the gardener. . . . Have these facts checked, and don't even arrest me, for I give you my word of honour that I shall remain in your office until such time as you are convinced of my innocence.'

These sensible remarks, made without the slightest hesitation and with the assurance of a man who knew what he was talking about, made a considerable impression upon the magistrates.

'Very well then, we must subpoena all those people. We shall have to find them,' Monsieur Mouilleron said, 'but it will take time. So in your own interests, resign yourself to staying secretly at the Law Court.'

'Providing I can send a note to my mother, to put her mind at rest, the poor woman. . . . Oh! You can read the letter.'

This request was too fair not to be granted, and Joseph wrote the following note:

Dear Mother,

Please don't be anxious about me. This misunderstanding which has befallen me will easily be cleared up: I have given them information enabling them to do this. Tomorrow, or perhaps even this evening, I shall be released. With fondest love, and tell Monsieur and Madame Hochon how distressed I am by this bother for which I am in no way responsible. It is the result of some coincidence which I don't yet understand.

When the letter arrived, Madame Bridau was prostrated by an attack of nerves and the potions which Monsieur Goddet was trying to get her to drink were without effect. Reading this letter poured balm into her heart. After a few paroxysms, Agathe fell into the state of dejection which follows crises of this kind. When Monsieur Goddet came back to see his patient, he found her regretting that she had ever left Paris.

'God has punished me,' she said, with tears in her eyes. 'Oughtn't I to have trusted in Him, dear godmother, and relied on His goodness in the matter of my brother's inheritance?'

'Madame, if your son is innocent, Maxence is a most dastardly rascal,' Monsieur Hochon whispered into her ear, 'and we shan't get the better of him in this business; so you had better return to Paris.'

'Well,' Madame Hochon asked Monsieur Goddet, 'how is Monsieur Gilet?'

'Although his wound is serious, he hasn't been fatally injured. A month's treatment and convalescence will put him right. I left him writing to Monsieur Mouilleron asking for your son's release, Madame,' he told his patient. 'Oh! Max is a splendid fellow. I told him the condition you were in, and then he remembered a detail about the assassin's clothing which proved that it couldn't have been your son. The murderer was wearing list slippers, and it has definitely been established that your son was wearing boots when he went out.'

'Oh! May God forgive him the harm he has done me.'

During the night a man had brought Gilet a letter written in block letters, which read as follows:

Captain Gilet should not allow an innocent man to remain in the custody of the law. The man who did the deed promises never to repeat it, if Monsieur Gilet releases Monsieur Joseph Bridau without naming the guilty man.

After reading and burning this letter, Max wrote to Monsieur Mouilleron informing him of the circumstances mentioned by Monsieur Goddet and begging him to release Joseph and call on him so that he could explain the whole business.

Just as this letter reached Monsieur Mouilleron, Lousteau-Prangin had already been able to establish – from evidence provided by the bell-ringer, a woman selling vegetables, some laundrywomen, some mill-hands at Landrôle mill and the gardener at Frapesle – that Joseph's account of his whereabouts that morning had been truthful: Max's letter set the seal on the accused's innocence, and Monsieur Mouilleron then took Joseph back personally to Monsieur Hochon's house. The poor young man whom people had so misunderstood was greeted by his mother with such a warm and effusive affection that, like the husband who thanks the thief in La Fontaine's fable, he gave thanks to fate for a vexation that had prompted such evidence of love.

'Yes,' said Monsieur Mouilleron competently, 'from the way you looked at the infuriated crowd, I immediately saw that you were innocent; but in spite of this, do you see, knowing Issoudun as I do, I realized that the best way of protecting you was to take you off, as we did. You certainly had a proud look on your face!'

'I was thinking of something else,' the artist replied simply. 'An officer I know told me that he was arrested in Dalmatia under very similar circumstances, by a rioting mob, one morning as he was coming back from a walk. This parallel intrigued me, and I was studying all their faces with a view to painting a riot scene of 1793. . . . I kept saying to myself: You rascal! You've only got what you deserve, chasing after people's inheritances instead of painting away in your studio.'

'If you will allow me to give a word of advice,' said the public prosecutor, 'at eleven o'clock this evening you will take a carriage lent by the postmaster and return to Paris by the coach which leaves from Bourges.'

'I agree,' said Monsieur Hochon who could hardly wait for his guest's departure.

'And my keenest wish is to get away from Issoudun even though it means leaving my only friend,' Agathe replied, taking hold of Madame Hochon's hand and kissing it. 'But when shall I see you again?'

'Ah! My dear girl, not until we are in heaven. . . .' (She whispered into her goddaughter's ear.) 'We have suffered so much on this earth that God will take pity on us.'

A moment later, after Monsieur Mouilleron had talked to Max, Gritte greatly surprised Monsieur and Madame Hochon, Agathe, Joseph and Adolphine by announcing that Monsieur Rouget had called. Jean-Jacques was coming to bid his sister farewell and to offer her his carriage as far as Bourges.

'Your pictures have caused us a lot of trouble!' Agathe told him.

'Keep them, my dear sister,' said the old man, who still did not believe in the pictures' value.

'Neighbour,' Monsieur Hochon said, 'our best friends and most reliable defences are our relations, especially when they are people like your sister Agathe and your nephew Joseph!'

'That may well be so,' replied the old man, with a dazed expression.

'You must think of ending your days in a Christian manner,' Madame Hochon added.

'Oh! Jean-Jacques,' said Agathe, 'what a day it has been!'

'Will you accept my carriage?' Rouget asked.

'No, thank you, dear brother,' she answered. 'I wish you the very best of health!'

Rouget allowed his sister and nephew to embrace him, and then left after bidding them a cool farewell. On his grandfather's instructions, Baruch had hurried over to the postmaster's office. At eleven in the evening, the two Parisians – huddled together in a basket-carriage drawn by a single horse and driven by a postilion – left Issoudun. Adolphine and Madame Hochon had tears in their eyes. They were the only people who regretted Agathe's and Joseph's departure.

'They have gone,' François Hochon said, coming into Max's bedroom at the same time as Flore.

'Well then, the trick has been played,' Max replied, low with fever.

'But what did you say to old Mouilleron?' François asked him.

'I told him that I had almost given my assassin the right to lie in wait for me at a street corner, and that – if they pursued this affair – the man was quite likely to kill me like a dog, before he could be arrested. So I asked Mouilleron and Prangin to set the most thorough investigations going on the surface, but to leave my assassin alone, unless they wanted me to be killed.'

'I hope, Max, you'll behave yourselves at nights for some little while now,' said Flore.

'Anyway, we've got rid of the Parisians,' Max cried. 'The man who stabbed me little knew what a favour he was doing us.'

Next day, apart from the extremely easy-going and reserved people who shared Monsieur and Madame Hochon's point of view, the Parisians' departure – though occasioned by a deplorable misunderstanding – was greeted by the whole town as a victory for the provinces over Paris. Some of Max's friends spoke of the Bridaus in fairly harsh terms.

'Well, those Parisians imagined we are imbeciles. They thought that you've only got to doff your hat for inheritances to pour into it!'

'They came looking for wool and are going back shorn; you see, the nephew isn't to his uncle's liking.'

'And, if you please, their adviser was a Parisian attorney.'

'Oh! So they had some sort of plan in mind?'

'Yes, their plan was to get old Rouget under their thumb;

but the Parisians weren't up to it, and their attorney won't have the laugh on us.'

'Don't you think it's abominable?'

'That's Paris people all over!'

'The Fisherwoman was being attacked, so she hit back.'

'And quite right too!'

Throughout the town, the Bridaus were thought of as the Parisians, the strangers: people much preferred Max and Flore.

20. *Philippe at Issoudun*

You can imagine how pleased Agathe and Joseph were to return to their little apartment in the Rue Mazarine, after this campaign. During the return journey the artist had recovered his gaiety, which had been disturbed by the scene of his arrest and by twenty hours of solitary confinement; but he was unable to raise his mother's spirits. Agathe found it extremely difficult to get over her emotions, especially as the Court of Peers was about to judge the case of the military conspiracy. Despite the ability of his defending counsel, whom Desroches had recommended, Philippe's conduct aroused unfavourable suspicions concerning his character. For this reason, as soon as he had informed Desroches of all that was going on at Issoudun, Joseph promptly went off with Mistigris to the Comte de Sérizy's country house, so as not to have any news of this case, which lasted for twenty days.

There is no need at this point to recapitulate facts that have become part and parcel of contemporary history. Either because he had played some prearranged role, or else because he was one of those who turned King's evidence, Philippe was sentenced to five years' police supervision and ordered to leave for Autun on the very day of his release, Autun being the town allocated to him by the Director-General of Police as his place of residence for the next five years. This sentence was equivalent to a period of detention, such as is given to prisoners on parole, to whom a town is assigned as their place of imprisonment. Learning that the Comte de Sérizy, one of the peers whom the Upper House appointed to conduct a preliminary investigation into the case, was employing Joseph to decorate his mansion at Presles, Desroches requested an audience with the Cabinet Minister and discovered that the Comte de Sérizy was most favourably disposed towards Joseph, whom he had accidentally met. Desroches explained the two brothers' financial position, recalling their father's services and the way in which these had been overlooked at the Restoration.

'Such injustices, my lord, are permanent causes of irritation and discontent,' said the attorney. 'You knew their father; at least put the sons into a position in life where they can make their fortune!'

And he succinctly described the family's position at Issoudun, requesting the all-powerful Vice-President of the Council of State to use his influence with the Director-General of Police, so as to change Philippe's place of confinement from Autun to Issoudun. He ended by referring to Philippe's terrible poverty, begging for an allowance of 60 francs a month, which in all decency the War Ministry ought to grant to a former lieutenant-colonel.

'I will obtain everything you have asked for, for it all seems reasonable,' said the Cabinet Minister.

Three days later, provided with the necessary papers, Desroches went to pick Philippe up at the prison of the Court of Peers, and took him back to his own home in the Rue de Béthizy. There, the young attorney gave this horrifying soldier one of those incontrovertible sermons in which lawyers assess everything at its true value, using plain words to assess people's conduct, and analysing and reducing to their simplest form the feelings of clients in whom they are interested enough to lecture them at all. After making the Emperor's aide-de-camp feel very small by taking him to task for his senseless dissipation, his mother's misfortunes and old Madame Descoings's death, he described the state of affairs at Issoudun, throwing much light on everything, as was his way, and fathoming the plan and characters of both Maxence Gilet and Flore. Gifted with the keenest understanding of these matters, the political detainee listened much more closely to the second part of Desroches's admonition than to the first.

'Things being as they are,' the attorney concluded, 'you can atone for what is atonable in the wrongs you have done your excellent family, for you cannot restore life to the poor woman whose death you caused; but only you can . . .'

'And what should I do?' asked Philippe.

'I have obtained permission for your place of residence to be changed from Autun to Issoudun.'

A look of joy flashed across Philippe's face, which was so thin and now almost sinister, so racked by illness, suffering and privation.

'Only you can recover your uncle Rouget's inheritance, half of which has already perhaps been wolfed by Gilet,' Desroches continued. 'You know all the details, now it's up to you to act accordingly. I am not going to outline any plan for you, I haven't any ideas in that direction; besides, everything changes when you are actually on the spot. You are up against a smart operator, this fellow is extremely cunning. The way he tried to get the pictures back when your uncle had given them to Joseph, the audacity of blaming your poor brother for a crime he hadn't committed – all this proves that you have here an enemy capable of anything. So you must be very careful, and try to show great caution – with calculated effort, if it doesn't come naturally to you. Without mentioning this to Joseph, whose artist's independence and pride would have been offended, I have returned the pictures to Monsieur Hochon, telling him only to hand them over to you. Maxence Gilet is a brave man . . .'

'That's just as well,' Philippe answered. 'I'm depending on this fellow's courage for the success of my plan: a coward would creep away from Issoudun.'

'Well, think of your mother who has been so adorably kind to you, and of your brother, whom you treated like a milch cow.'

'What, has he told you about those silly little episodes?' cried Philippe.

'Come on, an't I a friend of the family, and don't I know more than they do about you?'

'What do you know?'

'You have betrayed your comrades.'

'What do you mean, betrayed my comrades?' Philippe cried. 'I? One of the Emperor's aides-de-camp? What rubbish! We hoodwinked the House of Peers, the Ministry of

Justice, the Government and the whole damned shooting-match. The authorities were completely foxed!'

'That's all very well, if that's how it was,' the attorney replied; 'but, do you see, the Bourbons can't be overthrown, they've got Europe behind them, and you should think of making your peace with the War Ministry. Oh yes! You'll do that once you're rich! In order for you and your brother to become rich, you must lay hold of your uncle. And if you do wish to make a success of this business which calls for so much ability, discretion and patience, you have enough to occupy you during your five years.'

'No,' Philippe retorted, 'I must set to work quickly. Gilet might change the nature of my uncle's fortune, have it transferred to this woman's name, and then all would be lost.'

'Finally, Monsieur Hochon is a reliable adviser, who sees things clearly. Consult him, You have got your travel voucher. Your seat has been booked on the Orleans stage-coach leaving at half past seven. Your case is packed. Would you like to come to dinner?'

'I haven't got anything besides the clothes I'm wearing,' Philippe said, opening his horrible blue coat. 'But I am short of three things which you can ask Giroudeau, my friend Finot's uncle, to send me: my sabre, sword and pistols!'

'You're also short of something else, of a quite different kind,' the attorney said, shuddering as he looked at his client. 'You will be advanced three months of your allowance, to buy some decent clothes.'

'Ah! There you are, Godeschal!' cried Philippe, recognizing Mariette's brother, who was Desroches's senior clerk.

'Yes, I have been with Maître Desroches for two months.'

'I hope he'll stay until he gets a practice of his own,' Desroches intervened.

'And how is Mariette?' said Philippe, overcome with emotion as he recollected his memories.

'She is waiting for the new theatre to open.'

'It wouldn't cost her much to obtain my release,' Philippe replied. 'Anyway, it's up to her!'

After the frugal dinner offered him by Desroches, who

provided for his senior clerk's meals, the two lawyers saw the political detainee to his coach and wished him all the best.

On 2 November, All Souls' Day, Philippe Bridau called at the police superintendent's office in Issoudun, to have his travel voucher stamped with the day of his arrival. Then he went off to get lodgings (as advised by the official) in the Rue de l'Avenier. The news of the deportation of one of the officers who had been involved in the recent conspiracy spread through Issoudun in no time, and it caused even more of a sensation because this officer's brother was the artist who had been so unjustly accused. Maxence Gilet, who by now had completely recovered from the after-effects of his wound, had completed the very difficult operation of converting into ready money the sums which old Rouget had advanced on mortgages, and investing this money in a treasury scrip. The fact that the old man had borrowed 140,000 francs on his landed properties caused a great sensation, for everything is common knowledge in the provinces. In the Bridaus' interests, Monsieur Hochon, who was greatly shaken by this disaster, questioned old Monsieur Héron, Rouget's solicitor, as to the purpose behind this transfer of investments.

'I'll have been the salvation of old Rouget's family, if he changes his mind about them!' cried Monsieur Héron. 'Had it not been for me, the old man would have allowed the 50,000 francs a year interest to be put down in Maxence Gilet's name. I told Mademoiselle Brazier that she should merely concern herself with the will. Otherwise, in view of the weighty evidence concerning their manoeuvres which would be provided by the various transfers of money from all quarters, she would run the risk of an action alleging misappropriation. In order to gain time, I have advised Maxence and his mistress to allow time for this sudden change in the old man's habits to be forgotten.'

'Be the Bridaus' adviser and protector, for they are penniless,' Monsieur Hochon told Monsieur Héron; Hochon could not forgive Gilet for the anxieties he had experienced when he feared his house might be ransacked.

Maxence Gilet and Flore Brazier, seemingly immune from

all further attacks, joked when they learned of the arrival of old Rouget's second nephew. As soon as Philippe caused them any anxiety, they would be able to transfer the treasury scrip either to Maxence or Flore, by getting old Rouget to confer powers of attorney. If the will was revoked, an income of 50,000 francs a year was a handsome enough consolation, especially when the landed property itself had been encumbered with a mortgage of 140,000 francs.

The day after his arrival, at about ten o'clock, Philippe called at his uncle's house. He was anxious to be seen in his terrible garb. The result was that when the man who had been released from the Hôpital du Midi, and who had been imprisoned in the Luxembourg, entered Rouget's drawing-room, Flore Brazier shuddered at the very sight of his repulsive appearance. Gilet, likewise, felt that agitation of mind and senses which is Nature's way of warning us of some latent enmity, some impending danger.

Though the look on Philippe's face was due to his recent misfortunes, his clothes reinforced the sinister impression. His ragged blue coat was buttoned to the neck in military fashion, but for a pathetic reason; and even then it disclosed far too much of what it was supposed to conceal. The bottoms of his trousers, frayed like an invalid's garment, betokened extreme poverty. His boots, oozing muddy water out of their half-open soles, left wet marks wherever he trod. The grey hat which the colonel was holding showed a horribly greasy lining. His malacca cane, with its varnish all worn off, looked as if it had lain around in the corners of every café in Paris, and had poked its twisted ferrule through much mud and slime. Above a velvet collar through which the cardboard was showing was a head almost identical in expression to Frédérick-Lemaître's in the last act of *La Vie d'un Joueur*, a head in which the exhaustion of a still vigorous man is betrayed by a copper-coloured complexion, with patches of green. Such shades of colour are to be seen in the faces of debauchees who have passed many nights at the gaming-tables; dark rings circle their eyes, their eyelids are reddened rather than red; their foreheads have a threatening look, by the very fact that they indicate personal ruin. Philippe had barely recovered from his illness; his cheeks were wrinkled and almost hollow. He was nearly bald, but a few wisps of hair at the back of his head strayed around his ears. The pure blue of his sparkling eyes had taken on the icy tint of steel.

'How d'you do, uncle,' he said in a hoarse voice. 'I am your nephew, Philippe Bridau. This is how the Bourbons treat a lieutenant-colonel, one of the old guard, the man who carried the Emperor's orders at the Battle of Montereau. As Mademoiselle is present, I should be ashamed if my coat were to come undone. But, after all, that's the run of the game. We tried to start the war all over again, and lost. I have been confined to your town on police orders, on a special rate of pay of 60 francs a month. The townsfolk needn't be afraid that I'll push up the cost of living. I see that you are keeping the best of company.'

'So, you're my nephew,' said Jean-Jacques.

'Invite the colonel to breakfast,' cried Flore.

'No, thank you, Madame, I have already eaten. Besides, after the way my mother and brother were treated in this town, I would rather cut my hand off than ask uncle for a scrap of bread, or a farthing. Only, it didn't seem right, being in Issoudun, not to pay him my respects from time to time.'

Philippe held out his hand, into which Rouget placed his own, which Philippe shook.

'Whatever you do, I shall have no reason to complain so long as the Bridaus' honour is unscathed,' he added.

Gilet had had ample opportunity to scrutinize the lieutenant-colonel, for Philippe studiously avoided looking in his direction. Max's blood was boiling, yet he behaved with that statesmanlike prudence which sometimes resembles cowardice. He had too much to lose by flying into a temper, as a young man might have done; and so he remained outwardly calm and cold.

'It wouldn't be the proper thing,' said Flore, 'for you to live on 60 francs a month so close to your uncle when he has an income of 40,000 francs a year, and has already behaved so generously towards Major Gilet here, his natural relation.'

'Yes, Philippe,' the old man went on. 'We shall have to see what we can do about that.'

Flore introduced Philippe to Gilet, with whom he exchanged an almost timid handshake.

'Uncle, I have some pictures to return to you. They are at Monsieur Hochon's. You must give me the pleasure of coming over to verify them, sooner or later.'

Uttering these parting words in a staccato tone, Lieutenant-Colonel Philippe Bridau then left the house. His visit plunged both Flore and Gilet into an even more solemn state of mind than the shock they had had on first seeing this hideous war veteran. No sooner had Philippe slammed the door behind him, with the violence of an aggrieved heir, than Flore and Gilet ran to hide in the curtains and watch him as he walked back from his uncle's house to the Hochons'.

'What a ruffian!' said Flore, eying Gilet questioningly.

'Yes, I'm afraid there were a few like that in the Emperor's armies. I myself knocked off seven like that on the hulks,' replied Gilet.

'I hope, Max, that you won't get involved in a quarrel with him.'

'Him? Why, he's a mangy dog barking for a bone,' Max turned towards Rouget. 'And if his uncle listens to me, he will get rid of him by means of a donation. Otherwise, he'll never give you any peace, Papa Rouget.'

'He smelt of tobacco,' said the old man.

'He smelt your money,' Flore added peremptorily. 'My advice is: forgo the pleasure of seeing him.'

'Nothing would please me more,' Rouget replied.

'Monsieur,' Gritte said, coming into the room where the whole of the Hochon family was sitting after breakfast, 'here is the Monsieur Bridau whom you were talking about.'

Philippe politely entered the room and was met by profound silence – the result of general curiosity. Madame Hochon shuddered from head to foot at the sight of the man who had caused all Agathe's grief and who had been dear Madame Descoings's assassin. Adolphine, too, felt rather frightened. Baruch and François looked at each other in surprise. Old

Hochon kept his cool evenness of temper and invited Madame Bridau's son to sit down.

'The reason for my visit, Monsieur,' said Philippe, 'is to ask you for your sympathy and help. I now have to arrange matters so as to live for five years in this town on the 60 francs a month pension allowed me by the Government.'

'It can be done,' the octogenarian replied.

Philippe talked of indifferent things, and kept a perfectly becoming manner. He described the journalist Lousteau as an 'eagle'; Lousteau was old Madame Hochon's nephew, and Philippe won her approval by declaring that the name of Lousteau would become famous. Moreover, he did not hesitate to admit the mistakes he had made during his life. To a friendly reproach which Madame Hochon whispered to him, he replied that whilst in prison he had thought many things over and promised that from now on he would be a quite different man.

At Philippe's suggestion, Monsieur Hochon went outside with him. When the miser and the soldier were in the Boulevard Baron, at a spot where they could not be overheard, the colonel told the old man: 'If you wish to take my advice, we will never discuss business or people except when we are out walking in the country or in places where we can chat without being overheard. Maître Desroches has very clearly explained to me the influence of gossip in a small town. So I do not want people to suspect you of assisting me with your advice although Desroches has told me to ask you for it, and although I hope you will give me it. We are up against a powerful enemy and we must not overlook any precaution if we are to be successful in getting rid of him. To begin with, I hope you will forgive me if I do not call on you again. If we are rather cool towards each other, people will not suspect you of any influence over my conduct. When I need to consult you, I shall walk across the square at half past nine, just as you are finishing breakfast. If you see me holding my cane over my shoulder, that means we must meet, accidentally, in a public walk of your own choosing.'

'All this seems to me the plan of a prudent man who is determined to succeed,' the old man remarked.

'And I shall succeed, Monsieur. But most important of all, give me the names of the soldiers of the Imperial Army, here in Issoudun, who don't belong to Maxence Gilet's party, and whom I can contact.'

'To begin with, there is a captain of the Guards artillery, Monsieur Mignonnet, who trained at the École Polytechnique. He is forty years old and lives unpretentiously. He is a most honourable man and has criticized Max's behaviour, which he considers unworthy of a true soldier.'

'Good!' said the lieutenant-colonel.

'There aren't many soldiers of his stamp,' Monsieur Hochon went on, 'the only other one I can think of here is a former cavalry captain.'

'He's my man,' Philippe said. 'Was he in the Guards?'

'Yes,' replied Monsieur Hochon. 'In 1810 Carpentier was a squadron sergeant-major in the Dragoons; he left that position to become a sublieutenant in the infantry, where he was promoted captain.'

'Perhaps Giroudeau will know him,' thought Philippe.

'This Monsieur Carpentier has taken over the job at the Town Hall which Maxence did not want, and he is the friend of Major Mignonnet.'

'What can I do here to earn my living?'

'The Mutual Insurance Company of the Département du Cher are going to set up a branch office here, I believe, and you can obtain a job there; but it would only bring you in 50 francs a month at the most.'

'That will be enough.'

A week later, Philippe had obtained a new coat, a new pair of trousers and a new waistcoat all in good blue Elbeuf material, bought on credit terms repayable at so much a month, as well as boots, doeskin gloves and a hat. From Paris, Giroudeau sent him some linen, his weapons and a letter for Carpentier who had served under the former captain of dragoons. This letter won Carpentier over to Philippe; he introduced Philippe to Major Mignonnet, calling him a man of the highest merit and finest character. Philippe gained the admiration of these two worthy officers by a few confidential remarks about the conspiracy which had just been before the courts and which was – as people know – the Imperial Army's last attempt to overthrow the Bourbons, for the case involving the sergeants at La Rochelle belonged to another category of ideas. From 1822, soldiers were quite content to await developments: they had been put on their guard by the fate that befell the conspiracy of 19 August 1820 and by the Berton and Caron affairs. The latter conspiracy was a small-scale version of the one that took place on 19 August, but a conspiracy of the same type – though it contained better elements. Like the first, it was completely unsuspected by the Bourbon Government. But when they too were discovered, the conspirators had the sense to scale down their vast undertaking to the trivial proportions of a barracks plot. This conspiracy, in which several cavalry, infantry and artillery regiments were involved, was based in the North of France. The idea was that the fortified places along the frontier would be captured at a single go. In the event of success, the treaties of 1815 would have been violated by an immediate federation with Belgium, which would have broken away from the Holy Alliance in consequence of a military pact between soldiers. Two thrones were being simultaneously attacked in this rapid hurricane. But, rather than divulge such a formidable plan, which powerful minds had thought up and in which highly influential people were implicated, the conspirators revealed only a detail of it to the Court of Peers. Philippe Bridau agreed to cover up for his leaders, who disappeared as soon as the plots came to light either by treason or coincidence and who, sitting in one or other of the Houses of Parliament, could promise their co-operation only in the matter of completing the conspiracy's success within the Government itself. But to relate the plan which, since 1830, the admissions of Liberals have spelt out in all its depth, and in its immense ramifications which until then had been concealed from subordinate accomplices, would be to encroach on the domain of history and become involved in too long a digression. This rapid sketch is enough to explain the twofold part Philippe agreed to play in it. The Emperor's aide-de-camp was directed to lead a revolt that was planned to take place in Paris, and whose sole purpose was to conceal the true conspiracy and harass the Government at its centre whilst the real conspiracy was breaking out in the North. Philippe was then assigned the task of destroying all connexion between the two plots, by merely confessing secrets of a secondary nature; the terrifying destitution which both his dress and health indicated was a most powerful factor in discrediting the conspiracy in the Government's eyes, and reducing its apparent proportions. This double role suited the unprincipled gambler's precarious position. Feeling that he was astride both parties, the wily officer pretended to the Bourbon Government that he was an honest man, whilst retaining the respect of influential people within his own party; swearing to himself that later he would join forces with whichever of the two parties offered him the more advantages. These revelations both as to the true plot's immense scope and the role which some of the judges had played in it led Carpentier and Mignonnet to regard Philippe as a most distinguished man: his devotion to his cause showed that here was a politician worthy of the glorious days of the Convention. No wonder that within a few days the cunning Bonapartist became friendly with the two officers whose respectable position within the town reflected upon himself. On Monsieur Mignonnet's and Monsieur Carpentier's recommendation, he immediately obtained the post with the Mutual Insurance Company of the Département du Cher which old Hochon had pointed out to him. Given the tasks of keeping registers (as in a tax-collector's office), filling in names and figures on standard letters and sending these letters off, and issuing insurance policies, he had no more than three hours' work a day. Mignonnet and Carpentier secured his election to their Club, where his attitude and manners, in perfect harmony with Mignonnet's and Carpentier's high opinion of him, won him the respect often given to people with deceptive appearances. Philippe's behaviour was motivated by deep calculation; in prison, he had realised the drawbacks of leading a dissipated life. He therefore had had no need of Desroches's lecture to realize how necessary it was that he should win the middle

267

class's respect by leading an honest, decent and regular life. He was delighted to satirize Max by living in Mignonnet's fashion and he wished to allay Maxence's fears by deceiving him as to his true character. By appearing generous and disinterested, he hoped to be thought of as a fool, whilst all the time encircling his adversary and aiming to obtain his uncle's inheritance; whereas his mother and brother, who in fact were so disinterested, generous and great, had been accused of calculation when they were acting with naïve simplicity. Philippe's greed had grown keener when he learned the size of his uncle's fortune, which Monsieur Hochon explained to him. In his first secret conversation with Monsieur Hochon, both agreed on the necessity of not arousing Max's suspicions; for everything would be lost if Flore and Max only took their victim as far as Bourges. Once a week, the colonel dined with Captain Mignonnet, once with Carpentier and on Thursdays at Monsieur Hochon's. Three weeks after his arrival in Issoudun, he was already on visiting terms in two or three houses; he really only had to buy his breakfasts. At no time did he speak of either his uncle, or Flore, or Gilet, unless it was with a view to learning some detail of his mother's and brother's stay. The three officers, who were the only ones to have been decorated and amongst whom Philippe enjoyed the superiority of a rosette, which gave him particular prestige in all provincial people's eyes, used to go out for a walk together before dinner, always at the same time: to use a colloquial expression, they kept themselves to themselves. His attitude, reserve and peaceful appearance created an excellent impression in Issoudun. All Max's followers thought of Philippe as a swashbuckler, an expression which soldiers used to denote a very ordinary type of courage in officers whose gifts of leadership they denied. 'He's a very honourable fellow,' old Goddet would say to Max. 'Bah!' Major Gilet replied, 'from the way he behaved before the Court of Peers he's either a dupe or an informer; and, as you say, he's stupid enough to have been taken in by men who were playing for high stakes.' After getting his job with the insurance company, Philippe, aware of all the tittle-tattle that went on in the district, decided to conceal certain matters from the townsfolk as far as was in his power; he therefore took lodgings at the furthermost end of the Faubourg Saint-Paterne in a house with a very large garden behind it. There, in the greatest secrecy he could practise fencing with Carpentier, who had taught this skill in the infantry before his promotion to the Guards. He thus regained his old superiority in the exercise, without anyone being the wiser, and Carpentier then taught him secrets which enabled him to stand up to a first-rate opponent. After this, he took up pistol shooting with Mignonnet and Carpentier, allegedly for amusement, but really so as to give Maxence the idea that he would rely on this weapon if ever he became involved in a duel. Whenever Philippe met Gilet, he would wait to receive his greeting and reply by raising the brim of his hat in a cavalier fashion, as a colonel does when acknowledging a soldier's salute. Maxence Gilet never showed any sign of impatience or discontent; not a word on this subject had escaped his lips at La Cognette's, where he still gave suppers; for, since he had been stabbed by Fario, the pranks had been temporarily suspended. After a certain time, Lieutenant-Colonel Bridau's contempt for Major Gilet was an established fact, privately discussed by some of the Knights of Idleness who were not as close to Maxence as were Baruch, François and three or four others. There was general astonishment that the violent, impetuous Max should be behaving so reservedly. No one in Issoudun, not even Potel or Renard, dared to broach this delicate subject with Gilet. Potel, who was quite distressed by public disagreement between two officers of the Imperial Guards, spoke of Max as someone who might well hatch a plot to ensnare the colonel. In Potel's opinion, some new development was to be expected, after Max's efforts to hound out the brother and mother, for the Fario business was no longer a mystery. Monsieur Hochon had made a point of explaining Gilet's atrocious ruse to the wise old men in Issoudun. Besides, Monsieur Mouilleron, who was the hero of some of the bourgeois tittle-tattle, had privately mentioned the name of Gilet's assassin, if only so as to investigate the causes of Fario's and Max's enmity, and keep the law in a state of alert for any future developments. When discussing the lieutenant-colonel's position vis-à-vis Max, and trying to discover what would be the outcome of this hostility, the townsfolk therefore described them as enemies before they actually were. Philippe, who was carefully investigating the details of his brother's arrest, and Gilet's and Flore's antecedents, eventually struck up a fairly close relationship with Fario, his neighbour. After carefully studying the Spaniard, Philippe believed he could trust a man of this mettle. So closely were they allied in their hatred that Fario placed himself at Philippe's disposal, telling him everything he knew about the Knights of Idleness. In the event of his managing to obtain the same degree of influence over his uncle that Gilet at present enjoyed, Philippe promised to compensate Fario for his losses; he thus acquired a faithful supporter. Maxence was now faced with a formidable enemy; to use an expression that was popular in the district, he had found his match. Agog with gossip, the town of Issoudun had a foreboding that some struggle would ensue between these two men who, it should be added, despised one another.

PART THREE: WHO WILL GAIN
THE INHERITANCE?

21. *A chapter which all potential legatees should study*

One morning towards the end of November, Philippe met Monsieur Hochon in the long avenue of Frapesle, about midday. 'I have discovered that your two grandsons Baruch and François are Maxence Gilet's intimate friends,' he told him. 'These young rascals take part in all the pranks that go on in this town at night. That was how Maxence got to know everything that was said in your house whilst my mother and brother were staying with you.'

'And how did you obtain proof of these horrible allegations?'

'I heard them talking one night as they came out of an inn. Each of your grandsons owes Maxence 3,000 francs. The wretch told these poor lads to try and discover what our intentions are; reminding them that you had thought up a way of obtaining a hold on my uncle with the help of the priesthood, he told them that you alone were capable of guiding me, for fortunately he thinks I am only a swashbuckler.'

'What? My grandsons . . .'

'Keep a close eye on them,' Philippe went on. 'You will see them coming back across the Place Saint-Jean with Max, at two or three in the morning, as drunk as lords . . .'

'So that's why the little devils are so sober at home,' Monsieur Hochon remarked.

'Fario put me wise to their nightly merry-making,' Philippe continued; 'except for him, I would never have guessed it. My uncle is ruled with a rod of iron, judging by the few words

271

my Spaniard has heard Max saying to your grandsons. I
suspect that Max and Flore have formed a plan to nick the
50,000 francs a year interest in Treasury Bonds, and then go
off and get married heaven knows where, after feathering
their nest very nicely. It is high time we knew what is going
on in my uncle's household; but I don't know how to set
about it.'

'I'll think it over,' the old man promised.

Philippe and Monsieur Hochon took leave of each other, as
they saw a few people approaching.

Never, at any time in his life, did Jean-Jacques Rouget
suffer as much as after his nephew Philippe's first visit. Flore
was terror-stricken; she had a foreboding of the danger that
threatened Maxence. Tired of her master, and fearing that he
might live to a ripe old age, as she saw how well he was
standing up to her criminal onslaughts, she devised the very
simple plan of leaving the district altogether and going off to
marry Maxence in Paris, after having the investment of 50,000
francs a year in Government funds transferred to her own
name. Motivated not by any regard for his heirs nor even by
personal greed, but solely by his passion for Flore, the old
bachelor refused to transfer the investment income, arguing
that she was his sole heir. The unfortunate man knew how
deeply Flore loved Maxence, and foresaw that she would
desert him as soon as she could afford to marry. When Flore
was met with a refusal, even after the fondest cajoleries, she
resorted to harsh methods of treatment: she would no longer
speak to her master; he was now served by Védie, who found
him one morning with his eyes red and inflamed through
having wept during the night. Old Rouget had been breakfasting alone for a week, and none too well either! It is not
surprising that when Philippe decided to pay him a second
visit, on the day following his talk with Monsieur Hochon,
he found Jean-Jacques a changed man. Flore remained with
the old man, casting tender looks at him and speaking to him
affectionately; she played her part so well that Philippe realized
how dangerous the situation was, with so much attention
being showered on the old man in his presence. Gilet, whose

strategy was to avoid any possible collision with Philippe, did not put in an appearance. After shrewd observation of old Rouget and Flore, the colonel decided that the time had come to strike a powerful blow.

'Farewell, dear uncle,' he said, rising from his chair as if to leave the house.

'Oh! Don't go yet,' cried the old man, who was feeling much the better for Flore's pretended affection. 'Why not dine with us, Philippe?'

'All right, if you will come out with me for an hour's walk.'

'Monsieur is not at all well,' said Mademoiselle Brazier. 'A little while ago he didn't want to go out in his carriage,' she added, turning towards the old man and staring at him with the hard look that quells madmen.

Philippe took hold of Flore's arm, forcing her to look at him, and glared at her just as she had been glaring at her vicitim.

'Tell me, Mademoiselle, would my uncle, by any chance, not be free to come out with me on his own for a walk?'

'Of course he can,' she replied, scarcely able to reply otherwise.

'Well, come on then, uncle. Hurry up, Mademoiselle, get him his hat and cane.'

'But usually he doesn't go out except with me, do you, Monsieur?'

'Yes, Philippe, I always need her very much.'

'It would be better if we went in the carriage,' Flore said.

'Yes, let's go in the carriage,' the old man cried, in his desire to reconcile his two tyrants.

'Uncle, you will come out with me on foot and alone, or else I shall never come and see you again; for otherwise, the town would be right: you would be under Mademoiselle Flore Brazier's thumb. If uncle loves you, that's all right by me!' he continued, staring at Flore with a leaden look. 'If you don't love uncle, that's equally all right by me. But for you to make the poor old man unhappy. . . . No! That's not on! If you want to inherit a fortune, you must earn it. Are you coming, uncle?'

Philippe noted the painful hesitancy in the poor imbecile's expression, as his eyes kept wandering from himself to Flore.

'Oh! So that's how it is! Well, good-bye, uncle. My compliments, Mademoiselle.'

He turned round smartly on reaching the door and caught sight of another threatening gesture from Flore to his uncle.

'Uncle,' he said, 'if you do want to come for a walk with me, I will meet you at your front door. . . . I am going to call on Monsieur Hochon for ten minutes. If *we* don't go for a walk, I promise you I'll send the other people here for a very long walk.'

And Philippe crossed the Place Saint-Jean to visit the Hochons.

Everybody can imagine the scene which Philippe's disclosures to Monsieur Hochon were to bring about in his family. At nine o'clock, old Monsieur Héron turned up, armed with papers, and found that – contrary to habit – the old man had had a fire lit in the living-room. Already dressed at this unseasonable hour, Madame Hochon was sitting in her armchair by the fire. Her two grandsons, who had been warned by Adolphine of the storm that had been gathering over their heads since the previous day, were confined to the house. Summoned by Gritte, they were impressed by the kind of ceremonious formality displayed by their grandparents, whose coldness and anger had been louring for the last twenty-four hours

'Don't stand up when they come in,' the old man told Monsieur Héron, 'for they are two wretches who don't deserve to be forgiven.'

'Oh! Grandfather!' cried François.

'Silence!' Hochon continued solemnly. 'I know of your goings-on at night and your friendship with Monsieur Maxence Gilet; but you won't go and meet him again at La Cognette's at one in the morning, for the next time you both leave this house will be to go to your respective destinations. So you ruined Fario? Several times you nearly landed up at the Assizes! Silence,' he repeated, seeing that Baruch was about to speak. 'Both of you owe Monsieur Maxence money; for six years he has been financing your debauches. Each of you will now pay careful attention as I render my guardianship accounts, and we will discuss things afterwards. From these legal documents you will see whether you can play the fool with me, your family and its laws, by betraying the secrets of my house and reporting to a Monsieur Maxence Gilet everything that is said and done here. . . . For 3,000 francs you are prepared to become spies; no doubt for 30,000 francs you would commit murder! But haven't you nearly killed Madame Bridau already? For Monsieur Gilet well knew that it was Fario who stabbed him when he blamed the attempted assassination on to my guest, Joseph Bridau. And the reason why this gallows-bird committed such a crime was because he had learned from you that Madame Agathe intended to stay on here. You, *my* grandsons, to be spies for such a man! You, plundering honest people's money? Didn't you know that your worthy leader has already killed one poor young creature, at the outset of his career in 1806? I don't want any thieves or assassins in my family. You will pack your bags and go and get yourselves hanged somewhere else!'

The two young men went as white and motionless as plaster statues.

'Now then, Monsieur Héron,' the miser said to the solicitor.

The old solicitor read the first guardianship account, from which it appeared that the net total of the two Borniches' fortune was 70,000 francs, a sum representing their mother's dowry; but Monsieur Hochon had had some fairly large sums lent to his daughter and so had control of a portion of his Borniche grandchildren's fortune in the lenders' names. Baruch's share came down to 20,000 francs.

'So now you are rich,' the old man said. 'Take your fortune and stand on your own feet in the world! I reserve the right to bequeath my property and Madame Hochon's, who at this moment is fully in agreement with all my ideas, to whoever I wish, perhaps our dear Adolphine: yes, we can marry her to a peer's son if we so wish; for she will have all our capital!'

'And a very handsome fortune, too!' said Monsieur Héron.

'Monsieur Maxence Gilet will compensate you,' said Madame Hochon.

'Why should we scrape and save for rascals like you?' cried Monsieur Hochon.

'Please forgive us!' stammered Baruch.

'Sorry, won't do it again,' the old man mockingly repeated, in a childlike voice. 'But if I forgive you, you will go off and inform Monsieur Maxence of everything that has happened to you, so that he can be on his guard. . . . No, no, my little fellows. I have ways of discovering how you behave. As you behave, so will I. I shall judge you, not by a day's or a month's good behaviour but by your conduct over a period of several years! I have good feet and good eyes and I'm in excellent health. I hope to live long enough yet to know what future you carve out for yourselves. First, capitalist that you are, you will go to Paris to study banking in Monsieur Mongenod's bank. And woe betide you if you don't behave yourself: there'll be someone to keep an eye on you. Your fortune is banked with Mongenod and Son; here is their draft for the amount. Please absolve me from my guardianship by signing your guardianship accounts and the final receipt,' he said, taking the account out of Héron's hands and handing it to Baruch.

'Now, as far as you're concerned, François Hochon, you are owing me money rather than drawing any,' the old man said, looking at his other grandson. 'Monsieur Héron, read him his account; it is clear . . . very clear.'

There was a profound silence whilst the account was read.

'You will go to Poitiers on an allowance of 600 francs a year, and study law,' his grandfather said when the lawyer had finished reading. 'I was cutting you out for a fine life; now, you will have to become a barrister to earn your living. Yes! My fine ones, you have been deceiving me for six years! You must learn that I only needed an hour to catch up with you: I have seven-league boots.'

Just as old Monsieur Héron was leaving the room with the documents duly signed, Gritte ushered in Colonel Philippe Bridau. Madame Hochon left the room, taking her two grandsons with her to her bedroom so as to confess them (to use old Hochon's phrase) and discover what effect this scene had had upon them.

Philippe and the old man stood in a window-recess, talking in undertones.

'I have given your position careful thought,' Monsieur Hochon said, nodding towards Rouget's house. 'I have just been discussing it with Monsieur Héron. The treasury scrip for 50,000 francs a year can only be disposed of by the person in whose name it stands or else his proxy. Now, since you arrived in this town, your uncle has not conferred powers of attorney at any solicitor's office; and as he has not been out of Issoudun, he couldn't have conferred them elsewhere. If he does assign powers of attorney here, we shall know of it immediately; if he assigns them elsewhere, we shall also get to know about it, for a proxy has to be registered, and worthy Monsieur Héron has ways and means of finding out about that. So that if the old man leaves Issoudun, have him followed, find out where he has gone, and we shall think up some way of discovering what he has done.'

'No power of attorney has been conferred,' Philippe said. 'They want to obtain the proxy, but I hope to be able to prevent this. No, there won't be any power of attorney,' he shouted, seeing his uncle appear on the doorstep and pointing him out to Monsieur Hochon, to whom he succinctly explained the circumstances of his visit, circumstances that were so trivial and yet so important. 'Maxence is afraid of me, but he cannot avoid me. Mignonnet had told me that every year all the officers of the Imperial Army celebrate the anniversary of the Emperor's coronation. Well! In two days' time then, Maxence and I will meet.'

'If he has the power of attorney by the morning of 1 December, he will go post-haste to Paris and miss the anniversary celebrations.'

'Well, we must confine uncle to his room; but I have a way of looking at people that will turn imbeciles to lead,' Philippe replied, causing Monsieur Hochon to tremble, so atrocious was his expression.

'If they allowed him to go out for a walk with you, no doubt Maxence has discovered some way of winning the game,' the old miser observed.

'Oh! Fario is on the look-out,' Philippe replied, 'and he's not the only one. Somewhere near Vatan the Spaniard has discovered one of my old soldiers, to whom I once did a good turn. Without anyone being aware of it, Benjamin Bourdet is under my Spaniard's orders, and Fario himself has put one of his horses at Benjamin's disposal.'

'If you kill this monster who has led my grandsons astray, you will undoubtedly have done a good deed.'

'Today, thanks to me, the whole of Issoudun knows about Monsieur Maxence's nightly activities during these last six years,' Philippe replied. 'And the tittle-tattle, as you call it, is now in full flow about him. Morally speaking, he is a beaten man.'

As soon as Philippe left his uncle's house, Flore entered Maxence's bedroom to give him a detailed account of the visit which Rouget's bold nephew had just made. 'What ought we to do?' she asked.

'Before trying our last resort, which is to fight that great hulk, we must play double or quits, by thinking up some dramatic move. Let the old imbecile go out with his nephew!'

'But that big devil doesn't beat about the bush,' Flore cried. 'He'll tell him the true state of affairs.'

'Listen to me then,' Maxence said in a strident voice. 'Do you think I haven't eavesdropped and thought about our position? Ask old Cognet to get a stable-boy and a charabanc, we need them at once! Everything must be ready within five minutes! Load all your things into it, take Védie with you and hurry over to Vatan. Set yourself up there like a woman who intends to live there. Take the 20,000 francs he has in his desk. If I bring the old man to you at Vatan, you will only agree to return here after he has signed the proxy. I shall dash up to Paris whilst you return to Issoudun. When Jean-Jacques gets back from his walk and finds you are no longer here, he will lose his head and want to run after you. Then I'll make it my business to talk to him.'

Whilst this plot was being hatched, Philippe was walking arm in arm with his uncle along the Boulevard Baron.

'Two great politicians are at grips with one another,' old Hochon thought, following the colonel with his eyes, as he walked along supporting his uncle. 'I am very eager to see how this game will turn out, when a private income of 90,000 francs a year is at stake.'

'My dear uncle,' Philippe said to old Rouget, in phraseology that was strongly redolent of his Parisian connexions, 'you love this girl, and you are absolutely right, she's a real dazzler! Instead of making a fuss of you, she has treated you with contempt, and it's not hard to see why. She'd like to see you pushing up the daisies because then she could marry Maxence, whom she adores.'

'Yes, I know that, Philippe, but I still love her.'

'I have sworn on the body of my mother, who after all is your sister, to make your Fisherwoman as supple as a glove for you, and just as she must have been before this rascal, who wasn't worthy of serving in the Imperial Guards, came and made his home with you.'

'Oh! If only you could do that!'

'It's very simple,' Philippe replied, interrupting his uncle. 'I will kill Maxence for you like a dog ... but on one condition.'

'What's that?' asked old Rouget, looking at his nephew with a bewildered expression.

'Do not sign the proxy form they are asking you for until 3 December. Hang fire until then. These two tricksters want your permission to dispose of your 50,000 francs a year interest, and then they'll go off and get married in Paris and squander your million.'

'That's what I'm afraid of,' Rouget replied.

'Well, whatever they do to you, delay conferring the powers of attorney until next week.'

'Yes, but when Flore talks to me, she plucks my heartstrings and I lose all reason. When she looks at me in a certain way, her blue eyes seem like paradise itself and I'm no longer master of my own actions – especially after she has been harsh to me for several days.'

'Well, if she lays on the charm, just promise to confer powers of attorney, and let me know the day before you sign the form. That will be enough for me: either Maxence will not be your proxy, or else he will have killed me. If I kill him, you'll take me in to live with you in his place, and then I'll make the pretty girl do just as you want. Yes, Flore will love you, Heaven help me! And if you are not happy with her, I'll horse-whip her!'

'Oh! I shall never put up with that. Any blow struck at Flore would strike me to the heart.'

'Yes, but it's the only way of mastering women and horses. That is how a man makes himself feared, loved and respected. I just wanted to whisper this into your ear. ... Good day, gentlemen,' he said to Mignonnet and Carpentier, 'I am out for a walk with my uncle, as you can see, and I am trying to train him; for we are living in a century where children have to educate their grandparents.'

Everyone exchanged greetings.

'My dear uncle is reaping the consequences of an unfortunate passion,' the colonel continued. 'People are trying to rob him of his fortune and leave him like a shorn lamb; you know what I mean. The old man is not unaware of the plot, but he isn't strong-minded enough to foil it by doing without you know what for a few days.'

Philippe gave a clear outline of his uncle's position.

'Gentlemen,' he concluded, 'you see there is only one way of rescuing my uncle; either Colonel Bridau must kill Major Gilet or Major Gilet must kill Colonel Bridau. The day after tomorrow we are celebrating the Emperor's coronation. I rely upon you to arrange the seating at the banquet so that I am placed opposite Major Gilet. I hope you will do me the honour of being my seconds.'

'We shall appoint you president of the banquet, and sit on either side of you. Max, as vice-president, will sit opposite,' said Mignonnet.

'Oh! The rascal will have Major Potel and Captain Renard on his side,' Carpentier said. 'In spite of everything people in town are saying about his rampaging at nights, these two worthy men have already been his seconds, they'll still be faithful to him.'

'You see, uncle,' Philippe said, 'everything is falling into shape; so do not sign anything before 3 December, for the following day you will be free, happy, loved by Flore and untroubled by hangers-on.'

'You don't know him, nephew,' the old man said, with terror on his face. 'Maxence has killed nine men in duels.'

'Yes, but then there was no question of stealing a private income of 100,000 francs a year.'

'An evil conscience unsteadies the hand,' Mignonnet said sententiously.

'A few days from now,' Philippe went on, 'you and Flore will be living together like hearts in orange-blossom, once the mourning is over; for she will writhe like a worm, and yap and burst into tears; but . . . let the water flow!'

The two soldiers backed up Philippe's argument and tried to instil some courage into old Rouget, with whom they strolled for about two hours. Eventually Philippe accompanied his uncle back to his door, saying as his parting words: 'Do not come to any decision without first consulting me. I know women. I kept one once who cost me much more than Flore will ever cost you! She taught me how to treat the fair sex properly – and the lesson will stick for the rest of my life. Women are like naughty children. They are inferior animals to men, and you must make them afraid of you, for the worst plight that can befall us is to be governed by the brutes!'

It was about two o'clock in the afternoon when the old man returned home. Kouski opened the door weeping – or rather, on Maxence's orders, he pretended to be weeping.

'What is it?' asked Jean-Jacques.

'Ah! Monsieur! Madame has gone off, taking Védie with her!'

'Gon . . . ne o . . . o . . . off?' the old man stammered, in a choking voice.

It was such a violent blow that Rouget sat down on one of the stairs. A moment later he stood up again, looked round the sitting-room and kitchen, climbed upstairs to his bedroom, went into all the bedrooms, came back into the sitting-room again, threw himself into an armchair and burst into tears.

'Where is she?' he sobbed. 'Where is she? Where is Max?'

'I do not know,' replied Kouski. 'The major went out without telling me anything.'

Gilet, who was a very astute politician, had decided that it was necessary for him to go for a stroll round the town. Leaving the old man alone with his despair, he made him realize the extent of his abandonment, and so made him obedient to his advice. But to prevent Philippe from assisting his uncle in this crisis, Max had ordered Kouski not to open the door to anyone. With Flore absent, the old man had no one to check or guide him, and the situation was becoming exceedingly critical. During his walk round the town, Maxence Gilet was avoided by many people who, the previous day, would have gone out of their way to come and shake his hand. A general reaction was setting in against him. The doings of the Knights of Idleness were a general talking-point. The story of Joseph Bridau's arrest, now fully clarified, dishonoured Max; it took only a day for his character and actions to be assessed in their true light. Gilet met Major Potel, who was looking for him, frantic with anxiety.

'What's up, Potel?'

'My dear fellow, the Imperial Guards are degraded in the eyes of the whole town! The civilians are ganging up against you, and in consequence, it deeply upsets me.'

'What are they complaining about?' asked Max.

'About the practical jokes you used to play on them at night.'

'So we weren't allowed to have a bit of fun?'

'That's nothing,' said Potel.

Potel belonged to that category of officers who would reply to a burgomaster: 'We'll pay you for your town, if we burn it down!' For this reason the pranks played by the Order of Idleness scarcely disturbed him.

'What else?' asked Gilet.

'The Guards are divided amongst themselves! That's what's breaking my heart. It's Bridau who has unleashed all the townspeople against you. The Guards divided amongst themselves? No, that's bad! You can't draw back, Max, you'll have to have a duel with Bridau. I felt really inclined to pick a quarrel with that big skulk, and shoot him down; for then the townsfolk wouldn't have seen the Guards divided amongst themselves. In wartime I don't say anything against a duel: two Guardsmen have a quarrel; they fight but there are no civilians standing by to poke fun at them. No, that great ruffian has never served in the Guards. When there are townspeople looking on, a Guards Officer should not behave in the way he does towards another Guards Officer! Ah, the Guards are at sixes and sevens, and at Issoudun too, where they were respected!'

'Come on, Potel, don't get so worked up about it,' Max replied. 'Even if I didn't turn up to the anniversary banquet...'

'You mean you won't be at Lacroix's the day after to-morrow?' Potel cried, interrupting his friend. 'So you want to be thought of as a coward, you want people to think you're trying to keep out of Bridau's way? No! Infantrymen of the Guards mustn't give in to the dragoons. Make other arrangements, you must turn up!'

'Another man to knock off, then,' said Max. 'Well, I think I can turn up and still attend to my other business! For' (he thought) 'the powers of attorney mustn't be in my name. As old Héron has said, that would look too much like theft.'

Caught up in the nets woven around him by Philippe Bridau, this lion gave a violent shudder. He avoided everyone's eyes as he walked back along the Boulevard Vilatte saying to himself: 'Before I fight, I shall get the private income! If I am killed, at least the scrip won't go to this fellow Philippe, I shall have had it transferred to Flore's name. Following my instructions, the poor girl will go straight to Paris where, if she wishes, she can marry the son of some pensioned-off Marshal of the Empire. I'll arrange for Baruch to receive powers of attorney, and he will only transfer the scrip on my orders.'

To give him his due, Max was never calmer in outward appearance than when his blood and ideas were in a ferment.

No other soldier ever combined to this degree the qualities required in a great general. If captivity had not delayed him in his career, the Emperor would certainly have found that he was one of those men who are so necessary for the accomplishment of vast undertakings. Entering the room where Rouget, the victim of all these scenes which are so comic and yet so tragic, was still weeping, Max asked him why he was so despondent: he pretended to be surprised, said he knew nothing, and heard all about Flore's departure with well-feigned surprise.

He even questioned Kouski in order to obtain some light on the reason for this inexplicable journey!

'Madame just told me,' said Kouski, 'to tell Monsieur that she had taken the 20,000 francs in gold that was in the desk. She thought Monsieur would not begrudge her this as her wages over twenty-two years.'

'Wages?'

'Yes,' Kouski went on. ' "Ah! I shall never set foot in here again!" she said as she went off with Védie (for poor Védie, who is very fond of Monsieur, kept protesting to Madame). "No! No!" she said. "He hasn't got the slightest affection for me, he has allowed his nephew to treat me like the lowest of the low!" And didn't she weep! She wept bucketfuls!'

'Oh! I couldn't care less about Philippe!' cried the old man, whom Maxence was watching closely. 'Where is Flore? How can we find out where she is?'

'Philippe will help you. You are following his advice,' Maxence answered coldly.

'Philippe?' the old man replied. 'What can Philippe do to bring back this poor woman? Only you, dear Max, can find Flore. She will follow you, you will bring her back to me.'

'I don't want to fall out with Monsieur Bridau,' said Max.

'Heavens! If that's worrying you, he has promised me that he is going to kill you.'

'We'll see about that,' Gilet laughed.

'My dear friend, find Flore for me and tell her I'll do everything she wants!'

'Somebody must have seen her on her way through the town,' Maxence told Kouski. 'Serve our dinner. Put everything on the table, and then go and make inquiries in various places, so that by dessert we know what road Mademoiselle Brazier took.'

These instructions momentarily calmed the poor man, who was groaning like a child who has lost his nurse. At this moment, Maxence – whom Rouget hated as the cause of all his misfortune – seemed like an angel to him. A passion such as Rouget's infatuation with Flore is astonishingly like childhood. At six o'clock the Pole, who had simply been for a walk round the town, returned to the house and declared that Flore had taken the Vatan road.

'Madame is going back to her own birthplace, that's obvious,' said Kouski.

'Do you want to come to Vatan this evening?' Max asked the old man. 'The road is bad, but Kouski is a good driver, and you'll find it easier to make it up at eight o'clock tonight than it will be tomorrow morning.'

'Let's be off,' cried Rouget.

'Harness the horses quietly, and try not to let the town know anything about this silly little episode, for Monsieur Rouget's honour. Saddle my horse. I'll ride on ahead,' Max whispered to Kouski.

Monsieur Hochon had already informed Philippe Bridau of Mademoiselle Brazier's departure. Philippe jumped up from Monsieur Mignonnet's table to hurry over to the Place Saint-Jean; for he clearly understood the motive behind this able strategy. When Philippe knocked at the door, asking to be admitted to his uncle's house, Kouski answered from a first-floor window that Monsieur Rouget was unable to receive anybody.

'Fario,' Philippe said to the Spaniard, as he was walking along the Grande-Narette, 'go and tell Benjamin to fetch his horse. It is absolutely essential that I know what becomes of my uncle and Maxence.'

'They're harnessing the horse to the carriage,' said Fario, who was watching Rouget's house.

'If they go in the Vatan direction, get me a horse too, and come back with Benjamin to Monsieur Mignonnet's.'

'What are you intending to do?' asked Monsieur Hochon, who came out of his house on seeing Philippe and Fario standing in the square.

'A general's talent, my dear Monsieur Hochon, consists not only in keeping a close eye on the enemy's movements, but also in guessing from these movements what his intentions are, and constantly modifying his plan of attack whenever it is upset by some unexpected move on the enemy's part. Look, if my uncle and Maxence go out together in the carriage, they are going to Vatan; Maxence has promised to reconcile him with Flore, who *fugit ad salices*!, for this manœuvre was invented by General Virgil! If that is how things are, I don't know what I shall do; but I'll have a night to think it over, for my uncle won't confer any powers of attorney at ten in the evening – the solicitors have gone to bed. If, as the prancing of the second horse seems to indicate, Max is going to give Flore prior instructions by riding ahead of my uncle – and this seems both necessary and probable, the rascal has lost the game! You'll see how we old soldiers get our revenge in this gamble for an inheritance . . . and, as I shall need a second in the last round of the game, I am going back to Mignonnet's to make arrangements with my friend Carpentier.'

After shaking Monsieur Hochon's hand, Philippe walked down the Petite-Narette to see Major Mignonnet. Ten minutes later, Monsieur Hochon saw Maxence leaving Issoudun at a fast trot, and the old man's curiosity was so strongly aroused that he remained standing by his sitting-room window, awaiting the clatter of the old carriage, which followed not long afterwards. Such was Jean-Jacques's impatience that he followed Maxence after a time-lag of only twenty minutes. Kouski who was no doubt carrying out his real master's orders, drove the carriage at walking speed, at least in the town itself.

'If they are off to Paris, we've lost the game,' thought Monsieur Hochon.

Just at this moment a little boy from the Faubourg de

Rome arrived at Monsieur Hochon's house with a letter for Baruch. The old man's two grandsons, who had looked sheepish and crestfallen since the morning, had remained inside their grandfather's house of their own accord. Thinking carefully about their future, they had realized how much they ought to humour their grandparents. Baruch could scarcely be unaware of the influence which his grandfather Monsieur Hochon exercised over his Borniche grandparents; Monsieur Hochon would be sure to have all the Borniches' capital settled on Adolphine, if Baruch's behaviour gave them grounds for transferring their hopes on to the grand marriage with which the young man had been threatened that very morning. Richer than François, Baruch stood to lose a great deal; he decided, therefore, to yield completely to his grandfather's wishes, his only condition being that the debts he had incurred with Max should be paid off. François's future was in his grandfather's hands; the only fortune he could look forward to would come from him, since he was in debt to his grandfather, according to the guardianship accounts. Solemn promises were sworn by the two young men, whose repentance was given an additional inducement by the fact that they had compromised their future; and Madame Hochon reassured them about their debts to Maxence.

'You have done some very silly things,' she told them. 'Make up for it by good behaviour, and Monsieur Hochon will get over his anger.'

When therefore François had read Maxence's letter over Baruch's shoulder, he whispered to his cousin: 'Why not ask grandfather's advice?'

'Look,' Baruch said, bringing the old man the letter.

'Read it to me, I don't have my spectacles on me.'

My Dear Friend,
    In the grave circumstances I find myself in, I hope you won't hesitate to do me the favour of agreeing to become Monsieur Rouget's proxy. Be here by nine o'clock tomorrow morning at Vatan. No doubt I shall send you to Paris; but don't worry, I'll give you the money for the journey and I will join you there promptly, for it's virtually certain that I'll be forced to leave Issoudun

on 3 December. Farewell, I rely upon your friendship, and you can depend on mine.

MAXENCE

'Heaven be praised!' said Monsieur Hochon, 'the old imbecile's fortune has been saved from those devils' clutches!'

'It must be true if you say so,' said Madame Hochon, 'and I thank God for it. No doubt he has answered my prayers. The triumph of wicked men is always short-lived.'

'You will go to Vatan and agree to become Monsieur Rouget's proxy,' the old man told Baruch. 'A private income of 50,000 francs a year is going to be transferred to Mademoiselle Brazier's name. You will certainly leave for Paris, but you will halt at Orleans and wait to hear from me. Don't tell anyone where you are lodging, and take a room in the last inn along the Faubourg Bannier, even if it is only a waggoner's inn.'

'Here, what do you think's happened?' cried François, whom the sound of a carriage in the Grande-Narette had sent rushing to the window. 'Old Rouget and Monsieur Philippe Bridau are coming back together in the carriage, and Benjamin and Monsieur Carpentier are following on horseback!'

'I'm going to see,' cried Monsieur Hochon, carried away by curiosity.

Monsieur Hochon found old Rouget in his bedroom writing a letter which his nephew was dictating to him:

Mademoiselle,

If you do not come back to me as soon as you receive this letter, your conduct will show so much ingratitude after my many acts of kindness that I shall revoke the will I have made in your favour and bequeath my fortune to my nephew Philippe. You will also realize that Monsieur Gilet cannot be my guest any longer, now that he has rejoined you at Vatan. I have entrusted the present letter to Captain Carpentier and hope that you will heed his advice, for he will speak to you with my authority.

Your affectionate

J.-J. ROUGET

'Captain Carpentier and I met my uncle who was stupid enough to drive over to Vatan to meet Mademoiselle Brazier and Major Gilet,' Philippe explained to Monsieur Hochon with profound irony. 'I pointed out to my uncle that he was running headlong into a trap: wouldn't he be deserted by this woman, once he had signed over the proxy she is asking him for with a view to transferring into her own name a treasury scrip worth 40,000 francs a year? Now that he has written this letter, won't the beautiful fugitive return to his roof this very night? I promise I'll make Mademoiselle Brazier as pliable as a reed for the rest of her days, if my uncle allows me to take Monsieur Gilet's place, whose presence in this house is more than uncalled for, in my opinion. Am I right? And uncle is complaining!'

'Neighbour,' said Monsieur Hochon, 'you have adopted the best method of ensuring peace within your own house. My advice to you is to revoke your will, and then you'll see that Flore will become just as she used to be towards you in the early days.'

'No, because she will never forgive me for the distress I'll cause her,' the old man wept. 'She won't love me any more.'

'She will love you and promptly too. I'll make sure of that,' said Philippe.

'But can't you see?' Monsieur Hochon asked Rouget. 'They intend to rob you of your money and then leave you in the lurch.'

'Ah! If only I could be sure . . .' cried the imbecile.

'Look, here is a letter Maxence has written to my grandson Borniche,' old Hochon said. 'Read it!'

'How horrible!' Carpentier cried, on hearing the letter read aloud by Rouget, who was still weeping.

'Isn't that clear, uncle?' asked Philippe. 'Come now, keep this girl beholden to you out of self-interest, and she'll worship you . . . as can easily happen: you'll be two love-birds together.'

'She's too fond of Maxence, she'll leave me,' the old man said, seemingly terrified.

'But, uncle, the day after tomorrow either Maxence or I will have vanished from Issoudun without trace.'

'Well then! Monsieur Carpentier,' the old man went on, 'if

you promise me she'll come back, off you go! You are an honest man, tell her from me everything you think she needs to be told.'

'Captain Carpentier will whisper into her ear that I am bringing a woman from Paris whose youth and beauty are rather tantalizing,' Philippe Bridau said, 'and the hussy will come crawling back to you.'

The captain left, driving the old carriage himself. Benjamin went with him, riding on horseback, for Kouski was nowhere to be found. Though the two officers had threatened him with a court case and the loss of his job, the Pole had just escaped to Vatan on a hired horse, to tell Maxence and Flore of the surprise attack mounted by their opponent. After fulfilling his mission, Carpentier, who did not want to bring Flore back with him, was to ride back on Benjamin's horse.

On learning of Kouski's flight, Philippe said to Benjamin: 'As from this evening, you will take over the Pole's job. So try to climb on to the back of the carriage without Flore noticing, so that you are back here at the same time as her. . . . Things are beginning to warm up, Monsieur Hochon!' the lieutenant-colonel said. 'The banquet will be hilarious the day after tomorrow.'

'You are going to settle in here,' the old miser said.

'I have just told Fario to send all my things over here. I shall sleep in the bedroom which opens on to the landing outside Gilet's apartment. Uncle has agreed to that.'

'What will be the outcome of all this?' the old man asked, terror-stricken.

'The outcome will be that, in four hours from now, Mademoiselle Flore Brazier will come back to you as docile as a lamb,' Monsieur Hochon replied.

'May God bring that about!' the old man said, wiping away his tears.

'It is seven o'clock,' Philippe said. 'The queen of your heart will be here by about half past eleven. You won't see anything more of Gilet. Won't you be as happy as a king? If you want me to win,' Philippe whispered into Monsieur Hochon's ear, 'stay with us until this she-monkey arrives. Help me to keep up the old man's determination; then, between us, we'll bring home to Flore where her true interest lies.'

Monsieur Hochon remained with Philippe, realizing the appropriateness of his request; but both had a difficult task on their hands, for old Rouget kept on wailing childishly and would only stop when Philippe rehearsed the following argument, which he did ten times over: 'Uncle, if Flore comes back and behaves nicely towards you, you will realize I was right. You will be made a lot of, you will keep your private income, from now on you will act according to my advice, and everything will work to perfection.'

When the clatter of the carriage was heard in the Grande-Narette at half past eleven, the question in everyone's minds was whether it was returning full or empty. The horrible anguish on Rouget's face gave way to the prostration of extreme joy when he caught sight of the two women just as the carriage turned to enter the yard.

'Kouski, you are no longer in Monsieur Rouget's employment,' Philippe said as he helped Flore down from the carriage. 'You will not sleep here tonight, so pack your bags. Benjamin here is taking your place.'

'So you are the master here?' Flore asked ironically.

'With your permission,' Philippe answered, gripping Flore's hand as tightly as in a vice. 'Come this way. We'll have a little heart-to-heart talk.'

Philippe took the stupefied woman a few yards into the Place Saint-Jean.

'My dear girl, the day after tomorrow Gilet will be put out of harm's way by this arm of mine,' and he held out his right hand, 'or else he will have put paid to me. If I die, you will be the mistress in my poor imbecile of an uncle's house: *bene sit*! If I stay on my pins, you'll have to watch your step and serve him up with first-rate happiness. Otherwise, without meaning to be unpleasant to you, I know of prettier Fisherwomen in Paris, who are only seventeen; they will make my uncle exceedingly happy and support my interests. Get to work this evening, for if the old man isn't as merry as a cricket by tomorrow morning, I'll have just one word for you, do you understand? There's only one way of killing a man without the law being able to say anything about it and that's to fight him in a duel; but I know three ways of getting rid of a woman. So there, my darling!'

During this speech, Flore trembled like a person gripped by fever.

'Kill Max?' she said, looking at Philippe in the moonlight.

'Well, come on now. Here's my uncle.'

And indeed, despite everything Monsieur Hochon had said to him, old Rouget came out into the street to take Flore by the hand, like a miser seizing his gold; he went back into the house, took her upstairs to his bedroom and locked the door.

'Today is St Lambert's Day. Whoever leaves his job loses it,' Benjamin told the Pole.

'My master will shut all your traps,' Kouski replied as he went off to rejoin Max who took up residence at the Hôtel de la Poste.

22. *A duel to the death*

THE next day, between nine and eleven, women stood chatting on their doorsteps. Throughout the town there was only one topic of conversation: the strange revolution that had taken place overnight in old Rouget's household. Everybody was basically asking the same question.

'What will happen tomorrow between Max and Colonel Bridau at the coronation banquet?'

Philippe's words to Védie: '600 francs pension, or else you're sacked!' made her temporarily neutral between two powers as formidable as Philippe and Flore.

Knowing that Max's life was in danger, Flore became even more affectionate towards old Rouget than in the early days of their life together. Alas! Where love is concerned, self-interested deception is superior to the truth itself, which is why so many men pay so high a price to clever deceivers. Flore did not appear until breakfast time, when she came down with Rouget on her arm. Her eyes filled with tears as she saw the terrifying soldier, with his dark blue eyes and coldly sinister face, sitting where Max used to sit.

'What is the matter, Mademoiselle?' he said, after wishing his uncle good morning.

'The matter is, nephew, that she cannot bear the idea of your fighting Major Gilet.'

'I haven't the slightest wish to kill this fellow Gilet,' Philippe replied. 'All he has to do is get out of Issoudun and set sail for America with some private cargo, and I'll be the first to advise you to give him something with which to buy the best possible merchandise; I'll even wish him a good crossing! He'll make a fortune, and that will be far more honourable than kicking up a shindy in Issoudun at nights and letting the very devil loose in your house.'

'Well, that's nicely put, it really is!' Rouget said, looking at Flore.

'To A ... me ... e ... ri ... ca!' she sobbed.

'It is best to leg it to New York than moulder away in a pinewood coffin here in France. . . . No doubt your reply will be that he's very skilful: he may kill me!'

'Will you allow me to speak to him?' asked Flore in a humble, submissive tone of voice, imploring Philippe.

'Certainly, he may come and pick up his things. However, I will remain with my uncle during that time, for I am not leaving the old gentleman again,' Philippe replied.

'Védie,' Flore shouted, 'run over to the Hôtel de la Poste, my dear, and tell the Major that I would like him to . . .'

'To come and pick up his things,' Philippe said, interrupting Flore.

'Yes, yes, Védie. That will be the best excuse for him to see me. I wish to speak to him.'

Terror was repressing this woman's feelings of hatred to such an extent, and her shock was so great at now meeting a strong, implacable character after being adulated until then, that she was growing accustomed to yield to Philippe in the same way that poor Rouget had grown accustomed to yield to her. She anxiously awaited Védie's return, but Védie came back with a flat refusal from Max, who begged Mademoiselle Brazier to send him his things over to the Hôtel de la Poste.

'Will you allow me to go and take them over to him?' she asked Jean-Jacques Rouget.

'Yes, but mind you come back,' replied the old man.

'If Mademoiselle isn't back by midday, uncle, at one o'clock you must give me powers of attorney to dispose of your investment interest,' Philippe said, looking at Flore. 'Take Védie with you, for the sake of appearances, Mademoiselle. From now on you must keep my uncle's reputation in mind.'

Flore was unable to influence Maxence. Ashamed of having let himself be ousted from a position which the whole town considered disgraceful and unworthy, the major was too proud to flee from Philippe. Flore argued against him, suggesting that she and her lover should flee together to America; but Gilet, who did not want Flore without old Rouget's fortune and who did not wish to reveal his inner-most intentions to her, persisted in his determination to kill Philippe.

'We have committed a terrible blunder,' he confessed, 'we ought to have gone to Paris, all three of us, and spent the winter there; but how could we have known, when we first saw that great skulk, that things would turn out as they have? Events unfold dizzyingly fast. I thought the colonel was one of those swashbuckling types who haven't two ideas to put together: but I was mistaken. Since I wasn't smart enough to put him in his place at the very beginning, I should be a coward now if I ran away from the colonel. He has destroyed my reputation in the town. I can only recover my good name by killing him.'

'Go off to America with 40,000 francs, I shall find some way of getting rid of the brute. I shall join you, it will be much wiser.'

'What would people think of me?' he cried, impelled by the prejudice of the local gossip. 'No. Besides, I have knocked nine men off. That fellow doesn't seem much good to me: he left the Military Academy to go into the army: he was always fighting until 1815, since when he has been over to America. He hasn't ever set foot in a fencing-school whereas no one can match me with the sabre! The sabre is his weapon, I shall look generous if I offer it him, for I shall try to become the aggrieved party, and that way I'll get the upper hand. That's certainly the best course. Be calm: we shall be the masters the day after tomorrow.'

Thus, a stupid point of honour weighed more strongly in Max's judgement than sane political considerations. Flore returned to the house at one o'clock and shut herself up in her room to give full vent to her tears. All day long the gossip continued merrily in Issoudun, and a duel between Philippe and Maxence was regarded as inevitable.

'Ah! Monsieur Hochon,' said Mignonnet, who, accom-panied by Carpentier, met the old man in the Boulevard

Baron, we are very worried, for Gilet is extremely skilful with every weapon.'

'Never mind,' replied the old provincial diplomat, 'Philippe has conducted this business very well. . . . And I would never have believed that this big carefree devil would have succeeded so quickly. These two fellows have rolled towards one another like two thunderstorms.'

'Oh!' said Carpentier, 'Philippe is a deep-thinking man. His conduct before the Court of Peers was a masterpiece of diplomacy.'

'Well now, Captain Renard,' said one of the middle-class inhabitants, 'people used to say that wolf doesn't eat wolf. But it seems that Max is going to cross swords with Colonel Bridau. It will be serious between men of the Old Guard.'

'You think that's funny, you do. Because this poor boy used to get up to a little fun at nights, you have a grudge against him,' said Major Potel. 'But Gilet is the sort of man who could scarcely stay in a dead-alive place like Issoudun without getting involved in something!'

'Well, gentlemen,' a fourth person would intervene, 'Max and the colonel have had their little game. Oughtn't the colonel to have avenged his brother Joseph? Don't forget Max's treacherous behaviour towards that poor boy.'

'Bah! an artist!' Renard said.

'But old Rouget's fortune is at stake. People say that Monsieur Gilet was going to get hold of 50,000 francs a year interest, at the very moment when the colonel came to live with his uncle.'

'Gilet steal anybody's investment income? Now look here, don't say that, Monsieur Ganivet, anywhere else except here,' Potel cried, 'or else we would make you swallow your tongue – and without sauce, either!'

In all the middle-class houses of the town, people prayed for worthy Colonel Bridau's success.

On the following day about four o'clock, the officers of the Imperial Army who happened to be in Issoudun or in the neighbourhood were walking about the Place du Marché, in front of a certain Lacroix's restaurant, waiting for Philippe

Bridau. The banquet which was being held to celebrate the Emperor's coronation was due to begin at five, as is the military fashion. In every group people were talking about the Maxence affair and his expulsion from old Rouget's house, for the private soldiers had arranged to hold their gathering at a wine merchant's in the square. Amongst the officers, Potel and Renard were the only ones who tried to speak up for their friend.

'Ought we to bother about what goes on between rival heirs?' Renard was saying.

'Max has a soft spot for the ladies,' the cynical Potel observed.

'They'll soon be getting the sabres out,' said a former sub-lieutenant who was now cultivating a marsh in Haut-Baltan. 'As Monsieur Maxence Gilet was stupid enough to come and live in old Monsieur Rouget's house, he would be a coward if he let himself be chased out of it like a mere servant, without demanding satisfaction for the insult.'

'Certainly,' Mignonnet replied dryly. 'Better be a knave than a fool.'

Max, who now joined the other Napoleonic soldiers, was greeted with a very meaningful silence. Potel and Renard linked arms with their friend and walked a few paces to one side to have a word with him. Just at this moment, Philippe appeared in the distance in his full-dress uniform; he was dragging his cane along the pavement in a jaunty manner which contrasted with the close attention with which Max was forced to listen to the speeches of his two remaining friends. Mignonnet, Carpentier and a few others greeted Philippe with handshakes. This greeting, so different from the one Maxence had just received, finally banished from the latter's mind such ideas of cowardice or prudence, call it what you will, which Flore's entreaties and above all her affection had given rise to, once he was alone.

'We shall fight,' he told Captain Renard, 'and it will be a fight to the death! And so do not say anything more to me; let me play my part.'

After this parting word, pronounced in feverish tones, the

three Bonapartists came back and mingled with the group of officers. Max was the first to greet Philippe Bridau, who reciprocated his greeting with the coldest look.

'Well, gentlemen, let us sit down,' said Major Potel.

'Let us drink to the imperishable glory of Napoleon who is now in the Valhalla of the Brave,' cried Renard.

Feeling that the confrontation would be less embarrassing if all the guests were sitting at the table, everyone understood the little light-infantry captain's intention. They hurried into the long low dining-room of the Restaurant Lacroix whose windows opened out on to the market place. Every guest sat down immediately at the table, where, as Philippe had requested, the two adversaries found themselves facing one another. Several young men in the town, and especially some ex-Knights of Idleness, who were feeling fairly uneasy about what would take place at this banquet, walked up and down discussing the critical situation into which Philippe had forced Maxence Gilet. They deplored the clash between them, whilst at the same time regarding the duel as necessary. All went well until dessert, though despite the apparent verve of the dinner the two athletes remained in a state of watchfulness fairly closely resembling anxiety. Whilst waiting for the quarrel to flare up which both were bound to be contemplating, Philippe seemed admirably calm and Max dazzlingly gay; but, to those who understood the situation, each was playing a part.

As soon as the dessert had been served, Philippe said: 'Fill your glasses, my friends! I beg your permission to propose the first toast.'

'He said, *my friends*, don't fill your glass,' Renard whispered to Max.

Max poured himself some wine.

'The Grande-Armée!' Philippe cried, with true enthusiasm.

'The Grande-Armée!' was repeated as one voice by everybody.

At that moment, eleven private soldiers appeared on the threshold, amongst whom were Benjamin and Kouski, who repeated: 'The Grande-Armée!'

'Come in, my men! We're going to drink *his* health!' said Major Potel.

The ex-soldiers entered and all stood behind the officers.

'You can see *he* isn't dead!' Kouski remarked to a former sergeant, who no doubt had been bewailing the Emperor's death throes, finally concluded.

'I demand the second toast,' said Major Mignonnet.

The guests fidgeted with a few dessert dishes to keep up an appearance of composure. Mignonnet stood up.

'To those who tried to restore *his* son,' he said.

All except Maxence Gilet saluted Philippe Bridau, raising their glasses to him.

'Now it's my turn,' said Max, standing up.

'It's Max! It's Max!' people were saying outside. A deep silence descended on the room and the square outside, for Gilet's character was such that people expected some act of provocation.

'May we *all* meet here again, on the same date next year!' And he saluted Philippe ironically.

'Things are warming up,' Kouski said to his neighbour.

'The police in Paris didn't allow you to attend banquets like this,' Major Potel said to Philippe.

'Why the hell are you talking about police to Colonel Bridau?' Maxence Gilet asked insolently.

'Major Potel didn't mean any harm, *he* didn't!' Philippe replied with a bitter smile. (The hush was so deep that you could have heard a pin drop.) 'The police are so afraid of me,' Philippe went on, 'that they've sent me to Issoudun, where I've had the pleasure of meeting up with some old comrades; but, let us admit it, there aren't many amusements here. As I'm a man who never exactly objected to women's company, I now feel fairly deprived. Anyhow, I'll save up for some of these young ladies – I'm not one of those whose feather beds contain investment incomes, and Mariette at the Paris Opéra cost me an enormous amount of money.'

'Are you saying that for my benefit, my dear colonel?' Max asked, darting a glance at Philippe which worked like an electric shock.

'Take it whichever way you like, Major Gilet,' Philippe replied.

'Colonel, my two friends here, Renard and Potel, will arrange matters tomorrow . . .'

'With Mignonnet and Carpentier,' said Philippe, interrupting Gilet and pointing to his two friends.

'Now,' said Max, 'should we go on with the toasts?'

Neither of the opponents had departed from the ordinary tone of conversation. The only solemn thing about the occasion was the silence in which they were heard.

'Remember,' said Philippe, turning to the private soldiers, 'that our affairs are no concern of the townsfolk! Don't breathe a word about what has just happened. It's a secret that must remain within the Old Guard.'

'They will observe orders, Colonel,' said Renard, 'I'll make sure of that.'

'Long live his son! May he reign over France!' cried Potel.

'Death to the English!' cried Carpentier.

This toast enjoyed a prodigious success.

'Shame on Hudson Lowe!' said Captain Renard.

The dessert passed off very well, the libations were very copious. The two antagonists and their four seconds made it a point of honour that this duel, in which an immense fortune was at stake and which involved two men so distinguished for their courage, should have nothing in common with ordinary disputes. Two English gentlemen would not have behaved in a more exemplary manner than Max and Philippe; and thus the young men and other townsfolk who were standing about in groups in the square were disappointed in their expectations. In true military fashion, all the guests observed the deepest secrecy about the episode that had occurred over dessert. At ten o'clock, each of the opponents was informed that the agreed weapon was the sabre. The place chosen for the encounter was by the apse of the Capucin church, at eight in the morning. Goddet, who attended the banquet in the capacity of a former surgeon-major, had been asked to be present at the duel. Whatever the outcome was, the seconds decided that the fight would not last above ten minutes. At eleven in the evening, to the colonel's great surprise, Monsieur Hochon and his wife came to see him just as he was going to bed.

'We know what is going on,' said the old lady, her eyes brimming with tears, 'and I am coming to beg you not to go out tomorrow without saying your prayers. Uplift your soul to God.'

'Yes, Madame,' Philippe replied, prompted by old Hochon, who was standing behind his wife.

'There's something else!' said Agathe's godmother. 'I'm taking your poor mother's place, and parting with my most treasured possession. Look!' She handed Philippe a tooth attached to a piece of black velvet which was fringed with gold and on to which she had sewn two green ribbons; she then put it back again into a little bag after showing it to him. 'It's a relic of St Solange, the patron saint of Berry; I rescued it at the time of the Revolution; wear that round your neck tomorrow morning.'

'Can that protect you from sabre blows?' asked Philippe.

'Yes,' the old lady replied.

'I can't have that article on me any more than I could wear a breastplate.'

'What's he saying?' Madame Hochon asked her husband.

'He says he isn't allowed by the rules.'

'Well, then! Never mind! I shall pray for you.'

'But Madame, a prayer plus a good sword thrust can't do any harm,' said the colonel, pretending to stab Monsieur Hochon in the heart.

The old lady had to kiss Philippe's forehead. Then, as she was on her way downstairs, she gave Benjamin 30 francs – which was all the money she possessed in the world – to get him to stitch the relic into the waistband of his master's trousers. Which was done by Benjamin, not because he believed in the tooth's efficacy, for he said that his master had a much better weapon against Gilet, but because he felt bound to discharge a commission that had been so dearly bought. Madame Hochon left, feeling full of confidence in St Solange.

At eight o'clock the following morning, 3 December, under a grey sky, Max, accompanied by his two seconds and the Pole, arrived in the little meadow which at that time surrounded the apse of the former Capucin church. There they found Philippe and his seconds, together with Benjamin. Potel and Mignonnet paced out twenty-four feet. At each end of the length they marked two lines with a spade. On pain of being accused of cowardice, the opponents could not retreat beyond their respective lines; each of them had to stand on his mark, and walk forward (if he chose to) once the seconds had said: 'Go!'

'Should we take our coats off?' Philippe asked Gilet coldly.

'Certainly, colonel,' Maxence replied with a swashbuckler's self-confidence.

The two adversaries wore only their trousers: their pink flesh could be seen through the cambric of their shirts. Each man, armed with a regulation sabre of equal weight, about three pounds, and equal length, three feet, took a firm stance, holding his weapon point downwards as they awaited the signal. Everything was so calm on both sides that, in spite of the cold, the men's muscles quivered no more than if they had been bronze. Goddet, the four seconds and the two soldiers could not help feeling: 'They're splendid fellows!'

This exclamation fell from Major Potel's lips.

Just as the signal 'Go!' was given, Maxence noticed Fario's sinister face peeping out at them from the hole which the Knights of Idleness had made in the Church roof to let the pigeons into his warehouse. Max was dazzled by his eyes, which poured forth fire, hatred and vengeance. The colonel came straight at his opponent, putting himself on his guard so as to seize the advantage. Experts in the art of killing know that the cleverer of two opponents can get the upper hand – to use a metaphorical phrase which conveys the impression of the hilt-guard held high in the air. This posture, which to some extent enables a man to anticipate his antagonist's moves, so clearly indicates a first-rate duellist that a feeling of inferiority overwhelmed Max and produced that mental disorganization which demoralizes both gamblers and sportsmen when, faced with a master of the game or a man who is in luck, they falter and play below their usual standard.

'The devil!' Max thought, 'he's a first-class duellist; I'm done for!'

Max tried a moulinet, manoeuvring his sabre with the skill of a fencer; he wanted to make Philippe go dizzy and then strike his sabre and disarm him. But at the first blow he realized that the colonel's wrist was as strong as iron and as flexible as a steel spring. Maxence had to think of some other move and tried to reflect, the unfortunate man! Whereas Philippe, whose eyes were darting looks brighter even than the sabres themselves, warded off every attack as coolly and collectedly as a master practising in his fencing-jacket.

Between men as capable as these two combatants, a phenomenon is to be found which has its counterpart, amongst proletarian people, in the terrible combat known as foot boxing. Victory depends on a false move, an error in that calculation which must be as rapid as lightning and in which you must engage instinctively. During a period of time which is as short for the spectators as it seems long to the opponents, the struggle takes the form of a watchfulness that saps the strength of both soul and body, a watchfulness concealed beneath feints whose slow pace and apparent prudence seem intended to give the impression that neither of the opponents wishes to fight. This moment, which is followed by a rapid and decisive struggle, is a terrible experience for those onlookers who understand the game. Max parried badly, and the colonel knocked his sabre out of his hands.

'Pick it up!' he said, halting the fight. 'I am not the man to kill an enemy when he is disarmed.'

This was the sublimest expression of atrocity. This grandeur indicated so much superiority that the spectators considered it the shrewdest of calculations. And indeed, when Max took his guard again, he had lost his composure and inevitably found himself threatened once again with the hilt-guard raised high in the air, a position which exposed him to danger whilst keeping his opponent covered; he then tried to make up for his shameful defeat by some act of boldness; he no longer thought of keeping up his guard, but took hold of his sabre in both hands and launched furiously at the colonel, hoping to inflict some mortal wound on him in exchange for the loss of his own life. Though Philippe received a sabre blow which gashed his forehead and part of his face, he split open Max's head slantwise in a terrible return moulinet with which he countered the sledgehammer blow Max was intending for him. These two furious assaults put an end to the duel in its ninth minute. Fario came down and stood gloating over his enemy, who lay struggling in the grip of death, for in a man as strong as Max, the body muscles twitched appallingly. Philippe was carried off to his uncle's house.

So perished one of those men destined to accomplish great things, had he remained in a favourable environment; a man on whom nature had showered many qualities of character, for it had endowed him with courage, coolness and a political sense equal to Cesare Borgia's. But his education had not imparted to him that nobility of ideas and conduct without which nothing is possible in any career. He was not mourned, owing to the treacherous way in which his opponent, a less worthy man than himself, had managed to discredit him. His death put an end to the exploits of the Order of Idleness, to Issoudun's great satisfaction. In consequence of this, Philippe was in no way embarrassed by the duel, which in any case seemed like a stroke of divine retribution; the circumstances of the duel were told throughout the district with unanimous praise of both adversaries.

'They ought both to have been killed,' said Monsieur Mouilleron. 'It would have been good riddance for the Government.'

23. Madame Rouget

FLORE Brazier would have been in a most awkward position had it not been for the critical illness which she developed as a result of Max's death. She was stricken with delirium, added to which there was a dangerous inflammation caused by the complex events of the last three days; had she enjoyed her usual good health, she would perhaps have fled from the house where, above her room and in Max's bedroom and between Max's sheets, Max's murderer now lay. For three months she hovered between life and death, carefully tended by Monsieur Goddet, who also treated Philippe.

As soon as Philippe was strong enough to hold a pen, he wrote the following letters:

To Monsieur Desroches, attorney:

I have already killed the most poisonous of the two animals, but not without getting my head bashed in with a sabre blow; fortunately, however, the rascal did not put all his might into it. There is still another viper, with whom I am going to try to get on good terms, for my uncle is as fond of her as he is fond of his own gizzard. I was afraid that this woman Flore, who's a real beauty, would decamp from the scene, because then my uncle would have followed her; but the seizure she had at a serious juncture kept her in bed. If God wishes to protect me, he would call her soul into Paradise, whilst she is still feeling repentant about her wrongdoings. Meanwhile, thanks to Monsieur Hochon (who's a splendid old man!) I have the doctor, a man called Goddet, on my side – he's a sanctimonious devil who realizes that uncles' inheritances are better in their nephews' hands than in these hussies'. Besides, Monsieur Hochon has a certain amount of influence over someone named Fichet, whose daughter is rich, and whom Goddet would like his son to marry; so that the 1000-franc note which we have flourished in front of his eyes, if he can cure my head, is only a small factor in explaining his devotion to my interests. Also, this fellow Goddet, who at one time was a surgeon-major in the 3rd Infantry Regiment, has been cloistered with my friends, two splendid officers, Mignonnet and Carpentier; so that he now puts on religious airs with his female patient.

'After all, a God does exist, my child, do you see?' he says to her, taking her pulse. 'You have caused a great misfortune, and must now make amends. The finger of God is to be seen in this (it's incredible how many purposes the finger of God is made to serve!). Religion is religion; submit to the authority of the Church, practise the virtue of resignation; that will immediately calm you; it will cure you almost as effectively as my drugs. Above all, stay in this house and look after your master. Remember, forgetting and forgiving is the law of Christianity.'

Goddet has promised me he will keep Flore confined to her bed for three months. By slow degrees, she will perhaps get used to the idea of us all living together under the same roof. I have won the cook over to my side. That abominable old woman has been telling her mistress that Max would have led her a very difficult life. She says she heard the dead man say that even though he might be forced into marrying Flore on the old man's death, he didn't intend to let a woman handicap him in his ambitions. And the cook has even reached the stage of hinting to her mistress that Max would have got rid of her. So all is well. On old Hochon's advice, my uncle has torn up his will.

To Monsieur Giroudeau (c/o Mademoiselle Florentine),
Rue de Vendôme, Marais:

Dear Old Comrade,

Find out if that darling young ballet-girl Césarine is busy and try to persuade her to be ready to come down to Issoudun as soon as I ask for her. The minx would then arrive by the next available coach. She'll have to be decently dressed, and get rid of everything that reminds you of the theatre; for she must make out when she gets here that she's the daughter of a worthy soldier, killed in battle. So, plenty of respectable behaviour, a boarding-school girl's dress and top-quality virtue: those are your orders. If I do need Césarine and she turns out to be a success, there'll be 50,000 francs for her on my uncle's death; if she's busy, explain my requirements to Florentine; and both of you find me some ballet-dancer who's capable of playing this role. I have had my skull chipped in a duel with my legacy-hunter . . . who has kicked the bucket. I'll tell you all about that achievement! Ah, my dear fellow, we'll see prosperous days again, and have more fun yet, or Napoleon wouldn't be Napoleon.

If you can send me 500 cartridges, we'll get rid of them. Farewell, old chap. Use this letter to light a cigar. It's agreed that the officer's daughter will come from Châteauroux and will pretend to be asking for assistance. But I hope I shan't need to resort to this dangerous expedient. Remember me to Mariette and all our friends.

Agathe, informed of developments by a letter from Madame Hochon, hurried down to Issoudun and was received by her brother, who gave her Philippe's old room. The poor mother, whose maternal feeling for her wretched son found a new outlet, enjoyed a few happy days hearing the townsfolk's praises of the colonel.

'After all, my dear,' Madame Hochon told her on the day of her arrival, 'young men must sow their wild oats. The way-ward habits of soldiers of the Emperor's time cannot be quite the same as the habits of young men of good family who are carefully watched by their fathers. Ah, if only you knew the lengths that scoundrel Max went to here, in this town, at nights! Thanks to your son, Issoudun can breathe again and sleep peacefully. Philippe has seen reason at last, a little late in the day, but still it has come; as he used to say to us, three months' imprisonment in the Luxembourg knocks some sense into your head; anyway, Monsieur Hochon is delighted with his behaviour here, and he is respected by everyone. If your son can spend some time out of reach of the temptations of Paris, he will eventually give you great satisfaction.'

Madame Hochon saw tears of happiness well to her god-daughter's eyes on hearing these consoling words.

Philippe pretended to his mother that he was a changed man; he needed her. This crafty politician did not wish to resort to Césarine unless he actually filled Mademoiselle Brazier with horror. Realizing that Flore was an admirable instrument fashioned by Maxence, and a habit to which his uncle had grown accustomed, he wished to make use of her in preference to a Parisian girl, who might well induce the old man to marry her. Just as Fouché advised Louis XVIII to go to bed in Napoleon's arms rather than concede a People's Charter, Philippe wished to sleep between Gilet's sheets; but he was also loth to detract from the reputation he had built up for himself in Berry. To continue to play Max's role vis-à-vis Flore would be just as odious for her as for him. He could live on in his uncle's house and at his uncle's expense without incurring any dishonour, thanks to the laws of family hospitality; but Flore's reputation must be restored. Amid so many difficulties, and urged on by the hope of laying hold of the inheritance, he devised the admirable plan of making Flore his aunt. In furtherance of this secret design, he told his mother to go and see her and show her some marks of affection, treating her as a sister-in-law.

'I have to admit, dear mother,' he said, adopting a sanctimonious air and looking at Monsieur and Madame Hochon, who came to keep dear Agathe company, 'that uncle's way of life is hardly respectable, and he would only have to regularize it for Mademoiselle Brazier to enjoy the whole town's respect. Isn't it better for her to be Madame Rouget than an old bachelor's servant-cum-mistress? Isn't it easier to acquire clearly defined rights through a marriage settlement than to threaten to deprive a family of their rightful inheritance? If you or Monsieur Hochon or some good priest were willing to speak to her about this matter, you would put an end to a scandal which distresses respectable people. Besides, Mademoiselle Brazier would feel happy to be greeted by you as a sister and by me as an aunt.'

The next day, Mademoiselle Flore saw Agathe and Madame Hochon standing beside her bed; they revealed Philippe's admirable sentiments to Rouget and herself. The whole town spoke of the colonel as an excellent man, with a fine character – particularly in the light of his behaviour towards Flore. For a month Flore heard not only old Goddet, her doctor, whose profession wields so powerful an influence over the minds of sick people, but also respectable Madame Hochon, prompted by religious feelings, and Agathe, who was so gentle and pious, pointing out to her all the advantages she would derive from marrying Rouget. When – attracted by the idea of being Madame Rouget, a worthy and respectable middle-class woman – she keenly desired to recover from her illness and celebrate the marriage, it was no difficult task to get her to understand that she could not become a member of the old Rouget family and then turn Philippe out of the house.

'Besides,' old Goddet said to her one day, 'don't you owe this enormous good fortune to him? Max would never have allowed you to marry old Rouget. In any case' (he whispered into her ear) 'if you do have children, won't you avenge Max? For then the Bridaus will be disinherited.'

Two months after the fatal duel, in February 1823, the sick woman – on the advice of everyone in her immediate circle, and at Rouget's request — agreed to see Philippe. His scar made her weep, but she was soothed by his calmer, almost affectionate manner towards her. In accordance with Philippe's wish, he was left alone with his future aunt.

'My dear girl,' the soldier said to her. 'I have recommended your marriage to my uncle from the outset; if you agree to it, it will take place as soon as you are well again . . .'

'Yes, so people have told me,' she answered.

'As circumstances compelled me to cause you misfortune, it is natural that I should wish to do you the greatest possible good. A fortune, a family and the respect of everyone more than compensates for your loss. If my uncle had died, you wouldn't have been that young man's wife for long, for, according to what I have learned from his friends, he wasn't intending that you should have a happy future. Look, are we in agreement, my dear? We'll all live happily together. You will be my aunt, and nothing but my aunt. You will make sure that my uncle doesn't forget to mention me in his will; in return for this, just wait and see how I'll arrange for you to be treated in your marriage settlement. . . . Calm down, think it over and we'll talk about it again. You can see that the most sensible people and indeed the whole town are advising you to put an end to your irregular situation, and nobody blames you for receiving me into your house. People realize that in life self-interest must come before sentiment. On your wedding day you will be lovelier than you have ever been. By making you somewhat paler, your illness has given you an air of distinction again. If my uncle wasn't madly in love with you,' he said, rising from his chair and kissing her hand, 'then, upon my word of honour, you would be the wife of Colonel Bridau.'

Philippe left the bedroom leaving this last sentence in Flore's mind: it was intended to awaken a vague idea of revenge, which now beckoned to her smilingly. She was almost happy at having seen this terrifying person at her feet. Philippe had just played in miniature the scene which Richard III plays with the Queen whom he has just widowed. The significance of this scene is that calculation enters much further into the heart when it is concealed beneath an expression of feeling; then it can even overcome the most genuine grief. And so, in private life, Nature works in a way which is considered the highest expression of Art in works of genius: its method of operation is self-interest, whose motive power is money. It came as no surprise, therefore, when early in April 1823 Jean-Jacques Rouget's dining-room was the scene of a superb dinner given to celebrate the signing of the marriage settlement between Mademoiselle Flore Brazier and the old bachelor. The guests were Monsieur Héron, Monsieur Mignonnet, Monsieur Carpentier, Monsieur Hochon and old Monsieur Goddet, the four witnesses to the contract, the mayor and the parish priest, Agathe Bridau, and Madame Hochon and her friend Madame Borniche, in other words, the two old ladies who were the most highly respected in Issoudun. The bride was most appreciative of the concession Philippe had obtained from these ladies, who considered it necessary to bestow such a sign of protection upon a repentant woman. Flore was dazzlingly beautiful. The priest, who had been instructing the ignorant Fisherwoman for the last fortnight, was due to give her her first communion on the following day. The marriage was recorded and the following religious article published in the *Journal du Cher* at Bourges and the *Journal de l'Indre* at Châteauroux.

Issoudun

The religious movement is making progress in Berry. Yesterday all friends of the Church and all respectable people in this town witnessed a ceremony whereby one of the principal gentlemen in the district ended a scandalous situation that dated back to the time when religion was lacking in influence in our areas. This result, which is due to the enlightened zeal of the ecclesiastics in our town, will, we hope, inspire others to imitate it, thus doing away with the abuses of uncelebrated marriages, contracted in the most disastrous epochs of Revolutionary rule.

What is remarkable about the fact we are relating is that it has been brought about by the entreaties of a colonel of the Imperial Army, who was sent into our town by order of the Court of Peers and who stands to lose his uncle's inheritance as a result of this marriage. Such disinterestedness is rare enough in our time to be deserving of publicity.

By the terms of the marriage settlement, Rouget granted Flore a dowry of 100,000 francs and guaranteed her a jointure of 30,000 francs a year. After the sumptuous wedding reception Agathe returned to Paris the happiest of mothers, and informed Joseph and Desroches of what she called the 'good news'.

'Your son is too deep a man not to get his hands on the inheritance,' the attorney replied, after listening to Madame Bridau. 'You and poor Joseph will never obtain a sou of your brother's fortune.'

'You will always be unfair to the poor boy, just like Joseph,' the mother said. 'His behaviour at the Court of Peers was worthy of a great politician, he succeeded in saving many people's heads! Philippe's misdeeds stem from the inactivity which was paralysing his great abilities; but he has realized how harmful his faults of conduct were to any man who wants to get on in the world; and he has ambition, I am sure of that. I am not alone in foreseeing his future. Monsieur Hochon firmly believes that Philippe has a fine career ahead of him.'

'Oh! If he decides to apply his profoundly perverse intellect to making a fortune, he will certainly succeed, for he is capable of anything, and people like him make rapid progress,' said Desroches.

'Why don't you think he'll get on by honest means?' Madame Bridau asked.

'You'll see!' Desroches replied. 'However happy or unhappy his circumstances, Philippe will always be the man of the Rue Mazarine, the assassin of Madame Descoings and the domestic thief; but don't worry: he will always appear very honest to the outside world!'

On the day following the marriage, after breakfast, Philippe took Madame Rouget's arm when his uncle rose from the table to go upstairs and dress, for Flore had come downstairs in a housecoat and the old man in a dressing-gown.

'Dear aunt,' he said, taking her into the window-recess, 'now you belong to the family. Thanks to me, all the solicitors have had a hand in things. But I want no nonsense. I hope we'll behave frankly towards each other. I am well aware of the tricks you could try on; I'll keep a closer eye on you than any duenna. So you must never go out without giving me your arm and never leave my sight. As for what goes on in the house, damn it, I'll be like a spider inside its web. Here's something that will prove to you that, whilst you were confined to your bed unable to move hand or foot, I could have had you expelled from the house without a sou. Read this.'

And he handed this letter to the bewildered Flore:

My Dear Fellow,

Florentine, who at long last has just made her début in the new hall at the Opéra, dancing a *pas de trois* with Mariette and Tullia, hasn't forgotten about you, any more than Florine, who has dropped Lousteau for good and taken on Nathan. These two minxes have found you the most delightful creature you could possibly imagine, a young girl of seventeen who's as beautiful as any English-woman, and with the virtuous look of a lady who's fond of a bit of fun; she's as cunning as Desroches and as faithful as Godeschal; Mariette has trained her and wishes you the best of luck with her. No woman can stand up to this little angel who is a devil beneath the surface; she can play any role; she'll get the upper hand over your uncle and make him mad with love. She has the same celestial look as poor Coralie: she knows how and when to cry, and she has a voice that can drag a 1000-franc note out of even the most granite-like heart ... and the little hussy swigs champagne even better than we can. She's a useful person to know; she is under some obligation to Mariette which she wishes to discharge, after running through the fortunes of two Englishmen, a Russian, and a Roman prince. Mademoiselle Esther is now in the most terrible poverty; she'll be satisfied with 10,000 francs. She has just said, laughingly: 'Here, I've never fleeced any solid middle-class type, this'll teach me how!' She is a close friend of Finot, Bixiou, des Lupeaulx – all our circle in fact. Ah, if great fortunes still existed in France, she would be the greatest harlot of modern times. This letter has a ring of Nathan, Bixiou, Finot about it; they are just fooling around with the above-named Esther, in the most magnificent apartment you could find, which old Lord Dudley, de Marsay's true father, has just fixed up for Florine. He has been had by the witty actress, thanks to the costume she wears in her new part. Tullia is still with the Duc de Rhétoré, Mariette is still with the Duc de Maufrigneuse; so, between them they will get your police supervision remitted when the King's birthday comes round again. Try to get your uncle dead and buried by next St Louis's day, come back with the inherit-ance and enjoy some of it with Esther and your old friends who are all signing this letter together and wish to be remembered to you.

NATHAN, FLORINE, BIXIOU, FINOT, MARIETTE,
FLORENTINE, GIROUDEAU, TULLIA

Trembling in Madame Rouget's fingers, the letter was a clear indication of the terror that gripped her soul and body. The aunt did not dare look at her nephew, who glared at her with a terrible expression in his eyes.

'I trust you,' he said, 'as you can see; but I want something in return. I made you my aunt so that I could marry you one day. You are worth just as much to my uncle as Esther would be. A year from now, we must be in Paris, the only place where beauty is really in its element. You will enjoy yourself a bit more there than you would here, for there it's a perpetual round of amusements. I am going back into the army; I'll become a general and then you will be a great lady. That's the future that lies in store for us, now work towards it. . . . But I want a guarantee of our alliance. Within a month from now you will persuade my uncle to give me his full powers of attorney, on the pretext of saving both him and yourself the worry of managing his affairs. A month later, I want a special power of attorney to transfer his Treasury scrip to me. Once the scrip is in my name, we shall each have an equally good reason for getting married one day. All this, my dear aunt, is clear and obvious. There mustn't be any misunderstanding between us. I can marry my aunt after a year of widowhood, but I could never marry a dishonoured woman.'

He left the room without waiting for a reply. When Védie entered a quarter of an hour later to clear the table, she found her mistress pale and in a cold sweat, despite the time of year. Flore felt like a woman who has fallen to the bottom of a precipice. Looking into her future, she saw nothing but darkness; and in this darkness monstrous things were dimly visible, as if in the far distance – things which could only be perceived indistinctly, but which terrified her. She could feel the damp chill of underground passages. She was instinctively afraid of this man, and yet a voice cried out within her that he deserved to be her master. She could do nothing to change her destiny: whereas Flore Brazier had had a separate bedroom in old Rouget's house for decency's sake, Madame Rouget belonged to her husband, and so found herself deprived of that precious freedom of action which a housekeeper-mistress retains. In her horrible predicament, she hoped she might bear a child; but during the last five years, she had made Jean-Jacques the most decrepit of old men. Their marriage was to have the same effect on the poor man as Louis XII's second marriage had upon him. Besides, the close watchfulness of a man like Philippe, a man who had nothing else to occupy himself with, for he gave up his job, made any act of revenge quite impossible. Benjamin was an innocent and devoted spy. Védie trembled in Philippe's presence. Flore found that she was alone and without assistance! In the end, she grew afraid of dying; without knowing that Philippe could bring about her death, she guessed that any suspected pregnancy would be her death sentence. She trembled at the sound of his voice, at the veiled sparkle of his gambler's glance and at even the slightest movements of this soldier, who treated her with the politest brutality. As for the powers of attorney required by the fierce colonel, who was a hero in the eyes of the whole of Issoudun, it was given to him as soon as he needed it; for Flore fell under this man's domination as completely as France fell under Napoleon's. Like the moth whose feet are caught in the molten wax of a candle, Rouget rapidly used up his remaining energy.

As he witnessed his uncle's agony, the nephew remained as impassive and cold as the diplomats who, in 1814, witnessed the convulsions of Imperial France.

Philippe, who could scarcely believe there was any future for Napoleon II, then wrote the following letter to the War Minister, to whom – at Mariette's request – it was passed on by the Duc de Maufrigneuse:

My Lord,

Napoleon is no more. I wished to remain faithful to him after assuring him of my allegiance; now, I am free to proffer my services to His Majesty. If Your Excellency deigns to give His Majesty an account of my conduct, the King will no doubt consider my behaviour consonant with the laws of honour, if not with the laws of the realm. The King, who thought that it was natural for his aide-de-camp, General Rapp, to weep at his former master's death, will no doubt extend his indulgence to me: Napoleon was my benefactor.

I therefore beg Your Excellency to take into consideration my request for an appointment within my own rank, and assure you of my complete allegiance. I hope I have said enough, my Lord, to convince you that in me the King will have the most loyal of subjects.

Pray accept the respectful homage with which I have the honour of being

Your Excellency's most obedient and humble servant,

PHILIPPE BRIDAU

formerly a major in the Dragoon Guards,
Officer of the Legion of Honour, under police
supervision at Issoudun

With this letter was enclosed a request for permission to visit Paris for family reasons, to which Monsieur Mouilleron added letters from the Mayor, the Subprefect and the Police Superintendent of Issoudun, all of whom gave Philippe the highest praise, basing their testimonials on the article which had appeared in the Press on the occasion of his uncle's marriage.

A fortnight later, just as the Salon was opening, Philippe obtained the permission he had asked for, together with a letter from the Minister of War informing him that, on the King's instructions and as an initial mark of favour, he had been reinstated in the Army in his rank of lieutenant-colonel.

24. The repentance of a saintly woman

PHILIPPE brought his aunt and old Rouget to Paris. Three days after his arrival he took Rouget to the Treasury, to sign the document transferring the scrip which then became his property. Like Flore herself, the dying man was plunged by his nephew into the exorbitant delights offered by the dangerous company of tireless actresses, journalists, artists and dubious women where Philippe had already expended his own youth and where old Rouget had his fill of Fisherwomen. Giroudeau promised that he would assist old Rouget towards the pleasant death which a Marshal of France was later to make so illustrious (or so it is said). It was Lolotte, one of the loveliest figurantes at the Opéra, who amiably killed off the old man. But as Rouget died after a splendid supper given by Florentine, it was quite difficult to know whether it was the supper or Mademoiselle Lolotte who had finished off the old man from Berry. Lolotte attributed his death to a slice of pâté de foie gras; and, as the Strasbourg delicacy was in no position to reply, it became an established fact that the old man had died of indigestion. In this exceedingly free and easy world, Madame Rouget was in her element; but Philippe made Mariette her chaperone, and Mariette would not allow the widow to commit any stupidities – though a few flirtations alleviated her mourning.

In October 1823, duly furnished with his aunt's powers of attorney, Philippe returned to Issoudun to sell up his uncle's estate; the operation was rapidly completed, for he was back again in Paris by March 1824, with 1,600,000 francs, the net proceeds of his late uncle's property – quite apart from the precious pictures which had never left old Hochon's house. Philippe invested his money with Mongenod and Son, where young Baruch Borniche was working, and about whose solvency and integrity old Hochon had given him satisfactory assurances. The finance house allowed him 6 per cent a year on the 1,600,000 francs, with three months' notice of withdrawal.

One fine day, Philippe came to invite his mother to attend his wedding, at which Giroudeau, Finot, Nathan and Bixiou were the witnesses. By the terms of the marriage settlement the widowed Madame Rouget, whose matrimonial contribution was one million francs, made her property over to her future husband in the event of her dying childless. There were no wedding invitations and no reception and no show, for Philippe had a plan in mind: he set his wife up in the Rue Saint-Georges in an apartment which Lolotte sold him fully furnished, which Madame Bridau the younger found quite enchanting, and where her husband rarely came. Keeping everybody in ignorance of the fact, Philippe bought a magnificent town house in the Rue de Clichy for 250,000 francs, at a time when no one suspected the value which properties in this district would one day acquire; out of his income he paid 150,000 francs towards the cost of this house, agreeing to repay the balance within two years. He spent enormous amounts of money on furniture and interior decoration – in fact, two years' income. The superb pictures were restored, and estimated to be worth 300,000 francs; they shone forth in this house in their dazzling splendour.

At the accession of Charles X the Duc de Chaulieu's family enjoyed even more favour than they had previously done; Chaulieu's eldest son, the Duc de Rhétoré, often saw Philippe at Tullia's. During Charles X's reign, the elder branch of the Bourbons believed that they were permanently reinstated upon the throne; they followed Marshal Gouvion-Saint-Cyr's advice that they should attract soldiers from the Imperial Army on to their side. Philippe, who no doubt made valuable disclosures about the conspiracies of 1820 and 1822, was appointed a lieutenant-colonel in the Duc de Maufrigneuse's regiment. This charming nobleman felt himself morally bound to protect a man from whom he had stolen Mariette. The Ballet was not without a hand in this appointment. Besides, in its wisdom, the secret Cabinet of Charles X had already decided to give the Dauphin a slight tincture of liberalism. Philippe, who had virtually become the Duc de Maufrigneuse's personal favourite, was presented therefore not only to the Dauphin, but to the Dauphine, who was by no means displeased by rough characters and military men well known for their loyalty. Philippe weighed up the Dauphin's role very clearly, and used the first staging of this sham liberalism to get himself appointed aide-de-camp to a Marshal who was in favour with the Court. In January 1827 Philippe, promoted to lieutenant-colonel in the Royal Guards Regiment which at that time was commanded by the Duc de Maufrigneuse, requested the favour of ennoblement. During the Restoration, plebeian officers serving in the Guards regiments more or less had the right to petition for a title of nobility. Colonel Bridau, who had just bought the estate of Brambourg, asked for the privilege of entailing this estate with a count's title. He obtained this concession by making full use of his connexions in the highest society, where he would appear with a sumptuous retinue of carriages and liveries, in fact, all the paraphernalia of a great lord. No sooner did Philippe (a lieutenant-colonel in the finest cavalry regiment in the Guards) see his name recorded in the peerage under the title of Comte de Brambourg than he began to frequent the house of the Comte de Soulanges, a lieutenant-general in the artillery, to whose youngest daughter, Mademoiselle Amélie de Soulanges, he paid his addresses. Insatiable in his ambition and backed by the mistresses of every influential man, Philippe requested the honour of appointment as one of the Dauphin's aides-de-camp. He had the effrontery to tell Madame la Dauphine that 'an old officer who had been wounded on several battlefields and had experience of large-scale warfare would not be useless to His Royal Highness, when the need arose.' Philippe had the knack of adopting the tones of the most accomplished courtier; in this higher sphere he behaved exactly as was required, just as at Issoudun he had managed to win Mignonnet's support. Moreover, he lived on a magnificent scale and gave splendid receptions and dinners, to which he would not invite any of his old friends whose stations in life might have jeopardized his own future career. He was ruthless towards his boon companions. He absolutely refused to allow Bixiou to speak to him on behalf of Giroudeau, who wanted to go back into the army again after Florentine had dropped him.

'He's a man without any morals!' said Philippe.

'So that's what he called me!' cried Giroudeau, 'I who got rid of his uncle for him!'

'We'll have our revenge,' Bixiou answered.

Philippe wanted to marry Mademoiselle Amélie de Soulanges, become a general and command one of the regiments in the Royal Guards. He requested so many favours that, to silence him, he was appointed a commander of both the Legion of Honour and the Order of Saint-Louis. One evening, as Agathe and Joseph were walking home in the rain, they saw Philippe go by in full uniform, loaded with decorations and sitting upright in a corner of his handsome brougham, which was upholstered in yellow silk and had a coat of arms surmounted by a count's coronet; he was on his way to a reception at the Élysée-Bourbon. He splashed his mother and brother with mud, as he waved to them patronizingly.

'The rascal's getting on in the world, isn't he?' Joseph remarked to his mother. 'Even so, he ought to do better than splash mud in our faces.'

'He is in such a fine position, so high up, that we mustn't blame him for forgetting us,' said Madame Bridau. 'Climbing such a steep slope, he has so many duties to carry out and so many sacrifices to make that he can very easily not come to see us, even though he is still thinking about us.'

'My dear fellow,' the Duc de Maufrigneuse said one evening to the new Comte de Brambourg, 'I am sure your courtship will be favourably considered; but you would have to be free to marry Amélie de Soulanges. What have you done with your wife?'

'My wife?' said Philippe with a gesture, look and accent later discovered by Frédérick-Lemaître for one of his most terrifying roles. 'Alas! I'm afraid that I am certainly going to lose her. She hasn't a week to live. Ah! My dear duke, you have no idea what it's like to marry beneath yourself! A woman who was once a cook, who has the tastes of a cook, a woman who dishonours me, for I am very much to be pitied. But I have had the honour of explaining my position to Madame la Dauphine. It all happened through having to rescue a million francs which my uncle had bequeathed to this creature in his will. Fortunately my wife has developed a taste for liqueurs; at her death, I will obtain control of a million deposited at Mongenod's bank, besides which I have 30,000 francs a year invested in the 5 per cent, whilst my entailed estate brings in 40,000 francs a year. If Monsieur de Soulanges is given a Marshal's baton, as everything suggests he will be, then, with my title of Comte de Brambourg, I can become a general and a Peer of France. After being aide-de-camp to the Dauphin, that is the position I shall reach before I retire.'

At the Salon of 1823, the King's Principal Painter, one of the most excellent men of his time, had obtained a lottery office for Joseph's mother in the neighbourhood of La Halle. Later, Agathe was fortunate enough to change places, without having to make up for any difference in value, with the grantee of a lottery office in a house in the Rue de Seine where Joseph set up his studio. The widow now employed a manager and did not cost her son anything. By 1828, although in charge of an excellent lottery office for which she was indebted to Joseph's fame, Madame Bridau still did not believe in his fame, which was very much in dispute, as is all true fame in its beginnings. The great artist, who was still struggling against his passions, had enormous needs; he did not earn enough to maintain the luxurious standard of living demanded both by his social connexions and his distinguished position within the new school of painting. Though he received strong support from his friends in the Cénacle and from Mademoiselle des Touches, his work was not to middle-class people's taste. Middle-class people, who have the money nowadays, never spend a penny to support anyone whose talent is considered controversial, and Joseph had the Classical school, the Institut and the critics whose opinions flowed from these two other powers all ranged against him. The Comte de Brambourg feigned amazement whenever people spoke to him of Joseph.

Although supported by Gros and Gérard, who obtained him the Cross of the Legion of Honour at the Salon of 1827, the courageous artist had few commissions. The Home Office and the Royal Household were reluctant enough to buy his large canvases, but art dealers and wealthy foreigners were still less concerned about him. Besides, as is well known, Joseph falls a little too readily into whimsicalness, and this produces unevenness of quality, on the strength of which his enemies deny his ability.

'Large-scale painting is in a very sorry state,' said his friend Pierre Grassou, who painted daubs that were popular with the middle class, whose flats could not take large canvases.

'You need to decorate a whole cathedral,' Schinner often remarked to Joseph, 'you will silence the critics by painting some huge canvas.'

These words, which sounded so terrible to dear Agathe, bore out her early assessment of Joseph and Philippe. The facts supported her in her opinion (she was still provincial in outlook): had not Philippe, her favourite son, turned out to be the great man in the family? In his early mistakes she saw the waywardness of genius; Joseph, whose works left her coldly indifferent, for she saw too much of them in their formative stages to admire the finished product, did not seem to her to have advanced any further in his career by 1828 than in 1816. Poor Joseph owed people money, he was almost overwhelmed by his debts, he had chosen a thankless profession, which brought nothing in. Agathe could not even understand why Joseph had received the Legion of Honour. Philippe, who was now a count, who had developed enough self-control to give up gambling and who was invited to the receptions given by the Princess Royal, this brilliant colonel who, in military reviews or processions, would march past in a splendid uniform with two red ribbons across his chest – *he* was the embodiment of Agathe's maternal dreams. One day, on the occasion of some public ceremony, the odious spectacle of Philippe's destitution on the Seine embankment near the École des Beaux-Arts was wiped from his mother's mind as he passed her by, at the very same spot as before, now riding ahead of the Dauphin, with plumes on his shako and a dolman glittering with gold and fur! Agathe, who in her zealous loyalty had become a sort of grey-habited nun to the artist, only glowed with motherhood towards the bold aide-de-camp of His Royal Highness Monseigneur the Dauphin! In her pride for Philippe, she felt she could soon have him to thank for a comfortable retirement; she forgot that the lottery office from which she earned her livelihood had been obtained through Joseph. One day, Agathe found her poor artist so worried by the total amount owing on his colours merchant's invoice that – cursing the arts – she offered to pay off his debts. The poor woman, who paid the household expenses out of the profits from her lottery office, was most careful never to ask Joseph for a penny. She was therefore penniless; but she was relying on Philippe's good nature and open purse. For three years she had daily awaited a visit from her son; she pictured him bringing her some enormous sum, and delighted in advance in the pleasure it would give her to offer this money to Joseph, whose assessment of Philippe was still as inflexible as Desroches's.

Without telling Joseph about it, she wrote Philippe the following letter:

To Monsieur le Comte de Brambourg
My Dear Philippe,

You haven't given a thought to your mother once in five years! That is not right. You should think of the past sometimes, if only because of your excellent brother. Today Joseph is in need, whilst you are rolling in money; he is working, whilst you rush from one party to another. You have taken the whole of my brother's fortune. What's more, according to what young Borniche says, you have a private income of 200,000 francs a year. Well then, come and visit Joseph. During your visit, put a score of 100-franc notes in the death's-head; you owe us them, Philippe; but despite that, your brother will feel indebted to you, not to mention the pleasure you will give your mother.

AGATHE BRIDAU (née Rouget)

Two days later, the maid brought this terrible letter into the studio, where poor Agathe had just finished breakfasting with Joseph:

My Dear Mother,

A man doesn't marry Mademoisélle Amélie de Soulanges with only nutshells for a fortune, when concealed beneath the title of the Comte de Brambourg is the name of

Your son,

PHILIPPE BRIDAU

Falling back on to the studio divan, almost in a faint, Agathe dropped the letter. The rustle of the falling paper, together with Agathe's low but horrible cry, prompted Joseph to jump up, just when he had momentarily forgotten his mother's presence (he was working away furiously at a sketch); he craned his head over his canvas to see what was the matter. Seeing his mother outstretched on the floor, the artist let go of his palette and brushes, and ran to pick up the corpse-like figure! He put his arms round Agathe and carried her into his bedroom, where he laid her on his bed and sent the maid to fetch his friend Bianchon. As soon as Joseph was able to question his mother, she confessed to him about the letter she had written Philippe and the answer she had received. The artist rushed to pick up this reply whose brutal conciseness had just broken his poor mother's tender heart, smashing the grandiose illusions she had built up in support of her maternal preferences. When he returned to his mother's bed, Joseph had the sense to remain silent. He never mentioned his brother during the three weeks her illness, or rather her death throes, lasted. In fact, Bianchon, who came every day and tended the sick woman with the devotion of a true friend, had enlightened Joseph on the very first day as to the true state of things.

'At her age and in her circumstances,' he said, 'we can only think of making her death as painless as possible.'

Agathe, indeed, was so strongly convinced that God was calling her to the next life that on the very next day she asked for the ministrations of old Abbé Loraux, who for twenty-two years had been her confessor. No sooner was she left alone with him than she poured all her grief into his heart, and rehearsed all that she had told her godmother, which she often kept on repeating.

'In what way have I displeased God? Do not I love Him with all my heart? Have not I walked along the path of salvation? What have I done wrong? And if I am guilty of a wrong I am unaware of, do I still have time to make a requital for it?'

'No,' the old man answered in a quiet voice. 'Alas! Your life seems to be pure and your soul spotless; but God's eye, my poor afflicted creature, is more discerning than that of his ministers! I now see the truth a little too late, for you have even misled me.'

Hearing these words from a man who until then had only ever spoken peace and consolation, Agathe sat bolt upright in bed, opening her eyes wide with terror and anxiety.

'Tell me! Tell me!' she cried.

'Be consoled!' the aged priest continued. 'From the form your punishment has taken, I can see that you will be forgiven. God is only harsh on this earth towards his chosen people. Woe betide those whose misdeeds meet with a favourable reception in this world, they will be formed again within humanity until eventually their simple errors are harshly punished, and not until then will they reap the celestial harvest. Your life, my daughter, has been one long act of wrongdoing. You now fall into the pit you have dug for yourself; the only side of our characters in which we ever fail is the one we have weakened within ourselves. You have given your heart to a monster in whom you saw your own fame and glory, and failed to appreciate the son in whom your true glory shines forth! You have been so deeply unjust that you have overlooked the striking contrast between them: you derive your livelihood from Joseph, whereas your other son has constantly plundered you. The poor son who loves you without the reward of an equal love returned provides you with your daily bread, whereas the rich man who has never given you a single thought, and who despises you, hopes for your death.'

'Oh! I don't believe that!' she protested.

'But it is true. Your humble station in life upsets the hopes on which he has set his pride. There are your crimes as a mother! Your sufferings and torments as a woman foreshadow the peace you will enjoy in the Lord. Your son Joseph is so great a man that his love for you has never waned despite your unjust favouritism. Love him well! Give him your whole heart during these last days! Pray for him, and I shall pray for you.'

Unsealed by such powerful hands, the poor mother's eyes surveyed the whole course of her life. Enlightened by this ray of brightness, she realized the wrongs she had involuntarily done, and burst into tears. The aged priest was so deeply moved at the sight of such repentance in an errant heart, a heart that erred solely out of ignorance, that he left the bedroom to avoid revealing his compassion. Joseph came back into his mother's room about two hours after her confessor had departed. He had been to see one of his friends, to borrow money to pay off his most urgent debts, and tiptoed back into the room, believing that Agathe was asleep. He was thus able to sit down in his armchair without being seen by the sick woman.

A broken sob in which the words: 'Will he forgive me?' could be heard caused Joseph to jump up in a cold sweat, believing that his mother had fallen into the delirium that precedes death.

'What is it, mother?' he asked her, frightened by her tear-swollen eyes and grief-stricken face.

'Ah! Joseph! Will you forgive me, my son?' she cried.

'What do you mean?'

'I have not loved you as you deserved to be loved.'

'That's nonsense!' he cried. 'You haven't loved me? Haven't we been living under the same roof for seven years? For seven years haven't you been my housekeeper? Haven't I seen you every day? Haven't I heard your voice? Are you not the sweet and indulgent companion of my poverty-stricken life? What does it matter if you don't understand painting? Not everybody can have that gift! Only yesterday I was saying to Grassou: what consoles me in my struggles is the fact that I have a good mother; she is everything that an artist's wife must be, she takes care of everything, she looks after my material needs without causing me the slightest upset.'

'No, Joseph, no, you loved me, but I haven't loved you equally in return. Oh! How I would like to live on! Give me your hand.'

Agathe took hold of her son's hand, kissed it, held it to her heart and gazed at him with a glowing tenderness in the blue of her eyes that until then she had shown only to Philippe. Understanding facial expressions, the artist was so struck by this change and realized so clearly that his mother's heart was now opening up its treasures to him that he took her into his arms, holding her for some moments in his tight embrace, crying out like a madman:

'Oh, mother! mother!'

'I feel that you have forgiven me; God must confirm a son's forgiveness of his mother!'

'Just lie calm, don't worry yourself, and remember this: I feel that the love you are showing me now makes up for all the past,' and he laid his mother's head carefully on the pillow.

During the two weeks when life and death struggled for possession of this holy creature, she looked at Joseph in such loving ways, and showed such affectionate gestures and impulses, that in each of her outpourings a whole life seemed to flow forth. The mother now thought only of her son, holding herself in no esteem; elated by her love, she no longer felt any pain or suffering. She would say the innocent things children say. D'Arthez, Michel Chrestien, Fulgence Ridal, Pierre Grassou and Bianchon would come and keep Joseph company, and would often engage in whispered discussions in the sick woman's bedroom.

'Oh! How I would love to know what colour is!' she cried one evening, hearing them discuss a painting.

Joseph himself was sublime in the way he looked after his mother: he never left her room, he fondled Agathe in his heart, he responded to her tenderness with equal love. It was an unforgettable experience for the great artist's friends. These men, all of whom embodied the union of true talent and great character, were everything they ought to have been towards Joseph and his mother: angels that prayed, angels that wept with him, not mouthing prayers and raining tears but joining with him both in thought and action. Being as richly endowed with feeling as he was with genius, Joseph guessed from a few glances of his mother's that one desire lay buried within her heart; one day he said to d'Arthez: 'She has loved this rascal Philippe too much not to want to see him again before she dies.'

Joseph asked Bixiou, who was now launched in the Bohemian world which Philippe occasionally frequented, to persuade this wretched upstart to come out of pity and feign some affection, so that his poor mother's heart would be enveloped in a shroud threaded with illusions. As an observer of men and a mocking misanthropist, Bixiou was delighted to carry out such a mission. When he had explained Agathe's situation to the Comte de Brambourg, who received him in a bedroom hung with yellow water silk, the colonel started to laugh.

'What the devil do you want me to go there for? The only help the good woman can give me is to kick the bucket as soon as possible, for she'd cut a sad figure at my wedding to Mademoiselle de Soulanges. The less family I have, the better will be my position. You must realize that I should like to bury the name of Bridau under the grave stones of the Père-Lachaise! My brother is constantly killing my reputation by bringing my real name into the open! You have too much common sense not to understand my position, haven't you? Look, supposing you became a Member of Parliament, you have got a marvellous gift of the gab, you would be as feared as Chauvelin and you could become Comte Bixiou, Director of the School of Fine Arts. Once you had become that, would you be happy if your grandmother Madame Descoings was still alive, at having that worthy woman hanging around you, who was just like Madame Saint-Léon? Would you offer her your arm in the Tuileries? Would you introduce her to the aristocratic family into which you were trying to marry? Damn it! You'd hope to see her six feet below ground level, warmly wrapped up in a lead night-dress! Now, lunch with me and let's change the subject. I am a self-made man, my dear fellow, and I know it. I don't want people to see my dirty linen! My son will be more fortunate than I, he will be a great nobleman. The rascal will wish for my death, I fully expect that, or else he won't be my son.'

He rang the bell and said to a manservant: 'My friend is lunching with me, serve us an exquisite little lunch.'

'But smart society wouldn't see you in your mother's bedroom,' Bixiou protested. 'What harm would it do you to pretend to love the poor woman for a few hours?'

'I see what you're up to!' said Philippe, winking. 'You have been sent by them. I am an old warhorse who knows everything there is to know about genuflexions. My mother wants to diddle me out of some money for Joseph, as she is dying! No, thank you very much.'

When Bixiou related this scene to Joseph, the poor artist was chilled to the heart.

'Does Philippe know that I am ill?' asked Agathe, in a doleful voice, on the very evening of the day Bixiou gave an account of his mission.

Joseph left the room, stifled by tears. Abbé Loraux, who was sitting by her bedside, took her hand in his, clasped it tight and replied: 'Alas, my child, you have only ever had one son!'

On hearing this sentence, which she understood, Agathe fell into a crisis which was the first stage of her death-struggle. She died twenty hours later.

In the delirium that preceded her death, the words: 'Whom does Philippe take after?' escaped her lips.

Joseph was the only chief mourner at his mother's funeral. Philippe had gone on military business to Orleans, hounded out of Paris by the following letter which Joseph wrote to him just as their mother was breathing her last breath:

Monster, my poor mother has died from the shock caused by your letter; go into mourning for her, but pretend to be ill. I do not wish her assassin to be beside me at her coffin.

JOSEPH B.

Conclusion

THE artist who no longer felt he had the strength to paint, though in his deep grief he perhaps needed the kind of mechanical distraction which work affords, was surrounded by his friends who agreed never to leave him alone. A fortnight after the funeral, Bixiou – who was as fond of Joseph as a scoffing man can be of anyone – was one of the friends who gathered in the studio. At this moment, the maid hurried into the room, handing Joseph a letter which had been brought, she said, by an old woman who was awaiting a reply in the porter's lodge.

Monsieur

Although I dare not call you by the name of brother, I must make this appeal to you, if only because of the name I bear . . .

Joseph turned over the page and looked at the signature at the bottom of the last facing page. The words: 'Comtesse Flore de Brambourg' made him shudder, for he had a premonition of some horrible deed thought up by his brother.

'That rascal would catch even the devil out! And yet he's called a man of honour! And he wears a colonel's scalloped braid around the collar of his uniform! And struts about the Court with neck held high when instead he ought to be stretched by the neck! This rough neck actually calls himself a count!'

'And there are a lot more like him!' cried Bixiou.

'Still, Flore Brazier deserves everything she gets,' Joseph continued. 'She isn't worth putting oneself out for, she would have let me have my head cut off like a chicken, without saying: He is innocent!'

As Joseph threw the letter to the ground, Bixiou picked it up nimbly and read it out aloud:

Whatever wrong she may have done, is it right that Madame la Comtesse Bridau de Brambourg should die in the workhouse? If such is my fate, if such is the will of Monsieur le Comte and of yourself, then so be it; but if it is, as you are Dr Bianchon's friend, get him to give me his support so that I can find a bed at some workhouse. The bearer of this letter has been on eleven successive days to the Hôtel de Brambourg in the Rue de Clichy without obtaining any help from my husband. My condition does not permit me to summon an attorney, who would set about obtaining by legal processes what is morally due to me that I may die in peace. Besides, nothing can save me, I am aware of that. So, if you do not wish to concern yourself with your unfortunate sister-in-law give me the money to buy something with which to end my life; for, as I now realize, your brother desires my death, and has always desired it. Although he told me that he knew three infallible ways of killing a woman, I have not been intelligent enough to foresee which of these ways he has used.

In the event of your honouring me with your help, and seeing my pitiful plight for yourself, I am living at the corner of the Rue du Houssay and the Rue Chantereine, on the fifth floor. If I don't pay my arrears of rent by tomorrow, I must get out! And where can I go then . . .? I hope you will allow me to sign myself

Your sister-in-law
Comtesse FLORE DE BRAMBOURG

'What a catalogue of infamies!' cried Joseph. 'What is at the back of it all?'

'First let's call the woman in. I bet she's a famous preface to the story,' said Bixiou.

A moment later, there appeared a woman whom Bixiou described in these words: a walking rag bag! Indeed, she was a heap of linen and old dresses piled one on top of another, fringed with mud (on account of the season) – the whole of which was mounted on fat legs whose thick feet were badly wrapped in patched-up stockings and whose shoes oozed water out of their holes. Above this pile of tattered clothes was one of those heads you find in Charlet's pictures of sweeping women, tricked out in a horrible silk scarf whose very folds had worn thin.

'What is your name?' asked Joseph, whilst Bixiou was

sketching the woman as she leaned on an umbrella dating back to year II of the Republic.

'Madame Gruget, at your service, sir. I did have a private income,' she added, speaking to Bixiou, whose sly laugh offended her. 'If my poor daughter hadn't accidentally loved a fellow too much, I shouldn't be in the position I'm in today. She threw herself into the water, saving your presence, sir, my poor Ida did! So I was stupid enough to start backing a lottery number, and that's why at my time of life (I'm seventy-seven, sir!) I'm a sick-nurse earning ten sous a day, with food thrown in . . .'

'You're not dressed!' said Bixiou. 'My grandmother used to dress, she did! Even though she also backed her favourite lottery number.'

'But out of my ten sous I've got to pay for a furnished . . .'

'What's the matter with the lady you are looking after? What has she got?'

'Nothing, sir, if it's money you're meaning – her illness makes even the doctors shudder. She owes me for sixty days, that's why I am still looking after her. Her husband, who is a count, for she is a countess, will no doubt pay my bill when she is dead; so I've lent her everything I had . . . but I've nothing left: I've pawned all my things! She owes me forty-seven francs ten sous, besides my thirty francs nurse's wages; and, as she wants to kill herself with coal: it's not right, I tell her. . . . I've even told the concierge to sit up with her whilst I'm away, because she's capable of throwing herself out of the window.'

'But what's the matter with her?' asked Joseph.

'Ah, sir, the convent doctor has been, but as far as the illness was concerned,' Madame Gruget went on, adopting a shame-faced look, 'he said she must be taken to the workhouse . . . it's a fatal case.'

'We'll come at once!' said Bixiou.

'Here is ten francs!' said Joseph.

After plunging his hand into the famous death's-head to get all his cash, the artist went to the Rue Mazarine, leaped into a cab, and travelled to where Bianchon lived, whom he was fortunate enough to find at home; meanwhile, Bixiou was dashing to the Rue de Bussy, to pick up their friend Desroches. An hour later the four friends met in the Rue du Houssay.

'This Mephistopheles on horseback called Philippe Bridau has gone the right way about getting rid of his wife,' Bixiou said to his three friends as they climbed the stairs. 'As you are aware, our friend Lousteau, who was only too happy for Philippe to give him a 1,000-franc note every month, made sure that Madame Bridau associated with Florine, Mariette, Tullia and Madame du Val-Noble. When Philippe saw that his Fisherwoman had grown used to fine clothes and expensive pleasures, he gave her no further money, allowing her to obtain it . . . you realize how? After eighteen months Philippe had gradually pushed his wife along the downward path; finally with the aid of a dazzlingly handsome young warrant-officer, he gave her a taste for liqueurs. As he rose, his wife fell, and now the Countess is in the gutter. This girl, born in the countryside, has a tough constitution. I don't know how Philippe set about getting rid of her. I am eager to study this little drama, for I have to get my revenge on our friend. Alas, my friends,' Bixiou said in a tone of voice which left his three friends in doubt whether he was joking or talking seriously, 'you only have to give rein to a man's vice if you want to get rid of him. *Elle aimait trop le bal et c'est ce qui l'a tuée* (she loved dancing too much, and that is what killed her), as Hugo has said. There! My grandmother loved lotteries and Philippe killed her with them! Old Rouget loved larking about with women and Lolotte killed him! Madame Bridau, poor woman, loved Philippe; she died all because of him! Vice! Vice! My friends! Do you know what vice does? It panders to death!'

'So you'll die of joking!' Desroches smiled to Bixiou.

After reaching the fourth floor, the young men climbed one of those vertical staircases, rather like ladders, which you use to climb up to the attics of some Parisian houses. Joseph, who had seen Flore when she was so beautiful, expected some terrible contrast, but the artist could not have imagined the hideous sight that met his eyes. Beneath the sharp angle of an attic which did not even have any paper on the walls, and on a camp bed whose thin mattress was perhaps stuffed with flock, the three young men found a woman as green as a female corpse drowned two days ago, as thin as a consumptive two hours before death. This putrid corpse had a shabby square-patterned printed scarf over her bald head. Red rings encircled her hollow eyes and her eyelids were like the thin white skin of an egg. As for her body, which was once so ravishingly beautiful, no more than an ignoble bone structure remained. On seeing the visitors enter, Flore clasped against her chest a scrap of muslin which must once have been a small curtain, for it was edged with rust from the iron of the curtain-rod. Two chairs, a shabby sideboard with a tallow candle stuck into a potato, dishes scattered all over the floor, and an earthenware stove in the corner of an empty fireplace were the only furniture the young men could see. Bixiou noticed the remains of the pad of writing-paper which had been bought from the grocer's so that she could write the letter which the two women had very probably thought out together. The word 'disgusting' would only be the positive adjective, whose superlative form does not exist and by means of which – if it did exist – the impression caused by this destitution would need to be conveyed. When the dying woman saw Joseph, two huge tears rolled down her cheeks.

'She can still weep!' said Bixiou. 'That's rather a funny sight: tears coming from a set of dominoes! That explains the miracle of Moses.'

'Is she withered enough?' asked Joseph.

'Withered in the fire of repentance,' Flore replied. 'I cannot call a priest; I have nothing, not even a crucifix on which to see God's image! I am very sinful,' she cried, raising her arms, which were like two pieces of carved wood, 'but God has never punished anyone in the way he is punishing me! Philippe killed Max who had advised me to do horrible things and *he* is killing me as well. God is using *him* as a scourge! Lead a good life, for we each of us have our Philippe.'

'Leave me alone with her,' said Bianchon, 'then I can find out whether her illness is curable.'

'If she was cured Philippe Bridau would explode with

anger,' Desroches said; 'so I am going to have an official record made of his wife's condition. He hasn't ! ad her convicted of adultery, she enjoys full conjugal rights; he will have to face the scandal of a court case. First, we shall have the Countess moved to Dr Dubois's clinic in the Rue du Faubourg Saint-Denis; there she will be really well looked after. Then, I'll serve a writ on the Count for restitution of conjugal rights.'

'Bravo, Desroches!' cried Bixiou. 'How nice to think up a good action which will do so much harm!'

Ten minutes later, Bianchon came downstairs and said to his two friends: 'I am rushing over to Desplein, he can save this woman by an operation. Ah! He will have her very well looked after; drinking too many liqueurs has brought on a magnificent illness which we thought had died out.'

'You and your medical jokes, you're off again! Surely there's only one illness?' Bixiou asked.

But Bianchon was already in the courtyard, he was in so much of a hurry to inform Desplein of this great news. Two hours later, Joseph's unfortunate sister-in-law was taken to Dr Dubois's respectable clinic, which was bought later on by the Town of Paris. Three weeks afterwards, the *Gazette des Hôpitaux* published an account of one of the boldest ventures of modern surgery, performed on a patient who was referred to by the initials F.B. The patient died, less because of the operation's after-effects than because of the physical weakness caused by her poverty. Dressed in deep mourning, Colonel Comte de Brambourg immediately called on the Comte de Soulanges to inform him of his 'grievous loss'. It was whispered in high society that the Comte de Soulanges was marrying his daughter to a social upstart of great personal merit, who was due to be appointed colonel and brigadier-general of one of the regiments of the Royal Guards. De Marsay gave this news to Rastignac, who mentioned it at a supper at the Rocher de Cancale which Bixiou attended.

'But it won't happen!' the witty artist thought to himself.

Though some of the friends whom Philippe cut (Giroudeau,

for instance) were unable to retaliate, he had been misguided enough to offend Bixiou who, because of his wit, was invited everywhere and who was scarcely capable of showing forgiveness. Within the whole Rocher de Cancale's hearing, and in the presence of serious-minded people who were dining there, Philippe had said to Bixiou, when asked if the latter could come and see the Hôtel de Brambourg: 'You will only come to my house when you are a Minister!'

'Must I become a Protestant then to visit your house?' Bixiou replied jokingly; but he said to himself: 'If you are Goliath, I have my catapult and I'm not short of pebbles.'

Next day, the hoaxer dressed up at one of his actor friends' and, by the omnipotence of fancy dress, was transformed into a lapsed priest wearing green spectacles; he then hired a carriage and drove to the Hôtel de Soulanges. Bixiou, whom Philippe called a frivolous joker, wanted to play a joke on him. Allowed into Monsieur de Soulanges's house after insisting that he had a serious matter to discuss, Bixiou played the part of a venerable man entrusted with important secrets. In an assumed voice, he told the story of the deceased countess's illness, of whose horrible details Bianchon had secretly informed him, he explained the circumstances of Agathe's death, and old Rouget's death about which the Comte de Brambourg had boasted, and Madame Descoings's death, and the money borrowed from the till at the newspaper office, and he described the sort of life Philippe had led in his days of misfortune.

'Monsieur le Comte, do not marry your daugher to him until you have made the most searching inquiries; question his old friends, Bixiou, Captain Giroudeau, etc.'

Three months afterwards, Colonel Comte de Brambourg was giving a supper party at his home for Du Tillet, Nucingen, Rastignac, Maxime de Trailles and de Marsay. Their host listened with great unconcern as his friends spoke, half-consolingly, of his rupture with the Soulanges family.

'You can find someone better,' Maxime told him.

'What fortune would I need to marry one of the Grandlieu daughters?' Philippe inquired of de Marsay.

'You? You wouldn't get the ugliest of the six for less than ten million francs,' de Marsay answered insolently.

'But with a private income of 200,000 francs a year, you could get Mademoiselle de Langeais, the Marquis's daughter,' Rastignac butted in; 'she is an ugly woman aged thirty, with nothing in the way of a dowry; that would fit your bill.'

'I shall be worth ten million francs in two years from now.'

'Today is 16 January 1829!' said du Tillet, with a smile. 'I have been working for ten years, and I don't have that amount of money!'

'We'll advise each other, then you'll see how well I understand finance,' Bridau replied.

'What are you worth, altogether?' asked Nucingen.

'If I sold my funded property, but not my country estate or town house, which I cannot and do not wish to risk, as they are entailed, then I should certainly net three million francs.'

Nucingen and du Tillet looked at one another; following this subtle exchange of glances, du Tillet said to Philippe: 'My dear Count, we will work together if you so desire.'

De Marsay happened to notice the look du Tillet darted at Nucingen, a look which meant: 'The money's ours.' Indeed, these important merchant bankers were so well placed at the heart of political affairs that, within a given space of time and with absolute certainty of success, they could speculate against Philippe on the Stock Exchange, at a moment when all the probablities seemed to him to be in his favour whereas in fact the circumstances would favour them.

And this is precisely how things turned out. In July 1830, du Tillet and Nucingen had already made 1,500,000 francs for the Comte de Brambourg, who no longer mistrusted them, finding them both loyal and reliable advisers. Philippe, whose success had been due to the Restoration, was particularly mistaken in his deep contempt for civilians; he believed that the government proclamations of 25 July would succeed in their objective, and speculated for a rise; whereas Nucingen and du Tillet, judging that a revolution was imminent, moved against Philippe, anticipating a fall in share prices. These wily operators declared that they fully understood Colonel Comte de Brambourg's point of view, and seemed to share his convictions. They filled him with the hope of doubling his gigantic fortune, and took the necessary steps that would make him this amount of money. During the revolution of July 1830, Philippe fought like a man to whom victory meant four million francs. His loyalty was so noticeable that he was ordered to return with the Duc de Maufrigneuse to Saint-Cloud, where a council was being held. Philippe was saved by this mark of royal favour; for on 28 July he wanted to make a charge to clean up the boulevards, and would no doubt have been hit by a bullet from his friend Giroudeau, who was commanding a division of insurgents.

A month later, all that Colonel Bridau possessed of his former immense fortune was his town house, his country property, his pictures and furniture. Besides this, he was stupid enough, as he himself admitted, to believe that the elder branch of the Bourbon family would be restored, and remained loyal to them until 1834. Seeing that Giroudeau was now a colonel, an easily understandable jealousy led Philippe to go back into the army. In 1835 he was unfortunately sent out to a regiment in Algeria, where he remained for three years in an exceedingly dangerous post, hoping to be made a general; but an adverse influence – the influence of General Giroudeau – caused him to remain where he was. Philippe had become harsh; he carried the severity of military discipline to extreme lengths; despite his reckless courage, very similar to Murat's, he was detested. Early in the fatal year 1839, whilst leading an offensive against the Arabs during a retreat before superior numbers, he hurled himself against the enemy, with only a company following him, all of whom fell into the hands of a huge party of Arabs. The close combat was bloody and terrible; only a small number of the French cavalry escaped with their lives. Seeing their colonel surrounded, those who were some distance away did not think it advisable to lay down their lives in a fruitless attempt to free him from the enemy. They heard the words: 'Your colonel! Help me! A colonel of the Imperial Army!' after which came the most terrifying shrieks; but they returned to their regiment. Philippe had a horrible death: his head was cut off as he fell almost hacked to pieces with yataghans.

Thanks to the Comte de Sérizy's influence, Joseph married a retired farmer's daughter about this time, whose father was worth millions of francs; he inherited the Hôtel de Brambourg and the country estate which his brother, who was keen to debar him from inheriting this fortune, had never been able to settle on anyone. What gave most pleasure to the artist was the fine picture collection. Joseph, for whom his father-in-law, a sort of rural Hochon, is piling up banknotes every day, already has a private income of 60,000 francs a year. Though he paints magnificent pictures and gives much help to artists, he is still not a member of the Institut. By virtue of a clause in the deed of entailment he is now known as the Count de Brambourg, which often makes him howl with laughter when he is in his studio with his friends.

'You can always count on wealthy friends,' replies his friend Léon de Lora who, despite his fame as a landscapist, has not given up his old habit of twisting proverbs, and who, prompted by the modesty with which Joseph received these favours showered upon him by fate, reminds his friends that 'A man's appetite grows as he paints!'

Paris,
November 1842

FOR THE BEST IN PAPERBACKS, LOOK FOR THE 🐧

In every corner of the world, on every subject under the sun, Penguin represents quality and variety – the very best in publishing today.

For complete information about books available from Penguin – including Pelicans, Puffins, Peregrines and Penguin Classics – and how to order them, write to us at the appropriate address below. Please note that for copyright reasons the selection of books varies from country to country.

In the United Kingdom: Please write to *Dept E.P., Penguin Books Ltd, Harmondsworth, Middlesex, UB7 0DA*

In the United States: Please write to *Dept BA, Penguin, 299 Murray Hill Parkway, East Rutherford, New Jersey 07073*

In Canada: Please write to *Penguin Books Canada Ltd, 2801 John Street, Markham, Ontario L3R 1B4*

In Australia: Please write to the *Marketing Department, Penguin Books Australia Ltd, P.O. Box 257, Ringwood, Victoria 3134*

In New Zealand: Please write to the *Marketing Department, Penguin Books (NZ) Ltd, Private Bag, Takapuna, Auckland 9*

In India: Please write to *Penguin Overseas Ltd, 706 Eros Apartments, 56 Nehru Place, New Delhi, 110019*

In Holland: Please write to *Penguin Books Nederland B.V., Postbus 195, NL–1380AD Weesp, Netherlands*

In Germany: Please write to *Penguin Books Ltd, Friedrichstrasse 10–12, D–6000 Frankfurt Main 1, Federal Republic of Germany*

In Spain: Please write to *Longman Penguin España, Calle San Nicolas 15, E–28013 Madrid, Spain*

In France: Please write to *Penguin Books Ltd, 39 Rue de Montmorency, F-75003, Paris, France*

In Japan: Please write to *Longman Penguin Japan Co Ltd, Yamaguchi Building, 2–12–9 Kanda Jimbocho, Chiyoda-Ku, Tokyo 101, Japan*

BY THE SAME AUTHOR

Honoré de Balzac (1799–1850) was the author of a cycle of novels, the
Comédie Humaine, that analyse the motives underlying human action.
In his remorseless reality and the minute documentation of his
characters he foreshadowed the Realism of Flaubert and Zola.

The Chouans

The Chouans was the first volume of Balzac's long novel sequence. He
established the ground on which he was to become master, that of
enthralling narrative combined with the fascination of documentary
detail.

Eugénie Grandet

In provincial Saumur, after the revolution, the miser Grandet lives with
his daughter, Eugénie. The tragedy that follows the arrival of her cousin
Charles is described by Balzac with irony and psychological insight.

Cousin Bette

Bette is a poor relation of the rich Hulot family. She dreams of
destroying the people on whose patronage she is forced to rely.

Cousin Pons
A Harlot High and Low
History of the Thirteen
Lost Illusions
A Murky Business
Old Goriot
Ursule Mirouet
The Wild Ass's Skin
Selected Short Stories

FOR THE BEST IN PAPERBACKS, LOOK FOR THE 🐧

PENGUIN CLASSICS

Netochka Nezvanova   Fyodor Dostoyevsky

Dostoyevsky's first book tells the story of 'Nameless Nobody' and introduces many of the themes and issues which will dominate his great masterpieces.

Selections from the Carmina Burana   A verse translation by David Parlett

The famous songs from the *Carmina Burana* (made into an oratorio by Carl Orff) tell of lecherous monks and corrupt clerics, drinkers and gamblers, and the fleeting pleasures of youth.

Fear and Trembling   Søren Kierkegaard

A profound meditation on the nature of faith and submission to God's will which examines with startling originality the story of Abraham and Isaac.

Selected Prose   Charles Lamb

Lamb's famous essays (under the strange pseudonym of Elia) on anything and everything have long been celebrated for their apparently innocent charm; this major new edition allows readers to discover the darker and more interesting aspects of Lamb.

The Picture of Dorian Gray   Oscar Wilde

Wilde's superb and macabre novella, one of his supreme works, is reprinted here with a masterly Introduction and valuable Notes by Peter Ackroyd.

A Treatise of Human Nature   David Hume

A universally acknowledged masterpiece by 'the greatest of all British Philosophers' – A. J. Ayer

FOR THE BEST IN PAPERBACKS, LOOK FOR THE 🐧

PENGUIN CLASSICS

A Passage to India   E. M. Forster

Centred on the unresolved mystery in the Marabar Caves, Forster's great work provides the definitive evocation of the British Raj.

The Republic   Plato

The best-known of Plato's dialogues, *The Republic* is also one of the supreme masterpieces of Western philosophy whose influence cannot be overestimated.

The Life of Johnson   James Boswell

Perhaps the finest 'life' ever written, Boswell's *Johnson* captures for all time one of the most colourful and talented figures in English literary history.

Remembrance of Things Past (3 volumes)   Marcel Proust

This revised version by Terence Kilmartin of C. K. Scott Moncrieff's original translation has been universally acclaimed – available for the first time in paperback.

Metamorphoses   Ovid

A golden treasury of myths and legends which has proved a major influence on Western literature.

A Nietzsche Reader   Friedrich Nietzsche

A superb selection from all the major works of one of the greatest thinkers and writers in world literature, translated into clear, modern English.

PENGUIN CLASSICS

Honoré de Balzac	**Cousin Bette**
	Eugénie Grandet
	Lost Illusions
	Old Goriot
	Ursule Mirouet
Corneille	**The Cid/Cinna/The Theatrical Illusion**
Alphonse Daudet	**Letters from My Windmill**
René Descartes	**Discourse on Method and Other Writings**
Denis Diderot	**Jacques the Fatalist**
Gustave Flaubert	**Madame Bovary**
	Sentimental Education
	Three Tales
Jean de la Fontaine	**Selected Fables**
Jean Froissart	**The Chronicles**
Théophile Gautier	**Mademoiselle de Maupin**
Edmond and Jules de Goncourt	**Germinie Lacerteux**
Guy de Maupassant	**Selected Short Stories**
Molière	**The Misanthrope/The Sicilian/Tartuffe/A Doctor in Spite of Himself/The Imaginary Invalid**
Michel de Montaigne	**Essays**
Marguerite de Navarre	**The Heptameron**
Marie de France	**Lais**
Blaise Pascal	**Pensées**
Rabelais	**The Histories of Gargantua and Pantagruel**
Racine	**Iphigenia/Phaedra/Athaliah**
Arthur Rimbaud	**Collected Poems**
Jean-Jacques Rousseau	**The Confessions**
	Reveries of a Solitary Walker
Madame de Sevigné	**Selected Letters**
Voltaire	**Candide**
	Philosophical Dictionary
Émile Zola	**La Bête Humaine**
	Nana
	Thérèse Raquin

FOR THE BEST IN PAPERBACKS, LOOK FOR THE 🐧

PENGUIN CLASSICS

FOR THE BEST IN PAPERBACKS, LOOK FOR THE

PENGUIN CLASSICS

Matthew Arnold	**Selected Prose**
Jane Austen	**Emma**
	Lady Susan, The Watsons, Sanditon
	Mansfield Park
	Northanger Abbey
	Persuasion
	Pride and Prejudice
	Sense and Sensibility
Anne Brontë	**The Tenant of Wildfell Hall**
Charlotte Brontë	**Jane Eyre**
	Shirley
	Villette
Emily Brontë	**Wuthering Heights**
Samuel Butler	**Erewhon**
	The Way of All Flesh
Thomas Carlyle	**Selected Writings**
Wilkie Collins	**The Moonstone**
	The Woman in White
Charles Darwin	**The Origin of Species**
Charles Dickens	**American Notes for General Circulation**
	Barnaby Rudge
	Bleak House
	The Christmas Books
	David Copperfield
	Dombey and Son
	Great Expectations
	Hard Times
	Little Dorrit
	Martin Chuzzlewit
	The Mystery of Edwin Drood
	Nicholas Nickleby
	The Old Curiosity Shop
	Oliver Twist
	Our Mutual Friend
	The Pickwick Papers
	Selected Short Fiction
	A Tale of Two Cities

FOR THE BEST IN PAPERBACKS, LOOK FOR THE 🐧

PENGUIN CLASSICS

Horatio Alger, Jr.	**Ragged Dick** and **Struggling Upward**
Phineas T. Barnum	**Struggles and Triumphs**
Ambrose Bierce	**The Enlarged Devil's Dictionary**
Kate Chopin	**The Awakening and Selected Stories**
Stephen Crane	**The Red Badge of Courage**
Richard Henry Dana, Jr.	**Two Years Before the Mast**
Frederick Douglass	**Narrative of the Life of Frederick Douglass, An American Slave**
Theodore Dreiser	**Sister Carrie**
Ralph Waldo Emerson	**Selected Essays**
Joel Chandler Harris	**Uncle Remus**
Nathaniel Hawthorne	**Blithedale Romance**
	The House of the Seven Gables
	The Scarlet Letter and Selected Tales
William Dean Howells	**The Rise of Silas Lapham**
Alice James	**The Diary of Alice James**
William James	**Varieties of Religious Experience**
Jack London	**The Call of the Wild and Other Stories**
	Martin Eden
Herman Melville	**Billy Budd, Sailor and Other Stories**
	Moby-Dick
	Redburn
	Typee
Thomas Paine	**Common Sense**
Edgar Allan Poe	**The Narrative of Arthur Gordon Pym of Nantucket**
	The Other Poe
	The Science Fiction of Edgar Allan Poe
	Selected Writings
Harriet Beecher Stowe	**Uncle Tom's Cabin**
Henry David Thoreau	**Walden** and **Civil Disobedience**
Mark Twain	**The Adventures of Huckleberry Finn**
	A Connecticut Yankee at King Arthur's Court
	Life on the Mississippi
	Pudd'nhead Wilson
	Roughing It